THE LONELY HEARTS RESCUE

THE LONELY HEARTS RESCUE

by

Morgan Lee Miller, Nell Stark,
and Missouri Vaun

2022

THE LONELY HEARTS RESCUE

ISBN 13: 978-1-63679-231-6

This Trade Paperback Original Is Published By
Bold Strokes Books, Inc.
P.O. Box 249
Valley Falls, NY 12185

First Edition: October 2022

Credits
Editor: Barbara Ann Wright
Production Design: Stacia Seaman
Cover Design by Inkspiral Design

The Lonely Hearts Rescue

SOMETHING ABOUT YOU

Morgan Lee Miller

Chapter One

"Wait, stop. There's a cat right there on top of the car."

The speedboat slowed its juddering across the floodwater. About twenty-five yards away, Reese Shepard spotted a tuxedo cat balled up on the roof of a silver car that was three-quarters submerged in murky water. A pool of emotions accumulated in her from the last two days of work, and seeing the tuxedo cat trapped and terrified made her heart sink like an anchor. Its ears were pulled back, wide eyes steady on Reese and her team. She wondered how long the cat must have been there. At least two days with nothing to eat and only living off floodwater.

"Looks like we have one more to rescue," Reese said softly, making sure to tame the urgency in her voice so she didn't scare the tuxedo cat or the other three cats and two small dogs they had just rescued. The last empty kennel sat next to the one holding a Jack Russell terrier mix. The dog had a red collar and a tag that said "Russell" with a phone number engraved into it and had curled himself in the back of his cage. His rounded brown eyes revealed his fear, just like the other animals on the boat, like the tuxedo cat stranded on the car, like all the displaced and confused animals Reese and her team had rescued in the last two days. "We have one more cage."

Adam turned the steering wheel toward the submerged car that sat on a driveway, a ranch home behind it. The boat slowly inched forward until they were about twenty feet out from the car. Kelly and Claudia got ready along with Reese. Kelly grabbed the empty kennel, and Claudia and Reese grabbed long nets before gently sliding into the water. They all wore bright orange waterproof suits to prevent the contaminated floodwater from soaking into their clothes and their skin. They wore yellow helmets and thick waterproof gloves that protected them not only from the water but from animal scratches and bites. It added extra weight, but it offered the best protection.

Reese, Kelly, and Claudia cautiously waded through the water, keeping their stares fixed on the cat, who watched them as intently as they watched it. The closer they inched, the tighter the cat balled up. Claudia went on the opposite side of the car as Reese. That way, if the cat fell into the water, either Reese or Claudia would be able to quickly pull it out.

Just because this had been Reese's fifth hurricane season didn't mean the painful and terrifying looks in the animals' eyes got any easier to see. Her heart ached every time she came across one who needed to be rescued. While she soaked up the sight of the tuxedo cat, scared, alone, and trapped, the sinking feeling inside her was no different than all the others she'd experienced throughout her career. Her rescue organization, Paw Aid, had spent the last two days sweeping southern Louisiana towns that had been hit the hardest from Hurricane Sarah, a slow-moving category two that had tossed tons of rain on the Gulf Coast. Her team had rescued everything from rabbits, cats, and dogs to chickens, pigs, and even horses. The emergency shelter at the rec center had quickly filled with displaced animals waiting to be reunited with their families or waiting until it was safe to be released back into the wild.

As hard as it was finding animals who were alone and terrified, someone had to rescue them, and she was more than happy to be that person for them and their families.

"Hi, kitty, it's okay," Reese said, using a soft and steady voice. She stopped when she was a few feet in front of the side of the car. The cat stared at her with eyes fully dilated with fear.

When rescuing any animal, the ideal situation was for the animal to approach naturally. But many times, that didn't happen. The tuxedo cat had put itself into a great predicament on a car with water surrounding it, meaning it probably wouldn't feel safe enough to walk to Reese no matter how much she tried coaxing it over.

"What are you doing here? You scared, buddy? I know. It's scary out here."

The cat didn't have a collar, which, unlike a dog, didn't necessarily mean it was a stray. They wouldn't know until they ran a microchip scanner when they got back to the emergency shelter. The cat appeared thinner than it should have been, but it was a little hard to tell given its long coat. Its body was scrunched, revealing white paws that brought out its adorable long white whiskers and a white beard that started at its chin and went down his chest.

"We're going to get you out of here, okay? Get you safe and dry, some water that's not yucky like this, and lots of food and treats, I promise."

She took a step forward. Claudia followed, and Kelly waited at the front. Reese saw the cat's plans to bolt the second she took another step. Its whiskers twitched, its ears shot straight back, and it coiled into a tighter ball. They would have to act quickly. If the cat tried to run, it would land either on the trunk or in the water.

Reese gripped the net; she had to make this fast, or the cat would flail in floodwater contaminated with everything from raw sewage to pollutants. It was why rescuers like herself wore full-body suits and gloves; even something like a cat scratch could get infected. She and her team had to make sure they did everything they could to prevent the cat from exposing itself more.

She looked across the car at Claudia, who gave an understanding nod. Claudia tossed the net over the cat, but it was smart and ready to run. Right as the net was about to drop, the cat skidded along the roof of the car, the claws screeched against the steel, and it plummeted into the water.

"Damn it," Reese yelled, and her heart thudded like a brick.

As Claudia and Kelly trudged over, Reese's training and reflexes helped her react quickly. She slung her net over the cat and pulled it out right as Kelly appeared at her side with the kennel door open. Reese put the drenched cat inside, and Kelly locked the door. Reese breathed a giant sigh of relief that the cat was safe, though it was drenched from the tops of its black ears to the bottom of its tail. Even though it was only in the water for a few seconds, her heart still thrummed at the possibility of losing it.

"You can't do that, buddy," Reese said, peering inside the cage. The cat let out a miserable howl. "Yeah, you went swimming. That wasn't a good idea. But don't worry. We're gonna get you cleaned up." She petted the kennel cage with her thick black gloves. "I promise."

Adam directed their speedboat back to dry land where a truck was waiting to transport them to the emergency shelter situated inside the rec center. Out of the six animals they'd rescued in their last sweep, the tuxedo cat looked the most frightened. Curled up in the corner, it focused on the bottom of the cage instead of taking in its surroundings. It was like it wanted to do absolutely nothing but disappear from the world, and that yanked at Reese's heartstrings. The cat looked so ashamed, depressed, and defeated. She hoped that once they cleaned it up and got it checked out by the vet, they would find a microchip so they could find its family.

The poor thing just needed to go home.

It always amazed Reese how quickly the emergency shelter filled up. What was once a giant but quiet rec center gym when her organization had spent a day putting together kennels and a triage station was now flooded with displaced animals. Barking echoed around the gym so much, she couldn't hear someone talking right next to her. They used the separate racquetball courts for the cats, a much quieter room. Each animal had a blanket, food, water, and a toy. Cats had catnip and a litter box. Every animal had a small sign for the workers. Red meant do not approach. Yellow meant the animal was sick or injured. Orange meant the animal was shy, and green meant they were friendly. Each one was examined by veterinarians and treated for any issues. If they were microchipped, team members would call the families, and Reese assisted with reuniting families with their pets. Even though she had been at the job for five years, watching the families discover that their pets had survived and were back safely in their arms always made her eyes sting.

Her heart swelled when the owners of the Jack Russell terrier mix approached her. The mother and father had two young boys under ten who looked sad and scared as they soaked up the scene.

When Reese smiled, the kids' eyes rounded as if they were bracing themselves for the first good news they'd received in days. "Yes, I know Russell," Reese said and watched as the kids looked at their parents with hopeful smiles. "My team rescued him, and I can assure you, he's doing great. Come, follow me."

The boys cheered, and tears filled their eyes.

"He's been doing very well," Reese said over the sounds of barking as she navigated the rows of cages. "For all that he went through, he's in good spirits."

Once they approached the cage, the green sign let everyone know Russell was very friendly. He spun in circles and let out happy yelps when he saw his family. He ran up to the front and started clawing at the door, his tail wagging ferociously.

"Russell," the two boys yelled as they crouched and pressed their faces against the cage.

"Where did you find him? Was he okay?" the mother asked desperately.

"We found him on the second floor in one of the kids' bedrooms," Reese said. "He was on one of the twin beds, barking."

The mother shook her head. "We were rescued from the house just this morning. They didn't have enough room for him on the boat and told us they would notify Paw Aid about him being inside. Thank you for getting him. I wasn't expecting to get him back tonight."

In every disaster effort, humans were the priority. Not only did animal organizations have to wait until the people rescuing operations were underway before they came to the impacted areas, but if those people were found with animals, the people had to be rescued first. Sometimes, that meant the pet had to stay behind until another group could rescue it.

Reese opened the cage, and Russell leapt into the arms of the oldest son. The boy cradled him as the younger brother fell to his knees and showered the dog with petting. Russell flopped back and forth even more ecstatically than before.

"The house is a wreck, isn't it?" the father asked, low and soft as if he already knew the answer.

While the floodwater had mostly retreated by the time Reese's team had arrived, she'd noticed that the water line sat at least four feet from the ground. The furniture had floated and settled randomly around the living room. The house that had probably once smelled like fresh linens and warm cookies had reeked of pungent floodwater that didn't mix well with the early September humidity. As tragic as the state of their house was, Reese was grateful that the family and their dog were okay and had been reunited. It wasn't always a happy outcome.

"It was flooded pretty badly," Reese said quietly while the kids were lost in Russell's affection. "But Russell came right to us as if he knew we were there to help. Other than being hungry and thirsty, he was in amazing shape. All of you are really lucky."

The mom swiped at her eyes as she tossed a glance at her husband. He wrapped an arm around her and looked at his kids with their dog. A smile landed on his face while his dark brown eyes glistened. "We are. Thank you so much for saving our dog. He means everything to us, everything to the kids." He wiped away a falling tear. "We wouldn't know what to do without him."

"Can I please give you a hug?" the mom asked with her arms extended.

Reese nodded and hugged her. She could feel by the tightness how thankful the mom was for her taking care of their dog. Reese tried to hold back her own emotions, knowing she had to remain strong and calm around the families and the animals. This was the exact reason why she did what she did. Animals played a major role in humans' lives. They were the glue for families, for people. They gave people hope and peace when the world outside lacked it. Life was so much brighter and happier with a pet. It was telling with Russell's family. Their house had been destroyed. They probably knew mold would start growing, and they would have to start from scratch, buy a new house, new furniture. But it seemed like a blip on their radar right now. Their only concern was their dog. Everything else came second.

When certain jobs make you see the worst of the worst, those jobs also help show the best of the best.

Her last day in Hurricane Sarah's hardest hit area had been long and draining. Fourteen hours searching for animals who needed her help, going inside flooded homes, climbing on top of roofs to rescue animals that had desperately escaped the waters, and reuniting families with their fur babies. The tiredness weighed on her, her feet were sore, and her back started to ache. But she couldn't leave for her hotel until she'd checked on the tuxedo cat that she couldn't stop thinking about. The look in its eyes had pierced her heart, and she didn't think she would be able to let go until she knew that it had gone back to its family.

She searched up and down the rows in the racquetball court until she found the tuxedo cat's kennel. It had an orange sign on it, warning her that the cat was shy. Inside, she found it curled up on a bed. When the cat's eyes weren't dilated in fear, they were a beautiful bright green. She smiled. The cat was undeniably adorable.

"Hi, buddy, how are you doing?" Reese asked in a calm voice, hoping that would help to put it at ease.

She looked at the paperwork on top of the kennel. The cat was a boy, approximately two to three years, slightly underweight, but that probably had to do with being stranded on the car. Reese's stomach dropped when she found he wasn't microchipped, nor did he have a collar. Besides being dehydrated, hungry, and probably still upset that he had to endure a bath to scrub the gross water off his fur, skin, and claws, he had no other injuries and had started antibiotics to help recover from drinking floodwater. Because he was unclaimed, he would be taken back to a partner shelter where he would be put up for adoption. Reese checked the paper to find out her organization had already marked him as going back to the Lonely Hearts Rescue, a shelter a few miles away from her hometown.

She lowered the paperwork and peeked back into the kennel as hope forced her stomach to settle back into place. He had a bowl of dry food that looked like it had been nibbled on and a bowl of water that had definitely been used. While he might not have had anyone to take him here in Louisiana, she was glad that she could keep her eye on him as they traveled back to Lonely Hearts, where she would make sure he got the best loving home.

"It's okay, little guy. Looks like you're going to be coming back with me." She crouched to his level, and wide green eyes stared back at her. "You're going to find the best home, okay? I'll make sure of it, I promise."

He didn't look Reese in the eye. He just stared at his bed, blinked, and rested his head on his white paw.

That night, as Reese lay in her hotel bed, she reflected on her time spent helping the Hurricane Sarah recovery. It always transplanted her back to her Aunt Katy's house, where her love for animals had begun. Her five-year-old self had spent all her time out in the chicken coop, petting Aunt Katy's egg-laying chickens. Aunt Katy had treated them as pets, had given them names, and had let them play in her fenced-in backyard.

When Reese was nine, Aunt Katy had taken in a potbellied pig.

Apparently, the pig's owners had wanted a teacup pig. Aunt Katy had told Reese that teacups pigs were a hoax and were either underfed to stunt their growth or sold under false pretenses. So the family had found a potbellied pig in their house instead of the cute little lap pig they had expected. Since Aunt Katy had enough land, she'd taken in Wilbur on top of her chickens, two dogs, and three cats.

Aunt Katy had taught Reese how special animals were, how they were the only living things that didn't care about your wealth, your job, your clothes, your sexuality, or your religion. Animals only cared about the love you had to give.

"One of the greatest honors in life is having an animal trust you completely," Aunt Katy had told her. "And one of the most heart-breaking things is watching their trust be taken advantage of. It's important that we remind those animals of all the love they deserve, and in return, they'll give us the love we deserve."

It was a motto Reese still lived by. It swept through her mind with every animal she rescued. She'd promised the tuxedo cat and herself that she would find him the best home with all the love he deserved.

❖

"How are all the babies?" Reese asked Ashley Finch, the Lonely Hearts Rescue's adoption coordinator.

It was the morning after Reese and her team had returned home to Fairview with the truck of rescued animals assigned to go to the shelter. After spending a few hours helping the staff unload the animals and get them settled in their cages the day before, Reese returned the next morning. When it wasn't hurricane season, Reese tried to foster as many animals from Lonely Hearts as she could. Some needed extra care. They needed to learn how to trust humans. Reese considered herself a pretty patient person, and she absolutely adored animals, so she figured, why not help them even more by giving them a preview of the love they'd receive once they found their forever homes?

"Good. Mostly good," Ashley said with a friendly smile. "A few of them were looked at by Dr. Wu, and despite everything they've been through, things look like they're on the up for them. Some just need time adjusting."

"Like the tuxedo cat?"

"Like the tuxedo cat." Ashley lifted a curious blond eyebrow. "Have you been paying special attention to him?"

Reese shrugged. "I have. He just looked so miserable and ashamed. I haven't stopped thinking about him since I rescued him. We found him on top of an almost-submerged car."

Ashley deflated. "Really?"

"And then he fell into the water."

"No!"

"He hasn't had the best last couple of days."

Ashley's blue eyes sparkled as if she had just put all the pieces of the puzzle together. "Are you thinking about fostering him?"

"Do you think he needs to be fostered? Because I would love that."

"Little Apollo is going to need a lot of TLC."

Reese smiled at the cat's new name. Ashley made a fabulous adoption coordinator for many reasons. She knew everything about animals, and every fur baby who stepped through the Lonely Hearts's front door, Ashley loved them as if they were her own. Plus, she always gave the best names.

"He's very timid, probably the most of the batch," Ashley said. "So the fact that you're interested in fostering him makes me happy. I've been a bit worried about him too because…you know…shy and scared cats are the last ones to be adopted."

"I would really love to foster him."

Ashley put a hand over her heart. "This is reason number a-million-and-one why I love you, Reese Shepard. When are you able to take him home?"

"I have all the supplies from past cats, so I'm ready whenever. I think the next two weeks might offer us a bit of a break, in weather terms."

"Well, perfect. Let's go look at Apollo and see what he thinks."

Reese followed her to the cat room. Cages much bigger than the kennels offered the cats two levels to climb; each had a blanket, toys, food, water, and a litter box. Several times a day, the cats visited the free roam to run around, climb, scratch on the posts, and play.

Apollo was curled up on a fleece blanket on the second level, pressed against the back of the cage, his eyes still round in fear. The poor little guy had no idea what was going on, and it made Reese want to scoop him up even more and show him that everything was going to be okay.

"Here's your friend," Ashley said as they approached.

Apollo let out a soft hiss and buried himself underneath the light blue blanket.

There was something about him that tugged on her heart. The way he hid in the farthest corner, all balled up, the same way he'd lain in his cage at the emergency shelter back in Louisiana. How his fear for everyone and everything dilated his pupils to hide the beautiful green of his eyes. Reese also had a soft spot for tuxedo cats. She'd had one growing up named Sylvester after her favorite cartoon. Apollo looked like both Sylvesters, except he was all black with a white beard, had four white paws, and white whiskers popped against his long black fur. He was such a handsome boy, and Reese hoped he would eventually warm up to her so she could tell him so.

"He's going to need all the love you have to offer," Ashley said. "I'm sure with some Reese Shepard loving magic, he's going to be the perfect cat for someone."

Reese crouched to catch a peek. She used to be the quiet kid in school. She knew what it was like to be forced into social situations that made her uneasy. She didn't want Apollo to think he was alone. She would hold his paw and show him that the scariest part of his life was over.

"It's going to be okay, buddy. I promise to make you excited about life again."

Chapter Two

Hannah Marsh had no idea what to do.

One, she didn't know how to respond to the frantic email from Mason Hunt's mom on her phone, the one asking why Mason's score was so low on a homework assignment and saying Mason had been "too busy lately" to focus on homework.

Two, she had no idea how to navigate dating apps. Well, she knew how to navigate them when it came to talking to men. They messaged her, she could tell early on if they were serious about getting to know her or looking to hook up, and she didn't sit on the edge of her seat wondering if what she was typing back was good or not. Most of the time, the men said nothing of substance, so the conversation bar was low. She'd been on three dates with men now that she was recently single, and none had led to a second date. She was perfectly fine with that.

However, she didn't know how to message a beautiful woman. Unlike with men, she was constantly on the edge of her seat, worrying about finding the right words to say to the handful of women who'd actually initiated a conversation after they had matched. Hannah wasn't even worried about not getting a second date. She just wanted one. She was thirty-two and had just started putting the pieces together a few months back, realizing she was also attracted to women. She so badly wanted to explore the uncharted territory but had no idea where to start.

And last but not least, she wanted a pet but had no idea how that would work since the new school year had just started two weeks ago. She had been toying with the idea ever since she'd broken up with Mitch back in June, right at the start of summer vacation. Her breakup had made her think about a lot of things. It had made her question who she was just when she'd thought she had life figured out, and then out of nowhere, *bam*, an attraction to women. They were all so beautiful. And being home by herself made her feel so lonely. All her friends had partners, some had kids, and she only had Burnie Sanders, an aloe plant that she paid attention to once every three weeks when it needed watering.

But then she'd seen a picture on the front page of the *Fairview Gazette* of Lonely Hearts workers unloading cages from a truck. It had captured her attention, and the article had informed her about a bunch of animals rescued from Hurricane Sarah.

Hannah had taken the article as a sign that it was time to become a fur mom. She had the whole summer to think about it. With every night she spent alone in her house with Burnie Sanders, she was more determined to fix it.

Hannah put her phone away and decided to worry about Mrs. Hunt's email on Monday. She would also worry about mentally preparing herself to message the beautiful women she had matched with on the dating app later. She decided to focus on the now, sitting in the waiting room of the Lonely Hearts Rescue. She glanced up the two-story atrium and then noticed the pet supply store and the gift shop to the right. She hoped that as she left Lonely Hearts, she would have a reason to stop inside to grab a few things for her new fur baby, something cuddlier than Burnie Sanders to help her feel less lonely.

She believed in signs from the universe, and surely reading the article in the paper was one, right?

It doesn't hurt to look, she told herself.

"Oh my God, look at all these sweet babies," Hannah's mother said once the receptionist led them to the room of adoptable cats.

As they walked down the row of cages, some cats came to the front and rubbed up against it. Hannah's heart melted with each cat who looked at her and vied for her attention by sticking their paw out to touch her. As much as she loved teaching fifth grade, having all these sweet cats looking at her as if they already loved her made her consider quitting her job and buying a big plot of land so she could adopt all of them.

Her family had never had a cat. They'd adopted a golden retriever from Lonely Hearts when Hannah was eight. She'd named him Pongo.

Yes, she knew that Pongo wasn't a Dalmatian, that he didn't have a single spot on him, but she was eight and at the peak of her *101 Dalmatians* obsession. Pongo had lived to be thirteen and a half. He'd watched Hannah grow up, had been there for her during her heartbreaks and to send her off to college, and had always greeted her as enthusiastically as her parents whenever she'd walked through the door after months of being away.

As much as she loved dogs, it would be irresponsible of her to adopt one with her work schedule. She loved cats too. All animals, actually. Cats were easy and self-sufficient, a perfect fur baby that meshed with work.

"Hi there," a blond woman said. "Are we just looking today?"

Hannah and her mom exchanged a glance. It was a good question. What were they doing? "We're considering," Hannah said.

The blonde extended a hand. "I'm Ashley, the adoption coordinator. I can help with any questions you might have."

"I'm thinking about adopting a cat. I saw an article in the *Fairview Gazette* about the Hurricane Sarah animals."

Ashley's eyes lit up. "Of course! Some of them have already been adopted. We have a few others that are in foster homes, and I'd be happy to show you pictures. We would have to arrange a visit, but as you can see, we have so many cats here looking for homes too. I'll let you take a look, and we can bring over any of them to the playroom."

Hannah and her mom spent twenty minutes in the cat playroom, scratching chins, tossing mouse toys, petting any cat who walked up to them. How could she get paid to play with cats? That was the dream job right there. Maybe there was a cat café where she could work during the summers. Animals had magic powers to eliminate loneliness. She was positive that if she was surrounded by playful, adorable cats all day, she wouldn't dwell on the fact that she had nothing except her aloe plant to go home to. Her heart would have been stuffed with kitty love.

"We have this one tuxedo cat, Apollo, and his foster mom says he's adjusting really well," Ashley said. "He's very shy, but we know that when he finds the right person, he's going to make the best, most loyal cat. I can show you a picture if you're interested."

"I'm interested in all of the cats," Hannah said.

"Great. So here he is."

When Ashley showed her pictures of a longhaired tuxedo cat in his foster home, her heart swelled. Something about longhaired cats made her melt. She knew they would shed everywhere, but she didn't care. She was mesmerized by the soft green in his eyes and how his white whiskers stood out against his silky black fur. His cute white beard started right above his pink nose and dropped down to his chest. One picture of him with catnip clinging to his beard and a silly, googly look in his eyes was what did it for her.

"Oh my God, look how handsome he is," Hannah said.

"He is handsome, isn't he?" her mom said.

"He's making a lot of progress," Ashley said. "Again, he's pretty shy and timid, but he's been with his foster mom for two weeks, and he has proven that he just needs some patience, and he'll eventually warm up. His foster mom says he's very sweet, playful, and is starting to follow her around the house and loves sleeping snug against her feet at night. So after a bit of time, I'm sure he'll definitely be a perfect house cat."

"I would love to meet him."

"That's great. I can contact the foster mom right now and set up a time that works best."

Ashley stepped out of the playroom while Hannah and her mom tossed mouse toys at the cats. By the time they left Lonely Hearts, Ashley had scheduled a time with Apollo's foster mom for the next day. Hannah hoped it worked out. Although there were plenty of adorable cats in the cat room, something about Apollo drew her in. She wondered if the nerves fluttering inside her was a sign from the universe that she was about to meet her fur baby.

She hoped and willed it to be true.

"Lots of big changes are happening for you," her mom said in the passenger seat. "Good changes. I think a pet would be good for you, especially after Mitch."

Getting laid would be good for me, but getting a cat is a good start.

"Right when I thought I dodged the quarter-life crisis, it sprang out of nowhere." Hannah considered herself a late bloomer in almost everything. She had been the last of her childhood friends to have a boyfriend, the last to have her first kiss, didn't lose her virginity until she was twenty, and didn't even realize that she was bi until just a few months ago. Surely, the signs had been there, sprinkled throughout her life like breadcrumbs. But no, she didn't put the pieces together until a whole loaf fell on top of her.

"You act like delaying your quarter-life crisis is a bad thing," her mom said through a laugh. "All these changes seem good, though, right? You broke up with Mitch, and can I say how grateful your father and I are for that?" Hannah rolled her eyes despite the smile landing on her lips. She knew her parents hadn't liked Mitch because they'd seen how apathetic he was about everything.

She had been honest with them about the reasons why they'd broken up after six months. One, he was immature. Not in a fun way but emotionally and mentally. Sometimes, she'd felt like she was dating a kid right out of college instead of a thirty-six-year-old. Age really was just a number; their four-year age difference proved that Hannah, the younger one, was more responsible and mature. Two, he was lazy. She wanted to go on hikes and do things on the weekend if the weather was nice, but he'd never showed interest outside of watching sports, playing video games, and gambling. Finding things to do that they would both enjoy seemed more like a chore the longer they dated.

Three, girls were so pretty. Had they always been this pretty?

"Speaking of which, any updates in the dating department?" her mom asked.

Hannah loved that when she'd told her parents she was bi, they had been fully supportive and had cheered her on.

"Women are much smarter than men," her dad had said after she'd told them that she wanted to start dating women. "I think you'll have better success."

"You really think so?" Hannah had asked.

"Of course. What's not to like about you?" her mom had said.

Her parents had seemed just as excited as she was for her next dating adventure, especially her mom. Hannah was so grateful to have loving, accepting, and open-minded parents. That was why giving them info about her dating life was so easy.

"Zero updates," Hannah said and grunted. "Apparently, talking to women is a lot harder than talking to men."

"Just be yourself, honey."

"I don't know how to be myself when there's a beautiful woman trying to talk to me. And then there's a whole other layer of stress when neither of us initiates the conversation once we match."

"I don't know what any of that means, but you make small talk all the time with parents and ten-year-olds. I'm sure you're good at it."

"My small talk with parents revolves around their kids, and my small talk with kids revolves around school or their pets. I don't think I can apply those conversation starters to full-grown women. How am I supposed to date a woman when I can't even message one on a dating app?"

"I'm glad I met your father when I did without all the phone apps and…what is it called? Ghosting? I'm glad I lived in a simpler time."

"You should be glad. I think it's half of why millennials are stressed."

"Has anyone reached out to you?"

"I've matched with a few women, but a lot of them are like me and wait for the other person to speak. I've only talked to, like, three, and that's only because they've spoken first."

Her mom shook her head. "I don't understand. Why can't you speak first?"

"Because…they're *women.* I never had to worry about what I said to guys because they don't think. In the beginning, they care more about how you look. But women actually care about what you have to say." Her mom rolled her eyes. "Don't roll your eyes at me," Hannah said in her stern teacher voice.

"I can do whatever the hell I want. Now give me your phone."

"What?"

Her mom held out a hand and wiggled her fingers. "Hand over your phone, young lady."

"What? Why am I having high school flashbacks?"

"Because you're in trouble."

"But I'm…thirty-two? I have a mortgage." Her mom disconnected Hannah's phone from the USB cord playing Hannah's Spotify playlist. "Hey! That was a good song. You don't turn off the Civil Wars. That's a crime against music."

"Again, I don't know what that means."

Hannah wasn't sure what was riskier, checking on her mom while navigating the road or letting her mom go through her phone. It was so unfortunate that her mom wasn't like the other moms with an Android. Nope, her mom had an iPhone and knew how to break into one. Hannah rolled her eyes. She needed to think of a more complicated six-digit password than her birthday.

"What are you doing?" Hannah said. Her mom tapped on the screen, paused as if reading something, and then started typing. "Mom?"

"Hold on one second." After a few more moments, she finished whatever she was up to and flipped the phone over on her lap, screen-down. "There." She said it so casually, as if she'd done something as simple as change the radio station. "I messaged Erin."

Hannah's eyes widened. Erin was one of the girls who'd actually messaged her. She had been talking to her in small amounts for the last five days. For a woman who didn't know what "matching" or "ghosting" was, she sure knew her way around her daughter's dating app.

Hannah's heart thudded as a heat splashed onto her face. "You messaged Erin? Oh my God. Mom!"

"Oh, stop it. You're acting like I'm feral."

"I'm pretty sure a mother texting someone on her daughter's dating app is basically the equivalent of feral." A ding chimed on her phone, pulling their attention back to it. Her mom broke back into the phone and started texting again.

Hannah was grateful when she pulled into her parents' driveway and could devote all of her attention to whatever antics her mother had been up to. Once her mom hopped out of the car with the phone, Hannah chased her into the garage while she was still typing.

Geez, was she writing poor Erin a novel?

"Can I have my phone back, please?" Hannah said, unlocking several memories of her teenage years when she'd been grounded and had given the same kind of plea.

Her mom tapped the phone as if adding a last punctuation mark, then beamed when she gave the phone back. "Erin's typing. We're having a great chat. She sent me a winking face."

They stepped inside the house and were greeted by the smell of charcoal wafting from the patio through the first floor, cluing them in that Hannah's dad was trying to squeeze out a couple more dinners on the grill before retiring it for the winter.

She didn't have time to snoop and see what he was grilling. She had to snoop on her own dating app inbox to see what the hell her mother had sent to all the queer women within a fifty-mile radius.

She read her mom's text. *Hi Erin. I've noticed on your profile that you love hiking and the outdoors. My favorite hike is in Golsby Park. Have you been?*

Erin responded. *Oh, hi there! I've heard so many great things about Golsby Park, but I've never been.* Followed by the grimace emoji.

Mom disguised as Hannah: *If you're up for it, I can show you around. It's very beautiful. Gorgeous wildflowers. It's a hidden gem. If you're ever interested in hiking there, let me know.*

Erin: *I would love to go. The outdoors, wildflowers, and a cute tour guide?* Winky face. *Where do I sign up?*

Mom: *You sign up right here.*

A blush slammed onto her face as she sank into her chair at the kitchen table. Hannah lowered the phone and stole a glance at her mom filling up a glass of ice water from the Brita. How did she make it look so easy? How did her mom, who'd been happily married to her dad for thirty-four years—and had an insane crush on Tom Selleck for as long as Hannah had been alive—have more game with women than Hannah? She was easily making moves on queer women in their thirties as if *they* were Tom Selleck.

She needed to give her mom way more credit.

Her phone dinged with another message. *You say the date and time, and I'll be there.*

"Oh, did Erin respond?" Her mom rounded the counter and peered over Hannah's shoulder as if she truly believed she and Erin were best friends. Hannah didn't hide the phone. It would have been wrong. Her mom had done all the work, and she deserved to see the payout. "Looks like I just got you a date. You're welcome." Her mom nudged her shoulder.

"I can't believe this is happening right now."

"Lots of things to think about, dear. Should you get a cat? Should you go on a hike through the wildflowers with Erin? What are you going to do?"

Hannah exhaled deeply. She knew exactly what to do in both situations because she could feel it pressing in her gut. Her life was about to change in all the ways she'd wanted it to change. But even exciting changes were scary, like approaching the big hill of a roller coaster but suddenly becoming aware of its intimidating height. She was about to make that thrilling plummet, and the feeling already swirled in her gut.

If change was easy, then people wouldn't ever be stuck, and some people lived their whole lives willing things to be different. Some people were too afraid of the feeling of excitement meeting nerves like two oceans colliding.

But not Hannah. She wanted to ride out those waves and see where they took her because for all she knew, a collision could settle everything in place. After all the questions and confusion during the summer, all she wanted was to be settled in a place where she belonged.

She swallowed the nervous lump in her throat. "I want to get a cat, and I want to go hiking with Erin. That's what I want to do."

Chapter Three

"Buddy, they came here to see you," Reese whispered to Apollo, who was hiding underneath her bed. "You can't stay under here forever. You need to find your family."

Reese had made so much progress with him the last two weeks. It had started off very slow and had taken him a couple of days to explore her house, a whole week for him to come up to Reese and brush against her. Now, he slept by her feet every night, followed her around during the day, and curled up on his bed on her desk while she worked. She'd started calling him her little shadow. He was going to make the most loyal companion to someone or some family.

Four different families had stopped by with Ashley to meet him. One of those was in her living room with Ashley now, waiting for Apollo to come up to them. They had a five-year-old daughter who Reese sensed was one hundred percent over Apollo the second he'd hissed at them and sprinted to Reese's room.

She stretched her hand under the bed. He gave her one sandpaper kiss as if to thank her for checking in. She scratched his white chin as he extended it. "Come on, buddy. There are all these people who want to adopt you. You can't keep hiding from them."

When she took back her hand, Apollo stared and blinked. Reese took it as his way of telling her he could do whatever he wanted. She accepted his answer, let out a deep sigh, and went back to the living room where Ashley and the family waited.

"I'm sorry," Reese said, shaking her head. "He really is a sweet boy. He just needs time to adjust. He follows me around everywhere, loves to cuddle, and loves to play. Loves string and catnip and laser pointers. He just needs a few weeks to adjust. If he warmed up to me, I'm positive he could warm up to anyone."

The parents looked at her with sympathy. "It's okay. He just doesn't know us yet," the dad said.

"I like the orange kitty at the other place, Daddy," the five-year-old girl said, tugging on her dad's arm.

As defeated as Reese felt after hearing the brutally honest comment, she couldn't blame the girl. Hissing at her at really didn't help Apollo's case.

"Oh, sweetie. This kitty is just shy," the mom said and stroked her hair.

"The orange kitty liked to play with me. This one hissed at me."

"That's just because he's scared. He needs to get to know us."

The parents shot Reese an apologetic look. She thinned her smile. It was what came with fostering. She'd seen it before. People and families came to Lonely Hearts for an animal they'd seen on the website and left with a completely different one. Apollo didn't give the family a chance for them to fall in love with him, unlike Toby, the orange cat Reese remembered rescuing. While she was so happy that Toby had a girl who'd fallen madly in love with him, she couldn't tame the pang that rippled through her after hearing the little girl's plea for Toby and not giving Apollo the chance he deserved.

In the end, the parents apologized profusely and left without him. She knew they would go back to Lonely Hearts and at least adopt Toby, who deserved a loving home just as much as Apollo and the other cats.

However, Reese was biased. Apollo was her newest baby. Of course she was rooting for Apollo more.

Once the family left, she toppled on her couch and rested her head against the back of it, willing the sadness to subside. Ashley had scheduled for one more interested person to come by to meet Apollo, making it the fifth prospect to walk into her living room in the last week.

"He's going to find a home," Ashley said when she joined Reese on the couch. She patted her knee. "I know it."

Just like magic, when Reese opened her eyes, she found Apollo poking his head around the corner. She slid off the couch and onto the floor and sprinkled some catnip on her rug. His tail shot straight up, and he trotted over. He rammed his head against her hand and licked up his favorite treat. After he ate up the pinch, Reese decided to give him a big lump.

"Might as well loosen him up for the next visitor," she said, scratching his back as he cleaned up the catnip.

When he finished, he licked his lips and missed all the catnip stuck to his beard. He flopped over and showed off his belly. Reese ruffled the fur on his chest and laughed at the chaotic look in his eye.

She wished that the families who had walked away could see how happy and silly he was when he felt safe. She wished she could record him at his most comfortable and make everyone who stepped through her living room watch it so she could tell them this was how he was with some patience and love.

Then the doorbell rang. Apollo rolled back onto his stomach. He dug his claws into the rug and shrank himself into a frightened ball, ready to book it when the fifth person walked through the door.

"Want to answer it, Ashley?" Reese said and leaned in to pet him more in an attempt to calm him down. "I want to be next to him so he doesn't run."

"Sure thing."

As Ashley answered the door and greeted the person, Reese focused on Apollo and gave him his favorite chin scratches. He didn't stretch out his head. He was too concerned about the new person stepping inside. His pupils widened, and Reese could feel him tense. She heard a woman greeting Ashley and hoped that the sweet, gentle voice meant something. She wondered if it meant something to Apollo because he didn't flinch. His pupils dilated whenever he was scared or unsure, but he didn't run like with the other families.

"Aw, look at this little guy," the woman said, inching closer.

When Reese turned, she found familiar bright blue eyes staring at her that widened at the sudden contact.

A hot heat rushed down her back. Was that Hannah Marsh? The same Hannah Marsh who Reese had spent all of high school secretly crushing hard on?

Sweat beaded at Reese's hairline, and the surprise reunion unleashed all the forgotten memories like a broken dam.

"Reese Shepard? Oh my God."

Reese stood and paid extra attention to her knees. Seeing Hannah Marsh standing in front of her had her off-balance, as if she had stepped onto a tightrope without any warning. God, that friendly and contagious smile took her way back to when Reese would steal so many glances on the soccer field, in the hallways, in the locker room. Way back in the day, Hannah Marsh smiling at her would have made her whole day. It had been fourteen years since they had last seen or spoken to each other, but God, was she as beautiful as ever. She apparently still had the ability to make heat spiral up Reese's spine and land on her face.

"Hannah Marsh?" Reese said, hoping her nerves didn't make her words tremble too much. "Wow. It's been a minute. How have you been?"

"Not too bad. I can't complain, especially when I get to meet this little guy."

She pointed. Reese turned and found Apollo in the same spot. He still had a cautious grip on the rug, wide eyes firmly set on Hannah; one more move, and he would bolt. However, when Reese gestured for Hannah to sit, and she lowered to the ground next to Reese, Apollo widened his eyes, watching her. In that moment, with Hannah's knees brushing hers, Reese felt one hundred percent as nervous as him. Hannah Marsh sat an inch next to her and brought a wave of fruity shampoo with her.

Reese swallowed the lump in her throat and exchanged a glance with Ashley. For some reason, Apollo hadn't run. He stayed long enough for Hannah to sit and for the two of them to share the same space. Reese had no idea what was happening. This was already the longest he had been around someone without running away. She was afraid to move, scratch her nose, or say a word.

"You two know each other?" Ashley asked, keeping her voice soft.

Reese wanted to nod but decided against it. Apollo was skittish over the most random things. Plastic bags, headphones, hell, anything Reese held, he ran away from.

"We went to high school together," Reese said.

"We played soccer. She was my partner in crime."

Reese felt the blush slam onto her cheeks. "Oh, I don't know about that."

From the side of her eye, she saw Hannah face her with a shocked look. Apollo's stare was unwavering, but he still sat a foot in front of them.

"What are you talking about?" Hannah said. "It was you and me out there, Number Twenty-One."

"Hannah was significantly better than me. I was Robin to her Batman."

"That's absolutely not true." Hannah looked at Ashley. "Don't listen to her. She was pretty good."

Hannah was one year older, and Reese remembered dreading the end of her junior-year season because that meant Hannah would graduate and move on, most likely never to be seen again. They weren't best friends; they'd never hung out outside of their soccer team, but they had always been friendly. They followed each other on Facebook, though neither of them kept up with it. Even as Facebook friends after all this time, they'd still morphed into strangers.

"Never thought that next time we saw each other would be you adopting my foster cat," Reese said and pried her stare off Apollo to flash a smile.

When Hannah smiled back, Reese inflated like a balloon. All the feelings she'd dealt with on a daily basis in high school took hold again. One by one. Blush-infused cheeks, balloon in her chest, and every nerve ending lit up and flickered like the end of a cigarette.

Hannah pulled her glance off Reese and back to Apollo. She wiggled her fingers at him, and instead of caving to the greeting, he retracted his claws and tucked his paws under his chest in a perfect cat loaf.

"He's such a handsome cat. I bet tons of people are wanting to adopt him," Hannah said in a high-pitched voice directed at Apollo.

"I'm shocked he's still here," Reese said. He'd decided to settle into his spot with a complete stranger sitting inches in front of him and giving him attention. "He's been running away from everyone else. I just gave him a bunch of catnip. Maybe he's too high to run."

Reese handed Hannah a bag of salmon treats and his favorite string toy with fake pink feathers on the end. At the sound of the bag, he perked up and stared at Hannah's hands. She opened it and tossed one treat over. He jerked back and gave a displeased blink.

"I didn't mean to scare you," Hannah said. "I'm sorry. Here's another."

She grabbed another treat and slowly leaned in to place it next to the first one. Once she retreated back, Apollo appraised it from a distance for a few moments before taking one step. He cautiously sniffed as if he was a drug dog searching for something, and when he deemed them safe, he ate each treat in one swipe. He licked his lips and sat there, waiting for more. Hannah placed the third treat right in front of her. He didn't budge, too smart to fall into the trap.

Hannah reached out for him to sniff her hand. Reese was amazed when he inched forward, still keeping a safe distance, but sniffed her. His pink nose wiggled while he took his time surveying her and her whole life story.

Right as she reached for the bag of treats, Reese felt soft fingertips glide against hers. She looked over as the nerves started trickling in her stomach, and those bright blue eyes rounded at the contact. Pinpricks of heat popped up where Hannah touched her.

"Here, go ahead," Reese said and powered through the stutter dancing on the tip of her tongue.

Hannah flashed her a friendly smile and opened the bag. Reese tamed the fluttering in her stomach as Apollo perked up. He lowered his head and cautiously tiptoed forward. He snatched the treat and retreated back to his original spot to eat it. Hannah ditched the treats and offered his string toy. The little bell tied to the pink feathers jingled as she tossed it. He lowered himself in a pouncing position, and after a couple of string flicks, he lurched forward. He snapped at the feathers and swatted at the little bell.

Reese looked at Ashley, who seemed as surprised as she was.

Was Hannah Marsh really the chosen one?

Reese sat there in awe, observing how with each passing minute, Apollo loosened up. His tight, curled-up stance stretched out as he waited for another flick of the pink feather. His white paws flinched and swatted every time the feather moved. He was so entranced by the string that it was like he had forgotten how scared he was around people.

If he could let his guard down that easily because of his favorite toy, Reese was even more certain that he could warm up when he found the person he trusted.

In a matter of ten minutes of playing, Apollo plopped himself a few inches in front of Hannah. When she attempted a chin rub, he quickly lowered the last bit of his guard in a matter of a few scratches. He stretched out his head as if telling Hannah to give him more.

Reese's mouth hung open.

"This guy is so freakin' cute," Hannah said.

Apollo pulled away and brushed his cheek against Hannah's hands, and the sound of his purrs filled the small circle they'd formed around him. Those were the exact purrs he gave Reese when he lay at the foot of her bed at night while she massaged his back.

Reese relaxed against the couch. Seriously, what in the world was happening? Apollo was playing with someone after running away from a family just an hour ago? And not just anyone. Hannah Marsh.

Maybe Reese and Apollo had much more in common than Reese had originally thought. There was something about Hannah Marsh that had pulled them both right in.

"What are you thinking?" Ashley said, clasping her hands in front of her chest. "You two seem to be hitting it off."

Hannah shrugged innocently, and the cute, confused grin she flashed dug up the crush Reese had buried fourteen years ago. It came on so easily. All it took was being in Hannah Marsh's space, and she felt like a teenager all over again, sucked into Hannah Marsh's adorable charm. The most frustrating thing about it was that Hannah never had to try. She was just naturally adorable and charming.

"I really love him," Hannah said and moved her cheek scratches to his back.

He plopped on the ground and raised his butt in the air, giving them a view.

Reese was too stunned to pay attention. "Wait, seriously?" She felt like a mom whose child was invited to his first playdate. Except in this case, the playdate was permanent.

"Of course. What's not to love? He's sweet, he's funny, and I can already tell he has a very unique personality. I know he needs some patience, but I think I have it. I'm a fifth-grade teacher. It's basically a requirement. I would love to move forward with him."

Hannah glanced at Ashley, and she looked at Reese. Reese nodded her approval. Even as so much sadness settled in her like fallen leaves, she wanted to gather up the pile and toss them victoriously in the air. Apollo had found someone who understood him.

"Amazing," Ashley said. "I'll follow up with an interview. We like to vet those who adopt and make sure the animals are going to the best home."

Reese was so happy for Apollo. The little fluffball didn't even know how great a life he was about to have. "Did you hear that, buddy?" she said and reached to pet his head. "You chose your person. You're going to have a family."

He cheek-bumped Reese's hand. She liked to think it was his way to fist bump, as if saying, "Hey, Foster Mom. We did it. We found me a home."

Hannah stayed for ten more minutes, gave him a pinch of catnip, more chin scratches, and a few flicks of his string toy before Reese walked Hannah and Ashley to the door.

"I promise, he'll have the best home," Hannah said with a small smile, and it caused Reese's stomach to somersault. "He's going to be so spoiled. You can't see the shopping list in my head, but I promise that you would approve of everything this little guy is about to get."

"I know he will," Reese said and then checked behind her to find Apollo tucked in a cat loaf.

Although Reese was sad that her time with him wouldn't be hers anymore, she was sure that Hannah Marsh would give him the home he deserved. Everything about her had always been so kind. She was nice, genuine, and always had a smile. Reese couldn't help but wonder if Apollo's phenomenal animal instincts had led him to his chosen family.

"I'm just going to miss this guy, that's all," she said.

"This doesn't have to be the end, you know. Now that I know you live nearby, it would be great to catch up. See what's been happening since high school. And if everything works out with Apollo, you can come visit anytime."

"Yeah, I would love to catch up. Can I have your phone? I'll give you my number."

Hannah offered her phone.

Once she plugged in her number, Reese handed the phone back. "I welcome Apollo pictures. Actually, I insist on them. It's part of the adoption deal."

Hannah laughed. "Sounds good. I shall deliver. It was really nice seeing you again, Reese. I had no idea that by meeting Apollo, I would be reuniting with a long-lost high school friend." She glanced over Reese's shoulder. "Bye, sweet Apollo! I hope to see you soon."

After Hannah and Ashley left, Reese plopped on the rug, repeating Hannah's last words. She considered Reese a long-lost high school friend? That was a bold statement given the fact that they had been friendly acquaintances on the soccer team. Hannah's comment unveiled more of the crush Reese had buried with her youth. It could have just been Hannah being nice, but at that moment, Reese brushed that theory aside. She wanted to revel in Hannah while at the same time reveling in the fact her bestest buddy Apollo had picked out his new family.

She scooped him up and planted kisses all over his face. The sound of rolling purrs vibrated inside him.

"I think we found you a home, buddy. You did good. You found yourself a sweet…and super pretty mama. I'm so proud of you."

She hugged him again, and when he brushed his face against hers, her eyes stung with tears.

Chapter Four

The second Hannah opened Apollo's cage in her bedroom, he sprinted underneath her bed. She found his big eyes reflecting from the farthest corner. She let out a disappointed exhale. All the articles she'd read about introducing a cat to a new home said that cats didn't like change and needed a few days to adjust to their new surroundings. Reese had warned her when she'd first met Apollo, and Ashley had made sure during their phone interview that Hannah remained patient, but all the warnings didn't make it less disappointing and stressful that Apollo didn't immediately know how safe and loved he already was.

"I know, change is scary," Hannah said, sprawling on her stomach and resting her chin on her hand. "I'm going through a little bit of change myself. Maybe we can help each other?" He blinked and formed into a tight cat loaf. "I feel like you're kind of like me in a way. A little shy, but if given the chance, and surrounded by the right people, you'll open up. I understand that completely. However…" She got up, collected the mouse toys she'd bought and his favorite string toy that Reese had given her. She lined them up under the bed. "Look at all the toys you have." She whipped the string toy around, hoping that would make him come closer. Instead, he turned away and faced the wall. "Okay, I'll leave you alone, but I'll be right here. Whenever you want to come out."

Everything on the internet, as well as Ashley, said that for the first two days, keeping him secluded in one room would help him adjust. So that was what Hannah did the first night. She graded homework assignments and spread the papers across her bed. She messaged Erin to make sure they were still on for a walk tomorrow, and after Erin confirmed their evening stroll, Hannah got ready for bed. She checked on Apollo and found him passed out on the opposite corner of where she'd last seen him. At least he had moved around and found enough comfort to fall asleep, right?

❖

Hannah and Erin had spent almost two hours hiking the Golsby Park paths, immersed in effortless and never-ending conversation. Erin worked as a physical therapist, a job she absolutely loved. Hannah listened attentively as Erin smiled through the conversation about her close-knit and rather large family and the best places she had hiked and wished to walk in the future. When Erin's tone softened at the mention of her Akita mix dog, Clover, who she had adopted from Lonely Hearts four years back, Hannah felt a softness for her. There were no awkward silences, no overcompensating need to impress each other, and they both discovered they had quite a lot in common. There was something sweet and natural about Erin, and when their conversation turned flirtatious, Hannah relished in the warmth that streaked across her cheeks.

"This is a beautiful park," Erin said as they walked through the parking lot to their cars. "I can't believe I've never made it out here. Thank you for showing me around." She touched the back of Hannah's arm as they reached her CR-V.

When the eye contact held for a second longer than she anticipated, Hannah flitted her gaze away to the asphalt. "Oh, anytime. I had a lot of fun. Thanks for walking with me."

"Good luck with Apollo. This period is the hardest part. Clover was a bit scared too when I adopted her, but she came around, and now I can't imagine my life without her. She's the greatest decision I've ever made."

Hannah smiled. "Thank you for that. I have a feeling Apollo will warm up. It will be a good test of my patience."

"You're a teacher. I'm sure you have a lot of it."

"We will soon find out."

Erin rested her hand on the same spot that still burned from her touch moments before. "You get home safe, Hannah. Thanks for the great evening. Have a good night."

Erin leaned in and sent Hannah's heart into palpitations. She planted a soft kiss on Hannah's cheek. When she pulled back, she hovered just a couple of inches away. Shouldn't Hannah have felt desire tingling her lips? Shouldn't she have felt something magnetic zapping through her like a lightning bolt from being kissed by a beautiful woman?

Instead, she felt like a light-polluted night sky, the lack of chemistry clouding her ability to find one little spark out there in the abyss that she could reel in and run with. But since that wasn't there, she forced a friendly smile, backed away, and pulled her keys out of her pocket.

"You too." Hannah offered Erin a one-arm hug and got into her car. She sat in the driver's seat and watched Erin pull out of the parking lot. As Erin drove past, she smiled, gave Hannah a sly wave, and drove down the road.

Hannah expected to feel so much more. She felt the burning when Erin had touched her and liked how it felt having a woman slide a hand down the back of her arm. It was a reaction and a sign that confirmed Hannah's attraction and interest in women.

However, she wanted to feel so much more. Shouldn't she have felt something? A woman who was sweet, beautiful, caring, and who was also mature and responsible? She crossed off all the boxes, for crying out loud. So where the hell were the sparks when she'd kissed Hannah's cheek? Where was the desire skating on Hannah's lips, willing Erin to kiss her? Where was the riptide of anticipation of Erin's next text rather than the apathetic feelings Hannah already felt?

She needed to find some way to replicate the explosive firework feeling she'd always imagined she would feel when a woman kissed her. However, she'd already accepted that Erin wouldn't be the person to make her feel that way.

She was disappointed. She sighed her way back home, tiptoed into her bedroom, and lowered herself on the floor to check on Apollo underneath the bed. Erin might not have been meant for her, but Apollo definitely was, and she was so grateful that she got to come home to him. Instead of forming himself into a cat loaf, he sprawled on his side with one paw extended.

"I'm back. Did you miss me? It doesn't really look like it, but I'm glad you look comfortable."

He slowly opened his tired eyes. Hannah told herself the fact that he was in the middle of the floor, stretched out as if he was lying out on a lounge chair in the sun, and the fact that he didn't immediately run, was progress. She extended her hand to allow him to sniff. He perked up, smelled her hand, and then looked back at her.

"Does that mean you don't hate me?" He blinked and tucked his extended paw underneath him. "I don't know if the date went well. Like, shouldn't you know right away if there's something there? How can there be nothing there when she had everything I was looking for?" She waited for his response, but all he did was stare with a spark of curiosity. She took that as a sign to continue. "I don't know. I feel like we would make better friends, you know? I feel like you do know. You went on a few blind dates. Can you give me some tips on how to know when they're the right person? I guess I should follow my gut, huh? My own instincts?"

He let out a big yawn, flashing his full set of teeth, and then looked like a sweet, innocent ball of black-and-white fluff.

"Okay, sweet boy. I'm going to make some tea. I'll be right back."

She wandered into her kitchen to start the kettle, leaving her bedroom door cracked in case Apollo had the urge to sniff around. Her seven o'clock tea was an evening ritual she looked forward to. She loved something warm in her stomach while settling in for the night of either grading homework, reading a book, or indulging in trash TV that didn't use up any brainpower. It was quite the range of evening activities, but since she'd gotten ahead the night before with grading, she planned on watching trash. It would soon get better when Apollo adjusted to his new home so she could get his take on the *Selling Sunset* drama.

As she headed back into her room and set her steaming tea on her nightstand, she checked on him again. She couldn't help it. She loved knowing she had company underneath her bed. But as she poked her head underneath, she found it empty of an adorable fluffball. She perked up and searched behind her nightstands, then walked into her bathroom, checked behind the toilet, and the shower curtain. Nothing.

She scurried into her living room and peered underneath her couch and recliner. When she came up with nothing, she poked her head on the other side of her TV stand. When there was still no Apollo, her heart pounded, and the panic pressed against her sternum as her mind defaulted to the worst-case scenario.

Where the hell was he?

Day two of being a cat mom and she already lost him; it was as if he'd decided he hated her and had run away.

She rechecked all the spots, and when she still came up with no Apollo, tears threatened her eyes. The rational part of her brain told her that he had to be somewhere in the house. She hadn't opened the front door since she'd walked in from her date forty-five minutes ago. He had just found a good hiding spot. But the irrational part of her brain was not in the driver's seat. It told her he had unlocked the front door and darted back to Louisiana.

"Apollo! Come here, sweet boy," she said, jiggling the bag of salmon treats all over her house.

She had no idea what to do. Frantically call Ashley? Ashley might regret her decision to let Hannah adopt Apollo and round up all the other Lonely Hearts adoption coordinators so they could break into her house. They would snatch up Apollo in the middle of the night so they could find someone who wouldn't lose him on the second day.

Absolutely not. That wasn't an option.

She didn't know too much about who Reese Shepard was now, but she remembered her being sweet and quiet, and she hoped that meant she wouldn't judge Hannah for the frantic call she was about to place.

Her heart hammered, half with anxiety about Apollo and the other half with anxiety about Reese thinking that she didn't deserve to have her precious foster baby. "Hey, Reese? It's Hannah Marsh."

"Oh, hi, Hannah. What's up?" Hannah heard the friendly smile in her voice.

It's going to be the adoption coordinators and Reese breaking into your house. A whole team is going to save Apollo from you.

Hannah nervously scratched the back of her head as she paced in an erratic pattern across her living room. "You have any insight on really amazing cat hiding spots?"

Reese chuckled. "Is he hiding from you?"

"I think so? I mean, I left the bedroom door cracked open while I made tea, just in case he wanted to be adventurous, and when I came back, he wasn't underneath the bed."

"So he's definitely in the house somewhere," Reese said matter-of-factly. Her calmness and the chuckle from the second before alleviated some of the pressure in Hannah's chest. That must mean Reese didn't think she was a horrible cat mom, right?

"Has to be," Hannah said. "I know I'm already failing at being a cat mom, but I'm hoping that as his best friend, you could help me get into his head."

"I promise that you're not a horrible cat mom. Cats love to hide. I lost him for about ten minutes the first night I brought him back."

"Oh yeah? Where did you find him?"

"Under the bathroom sink, in the cabinet."

Hannah stopped pacing. "The cabinets?"

Reese laughed again, and it reassured Hannah that she was panicking over nothing, which was exactly what she needed. "Cats know how to open cabinets. Some can even open doors. Apollo apparently loves hiding in the cabinet underneath the sink. I found him sleeping in there countless times, like it was made for his naps."

Damn it. Hannah had no idea they had door-opening powers. Who needed opposable thumbs? Apparently, not cats.

"Okay, hold on," Hannah said.

She scurried into the bathroom, flipped on the light, and checked underneath the sink. Sure enough, there was Apollo, hidden in the farthest corner, big googly-eyes staring back at her behind a box of tampons. "What are you doing in here?" She reached her hand for him to sniff, but he stared at her blankly, as if he was pissed off at her for disturbing his peace.

"Found him?" Reese said.

"He's all the way in the back corner, hiding behind a box of tampons."

"Now you know how much he loves bathroom cabinets. He might even hide in the cabinets above your fridge…if you have them. One of my cats growing up would jump on top of the fridge and get himself into the cabinet above it. Cats are stealthy."

Hannah exhaled again. "It just makes me so sad that he's so scared."

"Cats hate change. You're only on your second day. Apollo didn't start braving outside my bedroom until day four. Didn't start playing with his string toy in my bedroom until day five. Didn't curl up on my lap until the second week. Apollo has his own time, but we know that he can eventually warm up. Remember when you met him, he didn't run away at all? You should have seen him with the four other families. He didn't give them a chance."

"Wasn't he high on catnip when he met me?"

"He was, but he still could have run. Give him a couple more days. He wasn't ever afraid of you. He's probably more scared of his new surroundings than he is with you specifically."

"I have been spending my evenings in the room with him, hoping one day soon he will hop up and watch some reality TV with me."

"Reality TV. Your love for *The OC* has morphed into reality TV?"

Hannah smiled, knowing exactly what Reese was referencing. "*The OC* was everything back in our day."

"You and Katie MacIntosh would have an episode debrief the next day with the whole team. God, I still remember everyone walking into the locker room in hysterics after Marissa shot Trey."

"It was a crazy episode," Hannah said, and they shared a laugh. "You were, like, the only one who didn't watch it."

"Well, after that episode, I started watching."

"Eh, but by then, the show was rapidly going downhill. You really missed its peak. Anyway, I think Apollo is settled under the sink for now. Forget the fact that he has a cat tree, two doughnut beds, and a human bed. He prefers the bathroom cabinet. Maybe it would help if he saw his best friend?"

"Really?"

Hannah heard the excitement in Reese's voice and smiled. "I'm serious about catching up, Number Twenty-One. Plus, I have someone here who would love to see you."

"I'm free tomorrow night if that works for you."

"It absolutely does. I'll text you my address and let you go. Thank you for helping me find Apollo. Now I know where to check next time he runs away."

"I foster cats all the time. I'm aware of all of their habits. Call anytime you need to ask a question. I'll see you tomorrow."

Hannah hung up and set the phone on her sink. Apollo lifted his head. "Do you want to stay here or head back to bed?"

When he lowered his head back onto his paws, she accepted his wishes and watched *Selling Sunset* by herself.

❖

"I come bearing gifts," Reese said on the other side of Hannah's front door, lifting a plastic bag in one hand and a bottle of red wine in the other.

Hannah gestured for her to come in. "Oh, you didn't have to do that."

"I know, but I want to spoil Apollo and figured I would treat the host. Not even sure what kind of wine you like, so I won't be offended at all if you don't want it."

"Please, I think this bottle of pinot is a major upgrade on the Target wine I had to offer. But please come in. Apollo is underneath the bed right now if you wanted to take a peek. The adventure under the bathroom sink really tired him out."

Hannah set the wine bottle and plastic bag filled with more catnip, catnip toys, and salmon treats on her coffee table before leading Reese to her bedroom. She flipped on the light, and they crouched to find Apollo in the same back corner. At least this time, instead of a tightly balled cat loaf, he rested his chin on the floor.

"What are you doing back there, buddy?" Reese said. He opened his eyes slowly and blinked. "You should come out and give me a tour of your new home. It's lovely. So much more than a box of tampons." Apollo closed his eyes, wanting nothing to do with Reese or Hannah. Reese stood. "I've noticed that he likes to sleep until nine-ish, and then he gets a burst of energy. I bet you he doesn't want to compromise his nap time."

"That *is* the time he emerges from underneath the bed and stares at me from the corner. Maybe he will grace us with his presence then. Until then, want to break into this bottle?"

"Absolutely."

They headed back to the living room. Hannah offered Reese a glass of pinot noir as they settled into the couch. "You know, we were on the same high school soccer team for three years, and I feel like this is one of the only times we've sat down one-on-one," Hannah said. "For being partners in crime, I find that truly unacceptable."

Reese pulled a drink. "I mean, we did have eighteen girls on the team, and you were Miss Popular. A seat by Captain Hannah Marsh was prime bus real estate."

"What? Absolutely not." Hannah felt the heat blossoming all over her face.

Reese must have noticed because she laughed. "It's true," she said. "Everyone loved you. Maybe Apollo picked up on it, and you can't argue with animal intuitions. It's scientific. So if you disagree, you're going against science."

"It's scientific that everybody loved me?"

"Yes, it's called chemistry." Reese laughed at her own joke.

Hannah shook her head and grinned. She drank a large gulp of pinot. She'd never learned how to take a compliment, but she did know how to divert from one like a pro. "Ashley told me that you save animals now?"

"I do." It was endearing that she acted so casual about it. "It's pretty amazing."

"What made you get into that?"

"Well, I had an aunt who rescued a bunch. She had chickens, two dogs, three cats, and even a pig."

"A pig?"

Reese grinned. "Yup. Wilbur. He was awesome. I was also obsessed with the movie *Free Willy*."

Hannah's eyebrow quirked. "As in, the kids' movie?"

"He was snatched from his family and all alone in a small tank. His dorsal fin was all flopped over from being in captivity. It wrecked me. I remember telling my parents I wanted to be like my Aunt Katy but save whales when I grew up, and they told me that it wasn't a career. I've never saved an orca but enough dogs and cats—and a few wildlife—that I'm sure is the equivalent to a few orcas."

"Why didn't anyone tell me that was a job I could do? I would have totally signed up for that."

"Don't get me wrong, I absolutely love my job. But it can be really hard sometimes."

Reese didn't need to say more. Hannah saw it all in her dark brown eyes and heard it in the tone of her voice. But even with the heaviness, Reese found a way to nonchalantly sip wine as if her job was the easiest thing in the world while Hannah sat completely in awe. She thought her job was hard at times. Dealing with out-of-control kids, out-of-control parents, even standardized testing, but she couldn't imagine what Reese's job entailed. She wasn't quite sure she wanted her brain to fill in the blanks at the moment. Not when she had good company and good wine.

"How do you even do what you do?" Hannah said. "I bet you see the worst of the worst. How does one even prepare for that? I'm still not over *Homeward Bound* or Mufasa's death, and turn off the TV when Sarah McLachlan starts singing."

"I'm not over Mufasa's death either. I watched the new *Lion King* with my niece and had to close my eyes during *that* scene. She cried. I cried. It was a whole journey talking about the circle of life for the rest of the day, pun intended. But someone's gotta do it, or all those animals will be stuck suffering."

"Stuck where? If they're not stranded from hurricanes, where do you rescue them?"

"All over. Hurricanes, floods, tornados, wildfires out west. Sometimes, we even get asked to travel overseas, so I've helped out in some Caribbean islands, India, Mexico, Guatemala. But most of our rescues are neglect situations, some hoarding, a couple of backyard breeders and puppy mills. Thank you for not going to a shitty breeder or Petland."

"Oh, I would never. We got my dog, Pongo, from Lonely Hearts when I was a kid."

Reese smiled. "I remember Pongo the Golden. How could I forget that name? Didn't he come to a few home games?"

"He did. He was a great dog. Lived to be thirteen and a half."

"A long time for a golden."

"I know. We were really lucky." Hannah paused for another drink. "How didn't I know you were this huge animal lover in high school?"

"I have no idea. I guess we were too busy talking about practice and games, *The OC*, and which boys' homes we were TP-ing that weekend."

As Hannah combed over everything she remembered about Reese, she realized how very little she knew. Were they really only friends on the soccer pitch, and that was it? Reese was a year younger, so that hadn't offered them many opportunities to be in the same class. Their school was quite big: two thousand kids total, which meant getting lost in the crowd was easy. Reese was quiet and was closer to the girls in her class on the team than Hannah and her group of friends. Sometimes, she and Reese had run into each other after the last bell and would walk to the locker room together, and that was the most time they'd had with each other. All their other moments were shared with teammates, and their conversations never dove deeper than soccer, pop culture, or school.

"Okay, so you rescue animals, no big deal," Hannah said jokingly. "And what about before? How did you get here, to this specific job?"

"Well, let's see," Reese said and looked up. "I went to college in North Carolina, didn't play soccer."

"Hey, neither did I. Probably because we couldn't find the kind of partners like what we had going on, right?" She playfully tapped Reese's knee and definitely didn't expect that the simple gesture would shoot something through her stomach.

What the hell was that, and why was it still reverberating on her palm?

She pulled her hand back. Was that the spark? No, it couldn't be. Maybe it was static. Static happened in mid-September, right? She made a mental note to google if static occurred when it was seventy-one degrees outside in mid-September.

Hannah glanced back at Reese, who smiled before pursing her lips as if diving back into thinking about Hannah's original question about her whereabouts. Hannah deflated. Apparently, only she had felt that flicker, and she pulled a long gulp to kill the lingering effects.

"I lived in Puerto Rico for three years and—"

Hannah lowered her glass. "You lived in Puerto Rico for three years? Whoa. Elaborate, please."

"It was my first job out of college. It was a nonprofit that helped with the street dog population down there. I did community outreach with their spay-neuter program."

"If you were living in Puerto Rico, why did you come back to Fairview? Were the palm trees, warmth, and ocean too boring?"

Reese smiled. "I really miss all of that, trust me. Living in San Juan was awesome. I also miss the colorful buildings, the architecture, and the food. But I came back because my family is here. My sister had a baby right after I moved down, and that was hard because I always wanted to be the fun aunt. I was only able to go home for Christmas, and that really wasn't enough time with them. I moved back about five years ago for this job. Now, tell me about you." It was her turn to pat Hannah's knee, and it flickered like a light show in Hannah's stomach again. She shot a look at Reese, willing for there to be some kind of indication that she felt it too. But when Reese casually retrieved her hand and slouched back into the arm of the couch, Hannah realized she was on an island with her feelings. "What have you been up to in the last fourteen years besides living a few blocks from the high school?"

Hannah cleared her throat. "I wish I could compete with you, but I haven't been anywhere exciting. I guess I became one of those people who never leaves her hometown. Lame, I know."

"Not lame at all."

"But." Hannah held up her finger for emphasis. "After this school year, my sister and I are going to celebrate my tenth year of teaching by traveling all over Europe: Ireland, England, France, Germany, and Italy. Soon, I'll see what's outside of Fairview, and then I'll have fascinating stories and won't have to live vicariously through you."

"Ten years of teaching?" Reese said with rounded eyes. "Wow. Sometimes, high school doesn't seem too long ago until something like this is brought up, and I'm reminded it's like a lifetime."

"Right? I started coaching youth soccer last year. I thought that by coaching nine-year-olds, I could get back into the sport I used to love, and let me tell you, I lost it completely. Those fourteen years are really starting to show."

Reese laughed. "I doubt that. You were the best one on the team."

"No, I'm serious. How did I forget so much? You would think twelve years of playing a sport would ingrain it in you forever."

"I hate to burst your bubble, Hannah, but you've been retired longer than you've been playing. It kind of makes sense."

Once Hannah double-checked Reese's math, her jaw dropped at the sudden new perspective. "How dare you age me like that? How dare you age *us*?"

Reese held up her hands in surrender. "I'm sorry. I'm just trying to say that it's been a while, and maybe you're being too hard on yourself."

"Is that what you're saying? Because I think you called me old instead."

Reese's face reddened as she made an I'm-in-trouble-face. Hannah wanted to take a mental picture. Was that a blush, or was her face red because Hannah had teasingly called her out? It was probably the latter, she thought. She'd never noticed Reese like that before. She had always been just Reese Shepard, a sweet, quiet girl on her soccer team whom Hannah had fun playing the sport with. Hannah had never thought about her in any capacity other than as a talented teammate, and because of that, she didn't expect Reese to think of her in any way that caused a blush.

You're just hoping something is there because you're new to this queer woman game, and everyone is shiny. Get back on the dating app and get laid instead.

Just then, a little meow paused their conversation. They turned, and Apollo was sitting on the other side of the coffee table, his fur all ruffled from a deep sleep and his eyes slowly starting to open.

"Oh, hello there, sweet boy," Hannah said and then checked the time on her phone. "You're out early."

"My bestest buddy," Reese said. She downed the last gulp of her wine and lowered herself to the ground. She extended her hand, and after needing a moment to recoup some energy, Apollo extended one paw, stretched out the rest of his sleep, and walked over to brush against her. She looked back at Hannah, her brown eyes melting at Apollo's cuteness.

Hannah couldn't blame her at all. She melted a bit too.

She joined Reese on the opposite side of the floor and opened the plastic bag of goodies. The crunching of the bag froze Apollo in a defensive stance, but once she pulled out the treats, he walked over to inspect it.

"He's already eyeing the catnip," Reese said through her laugh.

Hannah tossed his catnip-stuffed banana toy. He sniffed it once but was more interested in the salmon treats on her lap.

"Here, let me try this," Reese said.

When she reached over to grab the banana toy, a wave of perfume made its way to Hannah. It pulled her into a trance, trying to comb through her memory to see if Reese Shepard had always smelled so good and soft. Who was she kidding? They had been on a soccer team fourteen years ago. She couldn't remember if anyone on the team had smelled good because they'd always smelled like sweat and grass.

Was it because this was the first time Hannah had caught Reese smelling like something light and fruity that made her notice? That the quiet, reserved, and mysterious girl really turned out to have a heart of gold and a tough job that made her such a badass? Or was it because the more Hannah learned about her sexuality and just how attractive so many women were, she took notice of everything and everyone?

Reese pinched the ends of the banana toy together. "If you do this, you can get the catnip smelling stronger."

She tossed the banana back to Apollo. He smelled again, and this time, he plopped his furry body over it, held it between his two front paws, and started licking.

"You are a cat whisperer," Hannah said.

Reese shrugged, and something about her modesty made her even more alluring. "This isn't my first rodeo."

Hannah attempted to pet him, expecting him to lunge back, but he was so enthralled with the catnip, he either didn't notice the pets or truly didn't care as long as he had his toy. "Can you tell me his story?" Hannah asked. "Ashley said that you actually rescued him?"

"I did. I pulled him out of the floodwater and everything."

Hannah's eyes widened. "Pulled him out of the floodwater?"

Reese nodded and proceeded to tell the whole story. From when she first arrived in Louisiana to how her team was on their way back when she discovered him on top of a car. Hannah watched him lick the now-soaked banana and rub his cheeks against it. She pictured Reese wading through waist-deep floodwater, all her gear on, and breaking into homes to search for beloved pets trapped inside or on top of cars. Her heart broke at the same time it swelled from knowing Reese was able to put her emotions aside to save countless animals. Hearing her tell the Hurricane Sarah story made it easier for Hannah to imagine Reese combating wildfires on the West Coast, towns crumbled by tornados, and animals trapped in puppy mills.

Hannah didn't understand. She and Reese had spent three years on a team together, but just in the last hour, she had found out more about Reese than she'd ever bothered to learn during high school. Had Reese Shepard always been fascinating and alluring?

When Reese left an hour later, she hugged Apollo and then Hannah good-bye. Out of all the hugs, high fives, and team handshakes they'd shared, why did that hug catch Hannah's body on fire the way she'd expected Erin's kiss to do to her cheek?

Had Reese Shepard always been this pretty? Damn!

Chapter Five

"Did you rescue all those animals, Aunt Reese?" Nova's eyes lit up when she saw the Lonely Hearts volunteers holding the leashes of several excited dogs who were getting attention, pets, and belly scratches from the visitors.

It was one of Lonely Hearts' adoption events. With the intake of pets from Hurricane Sarah, there was no better place than the Madison Falls Rec Center to host an adoption event. A current of families coming and going filled the parking lot that Saturday. It was perfect exposure for the animals still needing homes.

"I rescued that black lab mix right there," Reese said, pointing to the dog getting pets from a girl Nova's age who wore a green soccer jersey with matching grass stains on her knees. Her dad talked to one of the volunteers standing by a table that had a Lonely Hearts banner hanging in the front. Reese hoped that the dad and his daughter were considering rescuing the dog Reese had found roaming a flooded street.

Off to the side of the parking lot sat the white van with a giant Lonely Hearts logo, the Kitty Mobile. Ashley was in there attending to curious people and families. A mother and daughter stepped out the doors, and it made Reese glad to know that all the animals were causing people to stop and look.

"I want a dog, but my mom says she's allergic," Nova said as the two of them continued walking toward the soccer fields.

This was the first Reese had heard of her older sister, Jenna, being allergic to dogs. In addition to their tuxedo cat, Sylvester, their family had also rescued a cat and dog when Reese was twelve: a beagle mix and an orange and white tabby whom Reese and Jenna had named

Copper and Tod after *The Fox and the Hound*. Not once did Jenna ever get hives or go into anaphylactic shock.

Reese swallowed her curiosity. She planned on interrogating Jenna on why she was lying to Nova and depriving her of a fur sibling. "Have you asked about getting a cat?"

"Mom says she doesn't want any pets. Didn't you guys have two cats and a dog growing up? She showed me pictures once."

"We did. Sylvester, Copper, and Tod. Tod the cat lived to be nineteen. Can you believe that?"

"Wow, that's old. I want to have a cat that lives to be that old."

"Let's talk to your mom and see what can happen."

Nova's brown eyes sparkled. "Really, Aunt Reese? All my friends have pets. I don't know why we don't have one. It's annoying."

"Because your mama is being a pet scrooge."

Nova laughed as they rounded the corner. All the parents and families for the next round of soccer games had already started unfolding lawn chairs along the sideline. Reese searched the fields to find a group with the same purple jersey Nova wore. When Jenna had asked Reese to pick up Nova for the game, she'd told her it was on Field Three, as if Reese knew exactly what that meant. Reese figured Nova would help guide them to the right place.

"There's my team," Nova said, tossed her soccer ball on the grass, and kicked it while heading in that direction. "My coach is right there."

Reese spotted Hannah in the same purple jersey as Nova, her dark blond hair pulled back in a ponytail, clipboard in hand, and a group of nine-year-olds circling her. "Nova, is that your coach?"

"Coach Hannah? Yeah. She's pretty awesome. She used to play soccer, you know."

"Oh, I do."

Nova looked up with a confused frown. "You do? How?"

"Because your favorite aunt used to play with her in high school."

Nova's eyes lit up. "You played soccer with Coach Hannah?" When Hannah and the rest of the team were within calling distance, Nova yelled, "Coach Hannah!"

Hannah turned, a smile already on her face. Her expression turned into an excited yet confused one when she met Reese's eyes.

Reese waved. "Oh, hi there. Apparently, you're my niece's soccer coach. Fun fact."

"And apparently, you two played soccer together," Nova said. "Was my Aunt Reese any good?"

Hannah's eyes locked with Reese's for an additional moment, and the smile that grew felt like it was just for her. At least, that was what she wanted to believe.

"She was," Hannah said to Nova.

"You should come to one of our practices, Aunt Reese."

"Maybe I will. Good luck, Nova." She ruffled Nova's hair before Nova kicked the ball to her teammates, who were sipping on juice boxes and eating orange slices.

Hannah inched forward. "Well, what a small world. I had absolutely no idea Nova was your niece."

"I had no idea that you crossed over to the dark side of Madison Falls."

Madison Falls was the next town over from Fairview, which naturally meant that the two towns had intense rivalries. Reese remembered how her toughest and most competitive games had been against the town. She'd gotten a total of four yellow cards in her high school career, and two of them had come from playing Madison Falls. The girls were more physical than the other schools in their division. Reese was certain it was due to the intense rivalry.

While Hannah Marsh was vivacious, outgoing, and kind to everyone, part of the reason she was so good at soccer was because she was a competitor at heart. She'd cared about the game, her performance, and her team and had expected others to respect the game and do their best in return, including the refs. Reese remembered that the last game of her junior year—Hannah's senior year—was against Madison Falls. The refs had made horrible calls. They had given both Reese and Hannah a yellow card during that game. Reese had never seen Hannah Marsh as angry as that until the last game of her soccer career.

"I figured I'd spread my wings outside of my school district," Hannah said and winced.

"You spread your wings to our rival school district? You're priming our alma mater's enemies. I'm questioning your loyalties." Reese nudged her arm, wanting a reason to touch her. She then wished her good luck and waited on the sidelines until Jenna and her husband, Frank, joined her on the field, both of them carrying a total of three chairs. "Hi. Why did you tell Nova you're allergic to dogs? We had Copper for twelve years."

Jenna laughed as she took a seat. "Hi, sis. My day's going well too," she said, not too seriously.

"Today would be a perfect day to find Nova a best friend."

"Absolutely not. I do not need to relive the pain of losing my pets again."

"But all the memories they gave us outweigh when they died. We had two amazing cats and a dog, plus Aunt Katy's whole farm. Don't you want Nova to experience that?"

Frank chuckled. "Reese, if you can get Jenna to change her mind, I would be forever in your debt."

"Both of them have been begging for a pet," Jenna said, unamused.

"Well, that's perfect, then," Reese said. "Lonely Hearts has so many animals right now."

"I know. I saw them in the parking lot." She patted Reese's knee. "Now, shh, Reese. The game is about to start."

Reese found herself very invested in the game. She'd seen Nova play when she'd first started soccer at five, and watching five-year-olds play had been interesting, to say the least. They'd hopped around the ball and had kicked it aimlessly, like a pebble in their way. Reese was glad those years were behind and that Nova was actually out there running up and down the field, passing to her open teammates and accepting passes from them.

"She's going to be a star midfielder," Reese said. "It's a shame that you chose Madison Falls schools over Fairview, but maybe you'll move out before she starts high school. You have five years."

"Oh my God, she's going to be in high school in five years," Jenna said, tossing a hand over her heart and exchanging a glance with her husband. "In five years, we're going to have a high schooler."

"Thank you for aging us, Reese," Frank said in a teasing tone.

"That's what I'm here for. I'm also here to strongly encourage you to move back to Fairview because I don't know if I can bring myself to cheer for my alma mater's rival. You should feel a little bit traitorous, Jenna. You're setting Nova up to be a Lion in blue and yellow." Reese added a cringe for comedic and dramatic effect.

Jenna hadn't played sports in high school. She'd devoted her life to being in the symphony orchestra, not knowing or fully understanding the intense rivalry.

As Reese thought about her only niece wearing an indigo and yellow soccer jersey, crushing her heart, she stole a glance of Hannah on the sidelines. She couldn't help it. The sight of her in a soccer jersey and a ponytail transported Reese to the lost memories of her youth. The days that had made her heart flutter whenever she'd gotten to simply share the same space as Hannah, the good days when Hannah had flashed her a smile, and the best days when they'd spoken. She had always watched Hannah from some kind of distance.

The warmth still clinging to the September air benefitted her because she was able to admire Hannah in shorts too. God, she'd always had amazing legs. Reese had always had to tame herself from stealing too many glances when they'd stretched before practice.

After fourteen years, Hannah Marsh still had sexy legs.

Reese forced herself to peel her eyes off Hannah. She faced Jenna. "You know, Nova's coach was on my soccer team in high school," Reese said.

"Was she really?" Jenna said and leaned forward to check out Hannah.

"She was the other forward. Once upon a time, she hated Madison Falls too. Like, what's even going on right now? She's coaching here. You moved here. I don't understand."

Jenna let out a "hmm" and settled back in her chair. "Explains why she's looking over here."

"Wait, what?"

"I've caught her looking over here a few times. I just thought maybe someone she knew was here." Jenna gestured to the other people watching the game. "Maybe it's you."

No, that couldn't be. She must have invited someone. Maybe her parents or whoever she was dating. Reese looked back at Hannah, hoping to catch her in the act, but her eyes were on the field as she cheered for one of her girls kicking the ball. Then Reese surveyed all the other people on the sidelines, trying to find some guy their age by himself so she could assume it was Hannah's boyfriend.

However, she just saw parents and a few grandparents, so at least she was able to breathe a relieved sigh, knowing Hannah hadn't brought her maybe-boyfriend to the game. She tried remembering what Hannah's parents looked like. She thought she had a decent memory of them, but when she scanned the sideline again, no faces matched the picture in her head.

When she glanced back at Hannah, their eyes locked. At the sudden contact, Hannah flitted her gaze back to the field as if she'd been caught doing something she wasn't supposed to do. Reese blinked a couple of times, trying to figure out if what she'd caught Hannah doing had actually happened or if she had done so much willing in her past that it had formed an illusion.

"See, told you," Jenna said and nudged Reese's arm. If it wasn't for Jenna confirming that what she'd seen was real, Reese would have believed she'd made it up.

For the rest of the game, Reese was either checking to see if she could catch Hannah in the act or clutching the arms of her seat whenever Nova ran closer to the other team's goal. With a minute left in the game, Nova scored a clean goal. Reese jumped out of her seat along with Jenna and Frank, and Nova flashed them a thumbs-up before celebrating with her team. Did this mean she was on track to become a star soccer player? If so, Reese would have to become more committed to getting her sister and brother-in-law to move out of the Madison Falls school district.

"Want to go check out some animals?" Reese said as she folded up her lawn chair after the game ended. "Or did you not take your allergy meds?"

Frank nodded at Jenna. "You know, it doesn't hurt to look."

"It does hurt to look because you know all those faces are going to be adorable, and you and Nova will just be more set on getting a pet."

"Are we going to look at the animals?" Nova said from behind them.

"That was an amazing goal, Nova," Reese said, holding out her hand for a high five. Nova smacked it and then flashed a proud orange-peel smile.

Jenna shook her head. "Nova, take the orange out of your mouth and tell Aunt Reese thank you."

Nova followed her mom's order and then said, "Thank you, Aunt Reese. Can we go look at the dogs and cats? Please?"

"I don't know, honey." Jenna said, stroking her daughter's ponytail.

"Just five minutes," Frank said.

Nova's smile widened. "I scored the only goal. I want to pet some animals. I think I deserve it."

"You do. Very much so," Reese said at the expense of Jenna shooting her a glare. "I'll go with you and your dad. Let your mom be a scrooge."

Nova giggled. "Yeah, Mom. You're a scrooge."

Right as Reese squeezed Nova's shoulder, she took one last glance to her left at Hannah. Their eyes connected once again as Hannah walked over with a mesh bag of soccer balls and orange cones slung over her shoulder.

Hannah smiled at Reese and then dropped her gaze to Nova. "You played well today, Nova. That was a beautiful goal."

"It's because I'm your good luck charm, right?" Reese said to Nova.

"Obviously," Nova said. "You should take me to practice next week, Aunt Reese, so you and Coach Hannah can show off your soccer moves." She kicked her ball to Reese and looked at her dad. "Can we go look at the animals now?"

Jenna exchanged a glance with Frank, who nodded as if encouraging her that they should go. "Okay, fine. Five minutes," Jenna said. "But we're not bringing one home today."

Nova jumped and hooked her arm around her dad's. "Come on, Aunt Reese. Show us all the animals you rescued."

"I'll be there in a second," Reese said.

Nova dragged Frank so they could move faster, and Jenna trailed behind, a couple of steps in front of Reese and Hannah.

Reese kicked Nova's ball to Hannah. She was impressed by Hannah's quick reflexes that stopped the ball before she kicked it in front of her as they walked. "Good win, Coach, and nice reflexes."

"You proud of that goal? I'm pretty proud of it. She's pretty advanced for a nine-year-old. Must have gotten it from you."

"Maybe, but I doubt it. It's just a bit tragic that my sister is forcing my poor niece to live in Madison Falls. Surely, we can't let her go to high school there. I'm starting a petition to get you and Nova back in Fairview."

Hannah winced. "I guess I'm a bit of a traitor, right?"

"Bit of a traitor? What happened to the Hannah Marsh who, during her last game of senior year, was ready to throw down because of those awful calls?"

"I know! What the hell was I thinking? You're absolutely right." She kicked the ball back to Reese as they rounded the corner of the rec center.

On the other side, the soccer families for the next block of games had gathered in front of the Lonely Hearts table, and there was even a line for the Kitty Mobile that was six people deep.

Hannah elbowed Reese's arm. "Look at all the attention the animals are getting. You're probably really excited seeing this."

Hannah smiled, and the spark coursed around Reese's spine like a growing wildfire at seeing another flicker of Hannah's beautiful and contagious smile, scanning her legs throughout the game, and ruminating over Jenna's observation.

"Definitely," Reese said and coughed, trying to loosen the nerves balling in her throat. "These events always help."

She spotted Nova and Frank petting the same black lab from before the game. The dog's tail wagged in unison with her butt as the dog licked the air while Nova petted her back. Nova's face lit up in one of those smiles only made possible by a happy animal. Reese wondered if Jenna noticed because she had the smallest grin on her face.

Maybe Jenna wasn't fully the pet scrooge she tried to make herself out to be.

And maybe Hannah Marsh had been looking at Reese the entire game.

❖

Reese had never watched Nova's soccer practices, but after the strong possibility of Hannah looking at her enough times for Jenna to notice during the last soccer game, of course Reese was quick to volunteer.

She liked thinking about the glances. It made her feel like she was in high school all over again. She loved how the smallest little things Hannah did added bold colors to her work days. As Paw Aid currently worked and planned with local authorities in Kentucky about a possible puppy mill raid while also keeping an eye on another storm system brewing in the Atlantic, Reese liked and needed the distraction. It didn't matter if she most likely had zero chance with her former crush; it was the anticipation of being in the presence of a beautiful woman that brought on the rush she had forgotten about. *Will she or won't she pat my knee, nudge my arm, or craft a perfectly wide smile just for me?*

It had been a while since Reese had put herself out there in the dating world, much to her mother's chagrin. Jenna had really set the bar high for their parents: finding her person in college, marrying him by twenty-four, and having Nova at twenty-six. At twenty-six, Reese was still living in San Juan, and her girlfriend of two years, Isabella, had broken up with her. The breakup was the catalyst for Reese moving back home. Though she had been debating moving back home for a few months by then, her relationship with Isabella had rooted her in place. When the breakup was done, she'd broken free from the roots and had come back home to restart another chapter of her life.

Though her current job was remote, it involved a lot of travel, especially during hurricane season. Reese didn't like the idea of leaving a pet by itself for long periods of time, and that meant jumping into the dating world was out of the question. Or at least, attempting to date between June through November was out of the question. It was a cycle for Reese. She devoted her summers to work, resurrected the dating apps in November, told herself that maybe this time, she would finally meet someone. There were plenty of first dates, a select few second dates, and by the time June rolled around, Reese was drained.

She knew she needed to try again. She knew that she was also probably open to the idea again because it was her typical cycle. November was six weeks away. Maybe it was her subconscious warming up for dating season.

However, Reese found some contentment being alone. She liked her space and the peace that came with it. But there were pockets of moments where it got too lonely, and the older she got, the larger the pockets became. They were starting to become very noticeable, to the point that the emptiness started to hold some weight. She really did want someone to fill in the loneliness. She just needed it to be the right woman.

Until her schedule allowed her to try dating again, she would enjoy the little moments with Hannah.

Reese popped open a chair off to the side of the Madison Falls Rec Center fields. Nova skipped over to her team and greeted them. Reese's eyes landed on an oblivious Hannah, who placed the cones strategically around the field. A few moments later, she headed back to the group of girls, and then her eyes landed on Reese. She smiled and waved, and the flutter awoke inside Reese.

Was it possible to get goose bumps in the stomach? If so, that must have been what was happening.

"You came to practice?" Hannah called.

"Nova required my presence."

"Depending on how this practice goes, I might require your presence on the field. I always like to end it with a ten-minute scrimmage."

"We should have my Aunt Reese join us," Nova said before turning back to her team. "She played soccer with Coach Hannah in high school. They were really good."

The rest of the team looked at Reese and nodded their approval, as if practice had just gotten a million times more interesting.

During the practice, Reese responded to a flood of work emails coming through after hours. The new hurricane, Timothy, was currently between Puerto Rico and Bermuda and had just been upgraded to a category three. The weather models showed it hitting the Carolinas in four days, and Paws Aid had started formulating their plan in Reese's inbox. As it stood now, she needed to brace herself to be deployed to Charleston in the coming days to help with the recovery efforts. The weather experts predicted Hurricane Timothy would bring lots of rain, despite it being expected to fall to a category one by the time it made landfall.

While catching up on the thread and replying, Reese occasionally looked up to admire Hannah in those black yoga pants that rounded her ass and legs perfectly. Those were a blessing as the years had progressed since her high school days: yoga pants. The tight ones didn't become a thing until after Reese had graduated, so checking Hannah Marsh out in a pair that shaped her bottom half was a brand-new sight. While Reese still tried to grasp her bearings at the sudden appearance of her long-lost crush, she reveled in the swarm of nerves Hannah's presence had always brought, the kind of nerves that woke up and energized her like a shot of espresso in the morning.

And she liked it. A lot.

"Hey, Reese?" She glanced up at the sound of Hannah's voice. "Wanna scrimmage?"

"Come on, Aunt Reese! Show us your moves," Nova called.

She knew she was about to embarrass herself in front of her crush and her niece. She was still deemed "cool" by Nova and wanted to keep it that way for as long as possible. However, the chances of her losing that title skyrocketed when she ran over to the field. Like Hannah, Reese hadn't played soccer since she was eighteen. Did she even know how to juggle anymore?

When Hannah passed the ball, Reese attempted. She rolled the ball back, flicked it up with her toes, and put herself to the test. She surprised herself by getting in a few juggles that apparently were good enough to impress the girls because they gasped and clapped. With the ball in the air, she tapped it over to Hannah, who caught it with her foot. The girls' mouths parted in awe, and their smiles grew as Hannah managed to get a couple in before kicking the ball back out on the field.

The girls clapped. "That was awesome," Nova said. "Can you teach us how to do that?"

"Next practice, I promise. For now, let's split up into teams. One team will be with me, and the other team will be with Nova's awesome Aunt Reese."

Those stomach goose bumps clambered up to the inside of her chest. She loved how her body reacted to anything Hannah did, and at the same time, she despised herself just a little bit.

After Hannah counted off the girls, she and Reese planted the small practice goals on the field and then met up in the middle. "We're the goalies," Hannah said. "You don't have to go easy on them. They're a U10 team. They can handle a challenge."

"The real question is, can we handle a challenge? Wanna make it fun? Losing team supplies a bottle of wine to the winner? Maybe we can have another Apollo hangout this weekend? I really miss him." Reese thought, why not? She liked the attention from Hannah, even if it had been innocent. But if she wanted more nudges, knee pats, and stolen glances, she had to create more opportunities for those to grow.

"I would love that," Hannah said. "He's doing so well. He's been sleeping on my bed, you know. I'll tell you about it after my team kicks your ass." She crafted a perfect grin and clapped to get the girls' attention. And something as simple as a smile made Reese's whole face burn.

Nova and her team brought Reese a victory. Two to one. Nova and another girl scored a goal each, further cementing Reese's plan to get Nova into the Fairview school district before she turned fourteen.

Reese helped Hannah collect the cones, balls, and goals while the girls guzzled water and chatted on the sideline. Hannah nudged Reese's arm again, the touch causing her heart to race like a herd of gazelles.

"Looks like Apollo and I owe you some wine," Hannah said, walking toward the sideline.

"Looks like it. I'm excited to see the little guy again. It looks like I might have to go to Charleston in a few days because of this new hurricane, and it would be great to check in on him before I leave."

"Well, like I said, you're welcome over any time. He's excited to tell you about how we've been cuddling for the last several nights. And by cuddling, I mean he's either at my feet or pressed up against the bend of my knees, but I'm not complaining."

"You got a couple bend-of-the-knees cuddles? I only got one of those in my two weeks of fostering him. That must mean he's really falling in love with you." She couldn't blame him. Hannah was so wonderful that the knowledge of it transcended species.

"That's good because I'm officially in love with him. I'm so glad I found him, and he chose me. How about you come over on Friday, and I'll try my best to convince Apollo to give you a cuddle before your big work week?"

Apollo cuddles and moments with Hannah Marsh? There was no other way Reese would rather spend her Friday night.

Chapter Six

Hannah checked herself in the mirror at least five times before Reese came over. She coiffed her naturally straight, dirty blond hair and made sure a strand didn't rebelliously go rogue and curl. She couldn't determine if her shirt was okay or too much. When Reese had come over the first time, Hannah had worn a Fairview Elementary shirt, not expecting that by the end of the night, she'd crave for more knee taps so she could feel her stomach light up in a fireworks display. She decided to upgrade from a T-shirt to a short-sleeve blouse that dipped to reveal a modest amount of cleavage. She didn't want to give it away that she was desperate for another touch. She just wanted it to be enough to suggest she'd be open to one.

Every time she checked herself, Apollo jumped up on the sink and watched her. He'd become her little shadow, and now, she couldn't go anywhere without him. She twirled around in her mirror, checking out her jeans and if they complemented her legs and butt, if they looked good with the blouse, and if her hair still looked decent.

"Do I look okay? Am I being too obvious?"

Apollo slowly blinked a few times, and based on Hannah's reading of the entire internet, that was a way of showing affection.

She scratched his chin. "Please tell me I don't need to desperately call my mom for approval. If I call her asking about my top, she will hound me over this, and this isn't anything. Just two former teammates hanging out."

She heard a knock at the door. Apollo leapt off the sink and rounded the hallway corner, half being a guard cat and half inspecting who he needed to run away from. When Hannah opened the door, Reese flashed a smile that made her insides twirl and dance.

"Hey, I come with pizza," Reese said, presenting a warm, delicious-smelling box.

"I'm pretty sure this negates your prize for the soccer practice win."

"True, but I was craving pizza, and I was almost positive it would excite you too. There's my bestest buddy!" She held out her arms and scurried over to Apollo, who was still sitting where the hallway pooled into the living room. When he saw her, he let out a meow, rubbed up against the corner, and greeted her with a head rub against her extended hand.

They caught up on each other's week over wine and pizza. Hannah listened to Reese explain what she would be doing in Charleston the next couple of days. She was thankful that Reese took control of the conversation because she was too preoccupied on loosening the large knots of nerves. Why was forming words so difficult right now?

After pizza, they moved to the couch, Hannah on one end, Reese on the other. A contented silence fell as they watched Apollo kneading invisible biscuits on his favorite fleece blanket in between them. Hannah stole a glance at Reese, watching her smile at Apollo as she stroked his back. For barely knowing much about each other, the silence was comfortable, a kind of peace that didn't need any words. Just the sound of Apollo's purrs. When Reese looked up and caught her staring, Hannah forced her gaze to Apollo. Damn it, she'd stared a little too long at Reese's soft smile and how her wavy, dark brown hair sat tousled a little past her collarbone. She had stolen so many glances, and Reese had caught several. Embarrassingly so. Hannah hadn't mastered being smooth around women yet. And when she glanced at Reese again, Hannah found her brown eyes fastened on her. She felt naked underneath that gaze. The vulnerability would have kept peeling away if it wasn't for the half grin that landed on Reese's lips before she darted her eyes back to Apollo.

"What?" Hannah said. Curiosity and panic fused in her chest.

But Reese's smile grew. "Nothing."

"What? Tell me. I see a bunch of thoughts behind your eyes."

She met Hannah's gaze. "It's embarrassing."

"Well, now you *have* to tell me."

"I do?"

"Of course you do. You can't tell me that and not say anything. That's not how it works."

Reese let out a long grunt and stopped petting Apollo to down a large portion of wine. Hannah smiled, amused by how quickly she became frustrated.

Oh, this has to be good, Hannah told herself, crossing her legs and bracing for the wonderful impact.

"Okay, but it's a bit embarrassing, and I hope it doesn't come off as creepy."

The fact that her voice dropped and she kept petting Apollo rather than looking Hannah in the eyes made Hannah more curious about what she was about to reveal. Hannah laughed. If Reese was trying to amp up her intrigue, then she was doing a fabulous job of it.

"You do realize I'm a fifth-grade teacher, right? I've been told many creepy things, many without warning. I have thick skin. Lay it on me."

"I'll lay it on you, but I need some more wine first," Reese said. "Liquid encouragement."

"Oh sure, if that's what it's going to take, I'll pour some." She snatched up Reese's glass and scampered into the kitchen. She thought of a number of possibilities as to what Reese was about to confess. From how frustratingly reticent she seemed, whatever she was about to say was going to be highly entertaining.

"Some liquid courage," Hannah said, handing Reese her glass and quickly settling back into her spot.

Reese took another gulp and stalled, continuing to watch Apollo as he closed his eyes and whipped his tail around contently. She blew out a heavy breath and dropped her stare to the glass. "I've been wanting to tell you this so we could laugh about it for a while. I almost did last time we hung out."

Hannah grunted. "Ugh, Reese, tell me. I'm dying over here."

One side of her mouth curled upward. "I had the biggest crush on you in high school."

Hannah's jaw dropped. The fluttering she'd first felt when Reese had stepped through her door a bit ago resurrected in her gut in a butterfly display of epic proportions. Did she hear Reese correctly? Did she just say she had a crush on her in high school? That couldn't be possible. No one had crushed on her in high school. "You...you had a crush on me?"

When Reese met her gaze, she noticed how Reese's confession must have stripped away her confidence because she had vulnerability in her dark brown eyes. "I did. I mean...I really didn't know what it was back then," she said. "I didn't know I was a lesbian until college, but yeah, in high school, I thought you were really cool and always wanted to be around you."

"You thought I was cool?"

"I thought you were cool *and* pretty, yes. You know, when we would find each other in the hallways and walk to the fields together after school?" Hannah nodded. "Those five minutes made my whole day. I woke up wishing every morning during the season that I would get the chance to walk to the field with you." She laughed and ran a hand through her hair. "Pathetic, I know."

A hot blush slammed onto Hannah's face as hard as Reese's confession hit her. She knew just how colorful it must have been because it pulled a wider smile from Reese that she hid behind her wineglass. Hannah never thought she would be jealous of a glass until Reese's lips pressed against it.

She flipped through all the memories, searching for something that would have given away Reese's crush. When she came back with nothing, she went through all their encounters since the day she'd adopted Apollo so she could overanalyze every look, every word, every smile, and every touch.

The knowledge of Reese's crush spread downward in an aching throb. Thank God Apollo was between them because he offered something to focus on rather than feeling the tension boiling between them.

"I...I had no idea," Hannah said, shaking her head.

"I hope that's not creepy or anything."

"That's not creepy at all. Why would it be?"

Reese shrugged. "I don't know. Because I just assumed you weren't into women and probably don't want to hear about a silly high school crush—"

"Why did you assume that?"

Reese shrugged. "There was a lot of boy talk in the locker room. I never partook...for obvious reasons. However, you did." She gave

Hannah a teasing smirk. "Also, we weren't really close, and yet, talking to you for five minutes made my whole freakin' day. It's a bit embarrassing."

"Well, one." Hannah raised her finger. "I'm offended that you didn't think we were close," she said playfully. "We were soccer friends. You were my partner in crime when our coach had us in a 4-4-2 formation. We played very well together. I loved having you as the other forward."

That was a fact; they had played well together. It happened so long ago that Hannah had forgotten about their on-pitch chemistry. She wondered if that meant the chemistry would translate as well with their lips pressed together.

She cleared her throat and added another finger to the tally. "Two, the fact that talking to me made your whole day is really sweet. Not pathetic."

It still hadn't fully sunk in. She was someone's big high school crush? That was a bold label. Forget all the girls Hannah had been afraid to message on her dating app. Reese Shepard, the mysterious, badass, and oh-so-sexy animal rescuer, had nursed a huge crush on her throughout high school. And by how Reese tripped over her words and the blush that darkened with each word she spoke, Hannah wondered if their reunion had revived it. She hoped it had because it would confirm what her body had been trying to tell her for the last week. All those nerves coiling inside her whenever she was near Reese were just the chemistry fusing them together.

"I have to ask, how long was this crush?" Hannah said. "Because this is huge news for me."

"The whole time. All three years."

The honesty and certainty undid Hannah. She needed more wine to ease all the emotions balling in her throat. The girl she'd been innocently crushing on for the last week had been massively crushing on her in high school? It unlocked so many feelings that she hadn't known she had. Reese was beautiful, hot, and sexy. She was reserved, still a bit quiet, though she'd seem to have grown out of her shell since high school. But Reese possessed a type of confidence Hannah wished she had, when the smallest amount was alluring and sexy.

Except in that moment, Reese's confidence flickered like a struggling light bulb. When Hannah noticed it fading, she gave Reese's knee a reassuring squeeze. There was a quick tug in her gut. She glanced up to find Reese staring at her delicately, as if worried about what her next words would be.

"I'm really flattered," Hannah said and pushed past the tugging inside. "If I would have known all this back then, I think that would have helped a lot of my insecurities."

Reese frowned. "Insecurities? What insecurities?"

"You know, just normal high school stuff."

"How did Hannah Marsh have insecurities? You were an amazing soccer player, everyone loved you, and you're pretty as fuck."

Hannah choked on her wine. Pretty as fuck? Had those words been used to describe her? "Wow, that's a statement…one I've never heard before."

"It *is* a statement. It's one hundred percent true." Reese's confidence was back and extremely contagious. She seemed so sure about her crush and her feelings that it rooted Hannah in place and stopped her from getting lost in her insecurities. The sudden and unexpected confidence boost skyrocketed her like an amusement park ride, and the nerves shifted in her gut from the friction.

"Well, thank you for that, really," Hannah said. "High school was a weird time. You defined yourself based on friendships and relationships, and back then, I had watched all my friends go through relationships, and I only had one boyfriend for two months."

"Oh, I remember that time," Reese said with the smallest smile. "Eric Boyd."

Hannah raised an eyebrow. "You do?"

"Absolutely. I remember because it crushed me whenever you held hands with him in the hallways."

Hannah laughed. "I'm sorry. If it makes you feel any better, it was barely anything. I think we kissed, like, twice."

"It was the longest two months of my high school life."

Hannah smiled as the confession unraveled the lingering insecurities still in her. "So there was that weird time with Eric Boyd, and then my senior year, I was the only one of my friends to go to homecoming with no date. I'd been the third wheel before, which was fine once or twice, but being the eleventh wheel at homecoming? It was, like, the worst feeling in the world. Little did I know that my fellow forward had a crush on me. I kind of thought I was very unnoticeable back then. Sometimes, I still do…but not as often."

As a silence fell, Reese directed her attention to Apollo. "I remember that homecoming," she said and reached to scratch Apollo's chin. He stretched out his head, his lips curved in a smile, and never once did he open his eyes. "It was my first high school dance."

"Your first?"

Reese lifted a shoulder. "I thought they were lame. I hated wearing dresses back then, and I definitely didn't want to wear makeup or have my hair done. I also didn't want to go with a boy because"—she gestured to herself—"lesbian, right here. Didn't quite understand it then but knew one hundred percent that I didn't want to go with a boy. Anyway, my friends finally convinced me to go to homecoming junior year. The five of us went solo. I specifically remember during one of the slow songs…" She paused to laugh, shaking her head. "Actually, this is going to be more embarrassing."

That made Hannah more excited. "What? Tell me."

Reese cleared her throat. "I remember during one of those slow songs, my friends and I walked off the dance floor, and I had this urge to find what you were doing. I wanted to know if you'd found someone to dance with or not, like Eric Boyd or some other guy. I saw you by the beverage stand. I think you were watching everyone else dance, but I was watching you. It was the first time I'd ever seen you in a dress, and you were, well…" She let out a long exhale. "You were very noticeable that night…to me, at least. Always had been. Still are, for the record."

The more she confessed, the more Hannah's chest inflated from the sincere compliments. For a second, Hannah wondered if her own imagination had pieced together Reese's words, a confession Hannah had always wanted to hear someone say to her, a desire that she never knew someone had for her.

The tension was so palpable, Hannah had to look at Apollo to steady herself. "Why didn't you walk over?"

"I just assumed that you would have rather had Eric or some other guy approach you than me. Plus, there was no way in hell my sixteen-year-old self would have womaned up and talked to you. Not when you looked that good in a dress. But now, I wish I could go back in time and tell you all this so you wouldn't have felt so insecure. You have no reason to be."

Hannah blinked several times as she tried to process all the words. Was it just her imagining things, or was there heavy tension vibrating between them? Something primal sprang inside her. She looked at Reese's lips, scanned every inch of them, and tamed the ravenous reaction bubbling behind her chest. She wanted to throw herself on Reese and kiss her senseless but wanted to hear more of what she had to say. None of this was what she'd expected when she'd invited Reese over, and here she was, sipping wine and reeling from Reese's high school emotions and feeling so affected in all the ways she'd wished she'd felt about Erin on their hike through Golsby Park.

She wondered if her insecurities were hindering her from fully diving into the queer dating world. Her very minimal dating life had made her question her beauty. And the men who were interested in her, well, she wondered how she always attracted the same type: emotionally immature men who didn't act like they were really attracted to her. And then she added the realization that she was bisexual just a couple of months ago. Were there women out there who were okay with dating a newly out thirty-two-year-old with zero experience?

"It should also help your insecurities that Apollo chose you out of all the people who attempted to meet him," Reese said, looking at Apollo, who was zonked out on his back, body twisted like a C, white beard toward the ceiling, and his paws dangling in front of him. "Obviously, there's something about you that's alluring to many."

Hannah raised an eyebrow. "Is that so?"

"One hundred percent. Must be those cat instincts, remember? Apollo probably picked up on the whole high school crush thing and just trusted me with you."

"That must have been it."

Their unexpected night shifted them to a whole different trajectory. The hooded look in Reese's dark eyes was a strong indication that this moment mattered more than the others.

The rest of the conversation drifted away from high school, and as easy and enjoyable as the chatting was, Hannah couldn't shake what Reese had told her. It dangled in her mind like a light and flickered anytime she started straying away to focus on the current topic, reminding her that this gorgeous woman sitting in front of her had spent three teenage years crushing hard on her.

When it was time for Reese to head out, she washed her glass in the kitchen before showering Apollo with so many kisses, he finally woke from his deep sleep and hopped off the couch to follow them to the front door. When Reese opened the door, the cool air swept inside, bringing a faint smell of fall.

"Thank you for inviting me over," Reese said. "I'm so glad Apollo's settling in and already claiming the blanket and couch as his. Anyway, I'm leaving in the morning. Can you keep me updated on him? I'll need plenty of pictures of him being adorable to get me through the week."

"I can do that. I promise."

"I'm glad. Good night, Hannah. Thanks again for the wine and company." She gave a small wave and stepped off the patio to the path that led to the driveway.

All of her words and compliments tumbled in Hannah's mind like a pile of bricks. No, she couldn't let the air around them surge all night with pockets of palpable tension just for her doubts and insecurities to douse the wonderful sparks. The night couldn't end with something as simple and innocent as a wave. Not when she'd felt anything but for the last two and a half hours. "Hey, Reese?"

She turned. "Yeah?"

Hannah walked down the steps and sucked in an encouraging breath of September air before she palmed Reese's face and kissed her. It was a gentle kiss, thanking her for everything she'd said and letting her know she was more than just flattered, that she'd felt it too. Hannah's stomach pleasantly swirled when she felt the lips she'd been admiring all night latch on to hers. As she felt Reese melting into her palms, she pulled away and steadied herself and her wobbly knees. Her lips buzzed against the cool air, wet from Reese's soft, wonderful kiss. She opened her eyes and noticed that Reese's eyes were still closed, as if she was savoring the kiss Hannah hoped that she'd thought about countless times before. Thinking that sent a jolt to her center.

"What…what was that for?" Reese said hoarsely when her eyes opened.

"I wanted you to know what it was like to kiss your high school crush…and to remind you that you shouldn't ever assume someone is straight just because they dated a boy for two months in high school." Hannah winked, and Reese's shocked expression helped the confidence straighten Hannah's back. "Good night, Reese."

When she walked back inside the house, she rested her back against the front door and deeply exhaled all the butterflies staggering in her chest. She ran a finger against her lips still tingling from the kiss.

Apollo sat in the hallway, his wide eyes questioning Hannah like a nosy parent.

"Yeah, I kissed her. Aren't you proud?"

He left his spot, let out a single, high-pitched meow, and threaded around her legs. He looked up with those adorable green eyes. She scooped him up and dotted kisses over his cheeks. They had come such a long way that he no longer squirmed in her arms. Instead, a rolling sound of purrs seeped out of him.

"You know how terrifying that was? But I had to. Everything she said was…perfect. Wasn't it perfect?"

She placed him back on the ground, and he laced around her left leg before sauntering down the hallway toward the bedroom. "You want to go to bed, snuggle, and overanalyze everything?" When he reached the bedroom, he turned and sat by the open door.

Hannah smiled. God, could her night get any better? A beautiful woman had admitted to secretly crushing on her for three years without her having any idea about it. She'd finally found the confidence to kiss a woman, and despite the kiss only lasting a few seconds, it had melted her. That three-second peck was better than her best make-out session with a guy, filling her stomach with butterflies that Erin's cheek kiss had only given her a speck of.

And to top it off, her new best friend and baby wanted nothing more than to cuddle her in bed.

Yeah, life was pretty good. Hannah wanted to bottle it up and save it.

Chapter Seven

By the time Timothy made landfall, it had been downgraded to a tropical storm. It still brought tons of rain to the Carolinas, and there were power outages up and down the coast.

Paw Aid spent the first three days searching the hardest-hit areas: Charleston, James Island, and Mount Pleasant. Those communities were still flooded with a few inches of water, and fallen trees littered the streets with leaves and branches. The rescue efforts were nowhere near as complicated as Hurricane Sarah but still involved long days of rescuing animals and some families with their animals alongside them.

But even as Reese stepped over fallen debris, snatched loose animals wandering the streets, and worked at the temporary shelter to help families with their pets, Hannah drifted through her mind, their kiss replayed, and Reese found herself in the middle of work with tingling lips. It kept playing, stopping, and rewinding, like Reese would do with the best part of her favorite song. She swatted away the memory and went back to work, rounding up loose animals, reuniting them with their families, and helping pass out pet food and supplies to people who came to the temporary shelter.

On the fourth day, she and her team checked out lesser hit areas, like John's Island and Gaslight Shores, a place Reese had always wanted to visit during the summer but hadn't had the chance to yet. She didn't count walking down its famous boardwalk while store owners cleaned up the debris as visiting. There were remnants of flooding, small debris on the roads, and downed power lines sagging throughout the town. The island was starting to get power back slowly but surely.

When Reese was deployed, her days were long. She ended every day by taking a long hot shower. She usually closed her eyes and turned on a relaxing indie folk playlist or a podcast. She relaxed her arms, legs, and entire body, sore from lifting, crouching, running, and standing.

Usually, she didn't miss home. She lived alone. Her parents lived fifteen minutes from her house and had each other. Jenna had Frank and Nova. Reese often considered traveling across the country, spending several weeks in different amazing US cities since her work was remote, until she was called in for a rescue. That was what the single life afforded her. She could do whatever she wanted, be away from home as long as she wanted because nothing rooted her to one specific place.

But the last couple of weeks had sparked excitement in Fairview. There was someone pulling her back to her hometown for the first time ever.

Instead of listening to her music or a podcast, she stood in the shower and allowed the hot stream of water to untangle the soreness that her muscles had collected from the day. Her brain moved boxes around to make space to think about Hannah and that kiss. Each time Hannah kissed her in her head, Reese's stomach flipped, and arousal zapped her center. God, how did the kiss she had been fantasizing about for years finally happen right before she was deployed for a week? She wanted more than anything to be home, show up at Hannah's, and ask what it had meant. Was it a sympathy kiss, or did it actually mean something?

She debated texting to ask. She debated asking Hannah if she was up for a FaceTime. Although her busy schedule didn't afford her much free time to text, she knew that by the time she went back to Fairview, she needed to have mustered up the courage to talk about the kiss, no matter how much the thought of it strained her throat. Hannah was single and probably on dating apps, like most singles in their early thirties. Reese waiting around would risk losing the chance she'd always wanted but had never thought she would get. Hannah Marsh, the girl she'd spent all of high school pining over, had kissed her, for crying out loud.

She couldn't sleep on her chance.

Her phone rang somewhere under the covers right after she put on her pajamas. She hoped it was Hannah calling to see how the last four days had been. It made her dig through the bed and fan the comforter when she couldn't find it fast enough. It flung and landed right in front of her. Instead of Hannah, she saw Jenna's name on her screen.

"Hey! How's Charleston?" Jenna said.

"Good," Reese said and flopped on her back. "But tiring. I'm ready to be home." For many reasons other than being just tired.

"I'm just calling to let you know I'm officially caving."

"What are you talking about?"

Jenna grunted. "I think I've been persuaded to adopt a dog."

When Reese heard Nova cheering in the distance, she smiled. She sat up, bracing for the impact that was Jenna finally acquiescing to an adorable fur baby. "Wait. Are you serious?"

"She's so serious," Nova said and let out a single shriek.

"Jenna? Really?"

"Really, and this is your fault, by the way. All your fault." Her voice only sounded half-bitter. "Frank and Nova couldn't stop thinking about that black lab after her soccer game the other week. And…well… we dropped off the adoption papers today at Lonely Hearts."

"Oh my God, Jenna! That's amazing."

"Nova said you rescued her?"

"I did. Damn, I'm making everyone fall in love with animals. I'm pretty proud of myself. Can't wait to tell my team tomorrow."

"You should be proud of yourself because I thought I would remain firm, and I didn't at all. All it took was five minutes of straight-up face kisses for Daisy to wipe away my tough exterior. I was hoping you could help us out by putting in a good word. We've been in touch with Brent, one of the adoption coordinators. He said a lot of people inquired about her that day."

"I'll send Ashley a text after I get off the phone with you and put in a good word. You know they have great resources at Lonely Hearts, right? There's a trainer, Rory Maclaren, who has dog classes called Academy of Dog. She's amazing. You should definitely sign up."

"Good to know. I'll need all the training. Thanks, Reese." She paused. "Didn't you help Nova's soccer coach find a pet? She mentioned something today at practice."

Reese's stomach bottomed out. "You talked to Hannah?"

"Yes, I usually say hi," Jenna said, sounding as if she knew she'd missed something. "She asked me how you were doing, and then we talked about the adoption event."

"She…she asked how I was doing?"

"Yes, am I missing something? You're acting strange."

Reese let out a long grunt and nervously scratched the back of her wet hair.

"Oh yeah, you're definitely telling me now."

"Okay, fine, but please don't tell Nova."

"Why would I tell my nine-year-old daughter anything? Spill."

Reese spilled, starting by mentioning how she'd withheld the juicy information of crushing hard on Nova's coach all throughout high school, how they'd reunited after all that time when she'd adopted Apollo, how every moment since had Reese reliving how she'd felt as a teenager, and how lucky she felt being on the receiving end of Hannah Marsh's attention.

And how Hannah had sort of kissed her out of nowhere five days ago.

"I knew it, I freakin' knew it," Jenna said, her enthusiasm almost as potent as Nova's from moments before. "I told you she kept looking at you during Nova's game."

"I had no idea she was looking at me. I didn't even know she was into women until she kissed me."

"You know, you're more than welcome to take Nova to practice anytime you want to flirt and get attention. Maybe sneak off for a little smooch."

"Jenna, shh. Nova doesn't need to know anything yet."

"Yet? Is there going to be a yet?"

Reese had no idea if it was anything, but if it was, of course she wanted there to be more than a quick good-bye kiss. Now that she knew what it was like to kiss Hannah, she was desperate to find how it felt to have her tongue dance with hers, have her lips on other parts of her body, have their bodies pressed together.

She wanted to know if Hannah wanted her as much as she had always wanted Hannah.

❖

Reese drove to Hannah's once she returned to Fairview the following weekend. During the drive, a memory swiped through her mind. It had been the last game of Reese's junior year, Hannah's last game of her soccer career. It was an away game against Madison Falls. Somehow, Reese had scored the seat next to Captain Hannah Marsh on the ride back. She'd been right behind Hannah when boarding, and when Hannah had slid into her seat, she'd smiled at Reese and waved for her to sit. It was the only time she'd sat with Hannah on the bus because a spot next to her had always been prime real estate. It might have only been a twenty-minute ride, but Reese still remembered how hard her heart had thudded, like a metronome made of a stone, consistently keeping a hard, yet steady, rhythm that she couldn't ignore if she'd tried. Those twenty minutes had made her feel like the luckiest girl on the team.

Flash forward fourteen years, and Reese's heart transformed into that same metronome, ticking fast as she stood outside Hannah's house. She had texted Hannah, asking if she was home, and Hannah had responded that she and Apollo were grading papers and watching *Selling Sunset*. Somehow, that had ended up convincing Reese to show up at Hannah's house, and as she stared at the doorbell glowing in the night, she questioned if she was doing this all wrong. Should she have texted that she was going to show up? What kind of millennial was she, just appearing at someone's front door without any notice? This wasn't the nineties.

She rolled her eyes. *You're already here. Act on it or miss your chance.* She rang the doorbell, and her metronome pendulum flung off and zapped around her chest like in a pinball game.

When Hannah opened the door, the ball lodged in her throat. "Hi," Hannah said, seeming surprised, but her smile let Reese know it wasn't a bad idea to show up. "This is a surprise. You're back."

"I'm back. I'm sorry, I didn't give you a heads-up. I was just in the area and…"

Hannah waved her off and opened the door wider. "Please, come on in."

Apollo was curled up on his fleece blanket on the couch. He perked up when he saw Reese, hopped down, and wrapped around her legs. She scooped him up and showered him with kisses before setting him back down. Hannah gestured for her to take a seat, so she did, right next to Apollo's blanket. When Hannah sat on the other side of the couch, Apollo jumped back up. He kneaded, staring at Reese as he slowly blinked. She scratched his chin, trying to find a way to stall while she sorted out the waves of nerves.

Hannah scratched his back, eliciting more loud purrs. "I don't understand cats," she said. "It's like he woke up one day and decided he wasn't scared."

"It's those cat instincts, remember? He chose you to feed him forever. That must mean you are his favorite out of everyone he met. All he needed was time to settle in."

"If he has those powerful instincts, then he definitely knows that I kissed you last weekend," Hannah said casually as she scratched Apollo's back. He lifted his butt straight in the air to encourage more. Like the little prince he was, he received more scratches. His eyes closed with contentment as the sudden and nonchalant reference stunned Reese.

Hannah had beaten her in bringing up the kiss, which had to mean she'd thought about it as often as Reese had, right? She attempted to clear the ball lodged in her throat. "Can we talk about that? It's been on my mind for the whole week."

Hannah lifted her gaze. "It has?"

"Of course it has, Hannah. You were on my mind constantly for three years. You better believe you kissing me is going to stick with me."

Reese had spent all of high school trying to tame her crush. *She doesn't like you like that. She doesn't like girls.* When they'd reunited, those same phrases had taken up residence in her brain again. She was fine with it because she'd had three years of practice as a teen, three years of taming under her belt. But apparently, everything she had ever thought since fourteen had been a lie. Or at least, time had given Hannah a perspective of herself that now greatly benefited Reese. Whatever the circumstances, Hannah was right. Reese couldn't assume anything about Hannah, and she was irritated with herself for just assuming heteronormativity when Hannah had left clues since she'd adopted Apollo. Looking back, it was clear as day. The wine dates, all the smiles, the touching. All those moments now felt a little heavier, a little more important than the others. Their meanings weren't fabricated by Reese's wild imagination. Everything had been real.

"It stuck with me too," Hannah said, offering the smallest hint of a smile that sent a ripple through Reese's midsection and then traveled lower.

"It did?"

"Oh yeah," she said so confidently. Reese wished she could share some of that confidence, or even better, inject some of it through her lips. "It really never left my mind. At all." It was her turn to clear her throat. "Wine? Do you want wine?"

Yes, that was what they needed. Wine. Maybe wine would help oil up the inextricable ball stuck in Reese's throat so she could form the proper words she'd been ruminating on all week.

Reese followed her into the kitchen. She rested her back against the kitchen counter as Hannah poured the wine. Her high school crush had kissed her. The short teaser of a kiss had consumed her high school crush's mind as much as Reese's crush had saturated her mind for three years. And now, here she was, finally in Hannah's house, in her presence, and what the hell was she doing on the other side of the kitchen?

Right as Hannah placed the cap back on the bottle, Reese propelled herself forward. She didn't want to taste the wine. She wanted to taste Hannah. She wanted to feel her tongue, her body pressed, and she wanted to comb her fingers through Hannah's soft, dark blond hair.

The days of imagining what it would be like to actually feel Hannah Marsh were over. All she had to do was grasp the moment.

Reese closed the space between them until she was so close that she could smell Hannah's floral body wash. Her blue eyes darkened as they dropped to Reese's lips and quickly flitted back up as if the lip scan was an accident. But Reese felt it in her chest, lighting up her stomach, and jolting down to her center. The simple movement was powerful enough to make her hyperaware of every nerve ending.

"I don't want wine," Reese said softly. Her confession dropped like an anchor in her pool of nerves.

Hannah's eyebrows furrowed. "You don't?"

"I don't." She allowed her fingers to glide across Hannah's soft cheek and watched how they blushed under her touch. She tucked a tendril of hair behind Hannah's ear. "Is this okay?"

Hannah scanned Reese's mouth again, bit her bottom lip, and nodded.

That lip bite did it. Reese gently guided Hannah's face to hers until their lips finally collided again, and when Hannah kissed her back, Reese had to pay special attention to her knees so they didn't collapse under her. The kiss started out as a gentle acquaintance, but once Reese opened her mouth and met Hannah's tongue, her whole body felt like fireworks seconds before takeoff, sizzling and ready to light up at any given moment. Hannah let out a soft murmur, and it encouraged Reese to deepen the kiss and let the fiery passion that swaddled them to fan open. She pinned Hannah against the fridge, one hand cupping her cheek, the other slipping between her shirt and warm skin before resting on the small of her back. They alternated between soft and sweet to hot and passionate kisses until standing became too uncomfortable.

As if Hannah had read Reese's mind, she pulled away. Her eyes stared back hooded and expressive. "Wow," Hannah said softly through ragged breaths. She held Reese's face against her palm and used a thumb to graze Reese's cheek. Reese leaned in, wanting and needing more than just her hand.

"Do you want to resume this somewhere else? Preferably not vertically?"

Hannah's eyes widened, but a salacious smile formed. She pulled Reese back in for a kiss that lingered. "Please," she said against her lips. She grabbed Reese's hand and led her into her bedroom. They passed Apollo, sound asleep on his blanket. When they slipped into Hannah's bed, everything started coming into focus, and everything started becoming real.

It had been a while since Reese had hooked up with someone. She wasn't sure if the nerves that stuttered in her chest were from her dry spell catching up to her or the fact that she was lying in Hannah Marsh's bed with Hannah staring at her with so much desire in her eyes.

Electricity and anticipation danced in the space between them. Hannah scooted closer, and Reese felt her hot breath on her lips. Following a trail of goose bumps, she skimmed her fingertips down Hannah's arm, paused at her elbow, and pulled Hannah back in. After a few moments of kissing, Reese decided to take charge and positioned herself on top. Hannah slid her hands underneath Reese's shirt, fingertips dancing their way along her spine. Then Hannah unexpectedly twisted her fingers in a deft motion that undid more than the strap of Reese's bra.

Reese spread Hannah's legs with a thigh, and her hips lifted as if encouraging Reese to relieve the pressure. Reese pressed a leg into Hannah's center and lowered herself back down to capture Hannah's mouth. At the contact, Hannah clawed at Reese's back, and the delicious pain sent a surge of arousal hard between her legs. God, did she need more pressure there, preferably Hannah's mouth.

Their bodies rocked in a motion more organic than rehearsed. Reese mapped the soft contours of Hannah's body, lifting her shirt and exposing more soft skin. When she disposed of the useless shirt, Reese kissed invisible paths downward, and Hannah rewarded her with breathy exhales and shudders of anticipation that she would always remember.

Reese loved how reactive Hannah was to her touch, and she became even sexier when she raised her hips to help Reese slip off her yoga pants and underwear. When Reese put her mouth on her, Hannah's cry filled the bedroom, and Reese slid inside her with ease. Reese's breath staggered, and her whole body came alive as a hot curl snaked its way from her stomach to her core. She got lost in the warmth of Hannah's body writhing beneath her and the soft moans that signaled Hannah's undoing. She cried out her orgasm, and Reese bit her lip to stop herself from following her over the edge. Reese watched as the aftershocks rattled through Hannah, amazed that she'd been able to send her to wherever she'd skyrocketed to.

Reese didn't have to wait too long to find out because Hannah was quick to take her there too. Soft tapping on her hip caused Reese to comply as Hannah pushed her jeans down her legs. Hannah teased her lips and tongue down Reese's naked torso and glided along her waist. Once she put her mouth on Reese, the flicks of tongue and fingers made Reese grip fistfuls of sheet, and all of the attraction, frustration, and pining she had suppressed for years unfurled all the knots. Hannah unwound her with ease, and she wasn't sure if how quickly she orgasmed was embarrassing or impressive.

As she collected her breath, she took in the sight of Hannah's coy smirk between her legs. She was perfection wrapped in soft bed sheets. "Wow, that was…amazing. That was really amazing," Reese said as she tried collecting her breath.

"Really?"

Reese had no idea why she heard doubt rattling Hannah's voice.

"Really. I…I forgot how to speak. Give me a second." The light kisses Hannah dotted from her center to her neck added to the bliss fizzling on her skin. "Why do you sound so unsure? Did you not hear?"

Hannah flopped onto her side and propped her head on her hand. "Oh, I did. It was sexy as hell. It's just that, um, that was my first time… with a woman."

It was Reese's turn to prop her head up. "Are you serious?"

Hannah nodded, and there was enough hallway light to reveal a thin layer of vulnerability in her eyes. "I didn't know I was bi until recently. I've been trying dating apps and…well, it's very difficult."

Reese laughed. "Oh, I'm well aware, trust me." She tucked a stray hair behind Hannah's ear. Hannah nuzzled her hand. "But I promise, you had a girl fooled just a few minutes ago. I would have never known."

"You're being nice…and maybe a little grateful that I just got you off? You're still glowing. Poor thing, you're in a daze."

Reese smiled. "I am still in a daze. I feel it in my legs, but that's not the point. The point is, regardless of your experience, I enjoyed it very much. See back to your dazed comment." She paused. "Can I tell you something?"

"What's that?"

"You were my first girl crush. My crush started at fourteen, and fourteen years later, I'm in bed with you. Funny to think that we were each other's firsts in some ways."

Hannah rolled back her lips as if she didn't want to show off a grin. "I like it. I like all of it."

"Oh yeah?"

"Yeah."

"Then can I be the first woman to take you to dinner? Because I would love that probably as much as this."

"I think you were supposed to ask me out before the fucking," Hannah said. "But because you're sexy and just made me feel things I've never felt before, I'll let it slide."

"So I can take you to dinner? Maybe tomorrow, if you're free?"

Apollo jumped on the bed and let out a soft meow that sounded like a question. Reese imagined him asking, "What the hell are you two doing in here and not paying attention to me on my throne?" He cautiously moved around their intertwined legs until he found a spot in the middle. He started kneading the covers in front of Reese's stomach.

"I think this is Apollo's way of asking your intentions," Hannah said.

Reese scratched his chin. He graciously accepted by extending his head. "My intentions are to treat your mama to a delicious meal. Maybe Italian. Maybe Indian. Maybe the new wine bar that opened up in town since she loves her wine. But, like, good wine. We need to upgrade her tastes."

Hannah playfully pushed her. "Hey! I like to think my taste is impeccable. I mean, I chose you, didn't I?"

Once Apollo kneaded all the biscuits, he curled up between them, rested his head on his paws, and filled the room with purrs. The scene unfolding settled on Reese like a warm blanket. She didn't think she could get more comfortable than at that precise moment. Curled up under the covers with Hannah and Apollo was the perfect way to end the long, busy week.

"Yeah, I guess you did."

Chapter Eight

When Hannah asked Reese to be her girlfriend six days before Christmas, deleting the dating apps off her phone was practically a present. No more worrying about what to say to women she'd matched with, no more feeling like she was going to die alone with fifteen rescued cats by her side, and no more worrying about her mom stealing her phone to set her up. Now she had to worry about her mom telling her girlfriend too many embarrassing childhood stories and revealing horrendous pictures of her awkward days with a is-this-supposed-to-be-a-bowl-cut-or-a-bob hairstyle. Her mom was apparently unaffected by all the teacher's scowls Hannah shot her way.

She still couldn't believe it. She had a girlfriend, and not only that, she was with someone who made her long for the chance to spend another day together. She dreaded the nights apart. She loved that with each passing day, she got more of Reese.

Reese would sometimes stay with her for a few days in a row, working from home on the couch with Apollo snug by her side, and Hannah would come home from work to a delicious dinner.

It was a cycle she wanted to wrap up in.

She really liked how her life had changed in a matter of months. Last year, she'd realized she was bi while in a relationship with a guy who'd never acted like she was anything special. She'd spent the summer putting herself out there and constantly feeling like she wouldn't ever meet someone right for her.

And then, somehow, the universe had brought Apollo, and for whatever reason, he had chosen her. He made coming home after a long day exciting. She would pull into the driveway, see Apollo staring out the window on the top of the couch, and by the time she opened the front door, he stood on the other side, greeting her with excited meows and leg rubs. For the rest of the night, he was her shadow like Reese had promised he would be if only Hannah gave him the time and patience to adjust. He was her sous chef in the kitchen, sprawling on the floor and flopping his tail while Hannah cooked and talked to him all about her day. He even had his own chair at the table, claiming the one to the right of Hannah's. At night, he curled against her on the couch while she graded papers or lay on her lap as they watched trashy TV.

And then there was her girlfriend, her amazing, wonderful, and beautiful girlfriend. Sometimes, Hannah caught herself watching Reese do the most normal or mundane things, like cleaning the dishes after dinner, typing on her computer answering late work messages, or petting and talking to Apollo while he lay on top of his cat tree. Hannah's heart swelled every time she looked at Reese. There was just something about her that was so gentle, comforting, and safe. Whenever Reese caught her staring, it sparked something magnetic in the air.

"It's weird when I catch you looking at me," Reese said, ditching Apollo on the cat tree to jump on top of Hannah on the couch. She planted kisses all over her face until Hannah giggled and gently pushed her away.

"Why is it weird?" Hannah asked.

"Because I feel like I spent forever looking at you when you weren't looking."

Hannah wrapped her legs around Reese's waist and flipped her over so she was on her back with Hannah on top. "That's sweet and all. Really." She leaned in to kiss her. "But it's my turn now." She hopped off and sat upright. Reese followed. Hannah locked an arm around Reese's and rested her head on her shoulder.

Reese kissed her forehead. "It's nice to have someone to come home to," she said, snuggling into the crook of Hannah's neck.

Hannah didn't think she could be more content. She had her beautiful girlfriend molded perfectly against her and her fur baby slowly blinking his affection at the top of the cat tree.

"I know that feeling well," Hannah said. "It's weird how everything just sort of came together at the same time."

"I blame that guy right there." Reese pointed to Apollo. He rested his chin on his crossed white paws. "I really believe that animals know when people have rescued them. He knows everything you've done for him. You can see it when he follows you around, when he cuddles on your lap, when he looks at you and stares like you hung the moon. I rescued him, and you gave him a home. He knows all of that. Cat instincts, remember?"

There was just something about a pet that sewed a person's seams and made them feel whole again, and for that, Hannah would be forever grateful for her newest best friend.

She'd had no idea what was missing from her life before. It had seemed okay, nothing really to complain about except the lack of a relationship. But the universe had a funny way of making things happen at the right time.

She closed her eyes and listened to the contented purrs of Apollo and the soft sighs from Reese. She had no idea how she'd gotten so lucky, but for whatever reason, the universe definitely knew what it was doing, and it had all happened while they weren't looking. Reese had found Apollo, Apollo had found Hannah, and Hannah and Reese had found each other again…all at the right time.

TEST OF FAITH

Nell Stark

Chapter One

Faith stumbled into the kitchen and stabbed at the button on the coffee grinder. The steely shriek that sliced the air made her clap both hands over her ears. Her quads burned as she crouched, staring blearily into the cabinet. After zoning out for a moment, she grabbed a fresh bag of coffee, then refilled the bean box and turned on the kettle. While it was heating, she opened the fridge.

One tall glass of green juice. A boiled egg that she had learned the hard way to microwave for only fifteen seconds. Damn it, she wanted a Pop-Tart. Or better yet, a shot of Jack.

Choking down a swallow, Faith reached for the kettle. It was empty. She had been heating air, not water. Cursing under her breath, she filled it, then went back to her lackluster breakfast. At least no one could accuse her of not making an effort. She might be terrible at trying, but she was still *trying*.

Which was the only reason she was awake at the ungodly hour of eight o'clock in the morning. Twice last week, Faith had been forced to cancel appointments at the animal shelter thanks to her flaky contractor. The incredibly patient pet adoption coordinator had offered to make a house call on her way in to work, but that meant scheduling their interview for 8:30.

Faith consoled herself by imagining how good it would feel to chew out Jameson later for his utter inability to keep an appointment. She wasn't actually going to yell at him—new!Faith didn't launch into tirades anymore—but playing out the scenario in her head was cathartic. Maybe she was being punished for trying to combine steps five and six of her eight-step "Growing Toward Actualization" program. In her defense, the decision to simultaneously "connect with community" and "commit to caring" had been motivated by the urgency of a natural disaster. Surely, that was forgivable?

For the thousandth time since she had submitted her adoption application, doubt seeped into the forefront of her mind. Yes, she had kept a plant alive for three whole months. But was that really enough time to prove that she could actually be a decent person? No. Definitely not. A dog was a *real* commitment. "Commit to commitment" might have become her therapist's favorite phrase, but it was a mantra for a reason. No way could she be trusted to care for a living being that didn't just sit on a windowsill.

As she poured hot water over the grounds, Faith reached for her phone. She could always cancel. Again. Given that she'd already missed her first two interview appointments, the shelter volunteer was probably ready to write her off, a fate Faith more than deserved. Why fight it? Fabricating an excuse wouldn't be hard: an urgent meeting, the sniffles, a friend's emergency. The volunteer wouldn't know she didn't actually have any friends.

Faith was scrolling down her contacts list for the woman's name—Jennifer? Jessie?—when the doorbell rang. Incredulous, she checked the time. 8:16. Worse yet, precisely zero caffeine was in her bloodstream.

Combing one hand through her unruly hair, Faith zombie-shuffled along the hallway. She would very politely tell what's-her-name that, upon reflection, it was absurd for her to ever even have considered being responsible for something that ate more than sunbeams. Taking a deep breath, she simultaneously opened her mouth and the door.

"You must be Faith!" The white-haired woman on the other side smiled like the world was a benevolent place. "I'm Jan, and I'm so glad you're interested in adopting one of our emergency pups."

Jan stepped over the threshold before Faith could utter a single syllable. Helpless before this display of brisk efficiency, Faith pulled the door shut and scrambled to keep up.

"Now, don't be nervous," Jan was saying. "I know these interviews can raise a person's blood pressure. I'm not here to judge you, just to make sure you're well prepared for your new best friend."

"Actually," Faith said, then had to clear her throat. "Um, about tha—"

"Oh!" Jan swerved into the living room. "What lovely bay windows. You should put your dog bed just there in that space between the chairs."

Dog bed? Dogs needed beds? Faith coughed.

"Right, but—"

"Do you have a yard?" Jan interrupted.

Faith found herself pointing toward the back of the house, where a small sunroom looked out over the deck. When Jan pulled open the sliding doors as though they belonged to her, Faith felt compelled to follow her out.

"Oh, it's fenced. I didn't notice that from the front. This is perfect."

Jan's wholesome smile persuaded Faith to look at the familiar expanse of green through fresh eyes. The shrubs her mother had planted along the fence needed trimming, and the grass was getting tall. What no one but she could see was the gauzy layer of memory that hung over the scene like a shroud. Maybe she needed to do to the yard what she was doing to the house, to herself. Demolish it down to the studs and start over.

"Your pup will love this. Have you ever owned a dog?"

"No," Faith heard herself say. "My mom wasn't a pet person."

"Oh, I feel sorry for her. The unconditional love of a pet is one of life's most profound joys."

"Yeah, she didn't have the first clue about unconditional love."

Only when Jan's expression softened into something approaching pity did Faith realize she had spoken out loud. Mortification rose like a flood. Then again, maybe this was the perfect opening to back herself out of this corner.

"That probably means I'm not qualified, right? Never had a dog. Clearly dealing with my own baggage." Faith tried out a smile of her own. She could feel it falling flat.

"On the contrary." There was a gentleness to Jan's expression that forced Faith to look away. "Dogs are incredibly empathic creatures. Some are even trained to work in therapeutic environments. But even without that training, they can help their owners decrease stress levels."

"Really?" The pressure behind Faith's eyes eased just enough, and she dared to meet Jan's gaze.

"I'll email you a few articles." Jan gestured toward the door. "May I see your kitchen?"

"Oh…sure." Faith led the way back inside.

"How lovely," Jan exclaimed. "The floor is gorgeous, and the backsplash tile picking up those accents? Just stunning."

"Thanks." The compliments restored a modicum of confidence. "The work isn't mine, but the palette is."

Jan gestured expansively. "You have beautiful taste. Now, how about the upstairs?"

Faith led the way to the stairs. "The whole thing is under construction. Or at least, it's supposed to be. I haven't heard from my contractor in days."

"Oh, that's a shame." Jan rested a hand on the banister. "Are you using Oscar?"

The grimace contorted Faith's lips before she could control herself. Quickly, she smoothed her expression. "No. I hired Jameson. Jameson Johnson."

Jan's brow furrowed. "Never heard of him." She leveled a critical look at the plastic drop cloths lining most of the staircase. "If you can't reach him, I'd suggest reaching out to Oscar Dalby. He's the best there is in this town."

Faith bit her tongue. Literally. The flash of pain was just distracting enough to stop her from saying something completely inappropriate. Swallowing hard, she tamped down her bitterness and resentment. This was *not* the time.

"How do you plan to keep your dog from venturing into the construction zone?" Jan was asking.

"I have a gate." Faith went to the hall closet and opened it, revealing her most recent impulse buy. She had grabbed it during an optimistic moment while running errands after her latest therapy session. She remembered feeling strong. Capable. Even a little confident.

The feeling hadn't lasted.

"You're prepared."

Faith knew she didn't deserve Jan's approving smile. "Well, I was a Girl Scout."

The smile broadened, and Jan held up one hand, fingers curling into the salute. "Me, too."

"Actually, I was kicked out after three months for building a fire in the church basement."

Jan's laugh was startlingly loud. "You didn't."

"I got too impatient to wait for the camping."

Jan wiped at the corners of her eyes. "Did you at least get your fire-building badge before you were banished?"

"Not so much."

"That's a travesty." She chuckled again.

As silence settled between them, Faith felt the nudge of her newly awakened conscience. "Did the receptionist tell you I'm moving back to the city as soon as I can? I mean, I know you need to ask questions about this place since I'll bring the dog here initially. But I won't be here long."

Jan nodded. "She mentioned it. We'll focus on city-appropriate dogs when you can make it over to the shelter."

When Faith's heart skipped a beat, she knew she'd gone soft. "Wait, does that mean—"

"Your application's approved? Yes." Jan stuck out her hand. "You're going to make a lucky canine-in-need very happy, Faith."

Jan's grip was gentle but firm. For the second time in ten minutes, Faith found herself fighting back tears. "I hope so."

After Jan left, Faith leaned hard against the door. Gravity pulled her down until she was curled against it and the floor, forehead pressed to her drawn-up knees. When the dam finally broke, Faith clenched her teeth and took short, shallow breaths, not wanting to hear the sound of her own sobs. The tears rolled down her cheeks slowly, silently. As the minutes passed, her jaw began to ache, and a dull pain blossomed behind her eyes.

Dully, she remembered her coffee still waiting in the kitchen. She raised her head and finally dared to take a slow, deep breath. She levered herself up, then angrily swiped at her eyes. In the past three months, she had cried more than she'd had in her entire *life*. And for what? Her mother didn't deserve a single drop. Maybe she was weeping for herself?

To escape that thought, she stumbled toward the kitchen. Setting aside the filter, she cupped her hands around the mug and took a long swallow. The coffee was still hot, but Faith took a perverse satisfaction in the pain that blossomed at the back of her throat. She deserved it.

No.

That was a lie.

Faith clutched her mug's handle as though it were the only thing keeping her afloat. Enduring her mother's emotional abuse had been hard enough. Hearing the same bullshit rhetoric in her own head was even worse. Panic was rising like a flood. Desperate, Faith reached for her tools.

"Everyone deserves goodness," she whispered, feeling like an idiot. "You deserve goodness."

Saying it was one thing, believing it quite another. Still, ridiculous as it was, the mantra anchored her. As she repeated it—first aloud, then silently—the tightness in her chest began to ease. Her breaths steadied, then slowed. She took another, more careful sip and forced herself to concentrate on the complex taste of the coffee: notes of chocolate and nut with the slightest hint of cherry.

"Okay." Bracing her hands on the counter, she stared out the window over the sink. She caught sight of an unknown neighbor on the sidewalk walking their fluffy white dog. Did she really want to have to do that every day, at least twice? A wave of anxiety soured her throat, bringing with it a bitter, angry voice. She could barely take care of herself. She would mess this up, just like she had every other relationship in her life.

Faith grimaced, resisting the urge to spiral into self-hatred. According to her therapist, her old self deserved compassion, not criticism. Every doubt came from fear, and it wasn't as though her fears were unfounded. But they weren't in control, not anymore. Slowly, painfully, she was forging new patterns and a healthier mindset. She *was* taking care of herself, and she *could* take care of a dog. Daily walks weren't something to be afraid of. They were something to welcome. Right now, she had no reason whatsoever to venture out of the house. A dog would force her to step outside every day and breathe fresh air.

As the wave receded, Faith took another, longer sip of coffee, then emptied the dishwasher to feel useful. Afterward, she sat at the island, phone propped on the marbled counter. She pulled up the thread with her agent and stared at it. She had last checked in five days ago. Was it too soon to send another text? Probably. Jolie was plenty incentivized to reach out as soon as she heard anything.

Not for the first time, Faith kicked herself for the way she had interpreted Step Four: Reach Higher. Why had she even tried? She had plenty of followers, and they were being patient with the current infrequency of her offerings. Yes, a larger fanbase would catapult her into the highest compensation tier, but did she really need the money? Or was this ambition a relic of old!Faith, who craved the spotlight as a surrogate for love?

Resting her chin on her hands, she stared at the phone's blank screen. *Fish Out of Water* wasn't her only shot. There would be other reality shows and better opportunities. For now, she had to bury the kernel of self-doubt and focus on keeping her ship afloat. Especially because she was teaching less than usual, she needed to run good classes that would have a long on-demand shelf life. Gritting her teeth, Faith pulled open her notes file. She had finalized her plan last night, but reviewing it never hurt. A high-intensity interval ride, this class was guaranteed to burn away any lingering dregs of anxiety. Anticipating the endorphin rush made her feel just the tiniest bit better.

When she finished and glanced at the clock, that precious seed of a good mood was crushed. Jameson had made all kinds of promises about showing up early this morning, but it was now almost ten o'clock, and his truck was not in the driveway. The burst of irritation propelled her past her natural antipathy to phone calls, and she dialed his number. This time, instead of his voice mail greeting, a robotic voice informed her the number had been discontinued.

A number flashed before her eyes: the amount of money she had already paid him to cover the cost of materials. With consummate care, Faith placed her phone on the table. Then, she stood, walked to the couch, and grabbed one of the throw pillows. Holding it against her own mouth, she screamed.

Once the worst of the rage had left her body, she dropped the pillow back on the couch and stood still, panting. A sheen of red tinged her vision. What was she supposed to do now? There was only one explanation for the discontinued number. Jameson hadn't gotten into an accident, and he wasn't having some kind of personal crisis. He had left town, and he'd taken her money with him. She'd been robbed.

She grabbed her phone from her pocket. As she raised it, she dimly noticed her hand was shaking. At first, she thought about dialing 9-1-1. This *was* a crime. But it wasn't an emergency, so instead, she settled for calling the closest police department. The woman who answered took down her name and number, then asked why she was calling. Faith explained.

"What is your contractor's name?"

"Jameson Johnson."

"Jameson like the whiskey?"

"That's right."

The woman clucked her tongue. "Never heard of him. You should have used Oscar Dalby. He's the best in town."

Faith bit one knuckle to keep herself from screaming. It hurt. When she pulled her finger out of her mouth, the ridges of her teeth prints were visible in the crinkled skin.

This day *sucked*, and it had barely even started.

Fortunately, the remainder of the conversation was actually useful. Faith took notes about contacting the state's licensing board and the Better Business Bureau. The woman also recommended she hire an attorney.

By the time the call finished, Faith had a numbered to-do list. After a few minutes of scowling at it, she added an item before number one. *Adopt dog.*

Maybe it was ridiculous. Maybe it was selfish. Maybe it was stupid. But wasn't her therapist always telling her that when the going inevitably got tough, she would need to *double down* on commitment instead of running away? Commit to community. Commit to caring. Jameson had taken enough from her. She wasn't going to let him set her back in any other way.

Del gave Scout the dalmatian one final ear scratch, then nodded to Gavin, who released his bear-hug hold on the dog. Del slipped one hand into the pocket of her scrubs for a treat, and as she held it up, Scout sat, tail whipping against Gavin's ankles.

"Ow!" Gavin stepped away, but he was smiling.

"He's well trained." Del gave Scout the treat, then slipped out of his kennel while he was distracted. "I'm surprised no one claimed him at the temp shelter."

Gavin reached for the tablet he'd left propped by the door. After a few moments of scrolling, he made a sympathetic noise. "It says here that his family's house was a total loss, and they had no place to keep him."

"That's so hard." Del tried to imagine what it must be like to have your entire home demolished and then have to give up your beloved pet. "Try taking off the cone tomorrow, but keep an eye on him. If he starts scratching or biting at the abrasion, put it back on."

As Gavin made a note, Del turned toward the last kennel in the row. The dog lying in a nest of blankets was probably about thirty pounds or so. Like Scout, she was wearing a cone. An absorbent pad on her left flank peeked out beyond the bright purple of the gauze wrapped around her abdomen.

"And who's this?" she asked.

"Her name is Buffy," Gavin said. "We think she's a cross between a cocker spaniel and a cavalier King Charles. Oh—"

"Oh?"

Gavin looked up with a stricken expression. "The notes say her owner died, and she was found next to the body."

In the years she'd spent working as an emergency vet, Del had witnessed more trauma than she cared to admit. Still, the thought of this sweet little dog—wet and hurting and cold, yet fiercely loyal—was enough to slip past her defenses. For the hundredth time today, she felt the keen edge of her own good fortune. She swallowed hard.

"Dr. Wu?" Gavin said. "Are you okay?"

"Sorry. Yes." Del rubbed at the back of her head where a headache was brewing.

"She suffered a puncture wound," Gavin continued. "The notes also say the vet at the temp shelter was worried about infection, so they left it open."

"Let's have a look. And we may as well change the dressing."

When Del unlatched the kennel door, Buffy raised her head. Her eyes were the color of coffee with just a splash of milk. A white patch of fur around her left eye and a vaguely heart-shaped splotch on the uninjured flank accented her silky, dark gold fur.

"Hi, sweetheart." Del moved slowly across the small space. When Buffy didn't stand, Del steeled herself for the worst. An injured dog trapped in a flooded area rife with bacteria was not a good combination. She sat cross-legged, then extended one hand. Buffy sniffed, then offered a tentative lick.

Del spoke softly as she reached forward. Careful not to jostle the wound, she scooped Buffy into her arms. The dog tensed slightly but otherwise did not protest. Slowly, Del turned and handed her to Gavin, then began to unwrap the gauze.

"There might be some Pomeranian in her, too."

Gavin looked skeptical. "Maybe, but she hasn't barked once since she got here."

"She hasn't had it easy." Del reached for the bandage. "Be ready. She might not like this."

Del was as careful and gentle as she could be, but the pad still stuck a little. She murmured softly to Buffy as she worked. As the wound became visible, a knot she hadn't even realized was in her throat melted away. While its edges still looked ugly, it was otherwise closing up well. Most importantly, there was no smell of necrosis.

"What do you think?"

"It looks good. She'll be fine." Del replaced the bandage and the gauze efficiently. "Keep her isolated for two more days, then let her out with the others." She leaned forward to kiss Buffy's forehead. The dog surprised her by licking her chin. "I think she might be lonely."

❖

Fifteen minutes later, as Del walked toward her car, Jada's ringtone pierced the air.

"Shit." Del fumbled for her phone. "Hello?"

"You stood me up. *Again.*"

"Sorry." Del walked faster. "I'm just leaving work."

"No, you're not." Jada's syllables were clipped, which meant her irritation was real. "I am literally standing outside the animal hospital, and no one's here."

"Not the hospital, the shelter." Del thumbed her key fob and got into the car. "I had to check on the pets rescued from the hurricane. I forgot to tell you. Sorry."

After several heartbeats of silence, Jada sighed gustily. "Now I'm annoyed that I can't be mad at you."

"Sorr—"

"Meet me at the restaurant, Del. And you're buying."

Del spent the drive to Vita's listening to a podcast on quirky science phenomena. Each episode was always interesting in some way, and she liked learning new things. More importantly, it had nothing to do with her job and stopped the insidious doubts of the day from taking root in her brain. She had discovered the coping mechanism while working as an emergency vet in the city. Haunted by the pets she had lost, Del had learned to force her own attention away from the void.

The parking lot at Vita's was hopping, and it took Del a while to find a spot. Once inside, she headed for the roof deck. She found Jada sitting at a table near the far corner of the deck, nursing a cosmo. A dirty vodka martini with extra olives waited on the empty place mat.

Jada looked up and met her gaze. "It's not fair how good you look in scrubs."

Del slid into the chair across from her. "You're gorgeous, and you know it. You're also engaged."

"Sweet talker."

"I really am sorry."

Jada huffed. "Will you stop?" She rested one hand on top of Del's. "Sisters for life, remember?"

Del acknowledged the familiar refrain with a smile. As the only two women of color in their organic chem class freshman year, they had bonded to survive. Necessity had, it turned out, proven a firm foundation for friendship. Jada might be her opposite in more ways than one, but in all the ways that mattered, they were on the same page.

A woman Del didn't recognize stopped by to take her order. She pinged Del's gaydar, but her gaydar was often on the fritz. When Jada leaned in with a conspiratorial smile, however, Del realized her own instincts had been right.

"She's cute. I'm getting her number for you."

"What?" Del spat, barely resisting the urge to turn and look at the woman. That was exactly what Jada *wanted* her to do. "No."

"Oh, I'm not asking." Jada crossed her arms. "It's happening."

"I know nothing about her. We currently have zero percent chance of compatibility."

Jada snorted. "That's a bleak way of looking at things. The other option is that you're at one hundred percent until proven otherwise."

Deflated, Del took a long sip, steeling herself for the conversation ahead. "I *have* been looking. Like I promised. I just haven't found the right person yet."

Jada scoffed. "*Dating* is how you find the right person."

"Maybe that's true for you, but it never has been for me." Del stared at the two olives pierced through their pimento hearts by a toothpick.

Jada's free hand covered hers. "All the more reason to give it a shot." She squeezed gently. "I know you got hurt. And I wish every day you'd let me cut off that bitch's tongue and—"

"Jada!"

She huffed out a sigh. "Not helping?"

"Not helping."

"Sorry."

Del filled the ensuing silence with a long, slow sip of her martini. She could feel Jada's stare like a laser.

"When I suggested you move out here, I was hoping the change of scene would be good for you."

"It has been." Del meant it. Moving out of the apartment she'd shared with Madison had been a financial necessity, but leaving the city had been good for her in ways she hadn't anticipated. There, she'd spent her time walking past and flinching away from memories: the Italian restaurant where they'd had date night every Thursday; the park where they'd sat and drank coffee on beautiful Saturday mornings; the bagel place where she had always stopped to grab Maddie a breakfast sandwich on her way home from a graveyard shift. Getting out of the city had meant leaving those constant reminders behind.

It had also meant leaving emergency medicine. Sometimes, Del had to admit, she missed the pace and challenge of it—the tunnel vision of trauma, the necessity of split-second decisions, the waves of adrenaline buoying her up. Her body was still having trouble adjusting to a normal and regular sleep schedule. Often, she woke after only a few hours, heart pounding, convinced she was in the on-call room at the hospital.

When she realized Jada was regarding her skeptically, Del sighed. "You were right. Getting out of there was a healthy decision. It's helping me move on."

"Move on? It's been six months. You haven't gone on a single date."

"So?" Despite Del's best efforts, irritation seeped into the syllable. "It's not like I've been a hermit. I've gotten involved. I put myself out there."

"I'm not talking about joining the board of the shelter or that thing you run in the park every week. That's work stuff." Jada leaned closer. "I'm talking about women. Putting yourself out there that way."

"Maddie and I were together for *five years*, Jada." The familiar pain knifed through Del as she said the words. "We were talking about marriage. Maybe you could turn your back on something like that after six months, but I can't."

As soon as she heard the words, Del winced. That had come out far harsher than she had intended. She opened her mouth to apologize, but Jada was faster.

"Del. Listen to me. *Maddie* turned *her* back on you. On everything you built together. Instead of doing the mature thing and telling you she was having doubts so you could work on them as a couple, she cheated on you."

Pain washed over Del, sour in its familiarity. Like always, it slipped through her armor, opening a chasm in her chest. "Just because she acted that way doesn't mean I'm going to."

Jada's jaw dropped. She shook her head slightly, then leaned closer. Del steeled herself, expecting another tirade, but this time, Jada's voice was quiet and serious, barely audible above the ambient noise.

"I want you to think about what you just said." Jada emphasized the point by stabbing one finger against the surface of the table. "It honestly worries me. You and Maddie aren't in a relationship anymore. You can't 'act that way' because you're not together. Taking the steps to find someone new is *healthy*, not a betrayal."

The words were heavy with truth, and the weight of them bowed Del's shoulders. She looked down, blinking back tears. Jada's hand entered her field of vision, reaching out to lace their fingers together.

"I'm not suggesting you try to replace Maddie. Just…try something *new*. You've never done casual. In the ten years we've known each other, you've had exactly two relationships. You deserve everything you want, Del, but tell me this. How the hell do you even *know* what you want?"

The question was a knife sliding between her ribs, finding its mark. For one horrible moment, she couldn't breathe. Some hint of panic must have surfaced in her face because Jada grabbed her upper arm, leaning close.

"Shit. Sorry. That was a bridge too far."

"No. You're fine." Somehow, her voice was strong. "You're... you're probably right."

"I'm no—"

"What if you are?" Del ran a hand through her hair. The texture was soft and heavy, starting to curl again. It would need straightening tomorrow. "I shouldn't be precious while I'm trying to figure it out."

Jada rubbed her arm gently. "Listen. I'm not saying you have to become a slut. And I swear I won't get that woman's number." She sighed. "Just...please. Relax. Flirt. Date. Go out with women for fun. No expectations. Not every encounter has to mean something."

Anger flashed through Del like lightning, sharp and hot. *But what if I want them to? What if I* need *them to?* The words burned her tongue. She reached for her drink, dousing the fire. The vodka tasted like ash.

Exhaustion seeped in, filling the empty spaces. She set down her drained glass with a sigh. "I'll try. I'll download one of those damn apps."

"That's a good place to start," Jada said. "But it's more important to just...be open."

Be open. Del bristled at Jada's implication that she was not. Not having gone on a date since her breakup didn't mean she was *closed.* It meant she was *processing.* And processing was important in the wake of breakup with a person she'd been intending to spend her life with.

Del was grateful when the food arrived, sparing her from having to reply right away. She stared at the noodles Jada had ordered for her because she knew they were her favorite. Suddenly, they seemed metaphorically resonant. She was stuck. And while eating spaghetti *fruits de mer* each time she came here might be healthy enough, the fact that she hadn't yet moved on from Maddie wasn't.

Chapter Two

Faith sat in her car, clutching the steering wheel as she stared at entrance to the Lonely Hearts Rescue Shelter. Sunlight glinted cheerfully from the windows as a family of four emerged with a large yellow dog on a leash. They all looked overjoyed.

Faith had to smile as she watched them. The act of smiling eased her own anxiety just enough that she was able to open the door. A warm breeze ruffled her hair, and she turned her face into it. She could do this. She could walk into that building and become a dog owner. She could give a traumatized animal comfort, support, and a safe place to live. Repeating the mantra as she crossed the parking lot got her to the front door. Before she could open it, someone else did, a recognizably queer woman holding it open for another woman clutching a cat carrier.

"Sorry," the first woman said. "Didn't mean to steamroll you."

"We're a little excited," the other said.

"No worries," Faith said. And then the door was closing behind her, and she was inside.

The atrium was airy and bright. To the left, a bank of windows revealed a roomful of cats. To the right was a similar room filled with dogs. The waiting area held a few more people, mostly in pairs or clusters. Faith stepped up to the front desk.

The woman sitting behind it looked up with a smile. "Welcome to Lonely Hearts. I'm Karri. Are you walking in, or do you have an appointment?"

"Thanks," Faith said because leading with gratitude was step one. "And I have an appointment. Faith Kincaid."

"Great, I see you on my list. Jan will be with you in just a few moments." Karri's smile was as brilliant as it was authentic. The old, nasty part of Faith wanted to make a snide comment just to rattle that smile. She breathed through the urge, thanked Karri again, and went to the window overlooking the dogs' play space.

At the sight of the romping canines, the tension in her chest began to ease. As she tracked the chasing and wrestling and snuffling, Faith felt her own smile return. Then, she heard the sound of her name. Jan approached her with a tablet in hand.

"I'm so glad you're here," she said. "Shall we go check out the pups?"

"Absolutely." Faith didn't really feel *that* confident, but "fake it till you make it" was sometimes a legitimate strategy.

As Jan led her through a side door and into a corridor, she chatted about the shelter's setup. They would start by looking at the dogs who were playing, but there were many other canines currently in their kennels.

"You can see them all," Jan said as she unlocked the first of two gates leading into the canine playroom. "We want you to find the friend who is the best fit for you."

Once inside the enclosure, they were greeted by a pack of all sizes. Jan laughed as she doled out pets and ear scratches, and Faith tried to follow her example. A striking dalmatian was particularly enthralled with her, and she smiled as the dog leaned against her legs while she petted it.

"Any interest in Scout?" Jan asked. "He's certainly taken a shine to you."

"Sorry. Too big," Faith said. "I don't think he'd do very well in the city."

With one last snuffle, the dalmatian ran off to join the pack playing in the middle of the room. As Faith turned to watch him go, her gaze fell on a much smaller dog curled up in the nearest corner. Its fur was mostly a tawny golden color, with a few white patches on its body and face. A plastic cone was around its neck. As though Faith had telepathically called its name, the dog raised its head and looked right at her. Heartbeats passed. The dog lowered its head and closed its eyes as though in defeat.

Ridiculous. She was projecting. Still, the space between her breasts ached. Faith pressed the heel of one palm to her sternum. "That one's hurt?"

"It must be only a minor injury, or the dog wouldn't be allowed out here with the others." Jan started walking. "Let's go say hello."

Faith trailed her. She had barely more than a clue about how to care for a healthy dog. Adopting an injured one was a terrible idea. There were probably all kinds of warning signs that a seasoned dog owner would recognize but that she would never pick up on. The thought of inadvertently neglecting or hurting an animal already in pain made her queasy.

Jan bent and allowed the dog to smell her fingers. She stroked its head, then stepped aside and consulted her tablet. Faith dropped into a crouch, then imitated Jan's greeting. The dog sniffed at her fingers, then licked them once. Carefully, Faith shifted her hand to scratch behind the dog's ears. Its fur was silky.

"Ah. Here we go. This one is Buffy."

Faith yanked her hand back, head whipping around. "Are you kidding me?"

"That's the name in her file," Jan said. "Is it some kind of problem?"

Faith realized she could hardly blame Jan for not getting the cultural reference. Still, the idea was ridiculous. "There's no way I can adopt a dog named *Buffy*."

Jan shrugged, unflappable as ever. "I think it's a cute name. But you can always change it, if you'd like."

Right. She could always change it. People changed their names all the time. This dog only thought her name was Buffy because someone had rewarded her with treats whenever she'd responded. Before Faith dropped out of college, she had taken Intro Psych. She knew how behaviorism worked.

Her thighs were tired of squatting. She sat and crossed her legs. Buffy scooted forward just enough to rest her chin on Faith's ankle. The plastic of the cone pressed uncomfortably against her calf muscle, but Faith found she didn't care. Buffy's eyes were the color of milk chocolate melting on a kitchen counter.

"It says here that Buffy's owner died when her house was hit by a tree." Jan's voice was subdued.

Faith winced. Without conscious thought, she reached for the dog, stroking the back of her head. When Buffy's eyes drooped in evident enjoyment, Faith couldn't hold back a smile. It disappeared when she realized both she and the dog had recently lost parents.

Craning her neck, she inspected Buffy's bandage. It didn't look very big, and Jan had said the shelter wouldn't make her available for adoption if she wasn't firmly on the path to healing. Still, she couldn't help but wonder if these goody-two-shoes animal-rescue types were trying to sucker her into some kind of scam.

"She's clearly not a hundred percent."

"You're right that she'll continue to need medical attention after you adopt her," Jan said. "Take her to Dr. Wu, the vet who examined her. Without approval, she wouldn't be up for adoption."

Buffy scooted a little closer. Her ears were so soft, and the ruff of fur below them was thick and curly. Faith ran her fingers through it. Her lips curved, held. Joy sifted through the mess of her emotions.

"Is she trained?"

Jan looked back at the tablet. "It says here that Buffy is fully house-trained and responds to 'sit,' 'stay,' and 'shake.' "

Buffy chose that precise moment to heave a heavy sigh, as though the weight of the world was resting on her tiny frame. Empathy flashed through Faith, swift and compelling. As she looked down, Buffy looked up. And in that moment, Faith couldn't imagine walking out of this building while Buffy was still inside it.

"Okay. Yes." Faith ran her free hand through her hair. "I want her."

Faith stood holding Buffy's leash in the lobby, waiting for the ancient machine to print out her receipt. In her other hand, she held a bag with the paperwork and one day's supply of food. The name of the brand was somewhere in the file folder. Apparently, if she wanted to switch Buffy's food, she had to do so gradually so as not to upset her stomach. Faith shrugged, trying to loosen her shoulders. Yes, there was a lot she didn't know. But she would learn. She could do this.

"You're all set," Karri said cheerfully. "I'm sure Jan reminded you, but don't forget to take"—she glanced down—"Buffy to the vet as soon as possible."

Right. "This Dr. Wu. The one Jan mentioned. Do you have his card?"

"Her," Karri said. "And yes." She reached under the desk.

Her. Faith shook her head, momentarily disgusted at herself. She kept trying to remember to use "they" whenever she didn't know a person's pronouns, and she kept failing. Way to reinforce damaging stereotypes. She thanked Karri for the card, then walked toward the door. As she crossed the threshold, the realization hit her: for the very first time in her life, she was a pet owner. The milestone rose up in her mind's eye like a mountaintop, inspirational and terrifying.

When she reached her car, Faith picked Buffy up, careful not to put her hands anywhere near the bandage. She watched as Buffy nosed around the back seat. Would she be safe enough back there without some kind of crate or leash? Faith reached into her pocket for her phone and wrote *look up how to take dog in car safely* in her notes file.

As she cautiously pulled out of the parking lot, her car's speakers announced an incoming call from her agent. Faith's thumb hovered over the *Decline* button. Right now, she was not in the mood for the aura of urgency that clouded every conversation with Jolie. Her priority was to get Buffy home, introduce her to the house, and start the process of teaching her to recognize a new name. Still, Jolie might have news. Or she could be peddling some kind of time-sensitive proposition that she would lay at another client's feet if Faith failed to pick up. With a sigh, she stabbed *Accept.*

"Hi, Jolie."

"Faith! Your day is about to get *so* much better. Are you sitting down?"

"Technically." As adrenaline washed through her, Faith took a tighter grip on the steering wheel. Jolie hyperbolized as a matter of principle. There was no reason to believe that—

"You've been selected as a finalist for *Fish Out of Water*!"

Only as Faith's jaw dropped did she realize she had stopped hoping a long time ago. And now, she was one step closer. *Finalist* didn't mean she would actually be on the show, but she had a fighting chance. And she was guaranteed a payout of five thousand dollars even if she didn't make the cut. That might be only a tenth of what she had lost to Jameson, but it wasn't nothing. It would pay some lawyer fees… for a little while, at least.

"Did I lose you, Faith? Are you there?"

Faith stared at the double yellow line twisting into her future. She swallowed hard, willing her voice to be steady. "I'm here. Just a little in shock."

"This is your big break, baby," Jolie enthused. "How soon can you make it back to the city to do the filming?"

Euphoria disappeared like a popped balloon. "I can't." Too late, she realized she had spoken the words aloud. Her stomach dropped.

"Why not?"

"The construction on my mom's house is nowhere near finished, and my contractor has gone AWOL with my money. There's no way I can pick up and leave right now." Faith glanced in her rearview mirror and caught a glimpse of Buffy curled up into as much of a ball as the cone would allow. "And I just adopted a dog. As in, I'm driving back from the shelter now."

The silence on the other end of the line was heavy with judgment. Faith clenched her teeth. Jolie was about to drop her for being difficult to work with, and she was going to have to find a new—

"This is the perfect narrative."

The distance between Jolie's reply and Faith's expectation gave her whiplash. "It…it is?"

"Yes. Faith, think about it. For years, you've been the party girl of Hype Cycle. 'No apologies' was practically your tagline. Now, grief and loss have inspired you to reevaluate your priorities. You've returned to your hometown to handle your mother's estate and embark on an internal journey of self-transformation. You're doing that whole eight-step fad thing, right? What's it called, again?"

Jolie didn't wait for her answer. As Faith listened to her prattle on, she felt a little nauseous. Jolie wasn't saying anything that wasn't true, but the *way* she was saying it made Faith feel like a caricature of herself. She would never have returned to Fairview if she could have avoided it. GTA wasn't a fad; it was legitimate and founded on the principles of cognitive behavioral therapy. And yes, she was trying to self-actualize, but it wasn't going very well. Besides, did she really want to exploit her own grief? *Could* you exploit yourself? The question made her head hurt.

"I don't suppose you're dating someone, are you?" Jolie was saying. "A steady relationship would *really* help this new image."

A welcome rush of anger halted the spiral of Faith's thoughts. Relationships were only allowed *after* step eight. The program was clear: jumping into one too early could lead to backsliding.

"*No.* And no fucking way am I getting into a relationship right now just because it's good for my image."

This time, there was no mistaking the tone of the silence that opened between them.

"I'm not suggesting you get engaged, Faith." The words were bitten off, sharp. "But your fans have never seen you with a steady girlfriend, and giving them a whiff of stability would be useful for your image right now."

The anger churned in her like a restless ocean, resisting platitudes. How dared Jolie try to control this part of her? She paid Jolie to find career opportunities, not pass judgment on her personal life.

Then again, in a reality show, was there really that much difference between the two? Jolie was trying to help her land this opportunity so they could both get paid. Faith didn't need to take every bit of her advice. And alienating her now, on the cusp of signing this deal, was the opposite of intelligent. She needed the money and the fame, and right now, that path went through Jolie. If she played her cards right, it wouldn't always.

Swallowing down her pride, Faith apologized. When Jolie finally hung up, Faith heaved a sigh. At the next stoplight, she glanced in her rearview mirror. Buffy was watching her with those soft, liquid eyes.

"How do you feel about maybe being famous?" Faith said.

When the dog yawned, Faith had to laugh.

Del ate her sandwich quickly, mechanically. The morning appointments had taken even longer than expected, and she was behind schedule. Between bites, she tried not to think about the expression on Mrs. Hayward's face at the news that her cat Stewart's condition was terminal.

Of course, she failed. And when she did, the bread stuck in her mouth. Raising her water bottle, Del took a long sip. When tears pricked her eyes, she blinked them back hastily. Damn it, she used to be stronger than this. Five minutes before her next appointment was no time to give way to grief. That was for later.

Her work phone buzzed with a text. *Patient Kincaid in room 3. New canine adoption.*

This news beat back the encroaching darkness. Any new adoption was always a good thing, but that was true more than ever now, with the surplus at the shelter. Del willed herself to think back to the dogs she'd examined, displacing the mental image of Stewart's distinctive face. A life lost, a life saved. That was something.

Del entered the room and stopped in surprise. Usually, visibly injured dogs were a hard sell, even to the bleeding hearts. She was beyond glad that someone had seen past the cone and bandage to the heart of gold beneath. And a coat of gold to match. Recognition sparked.

"Buffy!" The dog whirled and charged in her direction with barely a trace of a limp. As she scratched Buffy's ears, Del glanced at the wound on her hip. It seemed to be healing well, though she'd confirm that soon enough. As Buffy licked her hand, Del glanced up at her new owner. "So glad you found your forever—"

Del's mouth went dry. The woman was wearing a wide-collar T-shirt that hung off one shoulder and pulled across her breasts. Skinny black jeans clung to the contours of her sculpted legs. Strands of her dark, layered hair framed her pale face and clung to her neck. Her hips were cocked, and her lips were taut, but her eyes were wide and dark. For one charged moment, fear flickered like lightning. Then, it was gone.

"Well, you can't possibly be Dr. Wu," the woman said, sticking her free hand in her pocket.

The words were more effective than a bucket of water. Del stood. When the woman blinked and swallowed hard, Del knew she had seen the name stenciled over the pocket of her scrubs. A perverse satisfaction filled her. No, not perverse. *Deserved.*

"Actually, I am," Del said coolly, extending her hand. "And you are?"

"Uh, Faith. I..." Faith swallowed again. "I'm an idiot. Clearly." She dropped Del's hand, then rubbed at the back of her neck. "That was pretty horrible of me. Sorry."

Del's righteous anger melted away like snow in the springtime. Belatedly, she tried to cling to it. "Let's talk about Buffy."

"It's Pinot, actually." Faith tried out a laugh. "I mean, obviously, my dog can't be Buffy, right?"

A wave of self-consciousness prompted Del to laugh nervously in the way she absolutely hated. She was missing some joke again, just like always. "You've lost me."

Faith frowned, opened her mouth, and then closed it again. "My fault," she said. "Stupid joke."

Could this conversation get any more awkward? Del stifled a grimace and returned her attention to the dog, who was doing her best to sniff Del's shoes despite the interfering cone.

"So…Pinot? Big fan of the grape?"

When the moment of silence dragged on, Del realized she had blundered again. To avoid meeting Faith's gaze, she busied herself with lifting Bu—Pinot onto the exam table.

"Pinoe with an 'e' on the end, not a 't,'" Faith finally said. "It's a reference to Megan Rapinoe."

Del nodded as she pulled out her stethoscope, hoping the acknowledgment would end the conversation. It didn't.

"You know, the soccer player? And activist."

"Her name does sound familiar," Del said. That was true enough; she had definitely heard or seen it somewhere. She just couldn't remember the context.

"Damn." The syllable held a note of frustration. "I *really* thought you were queer."

The words slammed into Del like a punch, but the warm feeling they left behind wasn't pain. She stood there, blinking, as Faith clapped one hand over her mouth. The uncovered patches of her cheeks turned a vivid red.

"Fuck. I mean…shit. *No.* God da—" Faith clamped her lips together and squeezed her eyes shut, the skin around them crinkling.

Del felt as though someone had hit her on the head. She blinked hard, trying to dispel the mental fog. Her heart was beating quickly; she could hear it in her ears. Trapped between shock, annoyance, and arousal, she tried to muster a response. And failed.

Faith's eyes opened. She exhaled sharply. "I am so sorry. That was completely inappropriate. Do you want me to go? I should go."

A significant part of Del did want her to go, but Buffy—*Pinoe*—was already on the examination table. Not to mention the pesky voice in Del's head that wanted her to keep looking at Faith for as long as possible. Which was insane. This woman clearly had an issue with filters and boundaries. Del should listen to the part of herself that wanted to run away screaming.

"No," Del heard herself say.

"No?"

"Just...I need to do my job." Even to her own ears, her voice sounded hoarse.

"Right. Of course."

Del forced herself to block everything out except Buffy. No, Pinoe. Pinoe was still injured. Pinoe needed her. It didn't matter how stupidly attractive or infuriating her new owner was. Pinoe was all that mattered.

The exam didn't take long. Pinoe was already on the mend, and getting out of the shelter would be good for her. Still, Del noticed the way Faith shifted her weight and the desperation with which she was typing notes into her phone. An unwelcome wave of sympathy washed away some of Del's irritation. Faith was an obvious first-time dog owner, and her nervousness meant she was taking it seriously. Del could grudgingly respect that much.

"It's time to remove the bandage," she said. "But keep the cone on for a few more days. Then, you can try taking it off, but if you see her biting or scratching at the wound, put it back on."

Faith was nodding as her thumbs flew across the screen. "Right. Okay. Thank you." Suddenly, she glanced up. "Um, how do I take it off?"

Del beckoned brusquely. "I'll show you."

As Faith drew close, Del caught the scent of vetiver and lavender. The combination was fresh and earthy and appealing. When she caught herself starting to lean in, she braced one hand one the edge of the metal table. Through gritted teeth, she explained that the cone was fastened to a collar, then made Faith loosen and tighten it under her watch. All the while, Pinoe sat quietly, staring up at each of them in turn.

"It's probably obvious that I have no idea what I'm doing." As soon as the words were out of her mouth, Faith's eyes went wide. "I mean, I've done research. A lot of research. But I've never actually had any kind of pet, so I don't always know what I don't know."

Despite the many different layers of her annoyance, Del felt a wave of sympathy. "You're doing the right thing by asking questions."

Faith nodded. "She really is going to be okay?"

"There's still a risk of infection, but it's much lower now. As long as she doesn't reopen the wound, she should be fine." Del turned away to wash her hands. "You can boost her down."

When she turned, Faith was reattaching Pinoe's leash. Del held up a treat. "Okay if I give her this?"

"Sure, of course."

As she held up the treat, Pinoe sat without prompting. "Good girl," Del murmured. She steeled herself before looking back at Faith. "This practice runs a semi-weekly playdate at the Riverwalk dog park. Thursdays at six p.m., Sundays at noon. Bu…Pinoe can make some friends, and there will be plenty of people there to answer your questions. The vets here take turns stopping by, so you'll have access to an expert, too."

"That sounds great." Faith tucked the end of the leash under one arm and brought out her phone again.

Del watched her thumbs fly across the screen. "I'm usually there on Thursdays," she added, instantly hating herself.

Faith raised her head. "Oh. Okay. Thursdays."

"Mm." Del's self-consciousness was growing so quickly, she feared it would soon be visible, an extra shadow following her around.

As the corners of Faith's mouth turned up, the aura of her nervousness fell away. Del experienced the sudden, and not entirely uncomfortable, sensation of being backed into a corner, even though she hadn't moved a muscle.

"Thanks." Faith stuck out her free hand. "For everything."

What choice did she have? Del reached across the intervening space. The smooth heat of Faith's palm felt unaccountably good. She released her grip before her own palm could start sweating.

Swallowing hard, she gathered the shreds of her self-confidence like a tattered blanket. "Please check in with the receptionist on your way out. She'll schedule a follow-up."

"Right. Thanks." Faith sketched a wave. "See you Thursday."

When the door closed behind her, Del collapsed into the chair. She sat there for a moment, replaying the interaction. Mortifying. That really was the only accurate word. At least it was equally true for both of them.

Her phone buzzed with a text. The next patient was ready. Del rubbed briefly at her temples, then stood. She had a job to do.

Chapter Three

"Do you have any other questions for me, Faith?" Hallister asked, sitting back in his chair.

Faith looked down at the to-do list she had created on her phone. Send a registered letter. Call the bank. Take pictures of the unfinished work. Complete an application to the Contractor Recovery Fund.

Just looking at the list made her wish she hadn't kept this appointment. She had woken up with a headache that ibuprofen had never fully defeated. She should have crawled back into bed, pulled the covers over her head, and pretended everything was fine.

"Faith?"

She roused herself. "No, no questions. Thank you for your help."

"I'm sorry this happened." Hallister stood and extended his hand.

Faith felt the telltale pressure of her headache ramping up again as she returned to the waiting room. She was almost to the door when the receptionist called her name. With a sigh, Faith walked back to the front desk. The woman handed her a business card.

"This is the best contractor in town," she said.

Faith forced herself to glance at it, knowing the name she would find there. She smiled around her gritted teeth. "Thanks."

The day had been overcast when she'd entered Hallister's office. Now, it was pouring. Faith ran for her car. Even so, by the time she slid into the driver's seat, her hair was dripping, and her shirt was sopping.

"Figures," she muttered as she turned on the car.

The rhythm of the rain pounding against the windshield matched the drumbeat in her skull as she carefully navigated the roads. Faith muttered curses all the way home—curses at Jameson, at the rain, at her mother. The sting of guilt prompted her to direct a few at herself. No, she was not doing a good job of *Step 2: Embrace Positivity* today. Oh, fucking well.

When she finally reached her own front door, the sight of Pinoe framed by one of the sidelights momentarily arrested her slide back into self-loathing. Oblivious to Faith's infinite failures, the dog came bounding out to greet her. She had the uncanny realization that learning to see herself through Pinoe's eyes would probably be a helpful exercise. Maybe the therapy really *was* working.

Faith bent to pet her, then watched closely as Pinoe wandered out onto the lawn. She shook herself vigorously and squatted right away. At least the rain was good for *something*.

"It's miserable out here," Faith said. "Let's get inside."

Immediately, she headed toward the kitchen, desperate for more ibuprofen. Pinoe's collar jangled merrily as she followed. Faith stepped over the threshold only to yelp as she stepped on something hard. A crunching sound followed.

Pills were strewn all over the floor. The bottle was lying on its side near the dishwasher. Somehow, Pinoe must have knocked it down. Dread snaked down Faith's spine, cold and slithering. Had she eaten any of the pills? What did ibuprofen do to dogs?

She whirled to find Pinoe sniffing near the oven, perilously close to a cluster of capsules. Darting forward, Faith scooped her up, cradling her close.

"Are you okay?" She rubbed her cheek against the top of Pinoe's head. "*Fuck*, how do I tell if you're okay?"

When panic welled up in her throat, Faith desperately fought it back. She could feel Pinoe's heartbeat beneath her palm, and she allowed the steady rhythm to center her. Shifting the dog slightly to free up one hand, Faith extracted her phone from her pocket. Moments later, she was staring at the results of an internet search.

Ibuprofen is extremely dangerous to dogs, even in small quantities.

"Oh fuck. Oh no." Faith felt suddenly dizzy. Clutching Pinoe even more tightly, she staggered backward until she was leaning against the counter. The vet. She had to call the vet.

This time, her hand was shaking so hard it took her three times as long as it should have to pull up the number. The phone rang once, then twice.

"Pick up, pick up, pick—"

"Fairview Veterinary Hospital."

"I think my dog ate ibuprofen," Faith blurted. "What do I do? The internet says it's poison."

"I know this is scary," said the woman on the other end of the line. "Please stay calm so I can help you, okay?"

"Yeah. Okay." When Pinoe squirmed in her arms, she loosened her grip just a little.

"My name is Paula. Can you tell me your name and the name of your dog?"

Faith followed her instructions. "I just adopted Pinoe last week," she added. "I swear I thought the cap was sealed. I don't know what to—"

"My dog got into some of my medication once, too, Ms. Kincaid," Paula said. "We all try our best, but it happens. Dr. Wu is with me now, and I'm going to pass you over to her."

Faith's anxiety spiked higher. She had been such an ass to Dr. Wu at their first meeting. Surely, she wouldn't hold it against her? Did vets also have to swear some kind of Hippocratic oath?

"Hi, Ms. Kincaid. Can you tell me what happened?" The brisk efficiency in Dr. Wu's tone was reassuring.

Faith closed her eyes and forced herself to take a long, shuddering breath. She had to pull herself together and explain the situation clearly for Pinoe's sake. As she told the story, she tried to focus only on the facts. There would be plenty of time to beat herself up later.

"Okay," Dr. Wu said, once she had finished. "Is there any way for you to tell how many pills are missing?"

"It was a 500-pill bottle that I got only a few weeks ago. There were still hundreds of pills in there." Faith hurried over to where it was lying on the floor. She raised it and looked inside. "I think maybe half of them are still in the bottle? And there are pills all over the floor. I can try counting them all, but that will take a while. And I think some may have rolled under the oven."

"It's probably not worth taking the time to do that," Dr. Wu said. "You mentioned you were gone when she knocked over the bottle. How long was Pinoe alone?"

"I was out of the house for…an hour? Maybe an hour and a half."

"Okay. The safest option is to assume she ate at least some and bring her in. We can induce vomiting and give her activated charcoal, which will reduce how much of the ibuprofen is absorbed into her blood."

Faith exhaled shakily. That sounded horribly unpleasant for Pinoe, but it was much better than the alternative. The thought of losing her was like a knife flaying her open. Pinoe had survived a hurricane and the tragic passing of her previous owner. Faith had just lost her second parent. There would be no more death, not if she could help it.

"I can be there in ten minutes."

"We'll be waiting," Dr. Wu said.

Faith hurried to the hall closet and grabbed the dog carrier. She coaxed Pinoe inside, then dashed up to the bedroom to change her soaking shirt. As she pounded back down the stairs, she missed one and nearly fell, just barely catching herself against the railing. Fighting back a fresh surge of dizziness, she listened to the harsh panting of her own breath. Calm. She had to stay calm and cautious just long enough to get Pinoe to the vet.

"You've got this," she muttered as she began once again to descend the stairs, this time with slower, shaky steps.

For once, she didn't put any music on in the car. Instead, she focused intently on never going over four miles above the speed limit and on keeping multiple car lengths between herself and the driver in front of her. On each hill, she carefully pumped the brakes, mindful of the rain-slick streets. At each stoplight, she refined her apology to Dr. Wu, mentally exchanging and rearranging words, muttering phrases under her breath. Fortunately, she found a parking space near the front door to the animal hospital. Heart pounding, she opened the back door and crouched to check on Pinoe. When Faith pressed two fingers to the mesh across the front of the carrier, Pinoe's slick nose pressed back.

"Good girl," Faith murmured before carefully picking her up and whisking her inside.

Paula looked up as Faith pushed open the door. "Ms. Kincaid, right?" When Faith nodded, she offered a comforting smile. "We have an exam room all ready for you. Dr. Wu will be with you very soon."

Paula came out from behind the front desk and opened the door to the same room Faith had been in on Friday. Faith set Pinoe's carrier on the floor, then gingerly sat on the chair. Her head was all-out throbbing now. Bracing her elbows on her knees, she rubbed circles against her temples. When she closed her eyes, all she could see were the pills strewn across her kitchen floor like tiny land mines.

"You're going to be okay," she murmured, a prayer more than a promise.

❖

When Del's phone vibrated, she stopped typing in the middle of a sentence.

Ms. Kincaid and Pinoe are in exam room 1.

She stood. The sentence could wait, but Pinoe might not be able to. She had seen dogs come in to the ER with severe ibuprofen poisoning. After everything Pinoe had already been through, Del didn't want to waste a single second. She hurried into the hallway, pushed through the swinging door into the reception area, and gave Paula a wave before ducking into the room.

Faith sat on the chair with her face in her hands, and Del's heart lurched at her obvious despair. At the sound of the door, Faith looked up and ran her hands through her hair, shaking it back.

"Dr. Wu. Thank you so much for fitting us in on such short notice."

Del was already moving across the room. She crouched in front of the carrier. "Let's see how she's doing." When Del opened the zipper, Pinoe surged out to lick her face. Despite the circumstances, Del had to laugh. "That's a good sign."

She lifted Pinoe, then checked her heartbeat and the color of her gums. When she glanced over her shoulder, Faith was perched on the edge of the chair, legs tensed.

"I don't see any red flags at the moment," Del said. "But the problem with ibuprofen is that it stays in the body for a long time, getting recycled between the liver and intestines. The safest course of action is to assume she ingested some and stick to the plan."

"Yeah. Okay." Once Faith started nodding, she couldn't seem to stop. "So you'll induce vomiting and then, what was the other step?"

"Activated charcoal. Eating it will block the absorption of the ibuprofen, but I need to monitor her sodium levels while I administer it. It's also possible that at some point, she'll need to be put on an IV to help her regain fluids."

Faith visibly swallowed, and her eyes grew glassy with tears. When she blinked, two spilled over. But instead of bursting into sobs, she dashed them away and took a sharp breath, visibly pulling herself together.

"Whatever the best thing is—whatever's most likely to help her—I want to do that."

Del had seen many frantic and worried pet owners over many years. For some reason, the sight of Faith struggling to stay focused and coherent was deeply moving. She had none of the apathy or defensiveness Del sometimes saw in new pet owners who had gotten in over their heads. Faith might only have had Pinoe for a matter of days, but her commitment to the dog's well-being was entirely authentic.

"My team and I will take good care of her, Ms. Kincaid. We all want to see her pull through, and we have a lot of reasons to be hopeful."

"Thank you." Faith smoothed her palms against her thighs. "How long will she need to stay?"

"At least until the evening. Possibly overnight. I'll call you around five o'clock with an update."

"Okay." Faith stood, hands fidgeting at her sides. "Thank you so much."

When she stepped close to Del and leaned in to kiss Pinoe's forehead, Faith's distinctive scent caught at Del like the echo of a song she knew but couldn't place.

"I'm really sorry about what's going to happen in there," Faith continued, gently scratching behind Pinoe's ears. "But you're going to be okay. And *I'm* going to do better. Starting now."

The conviction in her voice struck Del with an almost physical force, snaring her breath. Faith looked up, and as their gazes met, Del was captivated by the intensity of her expression.

"I need to apologize for how I behaved to you on Friday, for the snap judgment I made and for what I blurted out. What I said was offensive." Faith exhaled sharply. "For…for a long time now, I've been deflecting my anxiety with humor. Usually at the expense of other people. It's something I'm working on, and I'm sorry."

Del could recognize a pre-rehearsed speech when she heard one. The thought of Faith committing the words to memory made her feel warm inside. "I appreciate that." Her initial impression of Faith had been *hot mess*, but the more they interacted, the less fair that assessment seemed to be. She might be struggling at the moment, but it was a struggle to grow. Del could see that now.

Before she could question the impulse, she reached out to squeeze Faith's shoulder. "I'll call within a few hours."

Faith nodded and sniffled, and Del, realizing she was *touching* a client, dropped her hand as though it were scalded. She left the room without a backward glance and didn't stop moving until she was in the intensive care and recovery area. Greg, one of the vet techs, was there checking in on Silus, who had been neutered earlier that morning.

"How's he doing?" Del asked.

"Looking good," Greg said. "Who do you have there?"

"This is Pinoe. She's one of the hurricane pups. She was adopted Friday but got into her new owner's ibuprofen today."

Greg grimaced. "How bad is it?"

"Not sure. The owner caught it early. I'll need the apomorphine." Del's phone buzzed, and she pulled it out of her scrubs pocket. "And I need you to stay with her during the emesis. I'll come back to check on her after my next appointment."

Del put Pinoe down on the large scale in the corner and told her to sit. The dog obeyed readily, looking up at her with caramel-colored eyes. The tip of her tail swished against the metal bed.

"Twenty-two pounds," Del called. The number was a little concerning; Pinoe should be closer to twenty-five, and she was only going to lose weight today. "You're a good girl. But if I give you a you-know-what, that will only make this worse."

She scooped up the dog and put her on the nearest exam table, petting her gently until Greg arrived with the syringe. Del injected the apomorphine subcutaneously, then lavished more love on Pinoe.

"This isn't going to be a fun day for you, but I promise you're going to get through it." She turned to Greg. "She's been through a lot since that hurricane hit."

Greg stepped close to scratch between her ears. "I'll hold her hair back."

Del scoffed and stepped away. Pinoe was in perfectly competent hands. Greg was the best tech at the practice. Still, for some reason, it felt wrong to walk away. She thought of Faith's stricken expression, of the tears she had brushed from her cheeks. Every animal was important to Del, but some were special. As she returned to the front desk, Del tried to untangle her own logic. Was Pinoe special because of what had happened during the hurricane? Or because she belonged to Faith?

As she approached the door leading out to the public area, Del straightened her shoulders. Pinoe would be fine. There were other animals and their people who needed her now. By the time she stepped across the threshold, a pleasant smile was plastered to her face. She acknowledged the waiting visitors with a quick wave, then stepped inside exam room two.

"Mr. Latimer? How is Cronkite doing today?"

The remainder of the day was a whirlwind. One client's cat scratched her just beneath her left eye. Another client's dog required sutures. When a twelve-year-old girl and her father visited with their obviously pregnant guinea pig, Del found herself having to explain how babies were made. It would have been easy to get caught up in the incessant waves of activity, but a part of Del was always thinking about Pinoe. Any time she had more than a minute between appointments, Del hurried back to the ICU. On her most recent visit, she had noticed signs of dehydration and decided to administer an IV.

By the time the final client left the building, Del was exhausted. She said good-bye to Paula, then hurried back into the depths of the building. Pinoe was lying in the corner of her enclosure, the fluids bag hanging from its side. Nearly empty. Despite all the dog had been through, her tail thumped at Del's approach.

"Hey, you," Del murmured. She extracted a treat from her pocket. "I can finally give you one."

Pinoe scooted forward to nose at the treat. After a moment, she took it from Del's hand.

"Good girl." When Del sat on the floor, Pinoe scooted forward again to rest her chin on Del's leg. "Let's call Faith, shall we?"

As she scratched between Pinoe's ears, Del scrolled through her contacts. The phone rang only once before Faith picked up with a breathy, "Hello?"

"Ms. Kincaid, this is Dr. Wu."

"How is she?" Faith's voice was rough, and Del wondered if, in the intervening hours, she had been crying.

"She's tired but stable. She was dehydrated, so we have her on an IV now."

"Do you think—" Faith's voice broke, and she cleared her throat. "Do you think she'll recover?"

"I do," Del said. "She hasn't exhibited any signs of poisoning yet. It could be that she didn't ingest any or that we were able to get it out of her system quickly enough. Either way, that's a positive sign."

"That's the best news." Faith sniffled. "Can I come pick her up, or does she need to stay the night?"

The wistfulness in her voice tugged at Del. "Let's give her another hour to recover. The office is about to close, but I'll give you my cell number so you can contact me."

"Are you sure?" Faith blurted. "I don't want to inconvenience you."

"If you abuse this privilege, I'll block you," Del said. When Faith didn't laugh, she sighed. "That was mostly a joke."

"Oh! Oh." Faith laughed weakly. "Sorry."

"See you in an hour."

Del hung up and looked down at Pinoe, whose eyes were closed. The weight of her head was a comfort, the regular puffs of her breath a reassurance. And yet, despite the demands of the day, Del felt strangely energized.

She didn't want the cause of her adrenaline to be Faith.

Faith's stomach growled as she carefully deposited the pizza on the passenger seat. As she pulled out of the parking lot, a horrifying thought occurred to her: what if Dr. Wu was vegan? Would she be offended by a cheese pizza? Or would she at least appreciate the gesture, even if she couldn't eat it?

"Oh, stop it," Faith said to the rearview mirror.

This day had already encompassed an eternity of fear, worry, and uncertainty, and it was just past six o'clock. As usual, she was being melodramatic and hyperbolic, allowing her imagination to conjure the worst-case scenarios instead of the best. At the next stoplight, she briefly closed her eyes, breathed in deeply through her nose, and then exhaled through her mouth as though cooling a cup of coffee.

"She might love cheese pizza," Faith said, pressing on the

accelerator. "Verona's might even be her favorite pizza place in town. *You* don't know."

The animal hospital's parking lot was deserted except for a van with the hospital's logo and an electric car. As Faith swung into a spot nearby, she felt another prickle of insecurity. Did an electric vehicle make it more likely that Dr. Wu would be vegan? Clenching her teeth, she shook her head, pulled out her phone, and scrolled to the bottom of her contacts list. The phone rang twice.

"Hello?" Dr. Wu's voice was crisp and guarded. Business-like.

"This is Faith Kincaid. Pinoe's owner?" Faith instantly hated herself for the interrogatory lilt. That was a bad habit she thought she had broken.

"Oh, Ms. Kincaid. Hello. Are you here?"

"Just pulled in." Faith drummed her fingers against the steering wheel. "Is Pinoe still okay to come home?"

"Yep. Meet me at the front door."

Faith waited awkwardly with the pizza, watching through the front windows. Dr. Wu was dressed in pale red scrubs today, a color that looked good on her. Her hair was pulled back into the same ponytail as last time. As she approached, Faith wondered what it would look like down, brushing her shoulders.

"Hi." Dr. Wu looked between her and the pizza as she opened the door.

"Hi." Faith hefted the pie. "I thought you might be hungry, especially since you're working late. It's cheese," she added belatedly.

"It smells great." Dr. Wu gestured for her to come inside. "I know I'm supposed to say 'You shouldn't have,' but honestly, I'm glad you did."

Relief pulled a smile to Faith's lips. "How is she?"

"Good." The certainty in Dr. Wu's voice was a balm. "She's perked up a lot since we put her on fluids. She'll probably be a little lethargic for the next few days, but I don't see any sign of poisoning."

Faith exhaled shakily. "I'm so glad. Thank you for taking such good care of her."

Dr. Wu took the outstretched pizza box. "Will you share this with me?"

Faith blinked at her. "I'm sorry?"

"I can't eat the whole thing myself." Dr. Wu shrugged. "It's never as good when it's reheated. And you probably haven't eaten anything all day."

"Guilty as charged. Okay, I'll have a slice."

"We'll use the break room." Dr. Wu gestured, and Faith followed her past the front desk, into the depths of the facility. Then, her steps slowed. As good as sharing that pizza sounded, she wouldn't be able to eat if she knew Pinoe was lying in a cage somewhere close by.

"Dr. Wu…I'd like to get Pinoe first. Is that okay?"

"Of course. I'd want the same thing." Dr. Wu led her into the break room and set the pizza on the table. "I'll be right back."

Set against one wall of the room was a counter, cabinets above it and drawers below. Faith opened a few until she found paper plates and napkins. Then, she paced to the windows at the far end. They looked out over a grassy, fenced-in area, some kind of dog run, if she had to guess. She made a mental note to find out whether the hospital boarded healthy dogs. If she was selected as a finalist for *Fish Out of Water*, she would need a place for Pinoe to stay while she was filming.

At the jangling sound of a collar, Faith turned so quickly, she became dizzy. As her vision cleared, Dr. Wu appeared in the doorway, Pinoe in her arms. There was a fond smile on Dr. Wu's face, a look unlike any expression Faith had previously witnessed. The softness of it tugged at her.

"She perked up ten feet away from the door," Dr. Wu said. "She knows her person."

When she stooped to deposit Pinoe on the floor, the dog ran for Faith not quite at full speed, but close. Faith dropped to one knee and held out her hands, tears stinging her eyes as Pinoe pushed her head into her palms and whined. Faith petted her gently, fingers sliding through the silk fur. As relief flooded through her, fatigue followed in its wake.

"I was so scared," she murmured. "I thought I might lose you, too."

When Pinoe jumped up, resting her paws against Faith's knee, she noticed the shaved patch of fur where Dr. Wu had inserted the IV. Avoiding the spot, Faith gathered Pinoe close and picked her up. She turned to find Dr. Wu watching her. The attention felt heavier than curiosity. Beneath her relief, she wondered at it.

"Thank you so much for taking care of her," she said.

"Of course." Dr. Wu pulled out a chair and sat down. "She's had a rough day, but she'll bounce back. She's lucky to have you."

Faith blinked across the table. How could Dr. Wu not believe her to be a hopeless failure? "And here I thought you were going to recommend I give Pinoe back to the shelter. Or call the SPCA on me for negligence." She tried to laugh, but no sound emerged.

Dr. Wu's eyes widened. "You were really worried about that?"

"Well…yes?"

"Ms. Kincaid—"

"Faith. Please. 'Ms. Kincaid' was my mother."

Dr. Wu nodded slowly in a way that made Faith believe she had recognized her use of the past tense. "I'm Del."

"Hi," Faith said. She felt stupidly self-aware under Del's scrutiny.

"Hi." Del regarded her seriously. "The last dog I owned ate a clock spring and required surgery. I'm a good surgeon, but I couldn't do it because I was her owner. The waiting and agonizing and self-flagellation were horrible."

"That's the truth," Faith murmured. "I'm sorry you had to go through that."

"Ditto." Del reached for a slice of pizza. "These things happen. They don't mean you're a bad person or pet owner. Especially because I'm sure you're already paranoid about sealing the Advil cap."

Faith had to laugh. "You have no idea. Except, of course, you do."

"I do. And that's my point. So please don't beat yourself up more than you have already."

Faith nodded and grabbed her own slice. When Pinoe didn't even raise her head, she frowned. "Usually, she shamelessly begs for food. Should I be worried?"

"No. She's stressed, and she might still be queasy from the emetic. But if she doesn't want to eat tomorrow, please call the office."

"Will do. Thanks."

An awkward silence descended. Faith ate her pizza one-handed while stroking Pinoe's fur. The adrenaline that had been her constant companion today was receding. Now that she had Pinoe on her lap and some food in her stomach, fatigue settled over her like a weighted blanket. When she glanced across the table, she noticed Del frowning at her phone.

"Is everything okay?"

Del rubbed at her eyes, telegraphing her own weariness. "Test results from another patient. Not good news." She set the phone face-down on the table. "I wish every story could end like Pinoe's."

There was real pain in her voice, and Faith wondered how she did it, how she kept coming back to this job that must be at least equal parts victory and defeat. She thought about her own relationship with loss and the imprint it could make. Consciously practicing the empathy she was trying to cultivate, Faith tried to imagine how difficult it must be to tell a worried pet owner that their cherished family member was dying.

"I'm sorry. It must be so hard to deliver bad news."

"It's the second hardest thing I do," Del said.

Faith could guess the first. She prodded the pizza crust on her plate with one finger. "This probably won't be comforting, but it's clear you care. That means a lot." She looked up to find Del staring at her thoughtfully. "Of course, I'm sure caring makes it all even harder."

Del laughed softly, but the sound was without humor. "I can't imagine the alternative." She shook her head. "Anyway. Sorry to get maudlin. I do love my job."

Faith could practically hear the clanking sounds of Del's shields and walls rising back into place. They were a coping mechanism—she knew that well enough—and also a sign that it was time for her to go.

Shifting Pinoe in her arms, she stood. "If I'm exhausted, I can only imagine how you feel. Thank you again."

"I'll walk you out." Del gestured for Faith to precede her, then fell into step down the hallway. "Aside from what happened today, how is everything going?"

"Good. Well. Mostly good." Faith brushed a kiss across the top of Pinoe's head. "It feels silly to mention after all the drama of today, but she's struggling to learn her new name."

Del nodded. "That can take a while." She held open the front door for Faith, then stood in the threshold. "If you'd like to talk with a training specialist, I can recommend a few."

"Thanks." Faith brushed aside a strand of hair, feeling suddenly awkward again. She wasn't accustomed to feeling this much gratitude. "Seriously. Thank you. You're a literal lifesaver."

Del's only response was a lopsided smile. "Have a good evening," she said, rubbing a gentle thumb across Pinoe's forehead. "And you, stay out of trouble."

"I hope you can get some rest," Faith said. "Good night."

As she walked across the parking lot, she tried to resist the urge to look back. When she failed, she found Del standing where she had left her. Del raised one hand, and a bubble of warmth manifested in Faith's chest, expanding to fill the heavy, aching void in her heart.

"Well," Faith said, as she slid into the driver's seat and glanced in the rearview mirror, "I somehow didn't permanently fuck up my relationship with your doctor." She double-checked for an oncoming car, even though the parking lot was still mostly empty. "Maybe there's hope for me yet."

CHAPTER FOUR

Pinoe, no. Stop. Stay!"

As Pinoe rocketed through the open door, Faith shouted everything she could think of. The dog remained willfully oblivious. Barefoot, Faith gave chase, offering an embarrassed wave to the woman—Sharon, she reminded herself—who was just stepping out of her car. Fortunately, instead of running across the street, Pinoe paused to sniff the mailbox. Faith scooped her up, cradling her to her chest.

"You can't *do* things like that," Faith exclaimed, burying her nose in Pinoe's ruff before turning to walk up the length of the driveway. "You'll give me a heart attack. Why won't you listen?"

Sharon watched in clear bemusement, pushing her sunglasses up to perch atop her head. Her glossy auburn hair was immaculately styled, and Faith took note of her designer shoes and jeans. Her look screamed, "Hollywood."

"Hi, Sharon." Faith stuck out a hand as she approached. "I'm Faith. Sorry about the drama."

"No worries. Glad the pup is safe."

"This is Pinoe," Faith said, angling her body so Sharon could pet Pinoe's head.

As Sharon crooned, Faith subtly took a deep breath, trying to regain her equilibrium. Okay, so the first minute of their interaction hadn't gone as planned. That was okay. Just because Pinoe had made a break for it didn't mean Sharon thought she was a negligent dog owner. Did it?

"Want to come inside?" Faith asked, relieved when her voice betrayed no hint of her internal freak-out.

"Lead the way."

Once in the foyer, with the door safely shut, Faith gently put Pinoe onto the floor. "Pinoe, sit."

The traitorous creature looked from Faith to Sharon but remained standing. Sharon laughed. "Stubborn little thing, isn't she?"

Now thoroughly mortified, Faith forced herself to laugh along. "I've had her for less than a week. We're still figuring each other out." She grabbed a treat from the bag on the table in the foyer. "And I've noticed she's very food motivated."

Food motivated was a term Faith hadn't known until two days ago, when she'd asked the internet why her dog only obeyed her when she offered a treat. Now, as soon as she held the nasty-smelling morsel before Pinoe, the dog's butt hit the floor without being asked. Sharon laughed again, then reached down to scratch Pinoe's ears.

"Me, too, Pinoe." She turned to Faith. "The notes from your agent mentioned she was abandoned in the hurricane?"

"Her owner died. They found Pinoe next to her body." Faith pointed to the raw scar on her flank. "She's still healing from the injuries she sustained during the flood."

"Oh no. That's so sad." Sharon gave the dog an extra scratch, then straightened. "And it'll make for a great story."

The comment jangled in Faith's ears. She could recognize the truth of it, but it also felt exploitative. She tried to tell herself she was being silly. Pinoe's owner was gone. No one was being exploited. Sharon was doing what *Fish Out of Water* paid her to do: turn Faith into a competitive candidate. Good stories were important.

She made a vaguely affirmative sound, then led Sharon deeper into the house. Pinoe's claws clicked against the wood floor. As Faith gave Sharon the tour, she was reminded of doing the same for Jan only a few days ago. Thinking of how her life had changed between then and now was dizzying.

"And this is your childhood home?" Sharon asked, leaning against the island as Faith made her a cup of coffee. "You grew up here?"

"I did." Faith felt her shoulders trying to tighten. Subtly, she rolled them back and down, hearing the tiny pop in her taut muscles. These questions were inevitable. She had prepared for them. She could do this. "I was born in the city, but we moved here when I was five."

"And I understand your mother passed recently? I'm so sorry."

"Yes, that's right." Faith poured another spiral of hot water on top of the grounds. The trickle reminded her of her own tears. She swallowed hard. "She died suddenly of a stroke last month. And my dad died when I was a teenager."

"That's so hard," Sharon murmured.

How the fuck would you know? The angry response bubbled up like magma. With an effort, Faith quashed it. Maybe Sharon did know. Maybe she didn't. Either way, she was being kind. Accepting kindness was step three. Step three was still a struggle sometimes. That was okay, Faith reminded herself. The steps weren't supposed to be easy because *change* wasn't easy.

"Your agent told me you're here fixing up the house to flip it?"

"That's right." The vise around Faith's chest eased a little. Talking about the house was solid ground, especially since she had decided that throwing Jameson under the bus was her best possible way to get her money back. "It's been rough, though. The first contractor I hired bolted with my money."

"Are you shitting me?"

Faith smiled to herself as she disposed of the grounds. By the time she turned to face Sharon, she had assumed the same carefully blank expression she had mastered while her mother was in one of her drunken rages.

"I wish. His phone is disconnected. I contacted the Better Business Bureau and hired an attorney."

As Sharon expressed anger and sympathy, Faith debated whether to share the rest of the story. It would add drama, which was probably good for her. On the other hand, no matter how little she liked him, Oscar was probably the best chance she had at actually getting the house in shape for a Realtor. She probably shouldn't do anything to alienate him. At least, not until she mustered the courage to actually have a conversation.

Coffees in hand, they relocated to the living room. Faith was gratified when, after she sat, Pinoe jumped into her lap. At least now, Sharon would see that her dog actually liked her. As Faith stroked Pinoe's silky fur, careful to avoid the healing wound, guilt seeped in to take the place of her complacence. Pinoe wasn't a prop to be used in the service of her ambition, no matter what Jolie might say. Pinoe was in pain, physically and emotionally. Pinoe was her responsibility to protect and nurture. Her priority.

When Sharon's questions returned to the subject of her youth, Faith was especially grateful to Pinoe for hiding the tremor in her hands. She tried to remain terse and objective. After her father's death, her mother had spiraled into alcoholism, and their relationship had deteriorated, particularly once she came out. Still, even as she maintained a steady voice, her mind swirled with memories.

Once the questions left Faith's childhood behind, she found herself able to relax a little. It was easy to talk about why she had decided to drop out of college to become a personal trainer, how she had been scouted by Hype Cycle and reached a certain measure of fame as part of their team. She was generous in her praise of them, citing the flexibility they had offered during her recent tragedy. But when Sharon steered the conversation toward Faith's decision to start the "Growing Toward Actualization" program, Faith tensed up again. Being honest to herself and others might be step one, but that honesty meant returning to the subject of her mother.

"If you look at my socials," Faith said, "you'll see I've cultivated a reputation as something of a wild child. My mom's death made me take a look in the mirror and reconsider my priorities. I've been angry and self-destructive for a long time. I'm trying to change that now. GTA is helping."

When Sharon finally stood to leave, Faith struggled not to betray her relief. She kept hold of Pinoe this time, not wanting a repeat of the door-dashing incident.

"Oh," Sharon said as she slipped on her shoes. "One more question. Do you have a significant other?"

"No!" Too late, Faith heard the vehemence in her own voice. She remembered Jolie's admonition that a girlfriend would be *useful for her image*.

Sharon's lips twisted. "That's too bad."

Faith felt suddenly distant from herself. She heard her mother's slurred voice, the oft-repeated words: *You're nothing. You'll never amount to anything.* Hovering above the scene in her own foyer, she watched the money, the fame, the opportunities slipping away.

Would telling one white lie be so bad? After all, she *could* easily be in a relationship. Finding women willing to date her had never been a challenge.

"Well…there is someone," she heard herself say. "But it's really new. Fragile."

"Oh." Sharon's smile was neon. "How sweet of you to be protective of this new love in your life."

New love. Faith swallowed hard, hating herself. "Yeah. I mean… I'm a mess." About this, at least, she could be honest. "I'm trying not to scare her off."

When Sharon squeezed her shoulder, Faith struggled not to grimace. "You're a catch, Faith," she said. "Don't worry so much. I'll be in touch."

Once the door was firmly shut behind her, Faith carefully returned Pinoe to the floor. Those warm brown eyes stared up at her, wholly oblivious to the fact that her owner had just allowed insecurity and fear to derail her into telling a stupid, selfish lie. When a wave of anxiety crashed over her, Faith braced herself against the door. She tried to take a deep breath, but it snarled in her mouth. She coughed and tried again, more slowly this time. In for four. Hold. Out for four. Hold. Repeat.

After a few minutes, the worst of the panic retreated, leaving the coarse sediment of guilt in its wake. After weeks of hard work, she had jeopardized all that progress at the drop of a pin. The back of her throat tasted sour. She swallowed hard. Retreating to the living room, she collapsed onto the sofa. Moments later, Pinoe jumped onto her chest, licked her chin, and then curled up on her sternum.

Faith blinked back tears as she stared at the ceiling. This was definitely what Jan had meant by *unconditional love*. And she definitely didn't deserve it.

Old!Faith's voice intruded, cynical and snarling. *You've lied a million times. Who cares about one more? And so what if GTA says you shouldn't date until after step eight? Fuck GTA. Find a girl; it won't be hard. Have some fun.*

"Shut up," Faith said loudly. When Pinoe raised her head in alarm, she whispered an apology and stroked her ears with extra gentleness.

"Okay," she said, keeping her voice even. "You're catastrophizing.

Yes, you made a mistake. Our mistakes don't define us. How we respond defines us."

Pinoe licked her chin again as if to punctuate the mantra. Faith felt her lips curve. The grip of the guilt eased, just a little, opening a space for strategy. How *was* she going to respond? She absolutely refused to drag some unsuspecting woman into a relationship she wasn't invested in. If only, she thought wistfully, it was possible to find someone *else* who wanted a fake relationship. Someone for whom the arrangement would also be beneficial. Yes, she would still be lying but only to the world. She wouldn't be hurting another person.

"Simple," she said, watching the word riffle the fur on Pinoe's forehead. "Now all I need to do is find a fake girlfriend."

Del leaned back against the chain-link fence of the dog park, enjoying the tug of the cool breeze in her hair. After a day in the office with it held taut in a ponytail, letting it down was a relief. On the folding table before her, the edges of flyers and pamphlets fluttered, each stack held down by a Fairview Veterinary Hospital mug.

She turned slightly to look out over the river. Sailboats dotted its surface, white sails crisp against the blue ribbon. The landscape was still lush and green, as though it were high summer instead of the verge of autumn. Del felt a sudden sense of foreboding at the thought of darkness encroaching subtly, steadily.

"Hi, Dr. Wu." Samantha, one of the regulars, waved to her. She bent to pick up a ball, then threw it for her Australian shepherd, Hugh.

"Hi, Samantha." Del waved back. She rolled her shoulders, hoping to shrug off the pessimistic thoughts.

An unfamiliar face approached the table. He introduced himself and Dexter, his yellow lab, as new to town and took one of the flyers. Del answered a few of his questions until he was distracted by the spectacle of Dexter being humped persistently by Cronkite the bulldog.

"Oh, don't worry about Cronk," Del reassured him. "Once he gets it out of his system, he and Dexter will be best friends."

The gate to the park swung open. Automatically, Del swung her gaze to the newest addition. *Buffy. No.* Pinoe. The dog almost glowed in the late afternoon sun, chestnut-golden fur glinting in the breeze. Behind her, Faith was every bit as attractive as Del remembered, though at least today, she wore a hoodie. Its slight bagginess made her look softer, less sealed off.

Faith paused just inside the gate. Pinoe sat close to her feet, mirroring her owner's uncertainty. Slowly, Faith's head turned. When she caught sight of Del, her shoulders relaxed, and she headed in the direction of the table. Del felt the butterflies in her stomach and busied herself with straightening the pamphlets. This was ridiculous. Faith knew she was attractive, and she had that kind of magnetic energy that appealed to everyone. She probably never dated the same woman twice. She was exactly the opposite of what Del wanted.

Go out with women for fun. No expectations. Jada's voice echoed in her brain.

"Shut up," Del hissed.

"I didn't say anything." Faith's voice. Coming from just a few feet away.

Mortified, Del jerked her head up. "Sorry. I..." When no convincing lies materialized, she defaulted to the truth. "I was talking to myself." She laughed, hoping the self-deprecation would be compelling. "Sometimes, my brain really needs to shut up."

Instead of finding an excuse to leave, Faith nodded. "I can empathize." She turned slightly, shading her eyes against the sun. "Also, hi. And...how does this work?"

"Hi." Grateful for the distraction, Del explained the rules of the park. Faith listened attentively, then crouched to unhook Pinoe's leash. She punctuated the movement with a caress of Pinoe's ears before standing again. Del had seen many people pet their dogs over many years, but there was something special about Faith's gentleness.

"Go have fun," she urged. After a moment of hesitation, Pinoe trotted away.

"So, how are thi—"

"Look, I just want—"

Del shut her mouth with a click at the same time Faith clamped her lips together. For a moment, they stared at each other. Then, Del tried to laugh the awkwardness away. "After you."

"Thanks." Faith rubbed at the back of her neck in a clear show of nerves. "I wanted to thank you again for taking such good care of Pinoe on Monday. You made yourself available right away, and then you went above and beyond. Thank you."

"I didn't give you special treatment, if that's what you're implying." As soon as the words were out of her mouth, Del regretted them. The feeling only sharpened when Faith flinched.

"I'm sorry. I didn't mean to—"

"No. Please don't apologize. I shouldn't have gotten defensive. It's just that fairness is important to me."

Faith nodded, her expression thoughtful. "I was referring to how you let me pick Pinoe up after-hours. It meant a lot to be able to take her home that day." She smiled in a quiet, wholly unselfconscious way. "I put her on the bed and watched her sleep for a while, and the next thing I knew, it was morning, and my teeth were all fuzzy-feeling."

Del's heart felt like a pat of melting butter. She could picture it: Faith's dark hair mussed on the bedspread, hands tucked under one cheek as she watched Pinoe's flank rise and fall. When she imagined Faith's lashes fluttering as exhaustion claimed her, the mental image made Del's chest ache.

"Anyway." Faith cleared her throat. "I'll let you get back to—"

They were interrupted by the sounds of Dexter vomiting loudly in the far corner. After he had emptied his belly, he slunk back toward his owner, tail between his legs.

"Please do pick that up," Del called. "If Dexter is sick, the other dogs could catch whatever he has if they get into the vomit."

When Faith took a step forward, the movement revealed Pinoe advancing toward the remains of Dexter's breakfast, ears pricked in curiosity. Del sucked in a deep breath to yell.

"Pinoe, come here," Faith called. The dog didn't so much as give her an ear flick. She kept moving forward, willfully oblivious. "Pinoe!" A note of desperation entered Faith's voice. "No. Leave it. Come here!"

A sudden thought flashed into Del's mind. Cupping her hands to her face, she shouted, "Buffy!" The dog stopped and looked back over her shoulder. "Come on, Buffy," Del called. "Leave it and come."

Obediently, the dog whirled and trotted over. Faith slipped the leash on, then rewarded her with a treat. When she rose from her crouch, she met Del's gaze. "How did you know?"

"Lucky guess," Del said.

"I'm starting to think changing her name might be hopeless."

"Would that be so bad? I didn't see a problem with her original name. Others might not, too."

Faith looked dubious. "I guess? The show is old now, but it *is* pretty popular among queer women."

"The show?"

Faith shook her head. "Right. Sorry. *Buffy the Vampire Slayer* was a television show that started in the late nineties. Buffy was the protagonist, a teenage girl with superpowers whose purpose on earth was to fight vampires and other kinds of demonic evil." Faith ran one hand through her hair. "But, you know, she had to balance that destiny with surviving high school."

Del couldn't keep the laughter out of her voice. "Sounds complicated."

Faith scoffed. "More like ridiculous. Which it was. But the show also recognized that and made fun of itself."

"That sounds refreshing." Not for the first time, Del wished her parents had been less vehement about minimizing her exposure to popular culture. "So where does Faith fit in?"

"Faith is another slayer who shows up in the third season. She and Buffy had super queer energy going on, but then—oh, shit." Faith's eyes went wide. "I should have asked if you wanted to be spoiled."

Del laughed at her deer-in-the-headlights expression. From what she could tell, Faith seemed to have two modes that she alternated between with dizzying speed: annoying smugness and deep vulnerability.

"Mostly, I like being spoiled. Better to be prepared for what's going to happen."

Faith cocked her head. "Not a fan of surprises?"

And there it was, a hint of that smugness. Only this time, instead of feeling annoyed, Del felt a pleasant prickling along her arms. Had this conversation just crossed over into flirtation?

"Nice ones are fine." She was proud of the words. They sounded relaxed. Casual.

Faith leaned against the table and crossed her arms. "Good to know."

Del forced her gaze away from Faith and out toward the dogs and their owners. She tried to be extra vigilant in her scrutiny, as though it would make up for the ridiculous thoughts she was having.

"So anyway," Faith continued, "in the show, Faith turns evil. And she's an antagonist to Buffy for most of the rest of the series until the very end."

"Do they end up together?" Del couldn't help herself from asking.

"Sadly, no."

"Unfair." Del cleared her throat. "I understand why you want to change her name to something else, but she really does seem attached to 'Buffy.' Would it really be so bad to stick with it?"

Faith shrugged. "Maybe not. At least if anyone calls me on it, I can say I tried, and she was too stubborn. Which is true. I've been calling her 'Pinoe' and plying her with treats for a week now, but she still won't listen to me."

Del thought of Buffy's owner and how she had died. "I realize that I of all people shouldn't anthropomorphize animals, but would it help if you thought she *wanted* to keep the name?"

Faith looked at her for a long moment, then nodded. "It might. And your secret's safe with me."

"Thanks." Del glanced around to make sure no one else was trying to flag her down. When she saw the coast was clear, she turned back to Faith. "Looks like Dexter's mess is gone. You can turn her loose again, if you want."

As Faith bent to detach the leash, Del caught herself admiring the way her skinny jeans clung to the lean contours of her legs. Not for the first time, she was grateful that blushes didn't register on her complexion.

"What a little extrovert," Faith said, watching Buffy trot confidently up to a group of larger dogs.

"She's a big dog on the inside." As a cool breeze blew from the river, Del reached for her own sweater. "Aside from the not listening thing, has everything else been going okay since the scare?"

"Yeah. She's settling in really well." Faith's smile was fond, genuine. "Her appetite is back to normal. And I like that she's a snuggler."

An image popped into Del's mind: Faith in bed, surrounded

by pillows, her back to the headboard, Buffy curled in her lap. She swallowed hard. "I can see that."

"There are going to be a bunch of strangers in my house next week," Faith continued, "and at first, I was worried about that. But so far, she seems easygoing with new people."

"I'm glad. What's the occasion?"

Faith jammed her hands in her pockets, clearly self-conscious. "This is going to sound silly, but…I'm in the running to be on a reality show. It's not a sure thing yet, but the producers collect preliminary footage of all the finalists. So that'll be my life for the next two weeks."

"Wow. Congratulations." Del racked her brains for everything she knew about reality television. It wasn't much. Jada enjoyed cooking shows, and she had tried to get Del to watch one with her when they were roommates, but all the yelling had been a turnoff. "That's a really big deal," she continued. She did at least know *that* much. "How are you feeling about it?"

"It's an amazing opportunity." Faith's shoulders hunched. "I really want it to work out."

Del couldn't fathom wanting to run toward that kind of notoriety. "That's very exciting, but it also sounds nerve-racking."

"Yeah." Faith exhaled sharply. "Getting on the show could change my life in some really powerful ways. But in the last talk I had with my agent, she said I'd be a more appealing candidate if I was in a relationship. That keeps haunting me, sapping my confidence."

Del struggled not to betray her surprise, fumbling for a safe answer. "I'm sorry you're being pressured. I know how that feels."

"Oh?" Faith angled her body toward Del.

"Your agent sounds like my best friend, who's always badgering me about the same topic." Del checked herself, then recognized just how ridiculous the comparison sounded. "In my case, the stakes are obviously much lower."

"Pressure is pressure," Faith said. "Why is she bugging you?"

"We're talking about you," Del protested, wishing she had kept her mouth shut.

Faith raised her eyebrows, one corner of her mouth lifting in a grin. "Not anymore."

Praying for a distraction, Del looked around again. Unfortunately, the dogs were playing peacefully, their humans apparently unplagued by burning questions. Her brain felt stuck, like a turntable arm stubbornly clinging to the groove of the truth.

"Hey." Faith touched her arm briefly. "You don't have to answer."

"It's fine." Del needlessly adjusted the nearest stack of pamphlets so they were perfectly aligned. "My ex and I broke up half a year ago. My best friend is pushing me to start dating again."

"Why don't they just want you to be happy?" The words held an edge.

"Jada does," Del hurried to clarify. "She just…thinks happiness means being in a relationship."

"That's not true of everyone," Faith muttered.

Del jumped on the chance to change the topic. "Is that the case for you?"

Faith sighed, then ran the fingers of one hand through her hair. It was a nervous, distracted sort of movement, yet also endearing. "I don't know. I'm working on creating new definitions of happiness." She rolled her eyes and let out a sharp laugh. "I know that sounds ridiculous."

"It doesn't."

For a long moment, they stood separated by only a few feet, looking in parallel across the river. As the silence stretched on, Del struggled with how or even whether to continue the conversation. The subtle current of vulnerability surrounding Faith leant her a magnetic quality. Del was drawn to beings in pain; she always had been. And pain surrounded Faith like a shadow, sometimes smothering, sometimes faded, but always present.

"Because I'm a coward, I hinted to one of the producers that I was seeing someone," Faith said. "And unless I find someone in less than a week, I'm going to have to fake a breakup."

Del maintained an expressionless mask until she saw Faith's lopsided grin. "That sounds complicated."

"Just a little." Faith held up her thumb and forefinger.

"I'm lucky. I have three whole weeks to find a date to Jada's wedding."

Faith cocked her head. "Why do you need a date?"

"*I* don't think I do," Del said, "but Jada does. It's because my ex will be there. She thinks I need to prove I've moved on."

"And have you?" Blunt as the question was, there was a gentleness to Faith's voice that softened the blow.

Del felt the telltale prickle behind her eyes. She shrugged. This time, Faith's touch on her arm was lingering, a gentle squeeze meant to reassure.

"I'm sure you know this, but no one gets to tell you when you're ready except you."

"Thanks." Del kept her focus on the river until she was certain she had pushed the tears back down. "Anyway. It sounds like we both need a miracle."

"Oh my God."

"What?" Del turned back to see Faith staring at her with a shocked, slightly manic expression.

"We can help each other."

Del looked at her blankly.

"Fake girlfriends."

If Del hadn't been braced against the table, she might have fallen over. "What?"

"We each need a girlfriend, but neither of us actually *wants* one. So we pretend to date each other until we don't need to anymore."

Del's brain felt like a car engine sputtering on a wintry day. "This is a thing people do?"

Faith cocked an eyebrow. "Queer people have been using beards forever."

"Well…yes."

The gate opened. Del swung her head around at the sound, then waved as Eduardo and Travis entered with their chocolate lab, Benny. He strained at his leash, desperate to join the pack playing beyond. Del experienced a sudden wave of gratitude that his owners didn't have to resort to beards to make their way in the world. The surge of emotion made her feel a little dizzy. Was she having some kind of breakdown?

"I know you have to work," Faith murmured. "How about this. Let's each go home and think about it. We can meet again soon to discuss."

"Okay." Del kept one hand on the table.

"Where and when?"

"Ah…" Gears in her brain whirred, then clicked into place. "The farmer's market on Saturday? Noon?"

"Perfect." Faith sketched a wave, then walked across the grass toward Buffy. Del watched her go, helplessly appreciating the swing of her sauntering hips. Grimacing, she forced herself to look away. With a bit of luck, maybe Faith would meet someone here, today, and the whole fake girlfriend idea would be off the table.

Del hoped so. She really did.

Chapter Five

As Faith carried Buffy down the stairs of the parking garage, she tried to laugh at herself for being nervous. The worst thing that could happen was that Del stood her up entirely. The second worst was that Del decided becoming fake girlfriends was idiotic. Either way, she'd be no worse off than she was before Thursday.

She set Buffy on the ground. Immediately, the dog strained at her leash, nose pointed toward where the market's distinctive white tents were ranged around the town hall. Was that a good omen? Faith wanted to believe. Then again, Buffy was probably responding to the smell of Sam's Sausage: the stall directly across the street proclaiming the "Sauciest Sausages in All the Land." Once the Walk sign illuminated, Faith let Buffy's momentum overcome her nerves.

After coaxing Buffy away from the sausages, Faith headed for the memorial statue where Del had suggested they meet. As she approached, she took the lay of the land. A few nearby stalls had attracted short lines of people, but Del wasn't among them. The benches scattered around the area similarly yielded no luck. Faith fished out her phone, but no new text message illuminated her screen. She rolled her shoulders, trying to ease a knot. She *was* a few minutes early. Early was a new thing she was trying.

She sat on one corner of the pedestal to wait. Buffy sat on her foot, and Faith buried her hands in the silky fur to avoid the impulse to reach for her phone. Be present, she thought, repeating her therapist's advice to avoid numbing herself to the world. It wasn't easy. When deep breaths alone didn't diminish her anxiety, she focused instead on tactile sensations—Buffy's soft coat, the heat of the sun against her bare arms, the slightly rough surface of the wooden bench. Closing her eyes would have helped, but she didn't want to miss the chance to spot Del.

Not that she was coming. Honestly, who in their right mind would agree to be her fake girlfriend? That was something that only happened in fiction. Del had probably thought better of ever having another conversation with her. Faith could picture it now: calling the veterinary practice only to be told she should take Buffy elsewhere. Surely, there *was* another vet in town?

"Hi, Faith." Del's voice interrupted her catastrophizing. She shook her head and glanced up to see Del standing just off to one side, a messenger bag slung across one shoulder. Her black hair glowed almost blue in the rays filtering through the trees.

"Hey. Hi." Faith's unaccountable nerves felt raw, exposed. "How are you?"

"Fine. It's a perfect day to be out here."

"Yeah. It's gorgeous."

Del saved them from more small talk by dropping into a crouch to greet Buffy. The dog's tail was moving so furiously that her entire rear end was wobbling. Faith had a new appreciation for the whole *tail wagging the dog* idiom. Buffy whined low in her throat as her front paws scrabbled against Del's knee. When she surged up to lick Del's chin, a beautiful smile rose to Del's lips.

"You were right, you know," Faith said. "She actually listens to me now that I'm calling her Buffy." As if to prove her point, Buffy looked over her shoulder. Faith quickly extracted a treat from her pocket, luring the dog away from her object of worship. If that was a mercenary move, so be it.

"I can see that." Del laughed, a warm sound. When she sat at the other end of the bench, Buffy jumped up and curled between them, then tucked her nose under her tail. Faith felt precariously…melty. Was that even a word?

"Now that she's made herself comfortable, I guess we're stuck here for a while."

"What a shame." Del's smile was muted this time, but it still seemed genuine.

Faith debated steering the conversation back into small talk before deciding she couldn't possibly endure it. "I wasn't sure you'd come." When Del said nothing, Faith pushed on. "I realize what I proposed sounds crazy."

"Just a little." Del acknowledged. "But it's also genius."

Faith blinked. "Genius?"

"The analogy you made to beards helped me contextualize it," Del said. "Thinking about it as a sort of business arrangement was useful."

There was a coldness to "business arrangement" that made Faith cringe inside, but she covered it with a nod. "Trade and barter?"

"Exactly." Del offered a small smile. "You'll be doing me a huge favor by coming to this wedding."

Faith wanted to return the expression but found she couldn't. "And you're really okay with appearing on national television? Because I'll be honest, the trade seems lopsided."

"I thought about that, too." Del looked away, across the undulating sea of people moving through the market. "It's going to be weird, but I doubt I'll attract a lot of interest. There won't be that much footage of me, right?"

"I've already told them my relationship is new, and I'm trying to protect it." Guilt curdled in Faith's stomach. "I swear, I'll do everything I can to make sure they use as little footage of you as possible."

After a long moment, during which Faith was sure Del was about to renege, she finally nodded. "Just, when we break up, I don't want it to be dramatic. That's all I ask."

Faith felt a twinge deep in her chest. Whatever had happened with Del's ex had clearly left a scar. Despite barely knowing her, she felt strangely protective. "Yeah, of course. We'll part ways amicably. No drama." When Del continued to stare into the distance, Faith touched her knee. She needed Del to know, to trust her. Or to start to. "Hey. I mean it. Even if the producers want drama, I won't play their game."

"Really?"

"Really."

Del swallowed hard. "All right. Thank you."

"No, God, don't *thank* me." Faith ran a hand through her hair. "I'm the one who should be thanking you. You've got the heavier lift."

This time, Del broke their gaze by focusing on Buffy. Faith

watched her slender fingers stroke through the long curly hairs of her ruff. "So," Del said. "If we're really doing this, we should probably get to know each other a little better, right?"

"Mm." Faith made a purposefully noncommittal noise. Where was Del going with this?

"We could grab a snack here and then pick up supplies for an early dinner. Want to come over to my place? I'm a decent cook."

Faith considered the offer. She didn't think Del was coming on to her in any way. In fact, her motivation was likely the opposite. She was probably inviting Faith to her home because that was a safe space.

"Sounds great," Faith said. "Is Buffy invited?"

Del's answering smile was genuine. "Always." She gestured toward the array of tents. "Is there any stall you're a particular fan of?"

Faith shook her head. When the grief bubbled up, she realized that for once, she didn't need to choke it back down. If they were going to be girlfriends, Del needed to know these details.

"I haven't been here in over a decade. My dad used to take me, when I was a kid. But…"

"But?"

"He died. When I was fourteen. Cancer."

Del squeezed Faith's shoulder. Her hand was warm, her grip firm but gentle. "I'm really sorry."

Faith had heard those same words a thousand times. Still, as Del spoke them, she knew they were authentic, offered by someone who knew loss intimately and understood its ripple effect.

"That must have been so hard," Del continued. "And I'm sure it continues to be."

Faith nodded. "Thanks. We were close." Unable to meet Del's sympathetic gaze, she reached to scratch behind Buffy's ears. When Buffy leaned against her leg, Faith felt strong enough to say the rest. "And just so it's not awkward when this comes up later, my mom passed two months ago. That's the whole reason I'm here…in Fairview, I mean. Dealing with her estate and the house and everything."

For the space of several heartbeats, Del said nothing. Then, she placed a gentle hand just above her knee. Faith found herself focusing on Del's fingers again, dark and slender, the nails neatly trimmed.

"That's a lot, Faith. It must be extra hard that they're both gone."

"Maybe," Faith said. "In some ways, I guess. My mom and I were estranged."

"If you ever want to talk about it, I'm ready to listen. No judgment."

"I appreciate that." Faith's eyes were stinging. She resisted the urge to tense up, forcing herself instead to take a deep breath. "Anyway. Food?"

"Definitely. Is there anything you don't eat or don't like?"

"I know too much about sausage," Faith said, watching closely for disappointment. Instead, her candor was rewarded with a deeply appealing belly laugh.

"Then let's go for the taco stand. Best tacos in town."

Faith resisted the urge to make a crass joke. She was pretty sure Del didn't have any kind of double entendre in mind. Instead, she focused on Buffy, rousing her gently by stroking her head. "C'mon, Buff. Time for tacos."

"This is going to sound so weird," Del said as Faith deposited Buffy on the ground. "But...ah...should we hold hands?"

Faith froze. The question was a reminder that she was flaunting GTA's rules about not dating until she had successfully completed the program. Then again, did fake dating really count? Even as the question crossed her mind, she had her answer. No. Her relationship with Del was a business transaction, not a romantic liaison. It was unorthodox, yes. But she wasn't breaking any rules. Still, they did need to be physically affectionate to convince both Maddie and Del's friend. What was her name? Jada.

Del's uncertainty and discomfort were obvious, but she had asked the question anyway. Faith felt a rush of admiration for her courage and beneath it, a current of newly minted affection.

"Good call. We should." She reached for Del's hand.

Their fingers interlaced easily. As Del's palm slid against hers, Faith felt her body, its needs so long denied by anyone but herself, come alive. Gritting her teeth, she forced down her libido. It was starved, misplaced, latching on to the closest host like some kind of parasite. None of this was real.

Belatedly, Faith realized Del hadn't said anything for a solid minute. "Is this okay?"

"Sure. Yes." Del glanced at her quickly, then away. "Sorry if I'm awkward. I haven't been, ah, affectionate with anyone for a while."

"Same. But we don't have to do this if you'd rather not."

"No, no. We should get used to it." Del forced a smile. "For the cameras. And for Jada."

As they queued up in front of the taco stand, Faith leaned her shoulder against Del's, just to see how it would feel. She liked the parity in their height. If anything, Del was slightly taller, something Faith wasn't used to.

"How about this? Still okay?"

"Yep." With her other hand, Del pointed toward the menu. "The *al pastor* is amazing."

"Sold," Faith said. "And I'm buying."

Del considered this. "Only if we trade off. And only if we keep all the receipts so we can balance out the spending once this is over."

"Perfect." Faith stepped up to the counter and leaned farther into Del's space. "What are you having?"

Food in hand, they wandered for a few minutes, looking for a place to sit. When a rickety table freed up, they grabbed it. Faith pulled out Buffy's collapsible bowl and a water bottle from her bag. She could feel Del watching her and wondered if she was impressed. Thanks to therapy, Faith had come to recognize that her public persona's devil-may-care attitude had been an unconscious defense mechanism to hide the fact that she cared far too much. Still, cultivating Del's good opinion didn't feel dangerous or problematic. Becoming the kind of person Del thought well of was fully aligned with Faith's own goals.

"So," Del said as Faith reached for her first taco, "I think we should formulate a strategy."

"It sounds like you've already given this some thought." Faith bit into her taco, then barely bit back a moan. "Holy shit, this is so good."

"Isn't it?" Del wiped her mouth. "And I do have some ideas. Once I decided to accept your offer, I started thinking about how to make it work."

Faith blinked hard. While she had been convincing herself Del would never agree to this plan, Del had been strategizing on how to execute it? "What did you come up with?"

"We haven't been dating long, which works in our favor," Del said. "But we still need a story about how we met. And some ground rules. And maybe a…a code of some kind that we can use in public if something's wrong."

"A safe word?" Even the question flew out of Faith's mouth, she froze.

Clearly taken aback, Del blinked hard. "That's…an interesting metaphor."

"Sorry," Faith said, fearing she might have ruined everything. "In case you can't tell, I have a bad habit of blurting out inappropriate comments. It's something I'm working on. Haven't made much progress yet."

Del's answering smile held welcome reassurance. "Well, it's not a *bad* metaphor. Any thoughts on what it should be?"

"Maybe…" Faith racked her brain, but every word she could think of was one that might actually come up in legitimate conversation. "Okay, no, I've got nothing."

"We'll put it on the back burner, then." Del sipped from her drink. "In terms of ground rules, how about this: we split all expenses related to being a couple. Public displays of PG-13-rated affection are fine, but no groping or indecency. Pet names are okay as long as they are previously agreed upon."

Part of Faith wanted to tease Del for saying "indecency," but this time, she was able to hold herself back. "Those sound good to me. And if we need to add to them, we can."

Del nodded. "The next question is, how did we meet?"

Faith took another bite as she considered. "I think we should stick as close to the truth as possible whenever we can."

"So we met when you brought Buffy in for her first checkup." Del's eyes glinted. "And you insulted me."

Faith's heart lurched both at the memory and at the way Del had described it. Her dismay must have shown, because Del's hand was suddenly on top of hers.

"Wait, hear me out. You begged Paula to give you my cell number so you could apologize. Then, you invited me out for coffee. The rest is history."

Faith sat back hard in her chair. Her heart was still pounding, but she had to admit the story was brilliant. She managed a breathy laugh. "You've done this before."

Del grinned. "I promise, I'm a fake dating rookie."

"Could've fooled me."

"When confronted with a puzzle, I'm a good problem-solver," Del said.

"You're nothing like the women I usually date." Faith caught herself. "Used to date."

"Oh?"

"They were just problems." Faith grimaced. "And so was I. No solutions in sight."

Del squeezed her hand, then withdrew. "I'm already facing the irony that this fake relationship might turn out to be the healthiest one I've had yet."

Faith laughed again, stronger this time. She raised her water bottle in a toast. "To us."

For a little while, they ate quietly. "No pressure to talk about this," Del began, "but you mentioned managing your mother's estate. How is that going?"

Faith let her anger over Jameson's disappearance burn away the familiar pang of grief. "It'd be going a lot better if my contractor hadn't split town with my down payment."

Del's jaw dropped. "Are you serious?"

"Unfortunately, yes. I called the police and the Better Business Bureau, and I have a lawyer. No luck finding him or getting the money back, yet."

"That's horrific." Del shook her head. "What's his name? I'll tell everyone I know to avoid him."

"Jameson Johnson."

"Easy to remember, at least." Del took another bite of her taco, her expression thoughtful. "I haven't been here long, but I have heard some of the hospital staff sing the praises of one contractor in particular. He has a memorable first name, too, Oscar. I'll see if I can find out his last name, if you want."

Faith was glad she was chewing. She took her time, trying to swallow her anger with the bite. She wiped her mouth, took a drink of water, and finally spoke.

"Dalby. Oscar Dalby. I know he's the best contractor in town."

Instead of asking why the hell she hadn't hired him, then, Del regarded her quietly. Steadily.

"Just shy of a year after my dad passed, my mom started dating him," Faith said. "He was good to her and to me. Hell, he treated me better than my mother did." Faith took another sip of water. "But I hated him for what felt like taking my dad's place. And I know it sounds ridiculous, but I've never been able to let that go."

Del touched her hand again briefly. "It doesn't sound ridiculous. That must have been so hard, given how close you were with your father."

To her mortification, Faith felt her eyes filling up. "Yeah," she said gruffly around the lump in her throat. "But if I had gotten over myself, I wouldn't be out fifty thousand dollars now."

"I hope you can recoup at least some of the money," Del said. "And who knows, maybe someday, you'll be able to mend fences with Oscar." She pulled a face. "Pun intended."

"Very funny," Faith muttered. But she was smiling, and that was a first when it came to hearing Oscar's name.

Del watched from her doorstep as Buffy sniffed around the shrubs bordering her walkway. Faith, holding the leash, was surveying the exterior of her townhouse. Once Buffy was finished with her inspection, she pulled Faith forward.

"Fair warning," Del said. "It's sparse in here. The place was pre-furnished, and I haven't made any changes."

"I'm the last person who will judge you for anything, ever," Faith said. She sounded serious.

"In that case, come on in."

As she followed Faith inside, Del tried to see the place through her eyes. Aside from a single piece of kinetic artwork—a framed, three-dimensional image of a butterfly that appeared to move as one walked past it—the walls were blank. That was one of the only possessions Del had taken with her, mostly because she had purchased it before Maddie came along. There was a TV on a stand in the corner, but Del hadn't turned it on even once. For all she knew, it was broken.

When Buffy jumped on the couch, Faith tried to shoo her off.

"It's fine," Del said. "If I minded a little dog hair, I'd be in the wrong line of work." She set the bags she was carrying just inside the kitchen. "Should we get cooking?"

"Just give me clear instructions," Faith said. "I can barely follow recipes."

Del grabbed a bowl from the cupboard next to the oven. "Well, your first job is to put the meat in this bowl and then dump the marinade we bought on top of it. I think you'll manage."

"Smartass," Faith muttered, but she was smiling.

Del took out a chopping board and her best knife. "Have you ever used a rice cooker?"

"I wouldn't recognize one if it slapped me."

"Well, prepare for your horizons to be expanded." Del pointed to where the rice cooker sat between the toaster and the sink. "Once you've finished the meat, make four cups of rice. The bag's in the pantry."

Faith mock saluted. "Bossy, aren't you?"

"That saying about cooks in a kitchen comes from somewhere." Del reached for the onion.

"Touché."

Silence descended, but it wasn't awkward. She and Faith didn't have much in common, and yet their banter was surprisingly fluid. Maybe it was easy to talk to her because they both had clear expectations? Which implied that Del only clammed up when she was afraid of disappointing someone. Something to reflect upon when she wasn't trying to navigate the beginning of a fake relationship.

"How long have you been in town?" Faith was measuring out the rice in tiny plinking sounds against the glass cup.

"Six months." Del carefully lined up her knife over the onion. "I was living in the city previously."

"Oh? Me, too. What made you decide to come out to the 'burbs?"

"My fiancée cheated on me." Del sliced down, quick and precise. If only her feelings for Maddie were as easy to separate as onion flesh. "When it happened, Jada—the friend who is getting married—told me I should get away for a while. Fortunately, there was a relief position available at the animal hospital."

"I'm really sorry." Faith touched her shoulder briefly. "If you want to talk more about it, now or anytime, I'm happy to listen."

Del paused. Hurt and vaguely ashamed, she had confided only in Jada. Still, it would be good for Faith to know a few of the details, especially since she was going to come face-to-face with Maddie in a few weeks.

"I met Maddie shortly after I moved to the city and started practicing emergency medicine. We moved in together after a year of dating. I proposed on our fifth anniversary. A few months later, I came home earlier than expected from a shift and found her in bed with someone she'd met at the gym."

"Shit." Faith abandoned the rice cooker to stand next to Del, leaning back against the counter. "I'm really sorry."

Del glanced over. Faith was watching her with a look of trepidation, arms crossed tightly. Even frowning and worrying at her lower lip with her teeth, she was stunning: a flawless face perched atop a perfect body. The kind of person who would have no compunctions about falling into bed with an engaged woman. The kind of person who had come between her and Maddie.

No sooner had the thought crossed Del's mind than she recoiled from it. She didn't *know* that. She was making unwarranted and damaging assumptions. Faith might be a mess, but she had good reasons to be that had nothing to do with Del's own trauma.

"Thanks," she said, turning back to the onion. As she sliced, its fumes made her eyes itch. Grateful for the excuse, she let a few tears well up and over. "I really thought she was the one. Being so wrong… it got to me."

Faith moved away just far enough to pluck a tissue from the box on the counter, then handed it over. "You deserve someone who prioritizes you," she said quietly. "Not who goes behind your back."

Del dabbed at her eyes again as a fresh round of tears sprang up. Shame at her uncharitable thoughts twisted her stomach. "Thanks."

Faith nodded. After a moment, she returned to the rice cooker. They both worked quietly for a while. Surreptitiously, Del watched her check and double-check the instructions, brow furrowing in concentration. The care she was taking not to mess up this simple task was endearing.

"I think some banal questions are in order," Faith said once the machine was active. "What kinds of music do you listen to?"

For a while, the conversation remained lighthearted as they exchanged valuable pieces of context. Eventually, Faith divulged a little more about her childhood, enough for Del to realize she was

Fairview born and raised, but she had never felt truly at home in the town. Attending college in the city had been a welcome escape. Del knew what had happened next because she had looked Faith up online after her crazy offer to embark upon a fake relationship. But Faith didn't know that.

"What do you do when you're not rescuing canines?" Del asked, hoping to make Faith smile.

"I'm a fitness instructor at Hype Cycle. It's an online fitness platform with physical gyms in most major cities."

"I've heard of it," Del said, though that wouldn't have been true three days ago. "What kinds of classes do you teach?"

"Cycling, mostly. I do some general fitness boot camps as well."

As she tended the stir-fry, Del asked how she had gotten started. She kept expecting Faith to tell her that she had more than four hundred thousand social media followers, but it never happened. Instead, Faith deftly redirected with a question about how Del had known she wanted to become a vet.

"I was raised in a commune of sorts. The community had its own school, its own farm. It tried to be as sustainable and independent as possible. This might sound crazy, but I had virtually no exposure to popular culture when I was growing up." Well aware at how strange this sounded to most people, Del glanced at Faith. Her expression was curious but not critical. Maybe she *had* been honest about never judging.

"Did you like growing up that way?"

"Mostly, yes. The commune was pretty insular, and I didn't really feel like I was missing out on anything. There were other kids my age, but I always gravitated toward the animals. I spent a lot of time at the farm and in the woods."

"Did you make a lot of animal friends?"

"So many." Del felt herself smile at the memories. "My father is a doctor, and whenever I found some injured creature, I'd take it home and beg him to help it. He had some creative solutions for insects, but he also knew his limitations. We took a lot of trips to the vet, and my fate was sealed."

"Well, Buffy and I are grateful."

"I'm glad she's doing so well." Del tested the stir-fry, then nodded. "This is ready."

"It smells amazing," Faith said.

"It's all the marinade."

Buffy followed as they sat at the table. "She's so shameless," Faith said. "I think her previous owner gave her table scraps."

Del locked eyes with Buffy. "Don't blame Faith for not spoiling you like that." The dog licked her chops. "She's doing the right thing."

Faith laughed. "Thanks for putting a good word in for me. Also, this tastes even better than it smells."

"There's nothing like cooking fresh." Del took a bite and savored it. "I'm going to be sad when the market disappears for the winter."

"Let's not think about it," Faith said. "What else should we know about each other?"

Del chewed thoughtfully. "Coming out stories?"

Faith grimaced. "I was thirteen. My dad tried to be supportive but called it a lifestyle. My mom was awful, and her emotional abuse got worse once she was a widow. I had one relationship in high school, and it was a completely codependent dumpster fire." She took another sip of wine. "Sorry to be a downer. This is why I'm in GTA."

"GTA?"

"Growing Toward Actualization." Faith rolled her eyes, then winced. "Sorry. I shouldn't do that. For a long time, I was dismissive of therapy and ridiculed self-help. Then, I hit rock bottom."

"I admire you," Del said, meaning it. "Change is incredibly hard."

"It really, really is." Fatigue crossed Faith's face like a shadow. In the next moment, it was gone. "Anyway, GTA is an eight-step program that you're supposed to complete over the course of six months…or longer, if you need to. Each step is designed to help you unlearn toxic habits and replace them with healthy behavior patterns." Faith stuck out her tongue. "I sound like a brochure."

"I asked for the explanation." Del hesitated, then rested her palm on top of Faith's hand. "And I meant what I said. I admire you for taking care of yourself, despite the stigma. That's a big deal." She ventured a smile. "You're reminding me that I should be back in therapy. I went after my first breakup, but I haven't managed to push myself back in since Maddie."

Faith turned her hand over and laced their fingers together. Her smile was lopsided. "I'm living proof that it's never too late."

"Duly noted." Del squeezed gently, then withdrew. Alone at this table last night, she had worried whether she would be able to exchange casual intimacies with someone who wasn't Maddie. Thankfully, that fear appeared to be unfounded.

"How about you?" Faith said. "Coming out story? Was that hard, being in such a tight-knit community?"

"No, fortunately. The group my parents belong to is very keen on self-expression." As always, Del experienced her good fortune in a visceral way. "I didn't realize I was queer until college, and telling them was still anxiety producing. But my parents encountered their own fair share of discrimination, and they felt strongly about not paying that forward."

"Sometimes, the opposite happens," Faith said. "I'm glad they were able to break the cycle."

"Me, too." Briefly, Del debated whether to say more before deciding that, yes, the bare bones of her family history was something even a recent girlfriend would know. "As you can probably guess, my dad is Chinese, and my mom is Black. I'm not sure if you're aware of this, but racism against Black and Brown people is very much alive and well in Asian cultures."

Faith's eyes widened. "I didn't know that."

"Broadly speaking, of course. Obviously, there are exceptions."

"Like your parents. Was it hard for them?"

Faith was looking at her as though she was the only person in the world. It was a new feeling, and unaccountably, Del felt herself on the edge of tears. Maddie had never given her that much undivided attention, not even at the beginning of their relationship. No sooner had the thought seared through her mind than Del began to question it. Was that really true? Or was she being ungenerous because of the way their relationship had ended?

"Del? Are you okay?"

The gentle question was a tether, guiding Del back to the conversation. "Sorry." When the word came out a little choked, she cleared her throat. "Lost in thought. Ah…my father's parents reacted badly when he started dating my mother. When they got engaged, his entire family cut off all contact. They didn't even go to the wedding."

Faith's hand closed around hers. Her palm, warm and dry, covered Del's knuckles like a weighted blanket. A fraction of the tension in her shoulders eased. Then, all thoughts flew out of her head when Faith began tracing tiny circles against the stretch of skin between her thumb and index finger.

"Have you ever met them?"

As she stared at the slow rotations of Faith's finger, Del's mouth went dry. The old grief collided with this new arousal, amplifying her confusion. Her skin felt too tight. "No."

"Their loss," Faith said. When she lifted her hand away, Del bit down on a gasp—whether of relief or disappointment, she didn't know.

Not trusting herself to speak, Del focused on eating. The only other people she had ever told those details to were Jada and Maddie. Almost immediately, Del found herself rationalizing the choice: it was true that the more Faith knew about her, the more effective their girlfriend performance would be. Still, Del had to admit that—their disastrous initial conversation in her office notwithstanding—Faith was easy to talk to. Well, good. That would only facilitate the success of their sham.

Thinking about the audiences they would need to convince was clarifying. Del sat back and wiped her mouth. "Okay. We know the basics about each other. What are the next steps, here?"

"I've been thinking about that," Faith said. "What if I ask my producer to film at the dog park this coming Thursday? That way, it won't be just us, and if you're feeling weird at any point, you can always make a work-related excuse to slip away."

Surprised at her considerateness, Del shifted on the couch to better meet Faith's eyes. "That's a really good idea. Thank you."

"I know this is going to be invasive. I'm sorry."

"Will it be for you, too? Or is it easier because this is something you want?"

"That helps," Faith said. "And it also helps that I'm used to performing in front of cameras in the studio. Though obviously, this will be more complicated than telling someone how hard to pedal and for how long."

Del laughed. "Just a little."

"How about for you?" Faith asked. "What should I do to prepare for the wedding?"

Del waved off the question. "Don't worry about that. All you have to do is show up."

"Do you know what you're wearing? I don't want to clash."

"I'm a bridesmaid," Del said dryly. "I don't get a choice."

Faith winced. "How bad is it?"

"Thankfully, the dress is simple. And it's a nice shade of burgundy. Jada has good taste."

Faith mimed wiping her forehead. "Okay…do you want me to wear a dress, too?"

"Wear whatever you want. I'm sure you'll look great."

"Oh?"

This had been a very extroverted day, and Del was too tired to prevaricate. "You're beautiful. You must know this?"

When Faith's jaw dropped a little, Del felt her face heat. Still, she maintained eye contact. She had spoken an objective truth, and she wasn't about to be embarrassed by it.

"I…thank you." Faith rose and reached for her plate and Del's. "I've got dishes."

"Oh, don't bother." Del stood and grabbed the cups. "I'll throw everything into the dishwasher."

Faith deposited the plates in the sink, then washed her hands. "I know this whole fake girlfriends thing is weird," she said, "but I had fun today. Thanks."

"Me, too." Del was slightly surprised that this was the truth. "In terms of next steps, you'll let me know when and where the crew wants to film?"

"I will."

Del watched as Faith clipped Buffy's leash on. As she walked them to the door, she wondered whether she and Faith needed to practice kissing, too. Bemused at the thought, she barely clamped down on a hysterical laugh. She had been the one to suggest hand-holding, and she had just pointed out Faith's aesthetic appeal. She was *not* about to initiate anything more today.

"Can I kiss you?"

The laugh escaped after all. When Faith shifted uncomfortably, Del hurried to explain. "I was just wondering whether we should practice that."

"It's probably for the best not to have our first kiss happen in front of a crowd." Faith raised the hand that wasn't holding Buffy's leash and cupped the side of Del's face.

"Probably," Del murmured.

Faith's mouth brushed against hers, mapping the contours of her lips. Only then did she press more firmly, her fingers stroking the short hairs at Del's temple. The kiss was slow and confident, and Del felt herself melting into the sensation. When the very tip of Faith's tongue darted out for a taste, Del heard her breathing stutter and felt her lips part, an unconscious invitation. Instead of taking her up on it, Faith eased the pressure of her mouth, gradually pulling away.

"Mm." Faith stepped back, brushing one thumb across Del's lips. "I think we'll be just fine."

"Yes," Del said, not daring to say any more lest her breathlessness betray her.

"See you soon."

Faith stepped out of the house, Buffy behind her, then turned and waved. Del waited to close the door until Faith was in her car. When she found herself pressing two fingers to her mouth, she dropped her hand.

"Yes, fine, it was a good kiss," she muttered. "But it's not real."

She couldn't help but think back to Maddie, then, though the pain felt duller than usual. Maddie's kisses had always been hurried, a necessary stop on the way to a different destination. But Faith had kissed her like it *was* the destination. And Del had enjoyed it. Still, good kisses were one thing. Real compatibility was quite another.

Del flopped onto the couch, already missing Buffy. Sometimes, she wished she had her own pet, but she had to foster animals frequently enough that it didn't make sense, especially in such a small space. Putting her feet up on the coffee table, she pulled out her phone and opened her text message thread with Jada.

All your prayers have been answered. I went on a date. Del contemplated the words, then deleted them. Maybe a touch too snarky.

You'll be relieved to know that I have a date to your wedding. No. Too stilted.

So I have a date to your wedding. She stared at the line of text until her vision blurred. Clear and direct, no frills, no-nonsense. Before she could second-guess herself, she hit send.

Within seconds, Jada was typing back: *OMG! Who?*

You don't know her. I met her through work. Her name is Faith.

Last name? Yes, I'm googling her.

Kincaid. I already did.

The Hype Cycle instructor?

Yep.

Jada's next message was completely unintelligible. Del rolled her eyes but felt herself smile.

We're too old to keysmash.

She's fucking hot.

I know.

I'm so proud of you!

When guilt curdled in Del's gut, she tried to ignore it. After this whole thing was over—after both she and Faith had gotten what they needed—maybe she could come clean. She wondered how angry Jada would be, then decided that was a problem for the Del of the future.

Thanks.

Chapter Six

Del arrived at the park to find a large van parked near the gate. Its back doors were open, and a woman was in the act of unloading equipment. As Del watched, she slung a camera onto her shoulder and balanced a box on her hip.

"Can I help?" Del asked.

"Oh…sure." The woman seemed relieved by her offer. "You can grab the box, if you want."

"You're with *Fish Out of Water*?" Del asked as they walked toward the gate.

"That's right." The woman looked at Del curiously. "How did you know?"

"I'm Faith's girlfriend." The words felt awkward on Del's lips. Over the past few days, she had told other people about dating Faith, but she had never introduced herself in *relation* to Faith.

"Oh!" The woman extended her hand. "Michelle. Camerawoman, obviously. Let me introduce you to Sharon, the producer. What's your name again?"

Having to make small talk did nothing to ease Del's nerves as they walked through the gate. A few dogs and their owners were milling about, but Faith was nowhere to be found. As promised, Michelle brokered a stilted introductory conversation between her and Sharon. Sharon was beautiful in that glossy way reminiscent of magazine covers, and Del felt unaccountably awkward in her presence. Angry at herself and resentful of Sharon's Hollywood aura, Del struggled to be personable, much less gregarious.

Then her peripheral vision caught sight of a golden blur streaking toward her from the direction of the gate. *Buffy.* She broke off what she had been saying mid-sentence, turned, and dropped to one knee.

Buffy arrived, tongue lolling, and rested her paws on Del's leg, straining to reach her face. Laughing but careful to keep her mouth shut, Del held still for the kisses.

"Should I be jealous?" Faith's voice was warm with amusement.

Del opened her eyes. As Faith walked toward her, she experienced sudden empathy with iron filings in the presence of a magnet. Gray jeans clung to Faith's muscular legs, and in deference to the coolness of the evening, she wore a black puffy vest over a crimson hoodie. A lapel mic was clipped to the neck of the sweatshirt. Surely, she was well aware she was being watched, yet she didn't look away from Del, and her smile was genuine, not performative.

A telltale flutter manifested in Del's chest, moth wings against a lampshade. Alarm bells followed, deafening inside her head. Acutely aware of the crew nearby, Del stood slowly, uncertain. Faith's smile never faltered, but when her eyes narrowed slightly, Del realized she had picked up on her discomfort.

The thought only made her more self-conscious, but then Faith was there, and Faith's arms were cupping her waist, and Faith was leaning in close for the kiss.

"Are you okay?" Faith whispered as she approached, lips barely moving.

"Yes," Del said. The word emerged breathless, but she had no time to care before Faith's mouth was on hers. She expected the kiss to be brief, but Faith lingered, sucking gently at her lower lip. Sparks skittered beneath Del's skin, redirecting her nervousness. For one long, perfect moment, Faith's kiss was her entire world.

She would process *that* particular reaction later, Del decided as Faith pulled away. For now, at least she had been distracted out of her paralysis.

"Hi," she said lamely, then laughed at herself.

"Hi." Faith, it turned out, had hooked one finger into a belt loop on Del's jeans. She tugged lightly before releasing her. "Can I help you get the table set up?"

The table. Right. Del shook her head slightly. She was there to do a job, not placate reality-show producers or kiss her fake girlfriend.

"No, it's okay. I've got it. You stay here." Del felt Faith's gaze on her as she turned and walked back toward the parking lot. She focused on keeping her shoulders squared, her gait brisk. Only when she was out of sight did she allow her posture to sag.

"Okay," she muttered. "Pull yourself together."

A part of Del wanted to get back into her car, drive away, and have Faith make some kind of excuse about her absence. The rest of her was disgusted by the thought. Anger compelled her to fling open the trunk with more force than was strictly necessary. Del hauled out the table and slung the messenger bag filled with promotional materials over one shoulder.

Once she was back inside the dog park, Del was relieved to see that the crew had followed Faith and Buffy toward the far end of the enclosure. The lack of attention was a relief, and Del focused on the small tasks: setting up the table, arranging the brochures and pamphlets.

By the time she had set up, the park was more crowded. Someone—an intern, Del guessed—was circulating with a clipboard, getting permission from the attendees in case their faces appeared in the aired footage. Samantha stopped by on her way out.

"Hollywood comes to Fairview," she said as Del petted Hugh. "So exciting."

"I hope Faith makes it," Del said. She could be earnest about that much.

"Me, too." Waving crossed fingers, Samantha turned to leave.

A few other regulars stopped by the table. Many wanted to exclaim over their brush with the entertainment industry, but a few had pet-related questions to ask. Slowly, Del relaxed into the familiar routine. She didn't even notice she was being filmed until Faith stepped into her field of view. The camera lens flickered in her peripheral vision.

"You've been busy," Faith said. She planted her palms on the table and leaned partway across it, inviting a kiss but not insisting.

Del froze. Hemmed in by the table, she was highly conscious of the fact that she was *working*. Then again, this was, by intention, a liminal space between the hospital and her personal life. She was supposed to be more casual here, more informal. Could one quick kiss hurt? Obviously, it would be helpful in the context of the show. She could feel the attention of the crew, their camera, the onlookers. The idea of kissing Faith for their benefit felt so wrong. But when she focused in on Faith herself, the creepy-crawling sensation retreated into the background. Del flashed back to their earlier kiss, felt its echo on her lips. She wanted that again. Not for anyone else, just for herself. And if that revelation could get her through this moment, she would let it. The panic could happen later.

Resting her own hands on top of Faith's, Del brushed her lips across Faith's mouth, then paused when she reached one corner. She breathed in, pulling Faith's scent into her lungs before drawing back. Del didn't have to manufacture her reluctance, and Faith seemed to share it. She swayed slightly, and for a few rapid heartbeats, there was a hint of awe in her expression. Then, she remembered herself, and the familiar mask clicked into place.

"Ah," Del said into the silence because someone had to say something. Her racing mind caught at the threads that had led to this moment. "Busy…is a good thing." No sooner had the inane words left her mouth than Del wished she could call them back.

"True," Faith said, nodding. "Want some help back there?"

Del wondered if she was asking because she actually wanted to help or because it would look good on camera. The ongoing uncertainty inspired a flare of irritation. She tried to shove it down.

"Sure," Del said. "Thanks."

Faith came around the edge of the table and leaned close. "I really do want to help," she murmured.

Before Del could accuse her of mind-reading, a young man holding the leash of a German shepherd puppy—just under a year old, by the look of him—approached the table.

"Dr. Wu, my dog just fetched a ball and came back limping," the man said. "Would you mind checking him out real quick, or do I need to wait to schedule something in your office?"

"I'll take a quick look." Del turned to Faith. "Good timing. You're in charge of the table."

"The power," Faith said with a laugh.

Del decided to kiss her on the cheek. "Don't let it go to your head."

By the time sunset approached, the dog park had emptied. Faith helped Del stack the brochures and fold up the table while Buffy lay in the grass nearby. When Michelle finally lowered the camera, Del blew out a long sigh. Her nerves were jangling from the prolonged scrutiny, and pressure mounted behind her eyes, heralding a headache.

"I've got a sweet tooth," Faith announced as they carried the table back to the car. "Want to walk over to Toppings and grab a cone?"

"Ice cream before dinner?" Del said. "What a rebel."

"Adulting should come with a few perks, don't you think?"

"Mind if we tag along?" asked Sharon.

Del tamped down the *Yes* that leapt to her lips. "You're welcome to," she said, "as long as Faith's up for it."

"Feel free," was Faith's reply. She reached for Del's hand, and as they walked, she was the one to keep the conversation going. Del was grateful for the respite.

When they reached the ice cream shop—more of a shack, really—Del announced the desserts were on her. Faith proclaimed a desire to wait with her while Sharon, Michelle, and the interns staked out tables. Once they were alone in the line, Faith leaned in closer.

"How are you holding up? I know this is hard."

Del thought about fibbing before remembering they had promised each other honesty. "I am a little tired."

"We can bail on this if you want." Faith's expression was serious. "I mean it."

"No. This is fine. But I do want to go home afterward."

Faith lightly kissed her jaw. "Want to come over to my place, instead? You haven't seen it yet, and it's never been cleaner. Well, except for the construction zone. I think I have a bottle of champagne somewhere—we can lie on the couch and watch…hmm." She squinted at Del. "Nature shows?"

Del had to laugh. "I have actually seen some nature shows. And predictably, I enjoy them."

"It's a date."

Laden with ice cream orders, they found the tables where *Fish Out of Water* had set up shop. Sure enough, Michelle was wielding her camera again. Del sat facing the river, knowing the sight of it would soothe her nerves. Faith sat across from her, talking about nature shows. Soon, the conversation shifted to focus on the strangest and most exotic animals Del had ever cared for during her time practicing emergency medicine, including a kinkajou and a hedgehog. As she told her stories, she warmed to the topic and gradually found it easier to ignore the crew.

"*Seven* stitches?" Faith asked, in response to a tale about a particularly bellicose iguana.

Del scooped up the final bite of her sundae. "Iguana bites are nasty."

Faith's gaze was suddenly focused on her lips. Del wasn't surprised when she leaned in, though her breath did catch at the intensity of her expression.

"I'm going to do the thing where I kiss ice cream off your face, okay?" Faith breathed.

"Mm," Del managed, and then Faith's lips were tracing hers, and Faith's tongue was flicking out to caress the corner of her mouth. Del didn't have to pretend her shiver. Then Faith's fingers were in her hair, and the kiss deepened. She tasted like peanut butter and chocolate and malt. A thought arrowed through Del with blinding intensity: she never wanted this kiss to end. Instinctively, she reached up to touch Faith's face, wanting to keep her close. All too soon, Faith pulled away, though she did turn to kiss Del's fingers as she withdrew.

Reality returned, filled with onlookers and their lenses. Faith started talking again, this time about her favorite ice cream places in the city. Del sat back in her chair, trying to focus. Her pulse was racing, her wits scattered. It was just a kiss, she told herself. Just a very, very good kiss.

It didn't mean anything.

❖

The next day, Faith woke to the twin sensations of a warm tongue lapping at her face and an insistent drumbeat of pain in the back of her head. She inhaled sharply, caught the smell of dog breath, and groaned. When Buffy resumed licking her chin, Faith finally muttered, "Okay, okay," and pushed herself into a sitting position. The throbbing grew worse.

Gritting her teeth, she pulled on sweats and a tank top, then stumbled to the door to let Buffy out. Blearily, she leaned against the doorjamb and cursed the bottle of cheap champagne she had found in the back of the bar cabinet. When Del had stopped at one glass, citing surgeries she had to perform in the morning, Faith had killed the bottle.

Which would have been fine, had the bottle been Veuve or better.

The bottle had not been Veuve or anything even remotely close.

When Buffy returned, Faith rewarded her with a treat and dragged herself into the kitchen. She turned the kettle on. While it heated, she downed three ibuprofen, then drank three tall glasses of water. Buffy, lying nearby, regarded her every movement with bright eyes. Faith double-checked the security of the bottle cap.

"Even thinking the word 'breakfast' is making me nauseous," she rasped. "But I hear you. I hear and obey."

Several minutes later, Faith sat at the island, clinging to her coffee as though it were her sanity. Only then did she look at her phone. A text from Sharon, confirming that the crew would be back that afternoon to shoot some extra house and neighborhood footage. A voice mail from the lawyer's office, asking her to call. Faith ignored both notifications. Instead, she pulled up her messages and clicked on her thread with Del.

How is ur day going? Sharon and crew will be here later to shoot more footage. Hope the surgeries r going smoothly. She sent the text with a "crossed fingers" emoji.

She filled up her water glass with green juice and drank it slowly, imagining it dissolving the knot of anxiety in her throat. She managed to force herself to reply to Sharon, but instead of immediately clicking on her lawyer's name, she opened her Solitaire app. Finally, after failing to win three times in a row, she decided the universe was punishing her for not returning Hallister's call. Gritting her teeth, she stabbed at his name in her contacts list.

"I have good news and bad news," he said once his receptionist had patched her through. "Which would you like first?"

Faith closed her eyes. "The bad."

"Jameson Johnson is in prison," he said.

Of course he was in prison. Faith wanted to scream. Instead, she made herself ask about the good news.

"We know exactly where he is, and he can't give us the slip."

She forced out a dry laugh. "Right. What happens next?"

"Unsurprisingly, you're not the only person he's defrauded," Hallister said. "It looks like he's been running something of a Ponzi scheme, taking on new work to reimburse prior clients for jobs he hasn't completed. There are multiple lawsuits against him, and we'll sign on as another plaintiff."

Faith couldn't hold in a sigh. "I'm never getting my money back, am I?"

"Never say never," Hallister said. "I'm transferring you back to my receptionist so we can set up a meeting to go over the next steps."

Once the appointment was on her calendar, Faith sat back in her chair and stared at the ceiling, resentment churning in her chest. The higher the waves of her anger swelled, the more she feared they might capsize her. Old!Faith wanted nothing more than to vent all these feelings on social media and subsequently drown them with another round of cheap booze. But she couldn't. She needed to be her very best new!Faith self today.

As if to punctuate the thought, her clock struck ten. Sharon would arrive in two hours. Faith chugged the remainder of her coffee and made herself return to her messages instead of succumbing to the temptation of social media. Ranting publicly would be self-destructive, but she could always vent to Del.

Ur never gonna believe this. My lying cheating snake of a contractor's already in prison facing multiple lawsuits.

She stared at the text box, willing Del to start typing. Nothing. When the screen went dark, Faith squeezed her eyes shut. She was being selfish. Del was probably in the operating room saving lives, while Faith was having a meltdown of her own making. None of this would have happened if she had simply gotten over ridiculous, nonsensical feelings of betrayal and hired Oscar instead.

At that moment, Buffy's cool wet nose pressed against her bare ankle. As Faith looked down, Buffy whined low in her throat. The tip of her tail wagged tentatively, and her brown eyes were almost… beseeching. Their plaintive expression jolted Faith from her spiral of self-flagellation. Was Buffy somehow responding to her mood? She thought back to what Jan had said in this very house only weeks ago: "Dogs are incredibly empathic creatures." With a gasp, she scooped Buffy up and cradled her close, burying her face in fur as a warm tongue bathed her neck.

She let the tears come, let Buffy's silky coat dry them. When she finally pulled back, Buffy was looking up at her expectantly. Despite the burn in her eyes, Faith felt a little lighter.

"I have less than two hours to pull myself together. Workout, then shower?"

Buffy yipped and licked her chin.

Faith carefully lowered her to the floor, grabbed a water bottle from the fridge, and got on her bike. She chose one of the most difficult classes on offer and channeled every ounce of her frustration into her pedal strokes, relishing the burn of her quadriceps and hamstrings. After a while, the endorphins kicked in. She imagined them swarming the gaps between her neurons, smoothing over the jagged edges of her psyche. Afterward, in the shower, she pictured the water washing away not only her sweat but also her resentment. She had plenty to be thankful for, after all. She had a decent financial safety net, a reasonably secure job, and an exciting opportunity ahead. Maybe she couldn't be her best self always, but she sure as hell could turn it on for the next few hours.

❖

By the time Sharon and her crew left, Faith's face hurt from holding a smile, and her headache was back in full force. Her eyes still stung from when Sharon had asked about her father. As she leaned against the door, listening to the sound of the crew's van pulling out of her driveway, fatigue came crashing down. She took another shower, then collapsed back onto the bed. Buffy jumped up next to her.

"We did it. It's all over." Faith shifted to be face-to-face with Buffy, who licked her nose. "Yeah, I know. If this works out, you get all the credit." She held up her hand. "High five."

Buffy raised her paw, and this time, Faith didn't have to manufacture her smile. She tousled the dog's fur gently, then reached for her phone. "Let's see what the rest of the world's been up to."

She opened her messages and flipped through. Still nothing from Del. It was past five o'clock, closing time for the animal hospital on Fridays. Sometimes, hours passed before Del could text her back, but since they had started talking, she had never gone a whole day without a message. Not to mention the fact that Del had read-receipts on, but none of Faith's messages had been read. Unease prickled the back of her neck.

She held the phone in her palm as though weighing it. If Del were her real girlfriend, Faith would call. Was that the right thing to do, or would Del consider that too invasive? Then, she checked herself. Step

Six was "commit to caring." She didn't need to be Del's real girlfriend to check in and see if she was okay.

The phone rang a few times, then went to voice mail. "Del. Hi. It's Faith. Obviously." She closed her eyes. Could she be more awkward? "Anyway, I just wanted to check in to see how you are. Talk to you soon."

She hung up and stared at her phone. Of course, Del had no obligation to reply to her messages or take her calls. But she had always done so in the past, and Faith couldn't escape the feeling that something was wrong. To distract herself, she did "maintenance" work on her socials. She replied to a few comments and wrote on some friends' posts. Fleetingly, she wished she could announce the big news about *Fish Out of Water*. The spots for each finalist were apparently going to air the week after next, so at least she didn't have to wait too long.

Once she had placated social media, she scrolled back to her messages. Still nothing. A sudden thought seared through her, burning away the fatigue. "Did I fuck up last night?"

Buffy raised her head, and Faith stared into her eyes. She thought back to the conversation with Del over their champagne. It had been light and triumphant, filled with relief. There had been a giddiness to it. She didn't remember saying or doing anything objectionable, but the possibility lingered. Worse, however, was the fear that Del had been physically hurt in some way, that she had been in some kind of accident last night or this morning. The possibilities warped and twisted inside her, souring her stomach.

She looked at her phone again. Still nothing. She looked back at Buffy. "Will we be total creepers if we drive by her house?" When Buffy stood and shook herself, Faith had to laugh. She held out her hand for another high five. "Then let's do this, wingman."

Just shy of twenty minutes later, Faith turned onto Del's street. She slowed as the driveway approached. When she spotted both Del's car and light spilling out the front windows, relief flooded through her. Moments later, the tide turned. What if Del had never left the house that morning? What if she was lying on the floor unconscious, just like Faith had found her father all those years ago? Even as a part of her recoiled from the memory, the rest of her resolved to act.

"We have to see if she's okay, Buff. You get that, right?"

Buffy whined. Faith nodded sharply and turned into Del's driveway, then cut the engine. She debated for an instant, then opened the back door and reached for Buffy. They were in this together. Cradling the dog against her chest, Faith rang the doorbell.

Her heartbeats drummed a cadence of fear. Faith tried to breathe slowly, steadily. One second. Two. Three. She glanced at her watch. How long should she wait before...before what? Was she seriously going to try kicking in—

The door opened. Del stood in the frame, backlit by the hall lamp. Her hair was down. The horrible visions in Faith's head vanished in the face of her physical presence.

"Hi." A rush of self-consciousness made Faith tongue-tied. "I hadn't heard from you, and I didn't know if you were okay, and...and I'm an idiot. Sorry to have bothered you."

Faith was about to turn away when Del shifted slightly. The light caught her face, revealing tear stains and puffiness. Instinctively, Faith reached to touch her shoulder.

"What's wrong?"

"Bad day," Del rasped. "I lost two animals in surgery."

Faith's heart clenched. Instinctively, she held out Buffy. Del took her automatically. For a moment, she stared at the dog as though she didn't recognize her. Then, with a gasp, Del buried her face in Buffy's fur and started crying again.

"Come on," Faith said softly. "Let's go inside."

She closed the door behind her and steered Del toward the couch. Along the way, she grabbed a few tissues. She sat beside Del for a little while, feeling awkward before tentatively reaching out to rub her lower back. Del didn't shrink from the touch, and Faith focused on making her movements slow and rhythmic. She might not have any idea what to say, but at least she could show Del that she wasn't alone in her pain.

When Faith's fingers brushed warm skin, she froze. She looked over and realized she had inadvertently bunched up Del's shirt. "Sorry."

Del sniffled and turned her face ever so slightly in Faith's direction. "Feels good," she murmured.

The words landed like a spark on dry tinder. Holding her breath, Faith eased her hand beneath the hem line. There was something profoundly intimate about resting her palm against Del's lower back, something soothing and protective. She let her fingertips trace slow, gentle circles and listened as Del's breathing gradually began to even out. When Del leaned across the space between them to rest her head on Faith's shoulder, Faith pressed her cheek against Del's hair.

They sat there for a long time, Faith watching Del's fingers comb rhythmically through Buffy's fur. Thoughts drifted in and out of Faith's mind, slow and random. Sitting still without a show to occupy her attention was usually excruciating, and she had *never* been a cuddler. But now, pressed against Del, Buffy touching both of them, Faith's restlessness never materialized. She closed her eyes and drifted, content for once to be still.

The doorbell rang. When Del jerked upright, Faith's instinct was to soothe her. "I'll get it." She looked at Buffy, who was now standing with her front paws on Del's knees. "Buffy, stay. Stay with Del."

Faith didn't have time to laugh at the surprisingly human sigh from Buffy as she settled back into Del's lap. She hurried toward the door and opened it to find a woman on the doorstep. Hair curling intricately around her shoulders and immaculately dressed in a gray suit with a blue dress shirt beneath, the woman projected an aura of sophisticated competence. Her pencil skirt clung to toned legs that Faith couldn't help but regard with a slightly more than professional admiration.

"Where's Del?" The woman's tone held hidden hostility on the cusp of breaking free.

Faith bristled and was about to retort in kind when she recognized the surge of anger and clamped down on it. She thought of her therapist, who had encouraged her to act from the assumption that everyone was doing their best, including herself. Only minutes ago, she had been where this woman was: on Del's doorstep, worried for her well-being.

Swallowing her irritation, Faith extended her hand. "She's here. She had a rough day. I'm Faith, Del's girlfriend."

The woman's expression relaxed into one of relief, and she clasped Faith's hand. "Jada. Her best friend."

"Jada?"

Faith turned to the sight of Del approaching while holding Buffy close. Faith took the dog, then stepped aside to let Jada enter.

Jada gripped Del's shoulders. "You scared the shit out of me," she said.

"I'm sorry."

"You know you can share the details or not, whatever you need. I'm just glad you're okay and not alone."

Del sniffled again. "Thanks. But I know I shouldn't disappear on you."

"And I know you need to 'turtle' sometimes." Jada reached for a tissue and handed it to her. "I'm glad you reached out to Faith. Next time, just…check in, if only briefly?"

Faith wasn't about to point out that Del had not, in fact, reached out to her. She was surprised when Del owned that.

"I didn't. Faith showed up half an hour ago."

Jada turned back to her, brows arched. She looked Faith up and down. "Oh. I *like* you."

Even as Faith curled one arm around Del's waist, she felt a pang for the time in the not-so-distant future when Jada would doubtless curse her name for letting go of Del.

"And is this the dog you adopted?"

"This is Buffy."

Jada froze in the act of reaching out. She stared incredulously. "You're Faith, and you named your dog Buffy?"

Faith turned to Del. "See? I told you this would happen."

Del's laughter was even sweeter than her vindication. "You were right. Though I still don't understand it."

Jada, who had extracted Buffy from Faith's arms and was now cradling her like a human baby, snorted. "That's because you're pop-culture illiterate." She looked between them. "So what's the story?"

Unsure whether to start narrating, Faith glanced at Del and caught a glimpse of Del's deep fatigue before her face returned to inscrutability. "Let's sit while we talk," she said. "And order some food."

"This is a day for treating ourselves," Jada said as she settled into the reclining chair that flanked the couch. "And you know what that means."

Panic showered Faith in sudden needles. Jada was acting like all three of them were in on whatever joke she was making. Was this something a real girlfriend was supposed to know? She rerouted every shred of concentration into the effort to keep her expression smooth. Was she about to ruin everything?

"I haven't introduced Faith to Vita's yet," Del said.

"That's absurd. Why not?"

Faith's anxiety ratcheted up another level. A cold sweat broke out on her palms, and she rested them on her leggings, wiping surreptitiously. Del glanced in her direction, but she didn't appear to share Faith's panic. Faith could only hope her own poker face was that good.

"I was waiting for a special occasion," Del said.

"Having a craving sounds like a special occasion to me. Here." Jada typed in her phone, then leaned across the space between them to hand it to Faith. "Check out the menu."

Once they placed their order, Jada recapitulated her request for the story. Del obliged, petting Buffy as she told it. Periodically, Faith interjected. Mostly, she watched Del. Exhaustion was plain to see in the set of her mouth and the glassiness of her eyes. Faith kept one hand on Del's knee, as much to reassure herself as to comfort Del.

That was a strange revelation. A strand of panic unfurled in Faith's throat, threatening to choke her. She swallowed hard. Of course she cared about Del. They were allies on a mission. And Del was Buffy's vet, who had already shepherded the dog through one crisis. Two, if she counted the aftermath of the hurricane. They could be friends, Faith thought, when this was all over.

All over. The phrase sent a pang through her, and she squeezed Del's leg without thinking. When Del turned an inquisitive look in her direction, Faith shook her head, embarrassment rushing to the fore. She channeled it by taking over the story, describing how Pinoe had refused to listen to her and how Del had finally diagnosed the problem at the dog park.

"This is the most adorable story I've ever heard in my life," Jada said. "And what a fucking metaphor. In learning to embrace Buffy, Faith reaches a higher level of self-awareness."

A *metaphor*? "That's, uh, very interesting," Faith muttered.

This time, Del was the one to squeeze her hand. "Jada majored in English. She's prone to metaphors."

"English?" Faith frowned. "I thought you were a doctor?"

She realized she had mis-stepped when Del and Jada exchanged a look.

"Doctors can major in anything they want in undergrad,"

Del explained after a moment. "They just need to also take certain prerequisite classes for med school. Vets, too."

Shame crashed over Faith in a hot flood. She could feel it in her face. Had Del told Jada she was a college dropout? Faith was suddenly and acutely reminded that they were *fake* dating. Obviously, Del would never want someone so uneducated.

On the heels of her embarrassment came the anger, wind gusting over the water. It made her want to lash out, to make them feel as low as she did. Instead, she clamped her mouth shut and surreptitiously worked through one of the breathing exercises she'd learned from her therapist. Just as her heart rate was finally starting to come down, the doorbell rang. Faith jumped up to get the food. She took the bag from the fresh-faced kid who delivered it. Then, once he was back in his car, she turned her face to the sky. A crescent moon hung over the roof of Del's townhome. The concrete slab of the doorstep was cool beneath her feet. Faith focused on the beauty above, the sensation below. She imagined her insecurities dissipating into the sky, the ground. She went back inside.

Jada was opening a bottle of wine. She looked up, a gleam in her eye. "I was just thinking. Maybe watching *Buffy* the show should be Del's penance for terrifying us today."

Faith grinned. "Perfect penance is perfect."

"Are you ganging up on me?" Del protested.

"Looks like it," said Jada.

They sat down to eat, and Faith asked how Jada and Del had met. Just as she hoped, that opened the floodgates to a series of stories. Del brightened as she talked about their college days. Faith ate slowly and listened carefully, trying to catalogue some of the details. They might come in handy at the wedding, when she would be around more of Jada and Del's college crowd. Faith wished she dared to take actual notes, but that would look bizarre. Once she was back home, she would have to jot down all the details she could remember.

After a while, Jada turned the tables to put the spotlight on Faith. When she asked about Hype Cycle, Del supplemented Faith's answers by throwing in the number of her social media followers and describing the popularity of Faith's classes. It was exactly the kind of thing a girlfriend was supposed to do, Faith realized. And yet, no one she'd ever dated for real had bothered to be her hype person in that way.

Self-absorbed. She had been, and the same was true of those she had associated with. Del, on the other hand, was thoughtful and generous. Once their "relationship" had run its course, she needed to find someone who would treat her like Del did. And she wanted—for the first time—to do the same in return.

Chapter Seven

Faith sat on the floor with her back to the couch, trying to meditate. Buffy was chewing on her hair, which wasn't helping. Or maybe it was. Faith had to laugh, which wasn't very helpful with the mental flow state she was trying to access. Then again, at least she was laughing.

In less than half an hour, the *Fish Out of Water Pre-Show* would air. Ten of the finalists would be selected. She had no foreknowledge, no spoilers. She would find out whether the show was her future at the same time everyone else did. After tonight, she would either be a reality show contestant or a footnote.

Fortunately, Del was coming over. They had decided that, if Faith was selected, she should share a selfie of the two of them, exultant. And if Faith wasn't selected…well, that was what the pristine tub of peanut-butter-cup ice cream in the freezer was for.

As the minutes ticked by, Faith gave up on trying to sit still. She paced the length of the living room, feeling like a tiger in a cage. Except the bars of the cage were fashioned from her low self-worth and her abject need to be admired and wanted, fused with her fear and self-loathing as a result of that neediness. At the thought, Faith paused. Huh. That was actually pretty insightful.

Buffy leapt from the couch, heralding the ring of the doorbell. Del. Faith hurried down the hall but paused to inspect herself in the mirror. When she caught herself, she shot her reflection an exasperated look and kept moving. Fleetingly, she wondered whether everyone who attempted a fake relationship experienced these little moments of forgetting it was fake. Surely, that was normal?

Normal. Fake dating. A hysterical laugh rose in the back of her throat. She swallowed it and opened the door. Del stood before her wearing sweats and a zip-up hoodie. Her hair was down, its ends slightly curly. The casual touches gave Del an aura of softness—vulnerability, almost—that Faith found intensely appealing. Realizing she was staring, she cleared her throat.

"Hi."

"How are you holding up?" Del asked as she crossed the threshold.

"Oh, you know. Panicking."

Del touched her shoulder briefly, then bent to greet Buffy. "You're going to be okay. We'll get through this together. Right, Buff?"

"I'm sorry in advance if I'm especially insane tonight," Faith said. "I'll try to keep my crazy under wraps."

"No need." Del scooped up Buffy. "Let it all out. I won't judge."

"Be careful what you wish for," Faith muttered. Del only laughed.

As she led the way into the living room, Faith found herself wondering how she'd gotten so lucky. *I won't judge.* Plenty of people said things like that, but by now, she knew Del truly meant it. She had also come to realize that all her friendships before Del had been *founded* on judgment and criticism. That was a sobering revelation, and yet one more thing she didn't want to revert back to.

"The pizza's on its way," she said as Del settled on the couch. "Want something to drink?"

Del asked for water, and Faith went to the kitchen. She opened the fridge. The beautiful cans of craft beers were calling to her, but the night was young, and her stress level was such that if she started drinking, she would have trouble stopping. Gritting her teeth, she reached for two seltzers instead.

When she returned to the living room, Del was sitting on the floor giving Buffy a belly rub. The dog was stretched out on her back, legs in the air, ears flopping to the ground.

"So shameless," Faith said, setting down their waters. "It must be a relief not to experience shame the way we do."

"Having a highly developed frontal cortex does come with disadvantages," Del said.

When Faith sat on the couch, Del joined her. Buffy regarded her balefully, then jumped up to curl between them. As the theme song for

Fish Out of Water began, Faith's phone pinged: Jolie, texting her with a series of crossed-finger emojis.

"My agent," Faith clarified at Del's curious glance.

The host of the show—a child actor who had ridden the coattails of his popularity about as far as possible—appeared on the screen. Faith tried to take slow sips of water as he explained the format: the pre-show would reveal the ten contestants in random order by showing a brief video vignette about each. The contestants would then be flown to Los Angeles, where they would participate in a live-streamed pre-broadcast event, allowing them to get to know each other before the competition began.

As the actor's chiseled face faded out to be replaced by the first of many commercial breaks, Del reached over Buffy's head to touch Faith's bouncing knee.

"Whatever you need tonight, I want to help."

A wildly inappropriate reply leapt to Faith's lips, and she clenched her teeth before it could escape. *Gratitude*, she reminded herself. *Empathy.*

"Thanks." She covered Del's hand. "How about you...is there anything you need?"

Del shrugged. "I don't think so. I double-checked my socials and warned the executive director of the shelter as well as my boss at the hospital. We're as ready as we can be."

Del's confidence that she would be selected made Faith feel warm inside. Before she could second-guess herself, she leaned over and kissed her. It was a quick kiss, but no one was watching. And that made all the difference.

The first vignette focused on a Latina woman who was a music executive by day and a DJ by night. Gorgeous and charismatic, generous and down-to-earth, she was sure to be a crowd favorite. Faith felt the familiar stirrings of insecurity. When bitterness tried to rise in its wake, she tried to breathe the negative emotion out of herself, allowing it to dissipate in the air.

"One down, nine to go."

Nine became eight. Eight became seven. She tried to watch the vignettes attentively, tried to imagine collaborating with and competing against the contestants. Seven became six. When the doorbell rang, Faith jumped up to get the pizza. Moving was so much easier than sitting, and she waved off Del's attempts to help with plates and fresh drinks.

The first hour passed. Five became four. Four became three. Faith couldn't sit at all, now. She paced the length of the living room, fists clenched.

"It's okay if you want to go," she told Del with forced lightness when the protagonist of the third-to-last vignette was revealed to be an elementary school math teacher who had pioneered a new way of helping children with math anxiety. "There's no way I made the cut."

"What makes you say that?" Del protested.

"Del. Honestly. Look at all these people. They're incredible."

Del and Buffy both stared at her from the couch. "As are you."

"Me?" Faith shook her head. "I'm a spin instructor with some internet fame, no. Notoriety. I am *nothing* like these people."

Del extended one hand. "You're not giving yourself enough credit, Faith. You're empowering. An inspiration. Now more than ever since you've fought through multiple tragedies to reclaim and reinvent yourself."

Faith stared at her. Reclaim and reinvent herself? Was that how it looked from the outside? "I'm disastrous," she protested.

Instead of rising to the bait, Del looked at her steadily. "Everyone's disastrous at some point. That's not important. What's important is what you decide to do about it."

For the space of several heartbeats, Faith stared, trying to detect any trace of pity or condescension. Finding none, she collapsed onto the couch in a thoroughly melodramatic fashion and buried her face in her hands. "You think way too highly of me."

"Or you don't think highly enough of yourself."

A new vignette began, the penultimate. Faith watched its story unfold dully. One more chance. Buffy crawled out of Del's lap and into hers. The sensation of soft fur between her fingers soothed the raw ache in her heart.

The spotlight ended. The ensuing advertisements were loud and jangling. As the last commercial faded out, Faith closed her eyes. "I can't look."

Her heart was pounding, her stomach twisted in knots. The sound of birds chirping emanated from the speakers. A simple piano melody began to play.

"*Faith.*" Del gripped her hand as she spoke. "It's you."

Faith's eyes flew open. She stared at the screen. There she was, seated on this very couch, Buffy in her lap, just as she was now. Faith heard herself tell her story. She watched as the video cut from the shelter to her backyard and then to the dog park. Del appeared, beautiful and competent and slightly self-conscious. The shot cut to Toppings. Del told the story about the iguana. They kissed. The way they kissed was beautiful. They looked like they were in love.

"You did it," Del was saying as the vignette cut to the studio where the host was waiting. "You did it, Faith."

Faith turned to her. Her heart was racing, but the world felt as though it was unfolding in slow motion. Del's eyes were bright with exultation. She was so very beautiful. So very *good.*

"I couldn't have done it without you," she said, hearing her own voice as if from far away.

Del's smile unfolded like a time-lapse flower. This time, she was the one to close the space between them. This time, the kiss wasn't quick. It was slow and deep, and Del's hand was cupping the back of her neck, and Del's tongue was questing between her lips, and Faith's hand was clutching the front of her shirt to pull her even closer. She could feel the zipper of the hoodie beneath her hand, and she wanted it *gone*, undone, wanted Del's skin bare before her. Her ears were buzzing with arousal, and her blood felt like it was burning, and—

"Faith." Del gasped, pressing their foreheads together. "Faith. Your…your phone. It's blowing up."

Panting, Faith turned to look at the table. Sure enough, her phone was rocking with vibrations, its screen lighting up with a new message every other second. She looked back at Del. God. She'd been about to *undress* her. Without asking.

"I'm so sorry," she gasped.

Some hint of panic must have surfaced in her eyes, because Del touched her mouth gently and shook her head. "You don't have to apologize," she breathed. "But you do need to talk to your agent."

"Okay," Faith said. "Okay."

She leaned in for one more fast, fierce kiss, then reached for her phone.

❖

As they meandered slowly through her neighborhood, Del tried to focus on the pleasant sensation of Faith's fingers entwined with hers instead of the creeping dread in her that bubbled up in her chest whenever she considered that within twelve hours, Faith would be on a plane flying across the country. At least Buffy would be staying with her while Faith was gone. That was something. She glanced down at where the dog was sniffing at a mailbox. They could miss Faith together. And unlike a human, Buffy could never betray the confusing miasma of Del's feelings.

The fact of the matter was that the kiss was haunting her. They hadn't kissed since, but that didn't seem to matter to Del's feelings. Faith had responded to her like a lover that night, and ever since then, Del was increasingly experiencing emotions she had no business feeling. Case in point: she had suggested a nice long walk around her neighborhood just so she could spend a little more time with Faith tonight. At least Buffy was the perfect excuse.

As they turned onto her street, Del passed a parked car that was the same model and color as Maddie's. Instinctively, she braced for sharp pain, but the reminder only inspired a dull ache.

"By the time I get home, Buffy's not going to remember me," Faith was saying.

Del squeezed her hand. "You'll be gone for less than a week. She'll remember you perfectly well. Promise."

Faith looked at her. "I'm being a whiny bitch, aren't I?"

"You're nervous about the trip," Del said. "That makes sense."

"You're right. I know. I guess I feel like an idiot for…for sort of dreading it and not being more excited. This is what I wanted, after all. And it's a good thing."

"Can you pinpoint what you're dreading? Or is it more of an aimless kind of dread?"

Faith was quiet for a long moment before answering. "I've made a lot of progress on myself these past few months. But I've also been in social exile."

"Ouch," Del said before she could stop herself.

"No. Shit. I didn't mean it like that." Faith stopped and tucked Buffy's leash under one arm so she could take Del's free hand, too. "Getting to know you has been the best part of being back here."

"I was joking," Del said, though she feared she hadn't been. "I'm not fishing for compliments."

"I'm not giving compliments. I'm telling the truth." Faith's thumbs moved gently across her knuckles. "Back in the city, I was always going out to clubs and bars. Partying hard—drinking too much, hooking up with women—that was my entire identity outside of my fitness persona."

Del couldn't imagine enjoying what Faith was describing. When disappointment swept over her, anger followed in its wake. She had always known that she and Faith weren't *actually* compatible. It made no sense to be sad about that.

"There's nothing wrong with that if it's what you want," she said, careful not to betray her own judgment.

"Maybe some people actually do enjoy living like that," Faith said, "but I didn't. I was fooling myself."

The disconnect between Del's thoughts and Faith's words felt like whiplash. "I'm…what?"

"I had all these friends who didn't *really* care about me," Faith said. "I was miserable and didn't know why. It took losing my mom and being forced to confront all my baggage around her to make me realize I wasn't actually happy."

Del felt her disappointment fading, giving way to something that felt suspiciously like relief. The implications of *that* were terrifying. A part of her wanted to pull away, to put real distance between herself and Faith. The rest of her wanted to pull Faith closer, to kiss her, even if no one was watching.

"Ugh. I'm rambling. Sorry." Faith dropped one of Del's hands and started walking again. "What I'm trying to say is that I'm worried being on this show is going to make me slide back into that lifestyle. I mean, obviously, it can't *make* me. But I guess I'm worried I won't be strong enough, and I'll lose all the progress I've made."

Hearing the distress in Faith's voice—knowing for sure that she truly didn't want to go back to her old self—finally tipped Del over the edge. The truth was staring her right in the face, and she couldn't hide from it any longer. She had feelings for Faith. Romantic feelings. *Real* feelings. They had been coming on slowly for a while, but now they were here, barreling down on her like a freight train. What was she supposed to do?

As they came abreast of Del's driveway, she fished her keys out of her pocket. In her distraction, she dropped them in the flower bed and bent to retrieve them. Should she say something? If so, what? "I think I've caught feelings?" "Do you want to be real girlfriends instead of fake girlfriends?" But if Faith didn't feel the same—which she probably didn't—what would happen? Would she still go to the wedding, or would Del be right back where she started: dateless and with no prospects?

"Del," Faith whispered. "There's someone waiting on your stoop."

Puzzle pieces she hadn't been consciously assembling clicked into place. The picture they'd revealed made the bottom drop out of her stomach. Time seemed to slow. Del didn't want to raise her head to the sight of Maddie sitting on her doorstep, but she knew that was what she would find.

She looked up to find Maddie looking back. The collar of a black turtleneck sweater peeked out from beneath her familiar blue puffer coat. As their gazes met, Maddie stood. Del remembered unbuttoning the jeans Maddie was wearing. She remembered seeing Maddie's boots in the hall of their apartment each day.

"Hi, Del," Maddie said.

"Maddie?" Del heard the tremor in her own voice and hated it. Hated herself.

At her side, Faith sucked in a breath and clutched her hand. The brief spike of pain from her grip broke through the strange emotional paralysis. Del swallowed hard and clutched back.

"Why are you here?" she asked, and this time, her voice was stronger.

Maddie looked at Del and Faith's joined hands. "I needed to see you, and I wasn't sure you'd take my call."

"You could have tried."

"Maybe I should have," Maddie acknowledged. "But I thought you might take me more seriously if we talked face-to-face."

Del's first reaction was skepticism. That might be part of the truth, but Maddie was also trying to make some kind of statement by surprising her. So far, the only effect it was having was to remind Del of just how self-absorbed Maddie was.

"Can we talk?" Maddie said as the silence went on. "Alone?"

Faith let go of Del and stepped forward, hand extended. "Hi. I'm Faith. Del's girlfriend."

Beneath the confidence in Faith's words was a current of hostility, and she had interposed herself between Del and Maddie, simultaneously drawing her attention and serving as a shield. Protecting. Faith was protecting her. Foundering as she was on a sea of emotion, that truth felt like a lifeline.

Faith cocked her head. "But you already know who I am because that's why you're here. You saw us on *Fish Out of Water*, and now you're having regrets."

Maddie waited a few heartbeats before shaking Faith's hand perfunctorily. "I appreciate how supportive you've been of Del when I couldn't be," she said, a hint of syrup to her voice. "I hope you'll respect the five years we had together and give us some time to speak privately."

Faith turned her head. "Del?"

Del stepped forward to stand beside Faith and reclaimed her hand, beyond grateful for the strength she was offering. "Not tonight, Maddie. I don't appreciate being ambushed."

Maddie's lips compressed into a thin line. "Tomorrow, then?"

A part of Del wanted to refuse. The rest of her knew she needed to have this confrontation, if only for the sake of closure. And to think that only a few weeks ago, she'd been torn up about Maddie's betrayal. So much had changed since then.

"I can do coffee in the late morning. I'll text you the place."

"All right." Maddie held Del's gaze for a long moment before walking away.

Del watched her go. When she turned, Faith was watching *her* with an intensity that made Del's heart flutter again. The beginnings of a headache thrummed in Del's temples. She stepped past Faith to open the door.

"How are you doing?" Faith asked as soon as the door was closed behind them.

"I'm okay," Del said, though she felt more than a little numb.

"Del." There was gentleness in the way Faith spoke her name and the slightest undercurrent of reproach.

"I am." Del heard the protest in her own voice.

"You're a strong, independent human who is really good at taking care of others," said Faith. "But that was hard, and I want you to talk to me about it."

"Why?" Del felt like she was suddenly on the precipice of panic. "What does it matter?"

"What does it—" Faith's face contorted. "Of course it matters. *You* matter. I care about you."

I care about you.

Del knew Faith meant the words to apply to their friendship, but instead, they blew the doors wide open on Del's feelings. Crush. Insanity. Whatever this was. Hadn't she acknowledged, right away, that she and Faith were incompatible? And now here she was, *pining*?

Fearing her expression might betray her, Del turned away and went to the couch. She sank onto it, and moments later, Buffy curled up against her thigh. Automatically, Del began to pet her. Faith sat at the other end of the couch, but Del kept her focus on Buffy. Exhaustion pressed down on her, as though Maddie's presence had eaten through the shields keeping it at bay.

"At the beginning, back when I had just moved out here," Del said. "All I wanted was what happened just now. To come home to the sight of her sitting on my doorstep."

"And now?" Faith's voice was even, the syllables free of judgment.

And now. When Del looked inside herself, all she found was uncertainty. She had gone from planning to spend the rest of her life with Maddie to having feelings for the woman who she was in a fake relationship with.

"I'm confused."

"That makes sense," Faith said. "It's all right to be confused."

Del laughed sharply. "All right, maybe. But also uncomfortable."

"I know." Faith reached over to squeeze her shoulder.

A shoulder squeeze was a far cry from the passionate kisses they had exchanged a few nights ago in Faith's living room. Still, Maddie's invasion had squelched any chance of an encore.

"You need to go home and finish packing," Del said. "I'm fine. Really."

Faith frowned at her. "Okay. But if you decide you want to talk…"

"I'll call you. Thanks." The headache was growing steadily worse.

"And if you decide you want to get back together with her, you will, right?" Faith's nose scrunched up in a way that was entirely adorable, and Del had to look away. "What I'm trying to say is, whenever you need us to 'break up' or whatever—"

Del couldn't bear to hear the end of that sentence. "I understand."

Faith nodded slowly. She reached across the space between them to pet her dog. "You take good care of Del, okay? And I'll see you soon."

When she bent to kiss the top of Buffy's head, Del tried, and failed, not to wish for a kiss of her own. Faith stood, then, and awkwardly stuck her hands in her pockets.

"Okay. Thanks again for looking after her."

"Of course."

"I'll see you. Less than a week."

"Yep."

"Good night," Faith said, sketching a wave as she headed for the door.

Once Faith had let herself out, Del sagged back against the couch and stared at the ceiling. Beside her, Buffy whined softly.

"Good-bye," Del whispered into the air.

Chapter Eight

Faith was trying to be good. She had been trying since she set foot off the plane yesterday. She'd had only two drinks in her hotel room. She had gone to bed before one o'clock. She had woken at eight and worked out in the gym. She had not indulged in the buffet for breakfast. She had consumed a lot of water. And now she was here, at a giant, fancy-ass house she had barely glimpsed before being whisked away into an underground room divided into cubicles. She was sitting before a slightly lopsided mirror undergoing hair and makeup, less than an hour away from the filming of *Fish Out of Water*'s pre-broadcast "Getting to Know You" event.

What was Del doing?

The thought had been intruding ever since she'd left Del's house two days ago. She had texted Del in the meantime, asking *how* she was doing, but the replies were less than satisfying. In response to how coffee with Maddie had gone, Del's response was, "Fine. No drama. She talked a lot." Faith, waiting for her flight to board, had agonized over her reply, typing and erasing and retyping until the plane's doors were about to close. She had finally gone with, "Glad there was no drama. How do you feel about the things she said?"

Then, cut off from communication, Faith had stared at the small screen on the seat back in front of her, dully watching it cycle through its advertisements and feeling her anxiety mount with each successive loop. Finally, she had thrown in the towel and purchased Wi-Fi access. When her phone reconnected to the internet, she saw Del had liked her message and replied, "My mind's all over the place. Trying to sort it out. Have a good flight."

What did *that* mean? Faith had been mulling over the message ever since, returning again and again to her own brief encounter with Maddie. Maddie's proprietary attitude toward Del had been grating, but she *was* beautiful, and she and Del had five years of shared history. They would probably get back together, wouldn't they?

Faith wondered whether Del had told Maddie about their fake dating arrangement. The thought made her feel cold inside. She didn't want Maddie wielding that kind of power over her. If she said something on social media once the show started, it might go viral and completely tank Faith's chances. She stared at her reflection in the mirror, seeing her panic there. Fortunately, Bruno, her stylist, was oblivious.

No. She was catastrophizing again. Faith closed her eyes and went through a few rounds of box breathing. Del was a good person. She wouldn't betray Faith to Maddie. The text messages made it sound like she was uncertain about what she wanted. If Faith had to guess, the likeliest scenario was that their fake breakup would happen sooner than expected. She tried to ignore the pang inspired by that thought. A breakup might actually be *good* for her chances. Plenty of viewers would be able to empathize with a person who was dumped in favor of an ex.

At the thought, her sadness shifted into sharp, stinging guilt. No. That could *never* be the narrative because then Del would reap all the blame. What a horrible thing to do to her. The fact that the thought had even entered Faith's mind made her want to be sick. She stared at her reflection and watched her own jaw flicker as she clenched her teeth. No drama. That had been her promise. If Del got back together with Maddie and needed them to break up, Faith would find a way to be the responsible party.

Bruno finally pronounced her fit for polite company. He fitted her with a small lapel mic and left her to her own devices in the little cubicle. *Fish Out of Water* was going to significant lengths to ensure the cast members didn't interact before the filming began, and Faith was more than happy to be left alone in the meantime. The only person she wanted to interact with was Del. Faith pulled out her phone, opened her messages, and stared at their thread. Should she reach out again, or was that ridiculous?

She was spared from making that choice by the arrival of a production assistant who ushered her into a corridor, up a flight of stairs, past a large, gleaming kitchen, and out a set of sliding doors. Faith stepped onto the immaculate white bricks of a three-tiered terrace overlooking the ocean. A warm breeze caressed her face as she stared out over the white-capped waves.

A burst of high-pitched laughter broke the spell. Faith looked around, registering several tables with umbrellas interspersed with clusters of chairs. At least three dozen people were gathered out there, most wearing headsets and wielding cameras or tablets. They swarmed across the terrace like ants. Everyone else, Faith realized, was like her: a contestant.

"Let me introduce you to Casey," the assistant who had fetched Faith enthused. "She's a life coach in Sedona. I think you two will hit it off."

Faith was about to protest when she realized she had set herself up for this. For the purpose of this show, her entire narrative was about healing and taking back control of her life. Of course the producers would think she wanted to hang out with a life coach. Clamping her lips together, she forced herself to meekly follow in the assistant's wake. This event was being live-streamed, and her mic would be hot the entire time. Even a muttered comment wasn't safe.

As it turned out, chatting with Casey wasn't nearly as challenging as Faith had feared, mostly because Casey loved to talk. All Faith had to do, she quickly realized, was act like she was listening and then periodically tune in just enough to ask a question. Casey was then more than happy to go haring off in a new conversational direction. Tuning out most of her chatter, Faith tried to piece together how the event was being streamed to the outside world. They were in the sights of multiple cameras, and several boom mics were angled in their direction. Once, an assistant with a tablet interrupted them with a question from a fan who was watching. The question, it turned out, was for Faith: how had adopting a dog affected her mission to become healthier mentally and physically?

Hearing it, Faith relaxed. Talking about Buffy was easy. As she answered, she thought of Del. It was a cold, rainy Saturday back in Fairview. Resolutely pushing past the mental images of Del entwined with Maddie, Faith tried to focus on more optimistic scenarios. What if Del and Buffy were, even at this very moment, curled on the couch under a blanket, watching the stream? When Faith tried to imagine how she might look through Del's eyes, a different species of fear coiled around her spine. What if Del didn't like what she saw?

As the thought took root, a new assistant interrupted their conversation, bringing over a contestant named Raoul to speak with Faith. Imagining Del observing from the ether made Faith want to try a little harder. She tried to stay focused on Raoul, the math teacher. Del had always made Faith feel like the most important and interesting person in the room, and she tried to make Raoul feel that way now.

Time passed. Faith's conversational partner changed, then changed again. And again. Periodically, an assistant would materialize with another question from the audience. For some reason, Faith's partners were rarely asked questions. One fan asked whether Buffy had made the trip to LA, prompting Faith to confess that Del was looking after her. Another questioned Buffy's name, prompting Faith to tell the full story, of which Del was a crucial part. Everywhere Faith turned, Del was waiting.

Except, of course, she was thousands of miles away.

Faith had fallen in love with Delphine Wu.

The realization felt like a physical blow, sharp and stinging. Dazed, Faith stared at the assistant who was asking yet another question. His lips were moving, but she couldn't hear a thing. A single imperative drowned out everything except its own urgency.

She had to go back and confess. Right now.

Maddie be damned. *Fish Out of Water* be damned. GTA be damned. In a blinding rush of clarity, Faith's priorities clicked into place. She had to try. Maybe it was too late, but she would never forgive herself if she didn't try.

"I know this is going to sound crazy, but I have to go."

The assistant blinked in confusion. "I'm sorry?"

"I have to leave. I'll come back, if you still want me. But right now, I have to go."

Faith turned on her heel, leaving the assistant spluttering in her wake. Pulling up her rideshare application, she headed for the top of the long, winding driveway. A car could pick her up in less than ten minutes. By the time her feet hit pavement, she was running.

By some miracle, traffic wasn't terrible. As the car wended its way back to her hotel, Faith checked the flight schedule. The last plane of the night was leaving in just less than three hours. She bought the flight, pairing it with a return trip on Monday evening. Then, she forwarded her email confirmation to both Sharon and Jolie with a note of apology. In it, she told them she'd had a fight with Del before leaving, and that the questions asked by the viewers had made her realize she needed to return home to apologize. There was, she thought, an outside chance that the white lie might even help her chances. Nothing increased ratings like a grand gesture.

At the very least, she hoped the clear evidence of her plan to return would save her from being dismissed from the show. Still, even if the worst happened, she still had Hype Cycle. Getting fired from *Fish Out of Water* was something she could live with. Not telling Del how she felt before Maddie sank her claws back in was not.

When the text came, Faith was not prepared. Apparently, way deep down, she hadn't actually believed Del was watching.

What happened? Are you okay?

Faith bit her lower lip. She didn't want to talk to Del right now. She didn't want to say the words in a text bubble or even over the phone. *Yes. Sorry 2 worry u.*

Why did you leave?

Faith squeezed her eyes shut. *I'll explain tmrrw.*

When her phone vibrated, Faith looked back at its screen, but all Del had done was to "like" the message. Faith stared at the thumbs-up until the screen went dark. Then, she stared out at the blurred landscape. She had wished so badly to get to Los Angeles. Now, for the first time ever, she wanted to return to Fairview. A sudden thought jolted her: what if she could make a life there? The thought was more than a little insane, since all she could remember wanting since she was a teenager was to get out. But now that she'd had the thought, it continued to pester her. What if she made a deal with Hype Cycle to start a studio in Fairview? There were plenty of soccer moms who would want to take her classes in person, weren't there? She didn't have to go back to the city, where Buffy wouldn't have a yard to play in. And then, crazy as it sounded…what if she started dating Del for real? What if—maybe—Del moved into her house?

Her house. Faith pictured the sheets of plastic covering the open wounds of unfinished construction. She felt the old anger like an infection, poisoning her blood. With a definitive head shake, she stabbed at her phone. No. That poison was only holding her back. A quick search online led her to the number she needed, and she punched in the digits before she could lose the will. It was Saturday afternoon in Fairview. No way would he answer his phone. Right?

"Oscar Dalby Contracting."

Shit. Sweat broke out across Faith's palms as shame rose to choke her.

"Hello?"

Faith cleared her throat. "Oscar?"

"Yes? Who's calling, please?"

"This is Faith. Faith Kincaid."

A pause. At first, Faith feared he had hung up. "Faith. It's been a long time. And…I was real sorry to hear about your mom."

"Thank you." Faith tried to speak the words, but they came out a whisper.

"So…what can I do for you?"

Faith swallowed hard. "Before I say anything else, I need to apologize. For how I treated you back when you were dating her."

Another long silence. "I appreciate that," he said. "But you were young and hurting. I understood that."

"You were always kind to me," she said. "Even when I didn't deserve it."

"Everyone deserves kindness, kiddo." Then, he laughed. "Though you're not a kiddo anymore, are you?"

"Not so much," Faith murmured. "But I know you're right."

"Well, listen," he said. "I appreciate your call. It's good to hear from you. And if there's ever anything I can do to help, just say the word."

"About that," Faith said. "Do you happen to have the bandwidth for another job in the near future?"

By the time she reached the airport, she had made a plan to meet with Oscar after her official return from the opening events of *Fish Out of Water*. On the plane, Faith put headphones in, curled up against the window, and tried to sleep. When insidious doubt crept into the corners of her mind, yanking her out of a fitful doze, she connected her headphones to the tiny screen and watched romantic comedies for the remainder of the trip. She landed, feeling grimy and exhausted, shortly after sunrise. The recent rain had given way to a beautiful autumnal day, and as her ride left the airport's barren parking lots, she soaked in the colors of the changing trees.

She had given the driver Del's address, but as they approached her driveway, she saw Maddie's car parked in the space. Fear sluiced down her spine, chilling her into alertness.

"Drive past," she exclaimed, then added a belated, "please."

As the car slowly passed Del's driveway, she saw that Maddie was, in fact, standing outside the door. Del, standing in the doorway, was talking with her. Hope leapt like flames, beating back her despair. Del wasn't letting her in.

"Good," Faith muttered fiercely.

"Where do you want me to stop?" asked the driver.

Faith had him drive to the next intersecting street. Then, she walked back toward Del's house, dragging her roller bag in her wake. As she approached Del's neighbor, she took stock of their darkened windows and empty driveway. Best yet, they had tall shrubberies separating part of their front yard from Del's.

"What even is my life right now?" Faith whispered to herself just before making the decision to hide behind the shrubberies. Surreptitiously, she peered through the leaves until she found a decent line-of-sight angle to Del's front door. Maddie was still there, but she was frowning. And Del appeared to be gesticulating, though with only one hand because she was cradling Buffy in the crook of her other arm. The sight gave Faith a welcome rush of confidence.

Ignoring the fatigue behind her eyes, she settled in to wait.

"Why are you throwing this away, Del?"

This was approximately the twentieth time Maddie had voiced the same sentiment over the past twenty-four hours, and Del was beyond tired of it. She had met Maddie for coffee yesterday morning, as promised. She had listened to Maddie's apologies, to Maddie's vision for what their life could be together, to Maddie's cajoling, wheedling pleas. Once, they were all she had ever wanted. Now, she only felt a dull regret beneath the sharp certainty that the two of them could never, would never, work.

"I'm not throwing this away, Maddie. You threw it away when you cheated. And then, you threw it away *again* when you didn't so much as look my way for months."

"But—"

"Now," Del said, refusing to be interrupted yet again, "you appear out of the woodwork saying you want to try again. You've barely apologized, and you're refusing to take no for an answer."

"But—"

"Why would I want to be with someone who refuses to take no for an answer?" Del wrapped both arms around Buffy. "I said no yesterday. I'm saying no today. We are finished. Good-bye."

Del stepped back inside the townhouse, shut the door, and locked it. Then, she leaned against it and buried her face in Buffy's fur. After several long moments of breathing in the aroma of dog, she set Buffy on the floor and returned to the kitchen. Maddie had ambushed her before she'd had more than a few sips of coffee, and Del took a long swig now.

The doorbell rang.

Del felt her tenuous grip on equanimity disappear. Irritation surged, fueled by the deep well of anger that had opened inside her when Maddie had cheated; that had grown deeper and broader with each subsequent failure of respect. She inhaled as she opened the door, intent on delivering a scathing lecture about boundaries and consent.

Only to feel her jaw drop.

Faith stood before her, rolling suitcase in hand. She looked surprisingly fragile: pale, with dark smudges beneath her eyes. Buffy, who had come to investigate, charged out the door. Faith dropped her bags and knelt on the dewy flagstones, petting Buffy gently as the dog whined and barked and nuzzled her palms.

"You really did miss me," Faith murmured, and there was real awe in her voice. It was a reminder, Del realized, that Faith still struggled with issues of self-worth.

"Of course she did," Del said. "You're her person."

Faith scooped Buffy into her arms and stood. Her gaze was shadowed. "When my car pulled up, Maddie was at your door."

She didn't sound happy about that. Why? Was it because Faith was a friend who didn't want Del to return to a problematic relationship? Or was it because Faith was jealous? The surge of hope was dizzying, and she surreptitiously clutched at the doorjamb to steady herself.

"She wouldn't take no for an answer," Del managed to say.

"What was the question?"

"She wants us to get back together."

Faith cocked her head. "And you refused?"

"I did." Del took a deep breath, willing the tightness in her chest to ease. "This past week has made me realize that I was holding on to the past because of inertia and fear. Not because it was actually good." She exhaled sharply. "That became abundantly clear when Maddie practically bullied me."

Faith took one step forward. "Practically?" Her gaze was intense. "Showing up at your door after you already said no doesn't feel like *practically*."

"You're right. And I know I should have seen her true colors earlier."

Faith's nostrils flared. "That sounds like you're still blaming yourself." The words were quiet, but they held an edge.

Irritation surged. "*You're* telling *me* not to self-flagellate?"

The crackling energy around Faith abruptly deflated. "Touché."

Del sighed. "Sorry. That came out harsher than I intended." She rubbed at the back of her neck. "I'm not at my level-headed best right now. It's been a morning."

"No, it's fine. You're not wrong." Faith squared her shoulders. "Is it okay if I come in? You asked yesterday why I left the event, and I want to tell you."

"Of course." Curiosity needled Del as she stepped aside, clearing a path to the foyer.

Faith crossed the threshold, then leaned her suitcase against the wall and gently deposited Buffy on the floor. When she straightened, that air of vulnerability was back. Del gestured for her to follow, then led her to the couch. When she settled on one end, Faith chose the opposite. Buffy immediately jumped into her lap and curled up there.

"You don't have to tell me if you don't want to," Del said.

"No, I do." Faith looked away, running one hand through her hair. Her other hand was rhythmically stroking Buffy's flank. "Telling you is literally the reason I left."

Del felt her heartbeat accelerate again as hope flamed higher. She managed to croak out an "Oh?" between suddenly dry lips.

When Faith turned back, her eyes were bright. Del watched her throat convulse as she swallowed. The fingers stroking Buffy trembled slightly. "I'm falling in love with you," Faith said.

Having anticipated this possibility did nothing to minimize Del's surprise. She felt her mouth fall open. Was it really possible? Faith was developing feelings—*real* feelings—for her?

"It started a while ago," Faith continued. "I'm not sure exactly when. The farmer's market, maybe?" She licked her lips. "Anyway…I finally realized yesterday what I was feeling."

"You ran out of the fancy party and flew back across the country to tell me this?"

Faith's shoulders slumped a little. "I know it was a crazy thing to do. It's just that…" She laughed, though the sound was without humor. "On my way to the airport to go to LA, the whole time I was in the air, sitting alone in that hotel room…no matter where I was, I couldn't stop thinking about you. And…and whether Maddie was going to convince you to get back together. When I realized just how much the idea bothered me, I had to confront the truth. Then, every move I made at the event reminded me of you in some way, every question I was asked, every answer I gave."

Del was starting to feel dizzy again. Belatedly, she realized she was holding her breath. She watched as Faith bent over Buffy, adjusting her position before meeting Del's gaze again.

"I don't mean to put any pressure on you," Faith said. Her fingertips picked at a stray thread on the nearest throw pillow. "This doesn't change anything. I just…I needed to tell you. Selfish, I know."

"Faith."

But either Faith didn't hear, or the sound of her name didn't register. "I promise, things won't get weird, and after the wedding, we can figure out how to break—"

"*Faith.*"

Finally, Faith clamped her lips together. She sat there, staring across the expanse of the couch, beautiful and exhausted and uncertain. After working so hard to make it on to *Fish Out of Water*, Faith had abandoned the pre-broadcast event. She had jumped on the next available flight, a red-eye, just to say those words. The surrealism of it all was overwhelming. But there weren't any cameras or crew to worry about right now. This wasn't scripted or planned or orchestrated to placate a reality show. This was reality itself.

Faith had feelings. *Real* feelings. And she wasn't alone.

"I'm falling for you, too." Del found herself smiling. She hadn't realized just how liberating it would be to speak the words aloud.

But Faith wasn't smiling back. She was blinking in clear disbelief. "Are…are you sure?" She cleared her throat. "I mean, look at you. You're kind and generous and beautiful and…and just *good.* So, so good. You do so much *good* for people. And I…I'm a mess. Working on it, sure, but still very much a mess."

Del scooted over on the couch until there was barely an inch of space between her thigh and Faith's. When Buffy raised her head, Del reached to stroke her ears. Exuberance bubbled up inside her—Faith had *real* feelings!—but it was tempered by Faith's uncertainty.

"Until very recently, I was hung up on a woman who—let's be honest—is toxic. Without you, I'm not sure I would have realized that."

"Really?" Faith's voice was small.

Del nodded. "And when I look at you, I don't see a mess. I see strength and resilience. I see an attractive face and stunning body but also a beautiful soul. I know you're working hard on yourself, and I respect you so much for that. But the core of you—the part of you that was drawn to adopting Buffy—that part doesn't need any work at all."

Faith stared, and Del waited for the words to sink in. She could tell when they finally did because the corners of Faith's mouth relaxed into a slight smile, and she shifted just enough to close the gap between their legs. Even that slight physical contact made Del shiver. She was struck by the fact that she didn't have to hold back, that she didn't have to raise shields against her own emotions. The realization was heady.

"I'd like to kiss you," Del said. "Is that what you want?"

"Yes," Faith whispered, and it was the sweetest word.

Del cupped her cheek, then leaned in slowly. Just before she was too close to see anything, Faith's eyes fluttered shut. Del kissed her as gently as she could, brushing Faith's lips with her own in a slow, gradual slide. Then, she pressed more firmly, finally allowing herself to relish the ways in which their mouths fit together. Faith followed her lead—something she had never done before—but there was no question of her responsiveness. When Del dared to flick her tongue against Faith's bottom lip, the breathy moan that greeted her sent heat pooling deep in her abdomen.

Only when Buffy squirmed against her stomach did Del realize she was lying partially on top of Faith, pressing her back into the couch cushion. Del shifted slightly, giving Buffy more room.

"Don't crush my dog," Faith murmured.

"Never," Del agreed and went back to kissing her.

Eventually, Faith squirmed enough that Buffy jumped down. Immediately, Del swung her leg all the way over, bracketing Faith's body with her knees. She combed her fingers through Faith's hair and kissed her harder. Faith's mouth was moving against hers, hot and soft and slow. Del pressed closer, instinctively trying to ease the ache between her legs. When she realized what her body was doing, she pulled back in a blaze of embarrassment.

"Sorry."

Faith looked up at her through hazy eyes. "What's wrong?"

"I was…practically humping you, there. Channeling Cronk the bulldog."

Del had only heard Faith's unrestrained laugh on a few other occasions. Silently, she promised to make sure Faith laughed that way much more frequently.

"Did it seem like I minded?"

"I don't know," Del said truthfully. "I got carried away."

"I like you carried away." Faith slid her fingers through Del's hair.

Del wanted to suggest they go upstairs. Instead, she said, "You must be so tired. Do you want me to drive you home so you can go to bed?"

When Faith arched one eyebrow, Del felt the power dynamic between them start to shift in the most delicious sort of way. "What if we go to bed here instead?" Then, Faith's nose wrinkled. "Though I need a shower first."

"If that's really what you want," Del said, and her voice quivered slightly, "I'll get you a towel."

"*You* are what I really want." Faith surged up to kiss her, and then Del was being pulled down, Faith's fingers lacing behind her neck. This was a kiss filled with fire, and yet behind the passion was real emotion. *Shared* emotion.

Faith's hands were moving, sliding along Del's shoulders and down the length of her back to cup her waist. She brought one thigh up, then pulled Del against it, and the friction between her legs made Del moan into her mouth.

Faith tore her lips away, gasping. "Upstairs."

Del stood on unsteady legs, then helped Faith up. She ascended the stairs as quickly as she could, thrilling to the sensation of Faith behind her. After grabbing a towel from the linen closet, she ushered Faith into the bedroom. Then, she closed the door before Buffy could slip inside, murmuring a quick apology.

"Do you want me to bring up your suitcase?"

Faith cocked her head, a slow smile spreading across her face. "Do I need clothes after I shower?"

Del's powers of speech temporarily abandoned her. All she could do was shake her head. Faith took the towel from her outstretched hand, then leaned in for a surprisingly chaste kiss on one cheek.

"See you soon."

Once Faith was in the bathroom, Del tidied up the bedroom in a flurry of activity. She bent down to sniff the sheets—she had changed them yesterday but was compelled to check—and, finding them still fresh-smelling, began to pace the width of the space. The shower sounded like the memory of warm summer rain. Del imagined Faith standing beneath the spray, water painting rivulets along her skin. Another rush of heat swept through her body, settling between her legs. Should she get undressed? Faith was going to be naked, but—

The shower turned off. Paralyzed by indecision, Del stood in the middle of the room. When Faith emerged wearing only the towel, Del reached for the dresser to steady herself. Then, Faith undid the loose knot that kept the towel wrapped around her body, and Del couldn't hold back a gasp.

Faith was perfection. That was the only word that fit. Her full breasts were tipped by dark pink nipples that made Del's mouth water. Her abdomen was a study in muscle, and Del found herself wanting nothing more than to trace the firm bands with her tongue, following them down, down until she reached the apex of Faith's thighs. A patch of neatly trimmed dark hair waited there, rosy lips peeking through to tempt Del's gaze. Faith's long legs looked as though a sculptor had chiseled them to portray an exemplar of female strength.

"I like the way you look at me," Faith murmured.

Blinking hard, Del focused on Faith's face. She knew she was blushing, but what was the point of embarrassment now? "You're gorgeous. So incredibly gorgeous."

Faith walked toward her slowly. "Let me undress you?"

Del nodded. She was wearing only a flannel shirt, and as Faith undid each button, her fingertips caressed the skin beneath. When Faith leaned closer, trailing hot kisses along the path her fingers had taken, Del couldn't suppress a whimper. By the time Faith pulled the shirt over her shoulders and let it fall to the ground, Del feared she was in real danger of combustion.

"Beautiful," Faith whispered. She stepped close, and the sensation of her breasts pressing against Del's was like sunbaked silk. When Del gasped, Faith slid her tongue deep inside Del's mouth. She ran her fingertips up along the contours of Del's back, caressing her inside and out. Faith was touching Del, kissing Del, as though she wanted both to devour and cherish her. Never before had anyone *claimed* her like this, Del realized through the haze of sensation. And she loved it. God, how she loved it.

Slowly, Faith gentled the kiss, then finally pulled away. She knelt before Del, hooking fingers into the waistband of her sweats. When she looked up, clearly seeking permission, Del nodded. She couldn't speak; she could barely breathe. Faith drew her pants and underwear down in the same smooth, slow movement until they reached the ground. Del stepped out of them carefully, mindful of the wobble in her legs.

"Let's lie down," Faith whispered, gently steering Del back until her thighs touched the mattress.

Then, Del was falling, and Faith was falling with her, and Faith's damp hair was a curtain around their faces as they kissed. Faith's body was hot and strong above her, and Del's head spun as Faith's nipples stroked across her breasts, as Faith's thigh pressed between her legs. Faith raised her head, and the heat of her gaze was a goad to Del's pleasure. Faith *wanted* her, and she could tell. The knowledge was beyond heady.

"I need to touch you, Del," Faith said hoarsely.

"Yes." Del whispered the word, hot and urgent. "Yes, please, yes."

With a groan, Faith bent to kiss Del's throat, her neck, her breasts. When she twined her tongue around one nipple Del felt the sensation between her legs, as though her nerves had become a network of live wires. Faith hummed in satisfaction, and all the while, one hand was tracing the ridges of Del's rib cage, the expanse of her belly. Del's insecurity flared—surely, Faith was used to touching bodies as perfect as her own? But even as the thought crossed her mind, Faith raised her head. Her eyes were dark, her lips taut. By now, Del knew her well enough to sense when she was pretending. She wasn't.

"I want you so much," Faith whispered, combing her fingertips through the coarse hair at the base of Del's abdomen. "So much."

The heat in her words burned away Del's fear. "Please," she said, and then Faith's fingers were dipping into her folds, skimming and tracing in a leisurely way that let Del know just how much Faith was enjoying her exploration. Two fingers slid slowly along the edges of her clit, and Del moaned, feeling herself grow even wetter.

Faith traced circles around her entrance, gathering moisture before continuing her exploration. Propping her head on one hand, she watched Del's face as she touched her—stroking with careful precision, paying attention to where she gave the most pleasure. The intimacy of her attention was breathtaking. Del's eyes wanted to close, and yet she pried them open, not wanting to lose sight of Faith's expression, almost fierce in its intensity. Then, finally, Faith made her touch firmer, and Del cried out as ecstasy coalesced inside her. She blinked hard, trying to stay focused on Faith, only to be caught up in the exquisite storm of sensation. Del cried out again, calling Faith's name, and then she was convulsing in the grip of the maelstrom as light and heat roared through her.

When Del finally came back to herself, she was lying on her back, Faith tucked along one side. Gentle fingers were caressing her abdomen, and soft lips were pressing kisses against her shoulder.

"Hi," Faith said softly.

"Hi," Del croaked. "You're amazing."

Faith smiled against her skin. "Watching you come apart for me was incredibly sexy. When can I do it again?"

"Soon," Del said. "But not yet."

She turned onto her side, subtly testing her own mettle. Much of her body still felt like gelatin, but her hands were rapidly regaining strength. And what she craved most of all relied on a different muscle entirely. She propped herself up on one elbow and reached out to trace Faith's jawline.

"I have this urge," she whispered. "To taste you."

Faith's eyes went dark again, the pupils swallowing the irises like a time-lapse eclipse, and a low whimper emerged from the back of her throat.

"Is that a yes?"

"Yes," Faith gasped, turning onto her back at Del's gentle encouragement.

Del slid one leg slowly over Faith's body, enjoying the harsh sound of her sucking in a breath as Del's wetness smeared across her abdomen.

"You did that to me," Del whispered, settling on top of her.

In the brief moments when Del had allowed herself to imagine them touching *for real*, she had always imagined feeling intimidated by Faith's experience. Now that it was happening, she felt only tenderness. Del kissed across her sternum, then down along the slope of one breast, smiling as Faith's hips twitched beneath her. She lingered on Faith's breasts, sucking gently at one nipple while rolling the other between thumb and forefinger. The movement of Faith's hips became more pronounced, and her head shifted restlessly against the pillow. Chin resting between Faith's breasts, Del paused for a moment, taking a mental snapshot. Then, gradually, she eased her way down, mouthing at the crests of Faith's ribs, tonguing at the troughs. By the time she reached Faith's stomach, her occasional moans had become near-constant gasps.

"You taste so good already," Del murmured. "I can't wait for what's next."

"Fuck," Faith groaned, and then Del's tongue was sliding down the rope of muscle along the side of her abdomen.

Del wanted to tease, but Faith's scent was so intoxicating that she couldn't muster the patience. Gently, she pressed Faith's legs apart, making room for her shoulders. Then, she brought her thumbs to Faith's labia, spreading her open with exquisite gentleness. The maze of her was a study in shades of crimson, and Del's mouth watered in anticipation. Faith's thighs twitched as Del blew a warm breath across her clit. When Del finally kissed it, Faith exhaled sharply.

Teasing them both, Del pulled away and licked at Faith's opening, dipping just inside. When Faith made a sound that was close to a sob, she pushed deeper, fluttering her tongue. Faith's internal muscles clenched, and the musky tang of her grew more pronounced. When Del groaned softly, Faith shuddered. Beneath Del's palms, the muscles in her thighs were quivering. Exhilarated, Del forced herself to go slowly. She licked her way up, thoroughly tracing the contours of Faith's sex until she was tormenting the head of her clit with the very tip of her tongue.

Incoherent sounds punctuated by guttural curses spilled from Faith's mouth. Delighted by her abandon, Del finally hollowed her lips and sucked, first lightly, then with delicious ferocity. Faith's entire body trembled violently, and then she was shuddering in the grip of orgasm, her opening contracting against Del's chin. She came for a long time, and Del exulted in each aftershock, prolonging them as much as she could.

When Faith's body finally went limp, Del kissed her clit one last time before sliding up to stroke her sweat-matted hair back from her forehead. Awe filled Del as she watched Faith slowly recover. She had only been with two other women, but neither had ever responded to her with such passion. The experience was intoxicating. She wanted to do it again. Every day.

"I think," Faith finally whispered, "you catapulted me into a different dimension."

"Oh?" Del could feel her smile growing wider. "And which dimension is that?"

Faith shook her head slightly. "Don't know its name. But it was good. A very good dimension."

Del laughed and kissed Faith's nose. "That's all right, then." She pulled the blankets up around them. "You're so tired. Sleep now, okay?"

But Faith opened her eyes, blinking heavily. "Want you again."

Del kissed her lips gently. "Me, too. But first, you need to rest."

Faith frowned. "Stay with me?"

Sliding one arm under Faith's neck, Del settled onto her back. Faith curled toward her, splaying one leg across Del's thighs. Within moments, Faith's breaths grew deep and even. Softly, Del kissed her forehead.

"There's nowhere I'd rather be."

❖

Faith woke to the smell of dog and the sensation of a rough tongue against her cheek. Buffy. Gently pushing her away, Faith struggled to sit up. At the pleasant ache in her stomach muscles, she remembered Del between her legs, strong hands clamped around her thighs, looking up at her in fierce concentration. She remembered her body convulsing repeatedly, caught in the grip of the strongest orgasm she had ever experienced.

Blinking hard in the light streaming through the curtains, Faith turned to her left. Del was asleep beside her, dark hair fanned out across the pillows. Her skin, illuminated by the sunbeams, was striking against the white sheets, and for several minutes, Faith was content to watch her. Then, nature's demands intervened. She slipped slowly from the bed, taking pride when Del remained asleep.

After using the bathroom, Faith pulled on Del's flannel shirt and padded downstairs, Buffy's nails clicking on the stairs as the dog shadowed her. Faith had kept her phone in airplane mode on the way back from the airport, not wanting to deal with the shitstorm she had precipitated. As soon as she reconnected to the internet, the messages came flooding in.

She sifted through them quickly before placing two calls, the first to Jolie and the second to Sharon. While she listened to each berate her, she grabbed a pair of shorts out of her bag, let Buffy out, and started a pot of coffee. The absence of a pour-over set only intensified her desire to have Del move in to her place. Still, that was probably a step they should wait on. For a little while, at least.

Del came into the kitchen just as she was apologizing to Sharon for what felt like the thousandth time. After pouring two mugs of coffee, Del slid her arms around Faith's waist and pulled her close. Faith leaned against her, enjoying the sensation of being held. Thankfully, the conversation ended shortly thereafter. With a sigh, Faith put down the phone.

"Hi," Del said.

"Hi." Faith turned in the circle of her arms, then leaned in for a kiss. "Mmm. You still taste like me. I like it."

"Me, too," Del said. "And you look good in my shirt." She gestured at the phone. "What's the word?"

"Fortunately, the producers are willing to go along with my plan to spin this little impromptu trip in a way that will help everyone."

"Oh?"

"You and I got into a fight before I left, and I flew home to apologize."

Del nodded. "That's good. I'm sure they love the drama."

"I realize I promised *no* drama." Faith watched Del closely. "I'm sorry I didn't run the idea by you first."

"I understand why you didn't. And besides, this isn't exactly the kind of drama we discussed avoiding." Del handed her a cup of coffee. "But from now on, we'll make decisions together, yes?"

"Yes," Faith said. She laughed as Buffy squeezed her way between them, tail wagging. "Oh, yes."

She bent and picked up Buffy, cradling her close. As the dog licked her neck, Del's arms came around her. Faith luxuriated in the sensation of holding and being held. Of family. The thought should have been frightening, but it wasn't.

"Adopting you was the best choice I ever made," she said to Buffy. And then, looking past her to Del, Faith sealed the words with a kiss.

FORCE OF NATURE

Missouri Vaun

Chapter One

The coffeehouse was buzzing with activity when Rebekah Hawks angled toward the door. The crowd inside spilled out to an orderly array of small café tables next to the sidewalk. This coffee spot was across the street from Riverwalk Park, so every seat had a great view of the water.

A light fog rose from the channel, as if the river itself had exhaled into the cool air. But that would be gone within the hour as the temperature warmed. The weather all week had been cool in the morning but warm by noon. This early autumn transition was Rebekah's favorite.

Living only a few blocks from the River Arts District meant she got to do her morning runs along the waterway every day. Splashes of bright autumn color reflected back from the water like a mirrored color wheel. Sure, there were more tourists in this part of the city, but that also meant there were more restaurants, bars, and shops. The river district was like a unique little village within the larger urban area of Fairview.

This was one of those mornings when she was glad she'd decided to cut her hair. Short hair was so much easier to deal with. The permanent lash extensions had also greatly shortened her morning routine. Rebekah hated to mess around with mascara in the morning. All she had to do now was add a little red lipstick and liquid liner, and she was out the door. Her father had always joked that she operated at the speed of a hummingbird. Maybe he was right. And maybe that was also why she really needed her morning boost of caffeine. She sometimes even preferred coffee to breakfast.

Getting a seat at the café would be a challenge this morning. Luckily, the line moved fairly quickly, so she didn't have to wait long.

"Getting your usual?" Gary smiled at her from behind the counter. He was a cute twentysomething, tall and lean, with dark hair and the beginnings of a beard. She came to this café often enough to know most of the baristas by name.

"I love that you always remember." She was playfully flirtatious. "It makes me feel special."

"You are special."

"Keep it up…you'll go far in this world." After paying, she dropped a generous tip in the glass jar near the register.

In another few moments, she was able to claim her chai latte with a shot of espresso. An energy jolt in a cup with a scone chaser. She scanned the room to see if any tables had opened up while she'd been waiting. She'd hoped to be able to sit and scan the news on her phone while she enjoyed her coffee, but that wouldn't work so well without an actual seat.

A familiar face came into focus.

Maggie Lawrence was sitting at a table for two by herself near the windows. Rebekah thought of her as a friend, but she was more of a professional acquaintance. Rebekah wasn't certain they'd ever spent time together apart from business or community events. But still, she knew Maggie well enough to share a table.

Maggie was probably ten years older, but she wore her age very well. She had straight dark hair that was just long enough to brush her shoulders. She was dressed in casual business attire, a white silk blouse and dark dress pants, as if she'd just come from a meeting. She tucked an errant strand of hair behind her ear absently.

Rebekah wove between tightly packed tables and presented herself in Maggie's line of vision. She was reading something on her phone so she didn't seem to see Rebekah until she was next to the table.

"Hi, Maggie, what a nice surprise to see you in my neighborhood."

"Rebekah…hello." Maggie smiled. "Please, join me." She shuffled a file folder of papers to one side to clear a spot.

"Thank you. This place is really packed today." Rebekah glanced around the crowded space before taking a seat.

"You look great. You make athleisure look sexy. How do you do it? I end up looking like a soccer mom no matter what I wear or how much Pilates I do." She was probably just feeling overworked and underappreciated, like most working moms. Maggie Lawrence was an attractive woman by any standard.

"Hey, don't shortchange yourself. You look great. I've seen soccer moms lately, and they could take tips from you…sexy." She wagged her finger in Maggie's direction in a sassy fashion.

"Hahaha. You're great for my ego. Maybe you should say that where my husband can overhear it."

They both laughed.

"*So*…do you come here often?" Rebekah quirked her eyebrows, her question playful.

Maggie smiled at the joke. "Actually, I don't, and I'm not sure why. This is such a fun area of town." She sipped her coffee. "I was at the arts center trying to talk their board into hosting a fundraising event. They turned me down."

"Oh, really, that's too bad." Rebekah nibbled her scone. "What's going on at the shelter?" She didn't want to say that Maggie looked tired. No woman wanted to hear that, even if it was true. But Maggie definitely had an air of stress around her.

"You know the most recent hurricane?"

"Yes." She didn't know details, but she'd seen it in her newsfeed. Fairview was a safe distance from hurricane zones, so the worst they had to worry about was spin-off storms. They'd had rain and a little wind but nothing too serious.

"I try my best to budget for these seasonal influxes of rescue animals, but the hurricane seasons are becoming longer and more intense." Maggie paused, her expression serious. "It's put the shelter under a bit of a strain. The short version is, we need money." She took a few swigs of coffee. "I'm afraid that I'm completely out of new ideas. Especially since today was a bust. Do you know anyone who might be available to help me put together a fundraiser?"

"Yeah, me."

"Seriously?" Maggie's expression brightened. She had the look of someone who spent more time helping others than herself. The notion that someone might actually come to her aid seemed to be a pleasant surprise.

"Yes, really. I'm between jobs, and I don't start my next position for six weeks. And frankly, I'm not doing so well with downtime."

Rebekah liked to be busy. She loved to have a problem to solve. She found it nearly impossible to sit still. Stillness made her mind spin with too many thoughts, and after the thoughts came the feelings. Suffice it to say, she preferred to be distracted with work.

Months ago, when she'd first planned for this transition, she and her girlfriend were going to use the weeks of free time to do some traveling. But an oversexed yoga instructor had derailed that plan. Her *girlfriend* was now her *ex*-girlfriend, and as far as Rebekah knew, was on a trip in Italy with her new plus-one. Rebekah had moved past the anger phase a few weeks ago, finally. Getting dumped right before the epic vacation trip was just icing on the breakup cake.

In moments of clarity, she rationalized that it was all for the best. At least, that was what she told herself during brief times of self-doubt. Things had been tense between them for months; Rebekah had simply been in denial about it. And besides, who wanted to have to start dating again? Dating was hard—miserable, in fact—which was why she was single at the moment.

"Honestly, Maggie, I could use a project." She'd been told by her ex that she was terrible at not being busy. So what? What was so great about downtime?

"Rebekah, thank you so much. I would love to have your expertise." Maggie scrunched her eyebrows and leaned forward. "I don't have a huge budget to pay you—"

"Please, don't worry about that." Rebekah waved her off. She had savings and was getting a raise and a signing bonus when she started the new job. Anything Maggie could pay her as a freelancer would just be extra cushion for some future vacation.

"Oh, I should run." Maggie checked her phone and began to gather her purse and papers. "Will you come by the shelter so that I can show you around, and we could talk more?" She hesitated. "I don't mean to seem desperate, but I sort of am."

"Don't worry. I'm happy to dive right in. I'm free this afternoon. Is that too soon?"

"My desperation says the sooner the better."

Rebekah laughed. "Perfect."

"I'll see you soon." Maggie smiled warmly.

❖

Two hours later, Rebekah parked along the circular drive in front of the Lonely Hearts Rescue. The entrance was two-storied, with windows extending up from the glass double doors. The main entrance opened into an atrium with exposed beams and lots of light. This building was fairly new. The shelter had reopened in this new building a decade ago, and the newness hadn't worn off yet.

When Rebekah first walked through the front doors, she took a moment to survey the space. There was a small sitting area to the left with a couple of love seats and chairs and a coffee table. To the right of the entrance was a small gift shop and pet supply store. They didn't seem to have bulk food items or lots of inventory. This was the sort of shop where one could purchase leashes and halters and beds: typical "new pet owner" items. A sign near the register told her that a percentage of the proceeds supported the shelter. Maggie was smart to have a small retail space on-site with a built-in consumer base.

Along each side of the great hall were windows where visitors could view dogs, cats, and even rabbits. When she looked more closely, she realized there were even a few guinea pigs up for adoption.

Dogs were on the right as she traversed the main room; cats and other small animals were on the left. It looked like there were other rooms behind the main viewing spaces where people could probably meet animals to see if they were a good match. She caught a glimpse of a young boy and his mom in one of the rooms with a rambunctious dog of the mutt variety. The jovial canine jumped up and almost knocked the kid down. He laughed and hugged the fluffy dog. Rebekah was no expert, but that seemed like a good match.

"Can I help you with something?" a woman behind the reception counter asked.

She'd probably lingered too long. She had felt the woman's eyes follow her as she'd moved around the main entrance area. She was near enough now to read the name tag that read *Karri*. She had shoulder-length brown hair, an easy smile, and a pleasant demeanor. The perfect sort of person to manage the front desk and greet visitors.

"Hi, Karri. I'm Rebekah, and I'm here to see Maggie Lawrence."

"Is she expecting you?"

"She is." Rebekah shifted her weight from foot to foot. She sometimes had a difficult time just *standing* still.

"If you'd like to take a seat, I'll let her know you are here."

"Thank you." But instead of sitting, she paced near the desk. She turned quickly on her heels and right into oncoming pedestrian traffic. "Oh!" Her hands were on the arms of the person she'd run into. She'd had to brace herself so that she didn't topple off her four-inch heels. "I'm so sorry."

She took a step back, but the stranger held on, possibly because she appeared unstable on her feet. How embarrassing but at the same time, a happy accident to bump into such an attractive stranger. Before she could regroup and introduce herself, she heard a familiar voice behind her.

"Rebekah, thank you for coming on such short notice." Maggie appeared from the hallway near the back of the reception desk. "Oh, and I see you've met Rory."

"Well, not officially." Rory smiled.

"Rebekah Hawks, meet Rory MacClaren," Maggie said. "Rory is one of our top dog trainers here at the shelter." She paused. "And this is Karri. She keeps things out front running smoothly for all of us."

"It's very nice to meet you both." Rebekah said *both*, but she was much more focused on Rory. She had regained most of her composure. She offered her hand to Karri first, then to Rory. This time, she clasped Rory's hand in greeting rather than in need of assistance.

Rory had short, thick, straight dark-auburn hair that was mostly slicked back, but a few strands fell casually over her eyes. She also had large, kind eyes almost the same color as her hair. Her clothing seemed to say *I'm a little quirky, and I shop at thrift stores*. She was wearing khaki cargo pants, a blazer, and a dark T-shirt with a plaid shirt over it.

"I'm sorry that I bumped into you a minute ago." Rory's smooth alto voice had an instantly calming effect.

"I'm pretty sure that was my fault." Rebekah shook her head. Flirtation was second nature to her, insignificant, and no guarantee to the listener of anything more than a pleasant exchange, but still, Rory seemed oddly oblivious to her charms, which almost felt like a challenge. Why did she care? Rory was definitely cute but not exactly her type. Besides, she was here to help Maggie, not meet women, even by accident.

"Shall I give you a quick tour?" Maggie asked.

"Absolutely." Rebekah gave a polite wave. "It was nice to meet you both."

❖

Rory stood for a few seconds, watching Rebekah and Maggie cross the length of the atrium. Who was Rebekah Hawks, and why was she here? She certainly wasn't on-site to work with animals. At least, that seemed like a safe assumption, based on her attire and choice of footwear.

Rebekah had platinum blond hair in a rather severe cut. As she walked away, Rory could see that it was shaved from ear to ear in back but from the front was longer and shiny blond on top with sleek bangs, parted at the side, that hung down to her eyebrows. She had an angular shaped face with a square jaw. They'd stood close long enough for Rory to notice the details. Rebekah had steely gray eyes with yellow flecks. She wore heels that made her almost as tall as Rory's five-foot-nine inches, with sleek, zippered, black, satin cigarette pants that accentuated her slender build, a sheer blouse, and a camisole underneath.

"Who *was* that?" Karri asked. They'd both been staring as Maggie and Rebekah walked away from the reception area.

"I really have no idea." Rory took a deep breath. "If you find out, let me know."

Rory walked toward the canine enclosures. She checked the paperwork in a clipboard that hung on the wall at the first room. Dillon, a three-month-old black lab puppy, was due for some basic training. She retrieved a leash and Dillon. They walked toward the nearest exit. His nails clicked on the linoleum floor as he practically danced and jumped his way to the door, trying to grab the leash with his mouth the entire time.

Behind the building were outdoor exercise pens and walking trails. Rory figured a walk would help calm Dillon a bit. She held the door for one of the volunteers returning from a walk with another of the hurricane rescues. The shelter had a supportive group of volunteers who assisted with pet care and dog walking. Volunteers really kept the whole place running smoothly, especially in times like this when the facility was literally at capacity.

Rory smiled at Dillon. She wanted him to feel safe. A puppy always had a choice of whether to interact with something in their surroundings. Rory's goal was to build confidence by rewarding the dog for making brave choices. This sort of socialization was essential while a puppy was in the early development phase, which ended at around twelve weeks. This guy had definitely been neglected in the training department. Improving his skills would help his eventual adoption be more successful.

As she led Dillon along the path, Rory couldn't help wondering if Rebekah Hawks was a pet owner of any kind. She highly doubted it.

❖

Forty-five minutes later, Rebekah emerged from the shelter in full brainstorming mode. After the tour with Maggie, she'd asked if she could just walk around a bit and think. She wanted to get a feel for the place and watch the staff at work.

As she exited, a woman was attempting to open the door with a kennel full of tiny puppies. Rebekah stepped through and held the door for her.

"Thank you."

"No problem." Rebekah smiled.

As she walked toward her car, she stopped to admire the sculpture she'd hardly noticed on the way in. There was a grassy area in the middle of the circular drive that featured a huge dog and cat sculpture made out of metal. The artist was Scott Allred. She'd met him at various art openings, but she hadn't seen him in a while. He was local and usually worked with found objects and scrap metal. The sculpture featured a cartoony-looking dog and cat seated side by side on a multicolored pedestal. The dog looked like a beagle, and the cat had orange stripes. She'd noticed the gift shop had images of the playful sculpture printed on T-shirts, calendars, and coffee mugs to raise money for the shelter. A drawing of the sculpture had become the shelter's unofficial logo. A playful way to let the community know that the shelter wasn't a scary place.

Something about the sculpture gave her an idea. Maybe it was the bright paint. Possibly it was the playful style.

She'd have to give this more thought and do a little sourcing and pricing of materials, but this idea might actually work. She climbed into her car feeling optimistic and energized.

Chapter Two

The next day, Rebekah was back at the shelter to present her plan. Maggie had gathered the manager, Derek Alvarez, and the Community Programs Director, Avery Hill. Derek had light brown skin and short dark hair. He was good-looking but seemed not to realize it. By contrast, Avery was fair-skinned, with blond hair cropped short so that it barely brushed the collar of her blouse. She had a very maternal vibe about her. She was full-figured and probably someone who doled out hugs on a regular basis.

Rebekah's basic concept was to get wooden doghouses donated from a couple of local vendors and then have a paint-athon by local artists in front of the shelter. Once finished, the doghouses would be sold at an auction. The promotion worked on multiple levels: Engaging well-known local artists raised visibility for the cause, and the more famous the artist, the more income they'd raise; press coverage would be a breeze, and extending the auction to online bidders would also increase the benefit's reach. An added bonus was that a bunch of lucky dogs would have newly painted houses to call home.

Avery was the first to speak. "I love this idea."

"I was able to get confirmation yesterday for donations of the doghouses. We'll have two size options." Rebekah was standing at the head of the table in the small conference room. When she was charged up about a project, it was hard to keep still. "Scott Allred has also agreed to paint one of the doghouses for auction. He'll do it ahead of time so that we can use his work to promote the fundraiser."

Derek nodded. "He's such a nice guy."

"I was thinking, you have the perfect staging area if we block off the circular drive out front and set up all the paint stations there. Then people will have a chance to watch the artists at work before the bidding begins."

"Are we only reaching out to professional artists?" asked Maggie.

"Good question. No, I think it would be great to involve kids in this project too." Rebekah rested her hands on her hips. "I reached out to the teen center in midtown. They have some graduates of their summer art program that they're going to send our way."

"This is very exciting." Maggie smiled. Rebekah's optimism seemed to be catching. "What's our time line?"

"Soon, right?" Avery glanced around the room. "I mean, the sooner the better."

"Yes, I know there's a sense of urgency about raising some funds." Rebekah took a deep breath. "I think we could pull this off in two weeks if we start promoting it now, like today. Scott is going to help me by reaching out to some of his contacts. That will definitely jump-start our list of stars." She paused. "If we're all in agreement, then I'll follow up with the vendors today and get the doghouses delivered. Derek, can I make you the primary contact for this since I'm not sure where these little houses should live until the event?"

"Sure, that works for me." He nodded. "I'll give you my cell number." He reached for a yellow notepad and scribbled his number.

"Rebekah, I can't thank you enough for spearheading this project." Maggie had hardly finished her sentence when someone knocked at the door.

"Hi, sorry to interrupt." Karri stuck her head in. "There's a problem with the cat playroom. Derek, can you come right away?"

"Sure." He was already on his feet.

Rebekah filed out of the room with Avery as Maggie headed back to her office. Maggie stopped before she reached her office door.

"Rebekah, please call me if you need anything or run into any snags."

"I will. Thanks, Maggie."

Avery and Rebekah rounded the corner from the hallway and turned toward the reception area. There seemed to be some sort of crisis at the front desk. A woman was in tears with a tiny dog on her arms.

Karri was trying to comfort her. "I'm so sorry, but don't worry, okay?"

"What's going on?" asked Avery.

"I had to bring him back. My landlord said absolutely no dogs." The young woman sniffed. "I feel so bad about this. I agreed to foster him, and now I can't. I feel terrible."

"Sometimes this happens, and it sounds like this was out of your control." Avery took the leash as the woman set the dog she'd been cradling on the floor. She nodded and wiped at tears as she turned to leave. She looked back once as she trudged toward the door, and then she was gone.

This was such a sad scene to witness. Rebekah felt bad for both the young woman and the dog. "What happens now?" She bent to pet the adorable, buff-colored dachshund. He had long silky hair, and the tag on his collar told her his name was Cotton.

"Well, he was one of the dogs we'd placed in a foster home while he waits for adoption into a more permanent situation." Avery explained. "With the most recent hurricane, we've literally run out of space, so we've had to place a few animals in foster care outside the shelter."

"Have you ever fostered a dog, Ms. Hawks? He really seems to like you." Karri rested her elbows on the counter as she smiled down at Rebekah.

"Me? Um, no." Rebekah stood quickly. She didn't want to give the impression that she was a dog person, which she wasn't. Was she?

"If you could take him, that would be amazing." Avery seemed to like the idea even though Rebekah was sure she hadn't agreed to anything.

Cotton looked up at her with big soulful eyes. Were those tears? Could dogs cry?

"I suppose I could help out as a temporary solution." She couldn't believe she was considering this, but Avery and Karri seemed so hopeful. Rebekah really hated to disappoint people. Plus, Cotton was seriously tugging at her heartstrings. How could she run a benefit for the shelter if she wasn't personally willing to at least foster one tiny dog? How much trouble could he be? Maybe small dogs were more like cats. Rebekah had a fleeting thought that possibly Cotton even knew how to use a litter box. She didn't actually have a litter box, but she could certainly get one.

"That's great news. Let me get one of the adoption coordinators, and she can help you fill out the paperwork." Avery reached across the counter for the phone and hit one of the internal extensions. "Ashley, can you come to the front desk? We need to get a new foster mom set up." Avery hung up and smiled. "Ashley is our adoption coordinator. She'll be right up to assist you and Cotton."

Rebekah had a sudden scared feeling that she had no idea what she was getting into.

An hour later, she was waddling toward her car with Cotton on a leash and an armload of supplies: a dog bed, food, and little green poop bags that she hoped never to use in public. Who knew fostering a dog was so complicated? She felt like she'd just filled out more paperwork than she'd had to do for her mortgage. Okay, that was a bit of an exaggeration, but still, in the interview, Ashley had asked about her house, her lifestyle, work schedule, family situation, and "potential pitfalls." Rebekah was beginning to feel like she was signing up for a dating service rather than as a dog sitter.

She had almost reached her car and was doing some mental gymnastics to figure out how she was possibly going to manage to get her keys out of her bag while juggling everything. She couldn't even see her purse for the plush dog bed she was hugging. She half spun in an attempt to reach for her keys and probably looked like a dog chasing her tail. The more she stretched for her keys, the farther they seemed to move away from her.

Cotton jerked the leash, heading in the opposite direction of her spin. She'd purchased one of those retractable leashes and now realized that had been a terrible miscalculation.

The dog trainer she'd met the previous day, Rory, appeared in her line of sight at the same moment that Cotton circled Rory's legs and doubled back. Rory became entwined with the leash, which also tightened around Rebekah's legs at about the same moment she toppled into Rory, again, dog bed and all.

"I'm so sorry!" Rebekah couldn't reel Cotton in. Apparently, the retractable part of the leash didn't work exactly as she'd anticipated. It was impossible to reel in.

"Hang on." Rory kept her from falling. "Let me hold the dog bed."

Rory started to laugh. “Or maybe I should assist you by taming this wild beast.”

“Would you? His name is Cotton.” Rebekah could not believe that she’d literally bumped into Rory for the second time. “I’m fairly certain now that I bought the wrong leash.”

“Yeah, you might want to start with a standard six-foot lead until you two understand each other.”

Rory tucked the dog bed under her arm and slowly traced the route of the leash until she could hold Cotton’s collar. “Okay, I’m going to unclip it. You should hold the button down so it doesn’t retract too quickly and hit you in the knuckles.” Rory motioned with her hand.

The cord of the leash shot back in Rebekah’s direction. At the last second, she squeezed the button near the handle, sparing her freshly manicured nails. “I see what you mean.” She exhaled loudly. “This thing should come with an owner’s manual.”

Rory held her free hand out for the leash, which she reattached to Cotton but without a Rory-Rebekah sandwich in the middle. Rebekah hated to appear as if she wasn’t in control of any situation. She’d been fostering this little pup for less than ten minutes, and she’d already almost face-planted in the parking lot and taken out one of the shelter’s trainers in the process.

Could this day just be over already? She still had vendor calls to make and emails to send.

“Let me help you get to your car.” Rory’s offer signaled nothing but kindness; still, Rebekah was feeling completely inept.

Rory hadn’t expected to see Rebekah again and was even more surprised to see that she was leaving the shelter with a dog. Rory trusted the adoption process. Surely, they wouldn’t allow Cotton to leave with Rebekah if the staff didn’t think she could handle it, but Rory had her doubts. Rebekah definitely seemed flustered and a bit unbalanced by the spill she’d nearly taken just now. Purchasing a retractable leash was a typical rookie mistake. New dog owners thought of the dog’s freedom to roam rather than their limited ability to control the animal. Especially until the animal was trained to respond to verbal commands or hand signals.

She maintained her grip on Cotton while Rebekah unlocked her car.

"Shall I toss this in the passenger seat for the dog?" Rory held up the dog bed as she asked.

"Thank you. That would be great." Rebekah swept her fingers through her hair and then propped her hands on her hips. She was standing in the open car door, watching.

"You'll get the hang of it." She closed the passenger door and smiled. "If you'll wait here, I'll get a shorter lead. You can borrow it while you and Cotton are getting used to each other."

Rory trotted to her car and came back with a much shorter, well-used leather leash.

"Are you sure you don't need this?" Rebekah studied her face. "Isn't doing this dog training thing your whole job?"

Rory laughed. "Trust me, I have a collection. I won't miss this one."

"How will I get it back to you?"

"I'm around here a lot. You can find me pretty easily." Rory started to walk away but turned back. "If you need any help with dog training, just call the shelter and ask for me."

Rory sat in her car for a minute, reflecting on her second encounter with the striking and intense Rebekah Hawks. Rebekah was stunning and confident and a bit of a whirlwind. Rory braced her arms across the steering wheel and watched Rebekah pull away. She hoped Cotton knew what he was getting into.

Chapter Three

Rebekah glanced over at Cotton, nestled in the dog bed in the passenger seat. His calm, comfortable demeanor suggested he'd been riding shotgun his entire life. What was this little guy's story? And how the hell had she gotten talked into fostering a dog? Well, it wasn't permanent. She was simply helping out in a crisis. Rebekah had already decided that she couldn't very well organize a fundraiser while at the same time not be willing to personally get involved. She smiled at Cotton. This seemed like a small price to pay. Surely, she'd only have to keep him for a couple of weeks before the shelter found him a permanent family.

Rebekah parked a few spots down the street from her condo. She decided to make two trips rather than repeat her earlier mistake and attempt to carry everything, plus Cotton, all at one time. She didn't want to leave him in the car, so she walked him to the house first.

He stared up at her as she unclipped the leash and left him sitting in the living room.

"Now, just be good. Stay right there." She spoke to the little dog as if he could understand. "I'll be right back."

A few moments later, she returned with the armload of supplies, but when she entered the condo, Cotton was nowhere in sight. She set the bag of dog food on the counter island that divided the living room from the kitchen and the dog bed on the floor. Rebekah rotated but didn't see him. What she did see was that he'd obviously run across the sofa and knocked all the throw pillows onto the floor.

"Cotton?" She picked up the pillows as she called, "Cotton, come here, boy."

She wondered if this dog actually knew his name or if that was simply a name given to him by the rescuers, in which case, she might as well just call him Dog. But Cotton *was* a much cuter name, and it seemed to fit him well. His fluffy fur was off-white and soft as downy feathers. His fur even curled up like feathers all along his stomach.

Rebekah looked toward the second floor. Could a dog with such short legs climb stairs? She cocked her head and listened but didn't hear anything. Not that she would be able to hear his light footsteps on the carpet, but she also didn't hear any whimpers or barks. Now that she thought about it, he hadn't made one sound since she'd picked him up.

"Cotton?" She kept calling as she climbed the carpeted steps to the second floor.

She came to a full stop in the doorway to her bedroom. Once again, throw pillows had been knocked to the floor, and there was a lump under the comforter right in the center of the bed. She lifted the edge of the comforter, and shiny black eyes looked back at her. Cotton had climbed the stairs and likely jumped from the quilted bench at the foot of the bed and tucked himself in.

"Get out of there." She reached under the covers and dislodged him. He braced all his weight in the opposite direction, determined to maintain his cozy position under the covers. Finally, she tugged him free and cradled him in her arm. He was very warm from being under the blankets. He probably only weighed ten pounds soaking wet.

"Yes, you're cute and cuddly, but dogs do not sleep in the bed."

Rebekah closed her bedroom door and carried him downstairs. She settled him into the cushy dog bed she'd purchased. It was near the laundry area at the edge of the kitchen. He obligingly sat there while she filled a bowl with water and a second dish with dry food. She put both bowls near him on the floor.

"Okay, now you just settle in while I get a little work done." There she was, talking to a dog again. She had a lot of phone calls to make if she was going to line up all the vendors for this event and expedite delivery of the doghouses. Not to mention lining up artists.

She needed to touch base with Scott and get his help to begin networking other painters to participate in the project. There were lots of things to do and only a few hours in the day left to do them. Tight deadlines were where she shined. Nothing got the adrenaline pumping like an impossible deadline, and she'd just given herself a big one.

Rebekah loved a challenge. And a challenge for a good cause was just icing on the biggest heart-shaped cookie ever.

❖

Rebekah rotated her shoulders and shifted her head from side to side. She'd been sitting on one of the high stools, working on her laptop at the counter, drinking tea, and had completely lost track of time. The shadows and orange light coming through the kitchen window behind her told her it was late afternoon. She stretched one more time and covered a yawn with her hand. And then she smelled something.

What was that awful smell?

She scrunched her nose and glanced around the kitchen. She got up and checked the garbage can under the sink. *No, not that.* Then opened the fridge. *No, not there either.* Then she turned toward the front door, which she could easily see from the kitchen.

There it was. On the small welcome mat just in front of the door—a tiny pile of poop!

"Cotton," she yelled, but he wasn't in the living room.

This was an emergency. She picked up her phone and dialed her best friend, Mary Beth.

"Hey there, what's up?" Mary Beth was relaxed, the exact opposite of how Rebekah was feeling at the moment.

"A disaster, that's what's up."

"Oh no, should I come over?" The question was laced with concern. "Where are you?"

"I'm at home, and there's poo in my living room." Her voice went up a notch; she couldn't help the pitch change when she was upset.

"Um…what? Is it yours?" Mary Beth's concern turned to humor, possibly laughter.

"No, of course not."

"Well, that's a huge relief." Mary Beth laughed.

"Stop laughing, this isn't funny." It was anything but. "I rescued a dog, and he pooped just inside the front door. Why would he do that?" Rebekah was truly at a loss.

"Well, I'm no dog expert, but did you walk him or take him out?"

The questions sounded ridiculously rational. Rebekah didn't respond immediately.

"Bekah, are you still there?"

"Yes, I'm here." She paused. "Maybe I should have walked him."

"Uh, yeah, probably." Humor had switched to sarcasm. "I have so many questions right now."

"What sort?" Rebekah retrieved the little roll of biodegradable clean-up bags and reached down to scoop up Cotton's deposit. She stretched as far from the mistake as she possibly could while still able to reach it with one hand. With her other, she held the phone at her ear and made tracks for the back door.

"What was that noise?"

"I'm going out back to put this in the dumpster." The lid banged loudly. "What are all these questions you have?"

"Well, first, how could you begin a new relationship without talking to me first?"

"It's not a relationship, it's a dog."

"And did you tell the people who gave you this dog that you are most definitely a cat person? Or possibly, a fish person, maybe, if it's only one fish, and you don't actually have to feed it?"

"Hahaha. Very funny." Rebekah took a deep breath and exhaled. "I couldn't say no. I'm helping the shelter do a fundraiser, and they are overrun with animals at the moment because of that hurricane that happened recently."

"Oh yeah, I read about that."

"I'm just fostering this dog. I get to take him back." She closed the door off the kitchen patio as she came back inside. "Maybe you should foster a dog too. Then we could take them for walks and playdates together."

"No thanks." Mary Beth snorted or laughed again.

"What's that supposed to mean?"

"This exact same thing happened to my sister, and now she has three dogs. The cutest miniature poodles you've ever seen."

"I didn't know Jane had dogs."

"She dumped Kenneth, he moved out, the dogs moved in, and now she never leaves the house except for short walks with the poodles, one of whom rides in a stroller. She's living her best life with those little fur babies. She even sleeps with them."

"Well, I draw the line at sleeping with a…hang on, I'm going to need to call you back." Rebekah realized where Cotton had probably gone. He had yet to materialize, even though she'd called his name. He clearly felt no remorse for his unseemly deed on the welcome mat.

She was pretty certain she'd closed the bedroom door, but as she reached the landing on the second floor, she could see that it was ajar. Sure enough, there was a lump again under the comforter in the center of the bed.

She gathered Cotton, all warm from snuggling under the covers and carried him to the door where she'd hung the leash that Rory had loaned her.

"Come on, we're going for a walk." She was annoyed with herself that she hadn't thought of it sooner, much sooner. It was not yet dark, but it would be soon. She took a right turn out of her place and headed toward the greenway path along the river. How far should she walk such a small dog? She had no idea.

"What a cute dog," an elderly woman commented as they passed.

It seemed people loved to talk when you had a dog in tow. Maybe walking a dog made a person seem more approachable, friendlier. Although, was she? It was probably too soon to tell. She wasn't big into small talk with total strangers, dog or no dog.

They had barely reached the greenway a few blocks from her condo when Cotton sat and refused to walk farther. No matter how much coaxing, he wouldn't budge. She wasn't even tugging his leash that hard. But eventually, to avoid glares from passing pedestrians, she picked him up and started for home. A middle-aged guy smiled as he passed them on the sidewalk.

"Who's walking whom?" he asked with a grin.

Very *not* funny, but she smiled thinly at his joke to be polite.

Once back at her place she phoned Mary Beth.

"I thought you were never going to call me back."

"Sorry, I had to take Cotton for a walk. I won't make that mistake again." Rebekah sank to the sofa. Cotton jumped up next to her and made himself at home, stretching out to his full wiener-dog length on the couch.

"Who's Cotton?"

"The little dog I was telling you about."

"Send me a photo."

"I have no idea why I wasted money on a dog bed. Apparently, he only likes people furniture." Rebekah snapped a shot of Cotton as he lounged on the sofa beside her. "I just texted you a photo."

"He's adorable. Look how fluffy he is! Is his fur as soft as it looks?"

"Not so loud. The compliments will go straight to his tiny head, and he already thinks he owns the place."

After dinner in front of the TV and then some light reading, Rebekah was ready to head upstairs. She plunked a very drowsy Cotton into the dog bed in the kitchen and switched off the light. She closed her bedroom door, changed into a baggy T-shirt, and scooted into bed.

Rebekah hadn't even had time to drift off when she heard a whine and scratching at the door. She was determined to ignore the noise.

First, he whimpered softly. Then the whimpers turned to little yips. Between each vocal appeal, he scratched at the bottom edge of the door, the scratching becoming more insistent the more time went by. Then he howled. For such a small dog, Cotton had a very healthy set of lungs and vocal cords.

Rebekah sat up. Maybe he was scared. Maybe she'd have to let him sleep with her until he got used to being in this new place. She exhaled loudly and got out of bed. Annoyed, she opened the door. Cotton trotted in and jumped from the padded bench to the bed just like before. And then as if he'd done it a million times, he used his long snout to root under the comforter until he'd burrowed underneath.

Rebekah sighed.

"Okay, just this once." She climbed in bed beside the tiny dog. "But don't get used to this."

She relaxed. She could feel the warmth of Cotton curled against her back. The sensation was surprisingly soothing, like a furry hot water bottle. She drifted off to sleep more easily than usual.

Chapter Four

Rory was just finishing up with a class of new puppy owners in one of the grassy areas behind the shelter when she saw the first delivery of doghouses. The big truck's arrival was actually great timing for the training class to have to deal with nervousness around loud noises. An array of different-sized, unpainted wooden doghouses was lined up neatly near the loading dock by the time Rory went back into the building.

"Hi, Karri, I was thinking of making a coffee run." Rory leaned against the reception desk. "Do you want me to get you anything?"

Before she could answer, the phone rang. "Hello? Yes, of course." Karri glanced up at Rory. "We normally don't respond to those sorts of calls unless Animal Control is unavailable."

"What's up?" Rory whispered.

Karri covered the receiver with her hand. "An animal in distress."

"Where?" Rory couldn't help asking.

"A condo near the River District." Karri was jotting down the address so she could pass it along to Animal Control.

"What condo near the River District?" Rebekah appeared out of nowhere. Rory hadn't even seen her coming.

"Sorry, ma'am, can you hold on for one moment?" Karri spoke into the phone as she held the address up to Rebekah.

"That's my house!" Rebekah claimed the yellow Post-it Note. "What did the person say, exactly?"

"That a dog had been howling all day, and she was afraid it was being abused. I was just about to pass along the call to Animal Control." Karri was reaching for the phone, but Rebekah stopped her.

"Wait…I'll go home right now and check." Rebekah glanced at Rory. "There's no need to call this in. I'll let my neighbor know when I get there."

"Would you like me to come with you?" Rory wasn't sure why she offered, but her classes were over for the day, and well, Rebekah just seemed like she might need help.

"You wouldn't mind?" Rebekah turned to face her. "Cotton and I don't quite understand each other yet."

"I'd be happy to go with you." The truth was, she'd been a little worried since the moment she'd helped Rebekah load Cotton into her car. She'd feel better knowing that things were going smoothly for him. He'd survived a hurricane evacuation and didn't really need more trauma in his life. Not that she thought Rebekah would do anything intentionally to disturb or unsettle him; simply being in a strange environment might be enough to set him off.

They rode in silence for the first part of the drive. Rory occasionally glanced over at Rebekah, who was beautiful and definitely out of her league. Not that she was interested in dating someone so obviously high-strung, or was she? Small talk seemed the safest course of action.

"Have you lived in the River District for very long?" That seemed like a safe question and a way to get to know a bit more about Ms. Rebekah Hawks without seeming too nosey.

"Only a little over a year. My girlfriend and I split up, and I decided I needed to live in a completely different part of town."

Her basic *safe* question had yielded some valuable intel after all.

"I get that." Not that she'd lived with any of her girlfriends; her place was too small. And not that she'd dated anyone seriously for a long time, but she could imagine what that might feel like. She could understand that a change of scenery might be part of the process of letting go and moving on.

They parked in front of a modern-looking, modular row of tall, narrow townhouses. She'd driven past these before and had thought they looked really interesting but were probably way out of her price range to rent, let alone own. The moment they stepped out of the car, Rory heard the unmistakable howl of a dog in distress, probably suffering from separation anxiety. Rebekah glanced at her with a worried expression as they walked toward the entrance. Or maybe her expression was annoyance. Rebekah was a little hard to read.

A woman who looked to be in her sixties stepped out onto her front stoop as they approached. "I'm sorry. I wouldn't have called if I'd known it was your dog. I was worried something was terribly wrong inside." The woman seemed sincere. "I didn't know you had a dog."

"That's okay, Mrs. Beeman. I'm glad you called someone." Rebekah smiled thinly as she fumbled with her keys. "I just got the dog. I'm fostering him for a couple of weeks."

It didn't really sound as if Rebekah was happy about it and might even be regretting her decision. She struck Rory as the sort of woman who liked her privacy. Rebekah opened the door to find Cotton near the front entrance amongst a pile of mismatched shoes, almost all of them what Rory would have described as dressy heels. Not all the shoes had been chewed, but at least a couple had teeth marks on the heels, and one of the strappy shoes was missing the strap.

"Oh no, did he eat it? Will that make him sick?" Rebekah held the shoe up to examine it.

It was nice to see that she was more concerned about Cotton's health than the shoe. Rory decided to check around the room for the missing strap in the hope he hadn't swallowed anything with a metal fastener.

"It's okay, I found it." Rory located it under a sofa pillow that was askew.

With the exception of the pile of mismatched shoes, the place was spotless and neat. The white shag carpet made Rory wonder why Rebekah had ever agreed to foster a dog in the first place. The townhouse was not dog-friendly in the least.

"Maybe this was a terrible idea." It was as if Rebekah had read her thoughts. "Should I take him back?"

Rory felt bad for both of them. Rebekah slumped to the sofa in defeat. Cotton stretched out on the carpet and rested his snout on his paws, facing the couch. He was an adorable dog, but Rory had had experience with dachshunds before. They were a tough breed to train sometimes, and who knew what Cotton's experiences had been before the hurricane?

"Why don't I help you out with Cotton?" Rory worried she might be getting in over her head, with both Rebekah and Cotton, but the shelter was completely out of space, and spending a little more time with Rebekah might help her understand why she felt an unexpected attraction.

Ever since they'd gotten tangled up in the parking lot, Rory couldn't quite shake the feeling that they were meant to meet each other. She just didn't quite know why yet. What was it about this intense woman that'd gotten under her skin? Maybe because she had a soft spot for anxious creatures. Rory always looked for cause and effect. She liked to soothe wounded spirits. Although she wouldn't have described Rebekah as wounded, there did seem to be something there, something behind the perfect facade that caused Rebekah to be so driven.

"How much do you charge?"

In that moment, Rory had been thinking of asking Rebekah out for dinner, so the mention of a fee caught her by surprise. She laughed.

"What's funny?" Rebekah cocked her head.

"Nothing."

"No, really, what's funny?" Now Rebekah sounded annoyed, as if she thought Rory was laughing at her. Or laughing at the situation Rebekah had gotten herself into.

"I was thinking of suggesting we get dinner somewhere, you know, a dog-friendly café, and then you asked how much I charge… you know, as if I'm an escort or something." Now that she'd voiced it out loud, even the suggestion that she could ask Rebekah out seemed ridiculous.

"Oh."

"It wasn't really that funny. It's just where my mind went." She was embarrassed and feeling awkward about the whole exchange.

"Do you normally have a fee for taking women out to dinner?" The corner of Rebekah's very kissable lips turned up into an almost smile.

Rory was glad that a small bit of humor had brightened the mood. "No, there's normally no fee for dinner out." She smiled. Rebekah's comment had buoyed her spirits.

"I *am* kind of hungry. And I know a nice café not far from here with outside seating." She stood and then looked at Cotton. "I should warn you that Cotton doesn't seem to enjoy walking very much."

"I can carry him if he gets tired. Too bad I didn't bring my doggie backpack when we left the shelter." Cotton perked up at the mention of his name and *walk* in the same sentence.

"I didn't even know there was such a thing as a doggie backpack."

"You clearly haven't known many dachshunds."

"Truth." Rebekah laughed.

The sun had dipped lower in the sky, but the air was still warm. They both had light jackets along in case the air cooled. It was a beautiful afternoon for a stroll and an early dinner. Rory had skipped lunch, so she was pretty hungry.

She wondered if Rebekah was strict about what she ate, or possibly, was a runner. She was leanly athletic. In fact, Rory worried she might be out of shape by comparison. She walked a lot of dogs but wasn't much of an athlete herself. She preferred to lounge in a coffeehouse with a good book when she found herself with any downtime on the weekends.

Rebekah marveled at how relaxed Cotton was while Rory held his leash. It was as if Cotton knew instinctively that Rory understood him, that she was indeed a dog person. Rebekah could have sworn that Cotton scowled at her during their stroll to the café. Could dogs scowl? She didn't know very much about dogs, except that Lassie was good, and Cujo was scary, and that one hundred and one dalmatians was way too many.

Rory stood casually near the entrance with Cotton while Rebekah went inside to check about outside seating. It was too early for dinner, so the hostess explained about the limited post-lunch, afternoon offerings. She left them with menus and returned with glasses of water and a bowl of water for Cotton. They had the patio to themselves. Having an early dinner in the middle of the week made Rebekah feel as if they were playing hooky from school or work or something.

She worked too much. She had moved to this terrific neighborhood partly for the restaurants, but in truth, rarely enjoyed them. Because who wanted to eat out alone? It was nice to be out with someone interesting.

Hmm, where had that thought come from? Since when did she find Rory interesting? Was Rory even her type? There was something unexplainably magnetic about her. A soothing, calming aura that pulled you in. Rory had an easy warmth. Rebekah actually could have sworn that her heart rate slowed a little more around Rory and that the tension she continually felt in her shoulders eased. All of these were details she noticed as the server took their orders.

Rebekah liked tidiness, method, and she liked to be in control. One pint-sized beast had thrown her world into chaos. As much as she hated to admit defeat, maybe she did need help. And the fact that Rory was a charming dinner companion just made swallowing her defeat that much more palatable.

"So how does this work, exactly?"

"Which part?" Rory paused with her water glass in midair.

"The dog training part." What had Rory thought she was talking about?

"Oh, right." Rory seemed momentarily flustered. "We can figure out a schedule. I can come to your house, or we could meet at the shelter. I also do phone consultations in a pinch."

"What's your hourly rate?"

"We can talk about that later." Rory seemed embarrassed by the question, but Rebekah wasn't sure why. "I'm just happy to help."

Two people were walking in their direction toward a nearby table. Cotton immediately growled and backed under the table, but his leash caught on a table leg and stopped his retreat. She tried to reach for him, but he was in an awkward spot beneath Rory's chair that she couldn't easily get to. Rory scooped him up and put him in her lap.

"Quiet." Rory was calm, her command soft but firm. "Leave it."

Cotton began to settle.

"How did you know that's what he needed?"

"It's my guess that he's a nervous dog. The howling when left alone and chewing your shoes, all of that is based in his anxiety of being left alone." Rory stroked Cotton and kissed the top of his head. "Possibly, he was left alone too often as a puppy or maybe even abandoned somewhere. He may have even been born nervous. It's almost impossible to know what his path has been. Now that he's here, it's important that we try to meet him where he is."

"You sound like a dog therapist." That wasn't necessarily a bad thing, and she hoped Rory didn't take it that way. She'd just sort of blurted it out.

"I suppose I am." Rory smiled. "My goal is to help dogs and people get along."

The server delivered the spring roll appetizer they'd ordered, then returned with the chicken club Rory had ordered and the spinach salad for Rebekah. Rory put Cotton back on the ground, where he wedged himself between Rory's feet, keeping an eye out for lurking danger.

"I think he prefers you to me." Rebekah was a little hurt, which surprised her. An hour ago, she'd been ready to take him back to the shelter for chewing her favorite shoes, and now, she was feeling left out because he clearly preferred Rory over her.

"He just doesn't know yet where he belongs." Rory reached across the table and touched the back of her hand. "He's figuring it out. It'll take a little time." Rory withdrew her hand abruptly, as if she'd realized what she'd done. "Dogs are very loyal, especially dachshunds. Just wait, you'll see."

Rory seemed to withdraw a bit as they sampled their entrees. The food was good, and Rebekah realized she'd been eating take-out too often lately. Eating out was fun. Plus, no cleanup to do after the meal.

"Did you always want to be a dog trainer?" That seemed like a safe question to draw Rory out. Plus, she was genuinely curious.

"I actually got a BA in creative writing with an emphasis in poetry. Not exactly the sort of degree that's easy to monetize. And I suppose I didn't really want to feel the pressure to write in order to pay the bills." Rory paused, her expression thoughtful. "I mean, maybe someday, but for now, I write for myself, and dog training pays the rent."

"Is there a school for learning to be a trainer?" Poetry was an interesting tidbit. Rebekah tabled that for later.

"I got my dog-training certificate at the Animal Behavior Institute. They have a balanced approach, which I really liked."

"As opposed to what?" She really had no idea about dogs or how to train them.

"Well, some trainers are super regimented and expect all dogs to adhere to the same results. I think, like people, all dogs are different. I like to treat each dog as an individual."

"I like that about you." The compliment simply popped out, but she sincerely meant it. "And it seems as if Cotton trusts you."

Cotton was even more relaxed across Rory's feet. He seemed like a different dog from when they'd first begun their walk to the café.

"What about you?" Rory asked.

"Me?"

"Are you planning to keep working at the shelter?"

"Oh, that." Rebekah smiled. "No, I work in marketing and PR. I'm between jobs, and Maggie asked for my help with the fundraiser." She took a bite, chewed, and swallowed. "I'm not so good with downtime, and I had a few weeks before I start my new job."

"I think I might be too much of an introvert to do PR or marketing."

"You might be surprised how similar the work is."

"How so?" Rory met her gaze and held it for a moment.

The direct eye contact triggered some fluttering in her stomach. "To be successful at marketing, you can't use a blanket, one-size-fits-all approach. You have to treat each scenario as you would an individual, special and unique."

"I never really thought of it that way."

Dinner with Rory was nice. It wasn't like it was a date or anything. And Rory did end up having to carry Cotton most of the way home, which she didn't seem to mind. Rebekah had enjoyed her company, so much so that she was about to suggest they meet up again. But as they stood on the front stoop to say good-bye, Rory beat her to it.

"If you'd like to start with a training session this weekend, there's a class I'm running you might enjoy."

"That could work. I have a meeting with the artists on Saturday, but it's in the morning around ten. I'll be free after that."

"This friend of mine has a small farm, and we set up an agility course and a space for puppies to play and socialize. There's also a huge dog run." Rory paused. "It's a little way out of town, but I could text you the address."

This was a clever way to get her number, if that was what Rory was after. She didn't mind. "Let me have your phone, and I'll input my contact info." She held out her hand.

Rory unlocked her phone and handed it over. "I'll text you the info." Rory smiled and stowed her phone in her pocket.

"Oh, wait, I just realized your car is at the shelter." She'd completely forgotten that they'd driven her car. "I can drive you back."

"No, I'm fine." Rory waved her off. "I'll just get an Uber."

"Are you sure?"

"Absolutely." Rory smiled. "I'll look forward to seeing you and Cotton on Saturday."

Rebekah closed the door and began to gather up the shoes that Cotton had carried downstairs. She wondered absently how many trips he'd made to get so many shoes piled together. She glanced toward the kitchen to see that he was sitting beside his dog dish. She trotted upstairs to stow the shoes in the closet. She'd organize them later and take stock of the damage. For now, she'd make sure to keep the closet door closed at all times.

Once she was back downstairs, she scooped food into the dish for Cotton and leaned against the counter while he ate. She decided to leave him and go upstairs to take a quick shower. She came out of the bath drying her hair. She wasn't a bit surprised to see that Cotton had already tucked himself in for the night. Why had she bothered spending money on a dog bed?

It was still early, but she wasn't really in the mood to watch a show. She retrieved her laptop from her briefcase and settled into bed next to Cotton to catch up on some email. Several of the artists she'd reached out to for the benefit had responded positively already. Things for the benefit were really coming together. Now all she needed to do was coordinate with Avery about community outreach so that the event received as much publicity as possible. They could enlist all the best local artists in the world, but if no one showed up to bid on the final pieces, then the whole event would be a bust.

Rebekah had just set her laptop on the bedside table when her phone rang. Mary Beth's number appeared on the screen.

"Hello." Rebekah sank into the pillows piled behind her.

"Hi." Mary Beth sounded chipper. "I called to see if you're still a dog owner."

"Yes, I'm still a dog owner." Rebekah laughed. "Not only do I still have a dog, I also now have a dog trainer. As a matter of fact, we had dinner tonight."

"Wait, you had a date?"

"I wouldn't call it a date."

"Is that because you don't think she's cute?"

"No, she's definitely cute." She paused. "Although maybe not my type."

"That's probably a good thing." Mary Beth sounded a little too excited.

"What's that supposed to mean?"

"Well, your *type* has a tendency to cheat and then break your heart."

There was truth to that statement, maybe too much truth. Mary Beth knew her too well. "Hey, listen, what are you doing tomorrow?"

"Not much, why?"

"Do you want to go to a farm with me in the afternoon?"

"You have a dog, and now you're going to a farm? Who are you?"

They both laughed. "Are you in or not?" Rebekah knew Mary Beth couldn't resist such an outlandish invitation, and she wanted a second opinion from someone she trusted about Rory.

"Are you kidding? Of course I'm in."

As if on cue, her phone chimed. It was a text from Rory with the time and location.

"I'll pick you up around one, okay?"

"Can't wait." Mary Beth made kissing sounds. "Love you."

"Love you too."

Rebekah leaned over to place the phone on top of her laptop on the bedside table. When she returned to her reclined position, just the tip of Cotton's nose was peeking out from beneath the covers. She was letting a dog sleep in her bed. It was crazy, and she hardly believed it herself, but he was pretty darn cute and almost impossible to say no to.

She switched off the lamp and snuggled down next to him.

"Good night." She rolled onto her side. "And stay away from my shoes."

Chapter Five

Rory parked in front of the barn and climbed out. She was the first to arrive for the training session, and that was the way she preferred it. She was about to walk to the house in search of her friend when she saw Bonnie coming out of the dark interior of the barn. Bonnie's long blond hair was pulled back into a ponytail. She was wearing riding boots with splatters of mud almost to the top. Her blue cotton blouse was tucked into snug-fitting jeans. Bonnie always managed to look sexy and outdoorsy at the same time. She was also comfortable in her own skin. She exuded calm confidence. All of which made her very good with horses and basically animals of all kinds, even dogs.

"Hey, there."

"Hi." Rory gave her a casual hug. They'd been friends since college. They'd been there for each other through good times and bad. She was lucky that Bonnie let her use space at the farm for classes. The dogs benefitted from a less-controlled environment surrounded by wide-open spaces.

"Are you expecting a big class today?" asked Bonnie.

"Not so far." Rory checked her phone. "I think I'm going to only have three. I guess the weather is too nice, and people are taking advantage of the day to do other things." There had been rain earlier in the week. There were a few puddles in the dog run and some wet spots in the agility course. But the sky was cloudless and sunny. It almost felt like summer.

"I was just going up to the house for a drink. Do you want anything?" Bonnie dusted hay debris from her jeans. "I think we might even have some lunch leftovers if you're hungry." Bonnie's wife, Anna, was a great cook, but at the moment, Rory wasn't in the mood to eat. The thought of spending more time with Rebekah had caused a flock of butterflies to set up shop in her stomach, and they showed no signs of settling down. She knew that at any moment, Rebekah was likely to show up. She tried to focus on calming down.

"I'm okay, but thanks." Rory shook her head. "I would take a sparkling water if you have one." Maybe that would help settle her nervous stomach.

Before Bonnie had time to walk away, Rebekah's dark blue BMW appeared in the driveway. She parked near Rory's Subaru and waved hello. She'd obviously come straight from meetings because she was wearing a blazer over a white jumpsuit and heels. Rory waved back.

"Who is that?" Bonnie asked.

"Rebekah Hawks."

"Wow."

"Yeah."

"And she thought that was the perfect outfit to wear to a dog-training class on a horse farm?"

Rory smiled. "She's a mystery I'm trying to solve."

"Good luck with that." Bonnie laughed. "I'll be back in a few with your drink."

Rebekah wasn't alone; another woman got out of the car, and they walked in her direction with Cotton in tow. Two other vehicles pulled in and parked next to Rebekah's car. It looked like everyone had arrived.

"I hope it's okay that I brought a friend," Rebekah said. "This is Mary Beth. And Mary Beth, this is Rory."

"When Bekah said she was visiting a farm, I had to see it for myself." Mary Beth smiled. She was wearing dark jeans and a green blouse that brought out the green in her eyes. She had long, wavy auburn hair and a slender figure that matched Rebekah's.

"It's nice to meet you." Rory extended her hand.

"I came straight from work, but now I'm thinking I should have changed." Rebekah looked at her classmates' jeans and casual shirts.

"We'll start you and Cotton with something simple." Rory stepped away to greet the others. "Just wait here. I'll be back once I get them set up on the agility course."

❖

Rebekah watched Rory saunter toward the fenced area. A middle-aged man with a golden retriever puppy and a woman and her daughter with a fluffy black dog waited near the fence. Cotton sat in the grass at her feet. She'd probably worn the wrong shoes too, but her choices had been limited to pairs without teeth marks.

"Oh yes, she's definitely cute."

Mary Beth's comment made her regain focus. "What?"

"Ms. Dog Trainer."

"Yeah, I told you she was."

"Uh-huh, but she's *really* cute." Mary Beth nodded as she watched Rory work with the other families. "And I think she likes you."

"Whatever." She shook her head. "Rory likes Cotton, not me."

"Keep telling yourself that." Mary Beth quirked an eyebrow. "Don't look now, but Hotty Dog Trainer is coming this way."

"Remind me why I invited you along?"

"So I could witness you on a farm." Mary Beth crossed her arms. "This day will be hard to top."

"Shush."

Rory rejoined them, and Rebekah tried hard to pretend they hadn't been talking about her. Rory directed Rebekah and Cotton to follow her to a grassy field opposite the other dogs while Mary Beth stood and watched. Rory suggested they work on some basic verbal commands.

"Verbal cues carry a lot of information. You have to be aware of tone as well as volume. This helps the dog determine your intent." Rory paused. "Once he learns them, it'll also make it easier for people who aren't Cotton's primary caregiver to deliver commands."

Cotton looked at Rory as if he understood what she was saying. Rebekah was beginning to figure out that doggie training wasn't only for the dog.

"It's good to remember that your dog may not know that you're angry or irritated by work or something other than his behavior. He might feel bad even if it's not his fault."

"Mixed messages are bad. Got it." This really was people training.

"The first command we'll work on is *come*." Rory had been holding something in her hand that looked like a much longer leash. She knelt and clipped it to Cotton's collar as she unclipped the shorter lead. "This works best by using a long lead. Let Cotton run around and go as far away as he wants. Then call him back with the command and give him a little treat when he obeys." Rory handed her a small bag of dog treats.

"What if he doesn't come back?"

"Then you just give the leash a light tug as you say the word *come*, and he should get the idea. You'll have to do it several times until he starts to get the hang of it." Rory started to walk away. "I'll be back to check on you in a bit. You've got this."

Rebekah felt utterly ridiculous waiting for Cotton to walk away. She was standing there with her heels sinking into the damp grass like an overdressed garden statue, and he didn't move. She glanced around for Mary Beth, who'd obviously already gotten bored. She was leaning against Rebekah's car and staring at her phone.

Rebekah started watching the other dogs and their owners in the adjacent field. The dogs were running up ramps and jumping over things. She'd only looked away for a moment when Cotton barked and took off at a dead run. He totally caught her by surprise and ran out the length of the tether and then jerked the lead easily from her relaxed fingers.

"Cotton! Come back!" She hadn't even gotten the chance to teach him the command, so of course, he ignored her. He was somehow running and hopping through the tall grass, barking frenetically the entire time. Every time he bounded up, his oversized ears flapped as if he might take flight.

Rebekah started to jog after him toward a small clump of trees and quickly realized that even her sensible square heels were no match for the thick grass, damp and slick in places. On the next step, her heel sank into the soft ground, so that when she lifted her foot, she left the shoe behind. She quickly took off the other one and continued barefoot. Cotton had obviously seen a squirrel or something; he was barking and circling. Yes, there was definitely something in the tree. She could see it was a squirrel as she drew closer. He was halfway down the tree facing the ground, chattering as if to taunt Cotton. And it was working. Cotton was going crazy.

She grabbed for the leash but realized it was tangled around more than one of the nearby trees like a string maze. She careful unwound it and was just about to reach Cotton's position when the squirrel jumped to another trunk, and Cotton took off again. This time, when he jerked the leash, she was just a wee bit off-balance. Barefoot and tiptoeing over a muddy patch of ground, she slipped. She sat down hard in the mud and dropped the leash, frozen. After a few seconds, she wrung her hands as if to shoo away the mud that had splattered all over her clothing and was seeping into the seat of her jumpsuit.

Rebekah started to cry. How did she get here, and why had she worn her new jumpsuit to a farm? Cotton hated her. Why had she agreed to foster a dog? She was ridiculous! No wonder her ex had dumped her for a yoga instructor. She was a hot mess, and now everyone knew it. No one liked long walks on the beach. Did anyone really care about world peace? Why was everything such a complete disaster?

Her vision was blurry from tears when Cotton returned to check on her. He jumped into her lap, tracking muddy footprints all over the white fabric that wasn't already dirty, which made her cry harder. He licked her face, and she tried to push him away.

"Hey, are you okay?" Rory's question was like a beacon in a storm. Even if it was a storm of her own making.

"Cotton ran away…and I tried to catch him…and then I lost a shoe…and then the mud." She took in a shaky breath, her statements punctuated by sobs.

"I have Cotton." Rory slipped her fingers through his collar and gently sidelined him. "Let's get you up on your feet." Rory tied Cotton's leash to her belt and then offered Rebekah both hands. "It's going to be okay. I've got you."

"Thank you." Rebekah sniffed loudly.

"Here, take this." Rory held out a bandana. "It's clean."

Rebekah dabbed her eyes with the soft cloth. It smelled like Rory, a mix of sandalwood and vanilla. She covered her face with it for a moment and inhaled. Like some sort of rustic aromatherapy, the scent calmed her frayed nerves.

"Careful now." Rory gently guided her by the elbow as they walked toward the less muddy grass.

"OMG, are you okay, Bekah?" Mary Beth hurried toward them. "I found your shoes." One of them was half-brown from getting submerged in mud.

"Don't say a word." She held her palm up in Mary Beth's direction.

"I wasn't gonna." Mary Beth swallowed a laugh.

Rebekah could only imagine how she looked: barefoot, muddy, and red-faced from bawling like a toddler.

"Mary Beth, why don't you walk Cotton to that fenced area over there? You can take the leash off and let him run around." Rory traded the leash for Rebekah's shoes. "I'll take Rebekah inside so she can, um, clean up."

"Sure thing." Mary Beth took Cotton and headed toward the grassy enclosure.

The gravel on the driveway was sharp underneath her bare feet. She winced and lifted her foot like a cat with an injured paw.

"Here, put these back on until we get to the office." Rory set Rebekah's shoes down so that she could easily slip into them. "I always keep a spare change of clothes in my car for…emergencies." Rory smiled, not in ridicule, more like a sympathetic friend. "I think this qualifies as an emergency, right?"

She nodded and sniffed again.

After a moment, Rory was back with a bundle of clothing under her arm.

"Come on. Bonnie won't mind if we change in her office. It's just inside the barn." Rory motioned toward the large entrance at the front of the building.

The space was small but tidy, with a desk and a couple of leather chairs. There was a half bath to the side. Rory laid the clothing on the counter and stepped back so Rebekah could enter.

"I'll be right out here if you need me." Rory lightly patted Rebekah's shoulder, possibly the only clean spot available. "I'm sorry those clothes probably aren't your style. But at least they'll get you home, cozy, and dry."

"Thank you for being so sweet." Rory really had come to her aid in her hour of need, without jokes and without making Rebekah feel stupid. She was feeling particularly vulnerable and way outside her ultra-controlled comfort zone. "I would hug you right now, but…" She looked at her mud-splotched clothing with dog prints all down the front.

"I'll be waiting for that hug whenever you feel ready." Rory was so sincere and sweet. "Hey, and the good news is that when you fell, Cotton came back to check on you."

"Oh yeah, I suppose he did."

"He's bonding with you. It just took a little time."

Rebekah nodded with a smile. She was feeling shy. Rory had seen her at her absolute most embarrassing. She needed a moment alone to process. She closed the door to the bathroom and looked at her disheveled self in the mirror. OMG indeed. She shook her head and slowly began to peel away the dirty clothing. She rolled the worst of the dirt inward so she could carry everything to the car and then began to dress.

❖

Rory was seated on the edge of the desk with her back to the door, so she didn't notice Bonnie until she was in the room.

"Hey, there you are." Bonnie walked over and handed her a can of sparkling water. "What are you doing in here?"

"Um, Rebekah took a spill and needed to change clothes."

Bonnie arched her eyebrows. Rory could see the questions, but she didn't want to encourage them because she didn't want to be talking about Rebekah the moment she reappeared.

"Hey, do you have some boots she could wear? I'll get them back to you."

"What size?" asked Bonnie.

"This size." Rory held up the shoe that'd been dipped in mud.

"I think I have something that might work." Bonnie smiled and then crossed the room to rummage in a closet.

Rebekah peeked out the door. And then slowly opened it to reveal her borrowed clothing. Rory's first thought was that she looked adorable wearing Rory's clothes. The pants were too big, cinched at the waist with a belt. The long-sleeved cotton shirt was tucked in with the sleeves rolled up partway, revealing Rebekah's elegant elbows. She looked like a runway model trying to impersonate a tomboy.

"Thank you for the clothes." Rebekah turned to retrieve her soiled things.

"I think these will work." Bonnie held out some slip-on boots. Not the sort to wear in the rain, but more like the sort of casual boots for a day hike or camping.

"Rebekah, this is my friend Bonnie. She owns the farm." Rory took the boots. "I asked her for some shoes because I don't think you'll want to wear these and risk ruining them."

"It might already be too late." Rebekah held up her suede pump that was half-covered in dried mud to examine it more closely. "Thank you, Bonnie. It's nice to meet you."

Rory could tell that Rebekah was feeling self-conscious. The glaring overconfidence that was usually there had dimmed due to her recent ungraceful fall.

"Don't give it a second thought." Bonnie smiled.

"I'll walk you out to your car." Rory placed her palm at the small of Rebekah's back and guided her past Bonnie and out of the office.

"Is class over for today?" There was humor in Rebekah's question.

"Well, I thought maybe we'd pick this up some other time." Rory figured it would be better to start over another day in a calmer situation.

"That sounds good to me." Rebekah opened the back door of her car and tossed the bundle of clothes on the back seat. "I feel like I'm having an out-of-body experience." She glanced down at the clothing and shook her head. "I really appreciate these. They just don't feel like me."

"I understand." Rory grinned. "I'm trying to imagine myself wearing your jumpsuit."

They both laughed. Rory was happy that she'd been able to lighten Rebekah's mood. Seriously, the sky was a shade bluer when Rebekah smiled.

Chapter Six

It had been almost a week since Rebekah had seen Rory. Five days since that awful, fateful farm disaster. Rebekah had washed the clothing she'd borrowed the very next day, and since then, the items had been neatly folded on a kitchen chair next to Bonnie's boots. Rebekah allowed herself to use the reason that she'd been too busy, but that excuse could only carry her so far. Maybe she was that busy for a day, or two, possibly three, but an entire week was just avoidance.

She had no reason to believe that Rory thought any less of her, but the entire episode had been so incredibly embarrassing. Mary Beth had confirmed the epic scale of the debacle repeatedly during the drive home from the farm. There was nothing like an overly honest friend to keep your ego in check.

Of course, Mary Beth had said that she was only joking, that no one would remember how silly she'd looked covered in muddy paw prints, and that Rory was a regular McDreamy in cargo pants. Mary Beth had gone on to say that Rory was clearly interested and had asked why Rebekah hadn't made her move.

What move? The move where she'd fallen on her ass? Or the move where she'd lost her shoe running after a maniacal tiny dog chasing a squirrel?

Rebekah stared at the small pile of clothing and exhaled loudly.

Today was the day. She'd texted Rory to get her address, and she was planning to gather a healthy dose of courage and drive over. Yes, that was exactly what she was going to do.

Rebekah had the clothes and the boots in hand and then had

another thought. Maybe she should bring a bottle of wine as a thank-you. She wasn't sure what Rory liked, but was wine ever a bad thing? She hoped not in this instance, at least.

"You be a good boy, and I'll be home soon." Rebekah had debated taking Cotton but decided that she didn't need the distraction. She wanted to have Rory to herself for once. She had wondered a few times if the only thing Rory liked about her was Cotton. Maybe she should sort out whether that was true or not.

Rebekah had invested in a baby gate to corral Cotton in the kitchen while she was out of the house. He stared at her from behind the mesh plastic barrier. She couldn't decide if he was glaring at her or not. They were obviously still figuring each other out.

"Don't be upset with me, okay?"

He continued to stare at her as if he was trying to inflict mind control with his gaze.

She forced herself to ignore him as she pulled the door closed behind her. He was a dog. He would be fine in the cozy warm kitchen. He had plenty of food and water, and besides, she would likely only be gone for an hour.

Rory's place was in the historic section of Fairview. Not downtown but an older neighborhood near the college. Most of the houses had been built in the thirties, but a few turn-of-the-century homes peppered the Midtown neighborhood. Rory's text had explained that she rented a granny unit behind the main house. The map app told Rebekah that she was approaching the address. She slowed and turned into a long driveway. These older homes had deep lots, actual yards, unlike a lot of the new construction in the suburbs. Rory had instructed her to park next to the free-standing garage. The cottage was behind it. The small structure was as adorable as Rory. The design felt more like something you'd find in a coastal village in New England. The siding was cedar shingles, punctuated with dark blue shutters and a light blue door. A flagstone walkway skirted the edge of the garage and arced through a grassy area to the front door of the dwelling.

This place was almost too cute to be real. Rebekah wondered how Rory had managed to find such a gem. She knocked lightly and took a step back.

"Hi, you found it." Rory smiled broadly as she swung open the door. She was wearing a crewneck cotton sweater over a T-shirt and jeans. She looked cozy and comfy, just like the cottage.

"It's such a cute place." She clutched the neck of the wine bottle as if it was a lifeline. "I'm sorry it took so long to return your things."

"Don't worry about it. Please, come in." Rory motioned for her to step inside. "I know you've probably been super busy with the fundraiser."

She handed the borrowed clothing over. "It has been a little crazy." It was nice to have a cover story, even if that wasn't the full picture. "Oh, and I brought this." She held the bottle out. "I hope you like wine."

"Thank you." Rory glanced at the bottle. "How about I get some glasses? Make yourself at home."

The cottage wasn't big, probably no more than six hundred square feet. She slowly gazed around the room. The bedroom was visible through an open door off the living room. The kitchen and living space were one large room divided by a table. The kitchen was galley-style, with everything along one wall facing the small kitchen table. The sofa was turned to face the kitchen, not quite in the center of the room but not against the wall either because of the built-in bookshelves.

Rebekah remembered that Rory wrote poetry. She rounded the sofa and read some of the titles. There were the usual suspects: Emily Dickinson, John Keats, Maya Angelou, W. H. Auden, and others she didn't recognize. She pulled one of the books off the shelf and examined the cover. The title of the vintage edition was *Bright Ambush*.

"You have a good eye." Rory offered a glass of red wine to her. "Audrey Wurdemann won the Pulitzer Prize for that book in 1934. She was only twenty-four when she wrote that collection."

"I've never heard of her, but now I want to know more." She sipped the wine and turned the book over to look at the back.

"You can borrow it if you like."

"It looks like it might be valuable."

"I trust you." Rory smiled. "Just don't read it in the bathtub."

Rebekah laughed. "How could you know that I'm notorious for drowning the occasional book?"

"I had the feeling that you might be the sort of person who multitasks, even when you're relaxing."

"Wow, you not only read books, you read dogs and people too."

She worried the statement sounded sharper than she'd meant, but Rory didn't seem to notice. Or maybe she did and was good at hiding her feelings.

"Occupational hazard, I'm afraid." Rory motioned toward the sofa with her glass. "Would you like to sit down?"

"Thanks." She sat, leaving a respectable amount of space between them. Why did she feel nervous? This wasn't even a date, but would it be such a bad thing if it was? Rebekah was drawn to Rory, and she couldn't figure out exactly why, because on the surface, they were complete opposites. She asked a question in order to redirect her thoughts. "Do you still write poetry?"

"That's a good question." Rory pondered for a moment. "I enjoy other writers' poetry. I have written things in the past but not in a long time." She took a sip of wine. "I suppose I've been suffering from writer's block. But can you call it writer's block if it lasts for years?"

"That sounds valid to me." She didn't really know many writers and even fewer poets…like, none.

"Thanks." Rory smiled. "I'm sort of surprised that Cotton isn't with you." She relaxed a little more into the cushions, which inspired Rebekah to relax also.

"I thought about it, but I didn't know what your situation here was."

"Well, all my situations are dog-friendly."

"I should have guessed. That seems obvious now." But the truth was, she'd wanted to be alone with Rory without the distraction of a dog in tow.

"How is it going with him?"

"Good, I think." She took a sip of wine. "Is it bad that I've been letting him sleep in the bed?" Rebekah seriously wondered if it was. "I didn't think I'd like that, but I do. He's like a little bed warmer with cuddly fur. He makes me feel safe, although I'm not sure how much protection he could provide against an actual intruder."

"You might be surprised." Rory laughed. "Small dogs have all the great qualities of big dogs. They just come in travel size."

"I had no idea." That was the truth. "I always thought of myself as a cat person. Owning a cat-sized dog never occurred to me."

"Dogs can be good for helping you slow down and live in the moment."

They were quiet for a minute or two. Rebekah didn't really know how to respond to that last comment. Was she talking about Rebekah or the universal *you*, as in everyone? Rory must have sensed the mood shift because she changed the subject. Rebekah had to give Rory points for that; she definitely knew how to read the room.

"Hey, should we go out for food?" Rory set her empty glass on the sofa table. "I should probably eat something before I have more of this wine, which is quite lovely, by the way."

❖

Rory noticed the change in Rebekah's expression; even her posture stiffened slightly. The remark about living in the moment had obviously hit a nerve. She hadn't meant it as a criticism, but she was afraid Rebekah had taken it that way.

"There's an Italian place only a few blocks from here that's really good. If you're up for dinner, we could walk."

"It's a little on the early side for me." Rebekah checked her phone. "But I did have a light lunch." She seemed to be calculating something in her head. "Okay, sure."

"Great." Rory stood up. "Let me get a jacket."

Rebekah was wearing dark leggings with a blouse and a flowy sweater thing that almost looked like a shawl. And for the first time since Rory had known her, Rebekah was wearing slip-on flats that made her a few inches shorter than Rory. She seriously looked sexy in anything, casual, dressy, or borrowed.

Rory's heart did a little hopscotch routine as she held the door for Rebekah, and the scent of her perfume softly lingered. Rory wanted to ask her out on a real date. Maybe she should just put it out there and see what happened, but she didn't want to scare her away.

Rebekah seemed to prefer a cushion of emotional space around her at all times. Rory had felt a tiny breach in that protective outer shell until she'd made the comment about living in the moment. She wanted to regain that minute of closeness.

They turned right out of the driveway and walked along the sidewalk. Rory loved to stroll around this well-established neighborhood. She'd wanted to live in a place with sidewalks. She'd grown up in an older suburban neighborhood along a two-lane highway.

As a kid, she'd sometimes ridden her bike on the shoulder of the road, but it had always been a little scary.

Rebekah was looking at houses as they passed. "This a great neighborhood."

"Yeah, I love it here." Rory's hands were in her pockets because she had the urge to reach for Rebekah's. "The older couple I rent from have owned the house since the forties. In fact, a lot of these houses still belong to the original owners. Well, except the ones built in the teens."

"I like the modern modular design of my condo, but there's a lot to be said for classic architecture like this." Rebekah hugged herself as they strolled. She seemed to be more relaxed.

The restaurant wasn't busy when they arrived. It was a classic Italian place with red leather booths, a nice bar area, and a bartender who always looked to Rory as if he'd been sent in from central casting for a movie set. The interior had dark paneling and stained glass light fixtures.

The hostess showed them to a booth at the back of the dimly lit restaurant and left menus for them.

"I can't believe I've never been here. This place is so great." Rebekah glanced around the room. "I keep expecting my grandfather to show up at the bar asking for a scotch and soda."

"Would this be his kind of place?"

"Most definitely."

"Does he live nearby?"

"No, he passed away a few years ago. My grandparents lived in Philadelphia."

"And your parents?" Rory wanted to know Rebekah's backstory.

"My parents grew up there, but both left for college and then ended up living in Connecticut." Rebekah opened the menu but kept talking. "Where did you grow up?"

"Is it obvious that I'm not a local?"

"Just that you have a slight accent that I can't quite place." Rebekah looked up from the menu.

"I grew up in North Carolina. I went to Chapel Hill and decided I needed to experience city life if I really wanted to be a writer." Her favorite professor had told her that in order to write about life, she needed to experience it. She'd taken his advice and had moved out of her comfort zone. The move had been good for her personal growth, but so far, not so good for her writing.

"Do you think that's really true?"

"What?" She worried that Rebekah could hear her internal monologue.

"That living in a city makes someone a better writer?"

"Oh, that…not really." Rory shrugged. "I was young and just wanted an excuse to move away from home." She paused. "I do think getting out on my own was a good thing."

The server took their orders and returned swiftly with two glasses of wine.

"What about you? How did you end up here?" Rory sipped her wine.

"I moved here for a job after college."

"Where did you go to school?"

"Northwestern." Rebekah leaned forward as if to whisper conspiratorially. "Is this like a first date?"

"I'm sorry. I'm asking too many questions." Rory felt heat rise to her cheeks.

"Because it would be okay with me if it *was* a first date, except for the fact that you haven't actually asked me out." Her tone was playfully flirtatious. She sipped her wine without taking her eyes off Rory.

"I would like to ask you out." Rory was being honest but hoped she didn't sound too serious. That sort of thing had a tendency to scare women off. "I mean, I did ask you to dinner. Can we rewind and pretend I asked you out on a date?"

"Hmm, I'm not sure…let's see…how am I feeling about a retroactive invitation for a first date?" Now Rebekah was teasing but in a sweet way. "I think I'm okay with that." She smiled and made eye contact, and Rory felt the intensity of the gaze pierce her chest.

"What a relief." She took a swig of water. Her throat was so dry. "Because I've wanted to ask you out ever since I saw you in those borrowed boots at the farm."

"Oh really, it was the boots that tipped the scale for you?"

"Absolutely." Rory arched her eyebrow and nodded. "Sexy."

Rebekah laughed, a sparkly, light-filled sound that danced in the air. Rory couldn't help smiling.

They finished dinner, and as they slowly walked back to Rory's place, Rebekah casually draped her arm through the crook of Rory's. Even this slight contact sent little tendrils of electricity all along her arm. Rebekah seemed unaffected, but maybe she was simply better at not showing things. Rory worried that everything she felt was written all over her face. She'd always been an open book, painfully so when displayed to the wrong person. She certainly hoped that Rebekah wasn't the wrong person.

This was only a first date. She coached herself to settle and not read into things, even when Rebekah tilted her head to rest on Rory's shoulder as she looked at the crescent moon. Antique streetlights lit warm circles of light as they passed from block to block. Ambient light from the houses added to the warmth of the evening stroll. Somewhere in the distance, a dog barked.

"Oh, that reminds me of Cotton. What time is it?" Rebekah fished her phone out of her bag and checked the screen. "I told him I'd only be gone an hour, and it's been three. I should probably check on him."

The unexpected, unplanned, and very pleasant first date was drawing to a close. Rory took a hand out of her pocket, and Rebekah allowed her palm to drift down Rory's arm until their fingers became entwined. They held hands all the way to Rebekah's car. And then the butterflies began to swarm in her stomach. Was a first kiss appropriate for this accidental date? Rory was still debating internally when Rebekah surprised her by making the first move.

Rebekah closed the space between them, braced her palms on Rory's forearms, and lightly kissed her. After the first brush of her lips, Rebekah pulled away only a little, as if she wanted to gauge Rory's response. Rory angled closer and tenderly returned the kiss. She slid her hands past Rebekah's hips and pressed them at the small of Rebekah's back, drawing her close. The kiss deepened, and she lost herself in Rebekah's embrace.

Rebekah broke the kiss after a few moments and leaned against her car as if she needed to regain her balance. "Thank you for a wonderful evening." She rubbed her thumb across Rory's lower lip. "I left a little lipstick there."

"I don't mind." Rory smiled.

Rebekah opened the door and climbed in. Rory closed it for her.

She stood in the driveway, shielding her eyes from the headlights as Rebekah backed out of the driveway and disappeared down the street.

❖

Rebekah parked not too far down the street from her place. This late in the evening, all the spots out front were already occupied. Her steps felt light as she trotted up the stairs to her front door. She couldn't help smiling as she placed the key in the lock and stepped inside.

"I'm sorry that I'm late." There she was, talking to Cotton again as if he understood what she was saying.

She quickly noticed he wasn't in the kitchen where she'd left him. Upon closer inspection of the baby gate, she could see that he'd chewed through the mesh and let himself out. She rotated slowly and looked toward the stairs. When she reached her bedroom and saw the little round lump under the comforter, she didn't even get upset. She simply shook her head as she kicked off her shoes and slipped into a T-shirt and silk boxers for bed.

Rebekah lifted up the covers and peeked underneath. Shiny black eyes peered back at her.

"Well, would you like to hear about my day?" She slid in next to him. She could feel his feathery soft fur against her legs. She sank into the pillow and smiled up at the ceiling. "It was a very good day."

She reached for the lamp switch and turned it off. The drapes were open. Pale moonlight filtered in, casting the room with a soft blue-white glow. Rebekah let her mind wander. It was fun to consider all the possibilities of things that might be. And it was all because she'd met this crazy little wiener dog. She slid her arm beneath the covers and placed her hand on his back.

"Good boy."

Chapter Seven

Rebekah had hoped to get a chance for a second date with Rory, but the days leading up to the fundraiser were intensely busy. She'd coordinated coverage in the paper, *Fairview City Weekly* Magazine, and even local radio and TV. She talked Maggie into doing a spot for the local morning show two days prior to the actual event. Maggie had been super nervous but had handled the live interview as if she'd been on TV her entire life. Maggie was a pro. Rebekah stood on the sideline, cheering her on.

The long hours had not been great for Cotton. Rebekah had decided after the first few days of chewed heels that if she didn't bring him along, she'd have no shoes left for the event. Not that she needed too much of an excuse for shoe shopping, but right now, she didn't really have time. She'd finally learned that the key was to put things at least three feet above floor level so he couldn't reach them. Cotton still had a good vertical jump for a short dog, but three feet seemed to be his threshold for mischief. Of course, she could also close doors, but she kept forgetting. The safest course of action was to keep things out of reach.

The day finally arrived when all Rebekah's hard work would either pay off or not. The circular drive in front of the shelter was staged with painting stations every ten feet. The artists began working around four o'clock. She'd enlisted a team of volunteers to prep the unfinished wooden doghouses with primer so that they would essentially be blank white canvases for the artists to work on.

Ace Hardware had provided most of the liquid acrylic paint, but a few of the artists brought their own supplies because they had specific techniques in mind.

The larger parking lot beside the building had been set up with picnic tables and food trucks. There was even a bandstand, and live music would start around six, just after sunset. Small white lights were strung at angles across the parking lot. If all went well, the band would play under a starry sky, and the sale of microbrews and food would bring the total donated to the shelter up even higher. All the vendors had agreed to donate a portion of their proceeds to the shelter, and the band had agreed to play for free.

Rebekah had waived her fee early on. It didn't feel right taking money from the cause when everyone else was donating so much of their time and energy. Giving back to the shelter just seemed like the right thing to do.

There were tons of folks milling about, watching the painting happen as they strolled from one artist's station to the next. The entire scene had great energy.

"Rebekah, this turnout is amazing." Maggie waved to someone she recognized in the crowd.

"You helped make it happen, Ms. TV Star."

"Hahaha, I hardly believe that. This is all you." Maggie put an arm around Rebekah's shoulders and gave her a friendly squeeze. "And I can't thank you enough. Really."

"I should be thanking you for my new roommate." She held up the leash and glanced down at where Cotton was seated at her feet. "Who knew I needed a dog?"

"Are you going to keep him, then?"

Rebekah had sort of forgotten that she was only fostering Cotton. The thought of letting him go to live with anyone but her made her queasy.

"I suppose Cotton and I are in this together forever."

"I'm so happy for both of you." Maggie's eyes sparkled. "Okay, I should probably mingle." She started to walk away. "Don't work all night. You should enjoy some food and music. You've earned it."

The crowd surged a bit, and Cotton was nervous, so Rebekah edged toward the grassy strip that separated the circular drive from the main parking lot. After a minute, she picked Cotton up and stroked his back.

"You're okay, boy." She kissed the top of his head. "Do you want to go sit in the car?"

"Wow, I've never been so jealous of a dog before."

Rebekah turned and smiled at the sound of Rory's voice. "I'm happy to see you."

"Are you kidding? I wouldn't miss this."

They hadn't seen each other since the dinner out, but Rory had texted her a few times with supportive messages. The encouragement meant a lot, especially coming from Rory, who had raised her usual casual attire up a notch. She was wearing dark dress pants and a blazer with an open-collared dress shirt and wingtips. Rory definitely cleaned up well.

The stress of making everything come together had gotten to Rebekah a few times, and she had seriously wondered if she'd overpromised on something she wasn't sure she could deliver. Like so many other events she'd worked on, all her planning paid off because everything just sort of fell into place at the last moment. The community had really come together to support the important work the shelter was doing. This entire project made her feel good, as if she was contributing to something truly worthwhile.

There were lots of dogs to welcome the crowd too. Volunteers walked around with some of the shelter's four-legged guests to hopefully inspire some adoptions during the evening. Not all dogs could handle the noise and the crowd, but some seemed to love the attention. Cotton wasn't one of them. She knew that if given the choice, he'd be burrowed under the comforter at home right now.

Rory could see that Cotton was a bit overstimulated by all the festivities and people.

"Hey, how about I take him to the dog run for a little break." She figured Rebekah might like to be freed up to walk around and check in with the artists.

As usual, Rebekah was impeccably dressed. Rory marveled at how she always looked so good and seemed to have the right outfit for every occasion, with the exception of farm wear. Tonight, she was wearing an emerald dress that hugged her hips and draped to mid-thigh.

She'd paired the dress with a lightweight cropped leather jacket and a sheer, shimmery silver scarf, dressy with a splash of fun.

"He might need a break. Are you sure you don't mind?"

"I'm sure." Rory held out her arms.

"I also brought his cozy bed. It's in the car in case you think he might prefer to wait out the festivities in there." Rebekah was catching on. Her empathy for Cotton touched Rory. This wasn't the same woman she'd run into that first day at the shelter.

"I think that's a great idea. I'll let him walk around a little while, and then I'll put him in your car."

"It's close to the front there, parked along the drive as you come in." Rebekah handed over the keys. "I got here early to set up, so I was able to find a close spot."

"I'll come find you in a few minutes." Rory cradled Cotton in one arm. She stood for a moment and watched Rebekah greet the artists working nearby. It was easy to see why she was so good at her job.

Rory carried Cotton away from the hubbub and set him in one of the long grassy dog runs behind the building. The hum of voices and music could still be heard, but the sounds were more muffled behind the building. Cotton tiptoed in the cool grass as if his paws were too delicate even for this cushy surface. After he sniffed around and did a little business, he returned to her and raised on his haunches for her to pick him up again.

"Someone is a very spoiled boy." She didn't mind. She picked him up and walked toward Rebekah's car.

He was a slightly nervous dog, but it was her professional opinion that he was simply born that way. Some dogs were nervous by nature. In his case, it didn't seem as if he'd suffered trauma. He liked people; it was crowds that bothered him. Rory could relate. She preferred small groups herself, so she understood exactly how he felt. But sometimes, a crowd was necessary to make things happen. This particular event had drawn huge support from the local community just when the shelter needed it most. Rory was very happy to see that all of Rebekah's hard work had paid off. She wanted to buy Rebekah a drink and help her celebrate.

Cotton curled up in the dog bed. He seemed very happy to take a nap. It was a cool evening, so Rory only felt the need to crack the windows for a bit of fresh air. The sun had just set, so there was no worry that he'd get too warm in the car. If anything, he'd probably prefer a blanket. But the dog bed was deep and pile-lined for extra soft cuddliness, so he would be fine until Rebekah was ready to leave.

Rory circled the painting area in search of Rebekah but also to see how the artists were doing. Some of the designs were abstract and brightly colored. Others had dog motifs. Most were almost finished, and the bidding had begun. Each station had a small table with a clipboard that included an artist bio and a suggested starting bid. Then people could write in their bids underneath until the auction closed. A couple of the doghouses had been set aside for online bids. It seemed that Rebekah had thought of everything.

She finally spotted her talking with Scott Allred. He'd been the lead artist contacted about this project and had graciously agreed to paint the first doghouse for use as promotion. He was a quirky fellow, with gray slightly shorter Albert Einstein hair and a blazer completely covered with various-sized buttons over a vintage Eagles T-shirt. Rory had never met him in person before, even though his metal sculpture graced the shelter grounds, but she'd seen photos of him.

"Hi." Rebekah smiled at Rory as she walked up. "Scott, this is Rory. She's one of the dog trainers at Lonely Hearts."

"Nice to meet you." Scott extended his hand.

"It's nice to meet you. I love your work and that jacket." Rory pointed at the button-covered blazer.

"Oh yes, my daughter made this for me to wear to art openings." He grinned and held the front of the jacket open a little farther. "It's a great conversation piece."

"Well, tell your daughter well done." Rory appreciated upcycled vintage clothing, probably more than most people.

"I should get going. I told my wife I'd meet her at a wine bar, and then we have late dinner reservations." He was talking to Rebekah. "As always, it was great to see you, Rebekah. And a pleasure to meet you, Rory."

"He seems really nice." Rory watched Scott walk away.

"He is. He's super talented, but he doesn't have a huge ego, and he's easy to work with."

"It looks like things are winding down with the auction." Rory scanned the scene. "Do you need to oversee this, or can I treat you to some food and maybe a drink?"

"Absolutely, I'm starved." Rebekah nodded and glanced toward the food trucks. "Avery and Derek are handling the auction, so I'm officially off the clock." Rebekah smiled.

"Excellent." Rory offered her elbow as they strolled toward the area where the party seemed to be beginning to ramp up.

There was an eighties cover band at the far end of the parking lot, and a dance area had been cleared. The tiny white lights strung across the scene created a magical feel. They'd each gotten a teriyaki bowl, and after finishing that and a couple of glasses of wine, Rory got up enough nerve to ask Rebekah to dance.

"It's been a while since I danced, so I make no promises." Rory extended her hand.

Rebekah accepted it. "I have confidence in you." They left their wineglasses on the nearest picnic table and found an empty space in front of the bandstand.

"I love the bands from the eighties," Rebekah shouted above the music.

"Me too." Rory began to move to the music. She felt super self-conscious so she tried to keep her movements to a minimum. Rebekah was obviously a much better dancer than she was. She decided to aspire to be the frame and allow Rebekah to be the art in this scenario. Rebekah lightly grasped Rory's fingers and spun herself around. Rory let her palm follow the curve of Rebekah's back until Rebekah was again facing her. They danced well together, almost as if this wasn't the first time.

After a little while, the band transitioned to a slow tune. "Holding Back the Years" by Simply Red. Rory hadn't heard the song in forever, but she'd always loved the lyrics, which were almost like stream-of-consciousness poetry. She wondered if Rebekah wanted to take a break, but as the easy, sultry tempo surrounded them, Rebekah stepped closer and draped her arms around Rory's shoulders. She rested her palms on Rebekah's hips as they swayed slowly to the music. Rebekah's heels made it so that they were almost eye to eye as they danced.

"This is nice." Rory kissed Rebekah gently on the lips. A sweet kiss, a kiss hopeful for more.

Rebekah rested her cheek on Rory's shoulder. Rory wrapped her arms around Rebekah in a swaying embrace. The press of Rebekah's body against hers was causing liquid warmth to pool in her center.

She wondered if Rebekah felt it too. Sometimes, it was hard to read Rebekah behind her practiced distance. Rory didn't mind. It was nice to take the time to get to know someone. She liked to peel back the layers and really understand a person. Superficial relationships didn't interest her.

When the song ended, they decided to get some dessert. There was a pie truck in the mix called Pie-To-Go. Rory retrieved two slices of apple and carried them back to the picnic table. Rebekah had purchased a couple of bottles of water. Rory was glad because the wine had been strong, and she was pretty sure she'd had enough if she planned to drive herself home.

"Well, how does it feel when an event you planned is such an obvious success?" Rory set the pie on the table and slid onto the bench seat.

"It feels pretty good." Rebekah held her bottled water up as a toast.

"All they had left was apple. I hope that's okay with you."

"I love apple." Rebekah sampled the dessert. "Actually, I'm pretty sure it's the crust I love."

"Me too. When I was a kid and my grandmother made pies, she would put the extra pieces into a skillet, sprinkle them with sugar, and bake them." The memory made her smile. It was also nice to notice the little things they had in common, since on the surface, they seemed so different. "I called them pie crust cookies, and they were delicious."

"Your grandmother sounds like my kind of woman."

They were quiet for a moment. Rory was in a thoughtful mood.

"Do you ever worry that life moves too fast? That if you slow down you might have to admit something is missing?"

Rebekah scrunched her eyebrows. It almost looked as if she was frowning.

"You know, you have this perfect life, or you think you do until you really reflect inward." She tried to explain the thought, but Rebekah seemed agitated.

"What are you trying to say?" Her expression had completely shifted from playful to pissed in the blink of an eye.

"I wasn't trying to say—"

"Oh, look at Rebekah and her perfect life and her perfect clothes. She stays so busy, she works so much because if she stops, she'll realize it's all empty? Is that what you're trying to say?"

"I wasn't talking about you—"

"Well, you don't know everything, Rory MacClaren." Rebekah abruptly stood. "And you certainly don't know me."

Rebekah stormed off. Rory sat in shocked silence. After a few seconds, she realized people at the next table had heard the angry exchange and were looking at her. She swallowed the lump in her throat, regretting the wine and the half-eaten dessert now sitting in the pit of her stomach like a stone.

She'd said one self-reflective thing; it wasn't even about Rebekah, although clearly, she'd hit a nerve of some kind. Rory had innocently said the wrong thing, and bitterness had slid between them like the razor edge of a sword, swiftly splitting them apart.

Rory felt sad and exposed. She cleared the table and walked along the edge of the crowd toward her car, trying to figure out how their fun evening had taken such a complete turn. She hadn't got very far when Rebekah filled her vision from nowhere.

"You still have my car keys." Rebekah held her hand out. It must have killed her to have to return for her keys after she'd stormed off in such an epic fashion. She seemed even more pissed off, if that was possible.

Rory fished the keys out of her pocket, offering nothing but lean, sharp silence.

Rebekah took the key fob and left without a word.

Now it was Rory's turn to get angry. She was slow to get mad or lose her temper, but she wasn't immune to callous, undeserved treatment any more than the next person.

Why did she care anyway? Why did she always try to save people? It was a bad habit that she needed to break free of. Dogs could be rescued but not always people. Rebekah obviously didn't want or need to be saved. And especially not by her.

She caught a glimpse of Rebekah's taillights as she neared the parking area. Sadness, hurt, and anger fought for dominance, and she wasn't quite sure yet which would win the night.

Chapter Eight

Rebekah was so angry. She white-knuckled the steering wheel all the way back to her place and screeched to a stop, parking right out front. She scooped Cotton up and was at the door when she realized that she should probably walk him first.

She set him down on the sidewalk and walked toward the river. It wasn't super late, but no one was out on her street. They were probably all having dinner or fun or—what the fuck?

Rebekah was so tired of people telling her she needed to slow down and feel things. Feel what? She liked being busy. There was no crime in packing as much into your day as was humanly possible. In truth, she had noticed that having a dog had forced her to think more about her schedule and leave open spaces for Cotton. Maybe that was a good thing, but she didn't need Rory telling her how to be in the world. Rory might know dogs, but she didn't know Rebekah.

They'd made it all the way down three blocks before Rebekah sensed the adrenaline ebb in her system. She'd gotten so pissed, and it had come out of nowhere. Why did she care what Rory thought anyway? It wasn't as if they were a couple. She didn't have anything to prove, and she certainly didn't have to change who she was to please some dog trainer.

Cotton trotted up the front steps upon their return. He looked up at her as she fumbled the house keys, nearly dropping them on his head. Once inside, she unclipped his leash, and he headed straight for the kitchen. Rebekah slumped to the sofa. She couldn't see him, but she could hear him crunching the kibble in his bowl.

She checked her phone. There were no messages from Rory. Why did that disappoint her a little? But there was a text from Mary Beth.

Good luck tonight! I'm sorry I can't be there. Mary Beth was out of town for work and hadn't been able to get back in time. *Be sure to slow down and enjoy the moment. You've earned it.*

What the hell? Why was everyone suddenly telling her to slow down? Rebekah started to text back but thought better of it. She didn't have the energy for a fight with Mary Beth on top of arguing with Rory. What was going on tonight? Had the planets slipped into some weird retrograde? Was that even a thing? She'd never been good at astrology.

Maybe she was just exhausted. She had been putting a lot of hours into this project. She set her phone on the coffee table and kicked her heels off as she crossed the carpet to the stairs. She didn't even care if Cotton chewed them. She was too mad and tired to care.

She tossed the leather jacket and scarf on a chair in her bedroom, then shimmied out of the dress and let it pool on the floor near the bed. She tossed her bra on the dresser where she rummaged for a T-shirt to sleep in.

She'd only just slid under the covers when Cotton hopped up from the foot of the bed. He trotted up the thick comforter as if he was walking on a cloud, then stuck his nose under the edge of the covering, his cue that he was ready to join her under the covers. She sank down to his level, and he curled up in the crook of her arm.

After a few minutes, lying in the dark, staring at the ceiling, Rebekah began to sob softly.

❖

Rory drove around a little before going home. She needed to cool off, and she knew if she went straight home, she'd just sit on the sofa and fume. She drove along the river for a little while, but that only made her think of Rebekah and the day they'd eaten at the café. By the time she got back to her neighborhood, she'd calmed down.

Maybe this was for the best. She and Rebekah were so incredibly different. They were bound to clash at some point. Rory felt bad that the clash had ended up being over something completely unintentional, a misunderstanding. But Rebekah hadn't even given her a chance to explain. Could she date someone like that? It didn't feel good to have someone lash out the way Rebekah had done. She was probably far too sensitive to date someone as volatile as Rebekah Hawks, regardless of how beautiful she was.

Rory parked and trudged around the garage to the cottage. It was times like this when she missed having a dog. Dogs were a great comfort when you needed someone to just sit and feel things with you. She'd lost her last companion animal a couple of years ago and hadn't been ready to adopt a new dog just yet. Losing a pet was hard, and she didn't want to rush into anything because that felt like she was trying to replace her beloved Olive.

After she tossed her blazer over a chair, she went to the bookcase and picked up a photo of Olive and traced the glass with her fingertips. Rory took a deep breath and placed the frame on the shelf. She went to the kitchen and put on the kettle to boil. Then she returned to the shelves to pick something to read. She searched for an old favorite, something to soothe the hurt, like spending time with an old friend. She could have called Bonnie, but what would she say? She wasn't even sure how to explain what had happened.

Just as the whistle signaled, she'd chosen a work of fiction by James Agee. He'd written *A Death in the Family* just before his own untimely death. It was a novel that read as if it was written by a poet because it was. Reading Agee's novel always transported her to another time and place, and somehow, despite the heavy subject matter, made her feel less alone.

She'd grown up in a rural area. This book always made her think of home.

Rory gathered the mug of tea and the book under her arm and kicked her shoes off on the way to the bedroom. She tossed the book onto the bed while she undressed and then slipped into a plaid flannel pajama shirt, along with her cotton boxers.

She sipped the tea and wondered for a moment what Rebekah was doing right now. She shook her head to dislodge the thought and opened the book. Whatever Rebekah was doing or thinking, it didn't matter. Rory considered herself lucky to find out they were incompatible sooner rather than later. Still, the thought made her sad and a little lonesome.

Rebekah hadn't let her explain that she'd been talking about herself.

Rory sank into the pillow. The weight of the well-read, weathered hardback was a comfort to her. She began to read of loss and family and of those we love, who despite closeness and relation can never tell you who you truly are.

Chapter Nine

Sunday after the fundraiser, Rory woke feeling as if she had a hangover. Not the alcohol-induced sort but the emotional sort. She'd tossed and turned all night, replaying the scene with Rebekah in a continuous loop, looking for clues about how it had gone so off the rails. She just couldn't decipher what had transpired.

Only a few people had signed up to use the agility and training course at Bonnie's farm. Rory arrived early so she'd have a chance to have coffee with Bonnie before the class started. Anna, Bonnie's wife, met her at the door.

"Hi, Rory. I was just running out to the market." Anna held the door open. She had curly dark hair and lots of curves. She had the energy of ten women and was always busy on her way to or from doing something. But Rory knew there was a lot to do on a farm, no shortage of tasks. "Bonnie's in the kitchen. We just made a fresh pot of coffee."

"Thanks."

Anna hugged her briefly before closing the door.

The old farmhouse had been gutted and redone over the last decade that they'd owned it. They had preserved some of the rustic features, like the exposed, rough-hewn beams along the ceiling. But they'd refinished the hardwood floors and had put a completely modern kitchen in. Rory couldn't imagine having a place like this, but she loved that, as Bonnie's best friend, she got to frequently enjoy it.

"Hey, how's it going…" Bonnie's question trailed off as she rotated to face Rory. "What happened to you?"

"Rough night." Rory was certain she was wearing disappointment all over her face.

"Does this have anything to do with Rebekah?" Bonnie slid a mug of coffee across the counter.

"Yeah." She took a seat at one of the barstools. "We got into a fight at the fundraiser last night."

"About what?"

"I wish I knew."

"I'm sorry we couldn't attend, by the way, but we did bid in the online auction." Bonnie paused. "We actually won one of the doghouses."

"Thanks for supporting the cause." Rory smiled thinly. She'd lost the forest for the trees. The important thing was that the shelter got the support it needed. Her failed attempt at dating Rebekah shouldn't overshadow that, but it was hard not to allow it to do exactly that.

"I'm sure you and Rebekah will sort out whatever happened." But Bonnie's statement didn't sound confident.

"Maybe it was bound to happen, and sooner is better than later." Rory sipped her coffee. "I can't explain it, but I really liked her." She paused. "I haven't been that interested in someone in a very long time."

"I can see why." Bonnie braced one arm on the edge of the counter and held her mug up with the other. She took a sip before continuing. "She's very pretty. And confident and capable and successful and a strong woman…I'd say she's a force of nature."

Force of nature. Yes, that was exactly what Rebekah was. With hurricane-force winds, she'd blown into Rory's life and out again with the same fury. She took a deep breath and exhaled. "She was out of my league anyway, I guess."

"What are you talking about?" Bonnie frowned. "You, my friend, are a catch. And don't you think otherwise. Rebekah would be lucky to have someone like you."

"You have to say that because you're my best friend." Even if it wasn't true, Bonnie's comment made her feel better.

"Since when do I sugarcoat things?"

"Never."

"Exactly." Bonnie nodded. "You should call her."

"I don't know."

"Well, give it a day or two. I'm telling you, she'll realize what she's missing out on, and she'll call you."

"I hope you're right."

A car appeared in the driveway; she could see it from the kitchen window. Her first client had arrived.

"I should get down there." Rory finished her coffee and put the cup in the sink. "Thanks for the coffee and the pep talk."

"Anytime."

As she walked the path from the house to the practice field near the barn, Rory felt lighter. Maybe Bonnie was right, and maybe she was just a little too close to see things clearly. Maybe Rebekah would call.

❖

Rebekah parked in an open spot in front of the shelter. Most of the paint stations from the previous night had been packed up except for three on the far side of the circular drive. Maggie happened to be standing near the entrance watching the cleanup when Rebekah arrived.

"Good morning." Maggie waved.

"Hello." Rebekah joined her near the entrance. "I left a little before the end last night, and I wanted to make sure all the cleanup got taken care of."

"Yes, everything is almost finished. The team you hired to do the breakdown has been great." Maggie grew serious for a moment. "Listen, I know I've said this before, but I really don't know how to thank you enough for what you created here."

"I was happy to do it. Truly." And she meant it. "Did the auction go well?" She was curious about the final numbers.

"Are you kidding?" Maggie smiled broadly. "We doubled our fundraising goal."

"That's really great news." At least something had gone well. Even if the whole evening with Rory had blown up. "Do you know if Rory is around?"

"No, she usually does trainings at the farm on Sundays."

"Oh, right, of course."

Mention of the farm reminded her of how sweet Rory had been to her when she'd fallen, and thinking of that made her stomach spin. Rory had been so kind, and last night, she worried she'd been terrible to her. She'd been so angry, but when she'd calmed down, she couldn't help replaying the exchange over and over in her head. She'd slept terribly.

"I should probably get back inside." Maggie motioned toward the door. "Are you coming in?"

"No, I should run." Rebekah had been completely lost in her own thoughts. "Besides, Cotton is in the car."

"How is that going?"

"I love having a dog." Rebekah smiled. Cotton was the one relationship that was going in the right direction. "Who knew I loved dogs?"

"Sometimes it just takes meeting the right pup." Maggie waved as the door swished closed behind her.

Maggie was probably right. And she'd been very grateful to have Cotton by her side when she was feeling so upset and unsettled. He'd been a calming presence during her restless night.

Rebekah sat in the car for a moment before driving. She looked over at Cotton, and he looked back at her from his cozy little dog bed on the passenger seat.

She knew in that moment that she'd overreacted. Rory's comment about slowing down had touched a nerve. And when someone touched a nerve, especially that one, she tended to go from zero to a thousand in seconds. She knew she needed to work on that, but she obviously hadn't mastered it yet. In the moment when it was happening, she was never able to step back to gain any clarity. She would simply react. With the stress of the event and two glasses of wine, she'd been wound up before Rory had even stepped on that little emotional landmine. In the light of day, she could see it clearly now. Rebekah owed Rory an apology, but how best to deliver it?

Chapter Ten

Rebekah parked in front of her condo but decided that she needed a walk to clear her head. Cotton was more agreeable than usual to walking, so once they reached the greenspace along the river, she turned right toward the coffee shop. As usual on a Sunday, the popular java spot was a bit of a beehive.

Only when she had her hand on the door did she see the notice: no dogs allowed. Since she'd never been a dog owner, she hadn't ever paid attention. But now that she was here, she really wanted a beverage and a scone. After the night she'd had, she felt she deserved it, but what about Cotton? She scanned the area. The outside tables were all full, but there was a bike rack not too far from the entrance with no bikes.

"Okay, boy, you stay and be a good dog. I'll be right back." She tied Cotton's leash to the bike rack, then hustled to the door. She didn't want to leave him unattended any longer than was necessary.

As luck would have it, there were only two patrons ahead of her in line. It didn't take more than ten minutes to get her drink. She ate a third of the scone while she waited, checking out the window a few times to make sure Cotton was okay. Rebekah claimed her latte, then tucked the remainder of the scone in a to-go bag and wound her way between tables to the door.

Once outside, she glanced toward the bike rack, and her heart sank.

Cotton was gone!

Rebekah was frozen in place. She blinked, hoping that when she opened her eyes again, he would be there. But he wasn't. She hurried to the bike rack where the leash and collar limply lay on the concrete. She picked up the collar and frantically searched up and down the street in both ways. He was nowhere in sight.

"Excuse me." Rebekah spoke to the man at the nearest table. He was intently working on his laptop. "I'm sorry to bother you, but did you see a little dog? He was tied here just a minute ago."

"No, sorry."

Her first thought was that someone had taken him. She was so stupid! Why would she leave such an adorable dog out for anyone to steal? But then it occurred to her that if someone had stolen Cotton, they'd have taken the leash. He must have slipped out of the collar and run away for some reason. Had something scared him? Cotton didn't like to be left alone, she knew that for a fact, but it had literally been ten minutes, and she'd checked on him multiple times. Whatever had happened, it had happened in the last three minutes. He couldn't have gone far.

Rebekah untied the leash and walked down the block, calling his name. Then she crossed the street and started to run along the path. She'd only taken a few sips of her latte, but she tossed it into a trash can so that she could move faster. Luckily, she'd worn her running shoes because she'd planned to do a workout after she dropped Cotton off at home.

After a few minutes with no luck, panic settled into her chest. She did the only thing she could think of. Before second-guessing herself, she dialed Rory's number.

"Hello." Rory sounded so calm.

Given Rebekah's panicked state, Rory's composure was annoying. And then her annoyance gave way to tears. Words never came, choked off by the lump in her throat.

"Rebekah?" Rory's calm sounded more like concern now, which only made Rebekah began to sob. Messy, gulping for air kind of sobs.

"Rebekah, where are you? What happened?"

"I'm at the corner…near the coffee shop…near my house." She tried to quiet the sobs enough to speak in broken phrases. "Cotton is gone."

"Stay where you are. I'll be right there."

Rebekah slid her phone in her pocket and wiped at her tears with the sleeve of her sweatshirt. She was hit with the realization that in her hour of need, the only person she'd wanted to call was Rory. Rebekah could rationalize that this was because Cotton was involved, but she knew the deeper truth. She cared about Rory. She wasn't sure she'd realized it until just now. The past few weeks, she'd grown attached. The transition had been so subtle. In the same way that the tide was invisible to someone who was out at sea, she'd missed all the signs of the ebb and flow of her own feelings.

Which was probably why she'd been so sensitive to Rory's comments the previous night.

Why was she so dumb about emotional things? She was a grown-up! Shouldn't she be figuring things out by now?

She wasn't sure how much time had passed, minutes or an eternity, when she finally saw Rory park nearby. Rebekah walked briskly in that direction. In a moment of spontaneous affection, as if Rory had been privy to her revelation, she flung her arms around Rory's neck and hugged her. Rory was slow to return the embrace, no doubt thinking that she didn't really know what Rebekah's embrace really meant.

"Rory, I'm so sorry about last night." She tucked her head under Rory's chin. "I'm an idiot, and I hope you can forgive me."

"Hey, it's okay."

"I promise to explain everything, but right now, will you help me find Cotton?" The tears were coming again. "I don't know what to do or where to look." She sniffed loudly. "What if he's been hit by a car? What if someone picked him up, and I'll never see him again?"

She was thinking the worst, and all her words came out in a rush.

"Cotton is a smart dog. He knows to avoid cars." Rory rubbed her hand on Rebekah's back in small circles. "We'll find him."

Rory couldn't see Rebekah's expression. She placed her finger under Rebekah's chin, angling Rebekah's face up so that she could see her eyes. Rebekah looked so frightened. She took a step back and nodded. Rory wanted to say things to make her feel better, even if she didn't know for sure they were true.

"Let's start from the beginning. Where did you see him last?"

"Over here." Rebekah started walking back toward the café. "I tied him up at the bike rack. I feel so stupid. Why did I do that?"

"We all make mistakes." She tried to comfort Rebekah. "You're still learning how to be a dog owner. For some dogs, that would have been a fine thing to do." There was no need to cross the street to the café. It was easier to see the street and the entire intersection from the grassy area near the walking path. "You checked the areas nearby?"

"Yes." Rebekah seemed so defeated that it made her heart ache.

"I think we might need to split up. I'll circle the block this way, and you go the other way. We'll meet back here."

Rebekah nodded.

"We'll find him." Rory strode with purpose in the opposite direction. She called Cotton's name. She checked doorways and trash cans. She dipped low to peer under parked cars. In a few moments, she'd rounded the entire block. Rory returned to the corner only a moment before Rebekah.

"You didn't see him either?" Rebekah's question was laced with unease.

"Let's walk back toward your condo." Rory was trying to think like Cotton. If he got spooked and ran for cover, where would that be? "I have an idea."

They walked toward Rebekah's condo at a fast clip, searching in every crack and crevice along the way. As they drew closer to Rebekah's place, Rebekah's pace quickened. Rory could see a glimpse of something on the top step, just in front of the door.

"Cotton!" At the sound of Rebekah's voice, Cotton's head popped up, his nose in the air. "Cotton!"

Rebekah jogged up the stairs and scooped the tiny dog into her arms. She hugged him tightly. He squirmed and licked her wet cheeks. Rory finally released a slow cleansing breath. Relief flooded her system. She climbed the steps slowly, not wanting to intrude on the little reunion scene.

Rebekah unlocked the door and she followed inside.

"Don't ever scare me like that again!" Rebekah laid Cotton on the couch and knelt beside him as she continued to stroke his fur. "How did you know he'd be here?" Rebekah looked up at Rory.

"I didn't know for sure, but I think Cotton knows this is home now, and home is where he wanted to be." Rory sank her hands in her pockets, unsure if she should stay or go.

"I can't thank you enough." Rebekah stood and stepped closer to Rory. "Especially after the way I behaved last night. I'm so sorry."

"Yeah, I'm not even sure what happened." She was reluctant to say very much until Rebekah explained. Rebekah's harsh words had stung, and she wasn't in a rush to feel that again.

"What you said about being afraid to slow down and if I did, I might have to feel things."

"Is that what I said?"

"Well, that's what I heard, and it was something my ex used to say, or at least something very similar." Rebekah took a breath. "I overreacted. I apologize."

"You know that I was talking about myself, right?"

"You were?" Rebekah seemed genuinely surprised.

"I meant that if I took time to slow down and look at my life, I'd realize I was missing something." She wasn't sure how honest she should be, but what did she have to lose at this point? "Rebekah, I really like you."

"I like you too, Rory." Rebekah tugged Rory's hand free from her pocket and held on to it. "I would really like to take you on a second date, maybe more, if you can forgive me for being such an oversensitive jerk."

Rory appreciated that Rebekah could own up to her behavior and be honest about what was behind the outburst. It was true that they were very different, but maybe difference was a good thing.

"To be honest, it was killing me not to call you." She brushed Rebekah's cheek with the back of her fingers. "Rebekah Hawks, you are an intense, fierce soul."

"I am?" Rebekah's question was soft as she moved into Rory's personal space.

"Yeah, and it's one of the things I like about you." Rory kissed her lightly. "Let's try this dating thing again, okay?"

"I'd like that very much."

Rebekah raised up on her tiptoes until her lips met Rory's. They kissed languorously until the kiss was broken by the yips of a neglected dog. Cotton sat up on his haunches, begging to be picked up.

"As for you, little man…" She stroked Cotton's fur as he snuggled in Rebekah's arms. "It's my professional opinion that your beautiful owner should invest in a very secure harness."

They both laughed.

Chapter Eleven

Two weeks had passed since Cotton had been lost and found. Rebekah and Rory had seen each other almost every day. Sometimes just for lunch or coffee; sometimes for dinner out. Most often at a dog-friendly restaurant. Something had shifted between them, and they were no longer trying to play it cool. At least, that was how Rebekah interpreted things. She was interested in knowing Rory, fully and completely. And Rory seemed to feel the same way about her.

They were easy together. Rebekah was more relaxed but still occasionally soothed and nervous at the same time. It felt good to want someone the way she wanted Rory.

Tonight, she had decided to invite Rory to her place for dinner. Not that she was actually going to cook. She didn't want to mislead Rory about her culinary skills. She'd ordered delivery from a local Japanese place, and it arrived shortly after Rory did.

She'd wanted to stay in for dinner because she was hoping Rory would spend the night. Rebekah was ready to take things to the next level or at least see where the next level might lead. Rory was so shy that Rebekah worried if she didn't take matters into her own hands, Rory might never make the next move. That thought amused her. She smiled as she gathered plates and returned to the living room.

Throw pillows were scattered around the coffee table. Rory took a seat on the floor and began opening food containers.

"Hey, I was thinking…I have a week off before I start my new job." Rebekah watched Rory deftly move sushi rolls to her plate with chopsticks. "Would you like to go somewhere?"

"Really?" Rory looked surprised.

"Yes, really. Why not?" Rebekah served herself, keeping her tone playfully flirtatious. "We could take things for a test run tonight before you commit to traveling with me."

Rory sputtered her drink and then coughed. Her cheeks flamed.

She was adorably easy to tease. Rebekah loved that she could have such an immediate effect on Rory with the slightest suggestion of sex. She was dying to have Rory all to herself for the entire night, although she hadn't broken this news to Cotton yet.

Rory had wisely suggested that she invest in a kennel in order to save her shoes and books and if she ever hoped to keep Cotton out of her bedroom in general. Cotton was taking the kennel training in stride so far.

"I would love to spend the night with you." Rory had regained her composure. She leaned over and kissed Rebekah gently. "I've dreamed of spending the night with you."

"Me too." She poured white wine into two glasses and handed one to Rory. "Here's to the Lonely Hearts Rescue and not feeling lonely anymore." She held her glass up.

"I'll drink to that." Rory lightly touched her glass to Rebekah's. She scooted closer on the cushions. Rory leaned against the sofa and put her arm around Rebekah's shoulders.

Rebekah sank against Rory, then she laughed and shook her head.

"What's so funny?"

"It wasn't anything funny really. I just had this thought." Rebekah grew serious. "You and Cotton have truly gotten into my heart." Rebekah paused and held Rory's gaze. "Maybe I'm the one who needed to be rescued all along."

Rory drew Rebekah into her arms.

She relaxed into Rory's embrace. This felt so right.

Rory's lips brushed her cheek as she whispered, "Every now and then, we all need to be rescued."

About the Authors

Morgan Lee Miller started writing at the age of five in the suburbs of Cleveland, Ohio. Since there is absolutely nothing to do there, she entertained herself by writing her first few novels by hand. During the day, Morgan works for an animal welfare nonprofit, and at night, she's procrastinating on her next novel. She currently resides in Washington, DC, with her two feline children, Milo and Elsa. She has a serious problem with oversharing pictures of her cats on Instagram and promises never to apologize for it.

Nell Stark is an award-winning author of lesbian romance. In 2013, *The Princess Affair* was a Lambda Literary finalist in the romance category, and in 2010, *everafter* (with Trinity Tam) won a Goldie Award in the paranormal romance category. In addition to the everafter series, she has published six standalone romances: *Running With the Wind*, *Homecoming*, *The Princess Affair*, *The Princess and the Prix*, *The Princess Deception*, and *All In*.

Missouri Vaun spent a large part of her childhood in southern Mississippi, before attending high school in North Carolina and college in Tennessee. Strong connections to her roots in the rural South have been a grounding force throughout her life. Vaun spent twelve years finding her voice working as a journalist in places as disparate as Chicago, Atlanta, and Jackson, Mississippi, all along filing away characters and their stories. Her novels are heartfelt, earthy, and speak of loyalty and our responsibility to others. She and her wife currently live in northern California.

Books Available From Bold Strokes Books

A Cutting Deceit by Cathy Dunnell. Undercover cop Athena takes a job at Valeria's hair salon to gather evidence to prove her husband's connections to organized crime. What starts as a tentative friendship quickly turns into a dangerous affair. (978-1-63679-208-8)

As Seen on TV! by CF Frizzell. Despite their objections, TV hosts Ronnie Sharp, a laid-back chef, and paranormal investigator Peyton Stanford have to work together. The public is watching. But joining forces is risky, contemptuous, unnerving, provocative—and ridiculously perfect. (978-1-63679-272-9)

Blood Memory by Sandra Barret. Can vampire Jade Murphy protect her friend from a human stalker and keep her dates with the gorgeous Beth Jenssen without revealing her secrets? (978-1-63679-307-8)

Foolproof by Leigh Hays. For Martine Roberts and Elliot Tillman, friends with benefits isn't a foolproof way to hide from the truth at the heart of an affair. (978-1-63679-184-5)

Glass and Stone by Renee Roman. Jordan must accept that she can't control everything that happens in life, and that includes her wayward heart. (978-1-63679-162-3)

Hard Pressed by Aurora Rey. When rivals Mira Lavigne and Dylan Miller are tapped to co-chair Finger Lakes Cider Week, competition gives way to compromise. But will their sexual chemistry lead to love? (978-1-63679-210-1)

The Laws of Magic by M. Ullrich. Nothing is ever what it seems, especially not in the small town of Bender, Massachusetts, where a witch lives to save lives and avoid love. (978-1-63679-222-4)

The Lonely Hearts Rescue by Morgan Lee Miller, Nell Stark & Missouri Vaun. In this novella collection, a hurricane hits the Gulf Coast, and the animals at the Lonely Hearts Rescue Shelter need love—and so do the humans who adopt them. (978-1-63679-231-6)

The Mage and the Monster by Barbara Ann Wright. Two powerful mages, one committed to magic and one controlled by it, strive to free each other and be together while the countries they serve descend into war. (978-1-63679-190-6)

Truly Wanted by J.J. Hale. Sam must decide if she's willing to risk losing her found family to find her happily ever after. (978-1-63679-333-7)

A Good Chance by Ali Vali. Harry, Desi, and Desi's sister Rachel are so close to getting everything they've ever wanted, but Desi's ex-husband is coming back to get his revenge and rip apart their chance at happiness. (978-1-63679-023-7)

A Perfect Fifth by Jaycie Morrison. Streetwise pianist Zara Keller and Lady Jillian Stansfield couldn't be more different, yet their connection brings a new awareness of who they are and what they truly want in their lives—including each other. (978-1-63679-132-6)

Catching Feelings by Ana Hartnett Reichardt. Andrea Foster expected to catch a lot of pitches from the Alder Lions' star pitcher, Maya, but she didn't expect to catch feelings. (978-1-63679-227-9)

Defiant Hearts by Lee Lynch. In these stories, you'll find your lovers, friends, and lesbians you wish you knew—maybe even yourself. (978-1-63679-237-8)

Love and Duty by Catherine Young. All Princess Roseli wants is to marry her three lovers, but with war looming, she must instead marry Princess Lucia to establish a military alliance between their planets. (978-1-63679-256-9)

Serendipity by Kris Bryant. Serendipity brings jingle writer Annie Foster and celebrity pop star Bristol Baines together, and their undeniable attraction keeps them close, but will their different paths drive them apart? (978-1-63679-224-8)

The Haunted Heart by Jane Kolven. A ghost, a ring, and a quest to find a missing psychic—it's a spell for love. (978-1-63679-245-3)

The Rules of Forever by Nan Campbell. After reconnecting at their high school reunion, Cara and Lauren agree to embark on a textbook definition friends-with-benefits relationship, but trying to keep it uncomplicated is harder than it seems. (978-1-63679-248-4)

Vision of Virtue by Brey Willows. When virtue and desire come together, be prepared for sparks in this next installment of the Memory's Muses series. (978-1-63679-118-0)

The Artist by Sheri Lewis Wohl. Detective Casey Wilson and reclusive artist Tula Crane are drawn together in a web of passion, intrigue, and art that might just hold the key to stopping a killer. (978-1-63679-150-0)

Cherry on Top by Georgia Beers. A chance meeting leaves Cherry and Ellis longing for a different life, but when Ellis's search for truth crashes into Cherry's insta-filter world, do they have any hope at all of a happily ever after? (978-1-63679-158-6)

Love and Other Rare Birds by Angie Williams. Ornithologist Dr. Jamie Martin and park ranger Rowan Fleming are searching the Alaskan wilderness for a bird thought to be extinct, and they're about to discover opposites really do attract. (978-1-63679-108-1)

Parallel Paradise by Mayapee Chowdhury. When their love affair is put to the test by the homophobia of their family, community, and culture, Bindi and Rimli will need to fight for a chance at love. (978-1-63679-203-3)

Perfectly Matched by Toni Logan. A beautiful Cupid named Hannah, a runaway arrow, and just seventy-two hours to fix a mishap that could be the best mistake she has ever made. (978-1-63679-120-3)

Slow Burn by Missouri Vaun. A wounded wildland firefighter from California and a struggling artist find solace and love in a small southern town. (978-1-63679-098-5)

The Inconvenient Heiress by Jane Walsh. An unlikely heiress and a spinster evade the Marriage Mart only to discover true love together. (978-1-63679-173-9)

The Value of Sylver and Gold by Michelle Larkin. When word gets out that former Boston Homicide Detective Reid Sylver can talk to the dead, the FBI solicits her help on a serial murder case, prompting Reid to assemble forces once again with Detective London Gold. (978-1-63679-093-0)

Wildflower by Cathleen Collins. When a plane crash leaves seven-year-old Lily Andrews stranded in the vast wilderness of Arkansas, will she be able to overcome the odds and make it back to civilization and the one person who holds the key to her future? (978-1-63679-244-6)